喚醒你的英文語感！

Get a Feel for English !

喚醒你的英文語感！

Get a Feel for English !

素養導向取材 × 英檢能力鍛鍊

實境英文練聽力

跟著做，聽&說
同步進化！

作者 / 劉怡均

突破連音、變音、弱讀、
重音、語調等發音變化難點
情境聽解、口語表達一舉搞定！

MP3
加值學更多
線上下載

本書包含三個章節共計 25 個單元，學習內容涵蓋簡單的生活情境、留學生活、情緒溝通、職場溝通及潮流時事。建議學習者以 Chapter 1 的生活情境作為入門與暖身，請留意會話中的粗體字部分為該生活情境常見之句型與詞彙，這種「對話亮點」對於學習者來說非常重要，務必仔細聆聽音檔，並且在反覆聆聽多次之後進行跟讀的練習。不斷地跟讀誦念是相當關鍵的步驟，不僅能夠加深對於常用句型與詞彙的印象，同時也能訓練實境生活中的口說反應能力，一舉數得。

語言的基礎是由聲音開始，而聲音又從模仿開始，如同我們小時候牙牙學語學習中文的時候，藉由不斷地模仿大人的聲音表現、歷經無數次將各種聲音詞彙排列組合的練習，長期累積下來，就會成為堅實的聽說能力基礎。然而，對於以英語作為第二外語的學習者來說，實在無法花那麼多時間去遨遊語言大海，慢慢摸索各種詞彙聲音進行拼湊練習，因此，本書的各種情境聽力設計就是為了讓學習者省去摸索的時間，在短時間內即能掌握實用句型與常見詞彙，只要能夠專注地反覆聆聽並且持續跟讀數次到熟記，必能在一般生活情境當中體會到一次溝通就上手的學習成就感。

從本書的 Chapter 2 開始，聽力技巧及聽力段落的複雜度會開始逐篇增加，循序漸進地介紹實境英文口語當中大量的發音變化，舉凡連音、消音、變音等規則，以及像是修正重述這類的口語表現，讓學習者能夠在實際生活情境中與英語母語人士溝通更加順利。許多人在練習英語聽力時普遍感到困惑的問題是，如果對話過程能像看電視一樣有「字幕」，那幾乎每一句話都看得懂，為什麼用聽的卻聽不太懂呢？會有這樣的問題，不單單只是因為語速過快而對聽力理解造成影響，更關鍵的原因是生活實境英語的發音與咬字其實與我們從書本上學到的詞彙音標有著非常大的差距，這是因為每一個單字分開來讀跟放到一個句子裡面讀會因為不同的發音變化而產生不同的聲音表現，學習者若能摸透這個從「點」（單字）到「線」（句子）的差距，必然能夠大幅提升聽力理解能力。因此，Chapter 2 將大量的英語口說發音變化巧妙地埋入每一個學習單元中，幫助學習者不但能熟習該情境的實用句型和詞彙，更能有效掌握英語聽力的重要技巧。

到了 Chapter 3 將會更進一步介紹如何模仿英語口說的抑揚頓挫，舉凡重音位置、語音語調以及句中語調重音等等聽力和口說重點都包含在內，學習者若能確實揣摩練習，必可同步提升聽力及口說力。此外，本書最後的潮流時事主題其聽力篇幅是本書所有單元中最長的，為的是讓學習者能夠挑戰進階，從「點」（單字）到「線」（句子）再到「面」（長段落），雖然難度較高，但是若能循序漸進、確實跟隨各個單元的內容做練習，自然能夠在這些長篇幅聽力段落中感受到自己的進步，既可說是本書自學旅程的成果檢測與驗收，亦是辛苦自學的歡呼收割。

Nana 劉怡均

CONTENTS

Chapter 3 習慣英語口語表達時的各種語調

了解並模仿基本的語音語調／重音位置為句子語意的重點

職場溝通

潮流時事

本書特色及使用說明

聆聽重點

在聆聽對話之前可先熟悉該情境常見的「對話亮點」有哪些，並且想像一下自己在真實生活中的類似語境。這個步驟有助於學習者在自學時更能融入該對話、提升聆聽過程的專注力，同時能夠加深對於「對話亮點」的印象。

整個聽力段落練習方式

建議看完「聆聽重點」當中的「對話亮點」之後，先以不看對話內容的方式「裸聽」第一次，接著可以重新播放錄音檔，並且跟著對話文本朗讀。可以假定自己是對話情境中的任何一方來進行跟讀，跟讀的時候請特別留意粗體字的位置，讀到粗體字可以特別提高音量來加深印象。這個步驟結束之後可以把書本闔上，再播放音檔第三次，這樣為一個循環的練習結束，這個循環可以重複多次，也可以根據個人學習情況斟酌增減調整。

粗體字

書中的粗體字位置都為實用例句以及該情境常見語彙，建議學習者在每一個單元反覆聆聽跟讀之後，另行針對這些粗體字內容背誦熟記，這樣有助於實際運用時能夠展現更為流暢的口說反應力。

搭乘捷運

聆聽重點

在捷運地鐵問路的「對話亮點」→捷運轉乘相關單字
例如：搭乘什麼路線、列車開往什麼方向、在哪裡轉車、在哪裡到站下車。

Track 0113　T = Tourist　P = Philip　★ 請特別注意粗體字的部分 ★

Ch 1

T **Excuse me, could you tell me how to get to** Diwa Street?
P Diwa Street? Diwa?
T Yes, Diwa Street, Taipei's [1]**oldest** street.
P Um, I don't… wait, **do you mean** Dihua Street, do you want to go to Dadaocheng?
T Yes, yes, Dadaocheng!
P [2]**Okay**, so… first, you **take the Blue Line bound for Nangang Exhibition Center**… and **get off** at Ximen. Then **transfer to** the Green Line bound for Songshan and take that to Beimen.
T Wow, thank you.
P [3]**Thank You**, I didn't even know that Dihua Street is the oldest street in Taipei.
T Well, I always do my homework before traveling abroad.
P Welcome to Taipei. I hope you [4]**enjoy** your stay.

聽力提點

1. **Old**
雙母音有兩段聲音，例如 old [ould] 的雙母音 [ou]，下顎會先往下發出 [o] 的聲音然後緊接著嘴型聚合回到 [u] 的位置，只是要注意雙母音的第一個聲音 [o] 是比較高且長的聲音，然後往下降音到第二個聲音 [u] 較短收尾，類似中文裡面的「ㄡㄨ」，old 這個字會很清楚的聽到雙母音 [ou] 的聲音。請比較第二個提點。

2. **Okay**

Unit 01／生活情境：搭乘捷運／ 023

聽力提點

該情境會話的聽力提點若只有一個，會以＊星號標記，若聽力提點不只一個，則以數字小標表示，方便學習者參照學習。套色字體為聽力提點當中特別要強調注意的發音咬字位置，可重複播放錄音檔來跟讀模仿道地口音。

2. **pay 和 celebrate**
雙母音 [eɪ] 在 pay [peɪ] 跟 celebrate ['sɛləbreɪt] 兩個字之間的差別：celebrate 的 [eɪ] 在非重音的位置，雙母音兩段聲音變得較短，[eɪ] 的尾音 [ɪ] 在口語聽力當中是沒有的。

延伸聽寫 | Exercise E ➲解答參見第 31 頁

Track 0117

1. Would you ①__________ __________ __________ __________ __________?
能請你走最快的路線嗎？
2. If the traffic isn't ②__________, can we ③__________ __________ the Longshan Temple on the way?
如果不塞車的話，我們中途可以順便經過龍山寺嗎？
3. I'll put your luggage ④__________ __________ __________.
我來幫你把行李放到後車廂。

實用字詞補充

1. **I'm afraid so.（情況或結果）恐怕就是這樣子**
例 A: Do we really have to leave now? 我們一定要現在離開嗎？
B: I'm afraid so. 恐怕是這樣沒錯。
2. **I'm afraid not.（情況或結果）恐怕不是如此喔**
例 A: What did he say? He agreed, right! 他怎麼說？他同意了，對吧！
B: I'm afraid not. 恐怕並非如此。

情境會話 E／翻譯

司機：女士，請問去哪裡呢？
乘客：海德公園，麻煩您。
司機：沒問題！
乘客：請問車程要多久？
司機：嗯，這就要看情況了，如果說我們很幸運的話，通常差不多 40 分鐘，你懂我的意思吧。
乘客：好的，我有點趕時間，可以走最快的路線嗎？
司機：好的，包在我身上。
乘客：那個，當然是安全第一。
司機：當然。
司機：噢……不……我想前面應該有發生車禍，女士，很抱歉，我想你可能從這邊用走路的會比較快喔。
乘客：恐怕是這樣沒錯啊！那好吧，我用走的，車錢可以刷卡嗎？
司機：當然可以。

Unit 01／生活情境：搭乘計程車／ 027

延伸聽寫

本書針對各單元設計豐富的延伸聽寫練習，讓學習者驗收單元學習成果並且體驗更多實用對話情境。

實用字詞補充

該單元的重要詞彙解析與相關例句。

情境會話翻譯

對話內容的中文翻譯為輔助參考使用，建議學習者切勿在練習聽力過程中反覆來回參照中文翻譯，此舉會影響聽力練習的整體效果。

加值學更多！

「路人問路，左轉右轉、直走到底、在左手邊還是右手邊 ......」超實用情境對話聽力練習內容，線上下載，隨時想聽就聽！

加值學更多

部分單元主題會提供更多豐富的相關學習情境供線上下載，請斟酌自身學習狀況及需求進行加深加廣的練習！

MP3曲目一覽表

Track	項目	頁碼
Unit 01	**生活情境**	
0101-0106	Conversation A	012
0107-0110	Conversation B	017
0111-0112	Conversation C	020
0113-0115	Conversation D	023
0116-0117	Conversation E	026
0118	Conversation F	028
0119	Conversation G	030
0120-0121	加值學更多	
Unit 02	**生活情境**	
0201-0203	Conversation A	034
0204-0207	Conversation B	038
0208-0210	Conversation C	041
0211-0212	Conversation D	044
0213	Conversation E	047
Unit 03	**生活情境**	
0301-0302	Conversation A	050
0303-0304	Conversation B	054
0305-0306	Conversation C	057
0307-0308	Conversation D	060
0309-0310	加值學更多	
Unit 04	**生活情境**	
0401-0404	Conversation A	066
0405-0408	Conversation B	069
0409-0411	Conversation C	073
0412	Conversation D	076
0413-0414	加值學更多	
Unit 05	**生活情境**	
0501-0502	Conversation A	080
0503-0504	Conversation B	083
0505-0506	Conversation C	086
0507-0508	Conversation D	088
Unit 06	**留學情境**	
0600	連音	093
0601-0605	Conversation A	098
0606-0608	Conversation B	106
Unit 07	**留學情境**	
0701-0703	Conversation A	114
0704-0706	Conversation B	119
0707-0708	Conversation C	123
0709-0710	加值學更多	
Unit 08	**留學情境**	
0801-0804	Conversation A	128
0805-0807	Conversation B	133

Track	項目	頁碼
Unit 09	**留學情境**	
0901-0902	Conversation A	142
0903-0904	Conversation B	145
0905-0907	Conversation C	148
0908-0909	加值學更多	
Unit 10	**留學情境**	
1001-1002	Conversation A	156
1003-1004	Conversation B	158
1005-1006	Conversation C	162
Unit 11	**情緒溝通**	
1101-1103	Conversation A	168
1104-1105	Conversation B	171
1106-1107	Conversation C	174
1108-1109	加值學更多	
Unit 12	**情緒溝通**	
1201-1202	Conversation A	180
1203-1204	Conversation B	182
1205-1206	Conversation C	185
1207-1208	加值學更多	
Unit 13	**情緒溝通**	
1301-1303	Conversation A	190
1304-1305	Conversation B	194
1306-1307	Conversation C	196
1308-1309	加值學更多	
Unit 14	**情緒溝通**	
1401-1402	Conversation A	202
1403-1404	Conversation B	204
1405-1406	Conversation C	206
1407-1408	Conversation D	208
1409-1410	加值學更多	
Unit 15	**情緒溝通**	
1501-1502	Conversation A	212
1503-1504	Conversation B	216
1505-1506	Conversation C	219
1507-1508	Conversation D	222
Unit 16	**職場溝通**	
1601-1605	Conversation A	228
1606-1607	Conversation B	234
1608-1609	Conversation C	237
Unit 17	**職場溝通**	
1701-1702	Conversation A	242
1703-1705	Conversation B	244
1706-1707	Conversation C	247
1708-1709	Conversation D	250
1710-1711	加值學更多	

Track	項目	頁碼
Unit 18	**職場溝通**	
1801-1802	Conversation A	256
1803-1804	Conversation B	258
1805-1806	Conversation C	260
1807-1808	Conversation D	263
1809-1810	Conversation E	266
1811-1813	加值學更多	
Unit 19	**職場溝通**	
1901-1902	Conversation A	270
1903-1904	Conversation B	273
1905-1906	Conversation C	275
1907-1908	Conversation D	277
1909-1910	Conversation E	279
1911-1912	加值學更多	
Unit 20	**職場溝通**	
2001-2002	Conversation A	284
2003-2005	Conversation B	287
2006-2010	Conversation C	289
2011-2012	Conversation D	292
2013-2015	加值學更多	
Unit 21	**潮流時事**	
2101-2102	Youtuber A	298
2103-2104	Youtuber B	301
2105-2106	Youtuber C	304
2107-2108	Youtuber D	306
2109-2110	Youtuber E	309
Unit 22	**潮流時事**	
2201-2202	Conversation A	314
2203-2204	Conversation B	317
2205-2206	Conversation C	320
2207-2208	Conversation D	323
Unit 23	**潮流時事**	
2301-2302	Podcast A	328
2303-2304	Podcast B	330
2305-2306	Podcast C	333
2307-2308	Podcast D	335
Unit 24	**潮流時事**	
2401	Conversation A	340
2402	Conversation B	344
2403-2404	Conversation C	347
2405	Conversation D	350
Unit 25	**潮流時事**	
2501-2502	Conversation A	354
2503-2504	Conversation B	357
2505-2506	Conversation C	361
2507	Conversation D	364

Chapter 1
熟習各種情境中的特定對話規則及變因

聽力重點：情境預測／習慣說話者因情緒而產生的不規則變因

五花八門、包羅萬象的生活情境，有許多常用的英文單字句型，如果能夠針對不同情境來練習聽力，並且配合跟讀練習加深印象，在實際生活中運用的時候，就可以大概預期會聽到什麼樣的內容。

1. 了解並且熟記生活常見情境當中特定的對話規則

從生活情境各單元介紹的實用句型開始進行聽力練習，並跟著音檔做跟讀練習，往後在真實生活中遇到類似情況的時候，即可透過預期心理來有效地提高自己在英語對話環境當中的理解能力，進而能應答如流。

2. 習慣實際口語情境當中的各種變因

我們在日常生活中使用中文與朋友聊天的時候，發音咬字會有許多含糊帶過的地方，比如我們說「你吃飯了嗎？」，以速度、咬字清晰這兩個面向來觀察，每個人說這句話的時候，在每一個字停留的時間長短都不一定，除了 Siri 之外，應該不會有人是每一個字都等速在發音咬字的。可能有人在「你」這個字上面拉長了一點時間，表示猶豫、有點害羞，或是在等待對方與自己眼神交會時再說出後面的資訊，這句話可能就會是「你～～吃飯了嗎？」；又或者當問出這句話的人是以一種很輕鬆熟悉的口氣時，「你」這個字的注音符號「ㄋ」也可能簡化，含糊的化在嘴裡只剩下一個很短、很快速的「ㄣ」的聲音，聽起來就很像是「ㄣ 吃飯了嗎？ 」，且這個「了」同樣也不會清晰的發「ㄌㄜ」的音，而是含糊滑過。同理，在英文口說時也一樣會有為了讓口語滑順而產生的發音調整與改變。

其他的變因還包括：在**內容表達上有重複的字眼或是更正重說**，像是「我本來就……我本來根本就沒有想要這樣子做啊……」、「你明明……你剛剛明明自己先承認的喔……」，或是**填補空白的語助詞**像是「嗯」、「那個齁」、「啊」以及插入式的短語像是「你懂我意思嗎？」、「我跟你說喔……」、「你知道嗎？」等等，此外也可能會有因為不同情緒而產生的重複，像是「真的，我沒騙你，真的，千真萬確！」。這些例子在中文的溝通當中十分常見，這類似「雜訊」的文字就像整段話裡面的小碎片或小雜質，有時還會使語言的表達變成很冗長、瑣碎、廢話連篇，甚至有可能造成溝通上的誤會。不過，因為我們身為母語使用者已經相當習慣這樣的表達方式，自然能夠在實際口語的各種紛亂詞語排列當中「迅速抓到溝通重點」，當聽到這些話，我們會注意的反而是後面的資訊。然而，當我們進入英語世界與他人溝通的時候，就必須做好心理準備，對方說話不可能會像帶著演講稿一樣，清晰地逐字完整鋪陳，很多時候都是片段的、來回重複的，甚至是天外飛來一筆的，更不要說有暗示、幽默開玩笑、比喻等等。要突破這個部分，最有效的方式之一就是從「有特定對話模式跟規則的生活情境」開始練習。

本書的聽力練習即以基礎生活情境作為開始，讓讀者可以先「熱身」，熟悉各種母音、雙母音的發音差別，其他比較複雜的發音規則，我們會在後續的篇章中一一揭開面紗。

Unit 01

機場・搭公車・搭火車・搭乘捷運
搭乘計程車・租車・加油站

情境會話 A 機場

聆聽重點

在機場辦理登機時的「對話亮點」→ 機場櫃檯相關單字
例如：辦理登機、護照、托運行李、手提行李、靠窗或是靠走道座位、超重、登機證、登機門。

Track 0101 G = Ground crew F = Felicia ★ 請特別注意粗體字的部分 ★

G Good afternoon, ma'am.

F Good afternoon. ***I would like to* check in, please.**

G **May I see your passport, please?**

F Sure, here you go.

G **How many pieces of baggage are you checking in?**

F Just one.

G Please put it on the scale, thanks. **Would you like a window or an aisle seat?**

F A window seat, please. And could you please mark this bag as **fragile**?

G No problem, but ma'am, I'm sorry but your bag is **overweight**. The limit is 20 kilos. You either need to pay for the excess or take something out.

F Oh, how much should I pay?

G 130 US dollars.

F Fine, **do you take credit cards**?

G Yes, just a moment… sign here please.
You have a **stopover** in Washington but your luggage will **go straight through to the final destination. Here are your boarding passes and your passport**. You will be boarding at gate C8 at 1:45pm. **Have a nice flight**.

F Thank you very much.

聽力提點

Track 0102

*** I would like to** check in, please.

針對 I would like to 不同的語速練習。

（咬字清晰的）**I would like to** check in, please.

就像中文表達「我想要做某件事……」的「我想要」三個字有可能會咬字清晰，這也是表達一種比較正式提出請求或比較有禮貌的語境。

（縮讀的）**I'd like to** check in, please.

中文的「我想要」三個字很多時候會含糊的滑過，嘴巴開合的幅度也大幅縮減，尤其是開頭的「我」不會發「ㄨㄛˇ」，反而會像是「ㄛ」，在英文中也有異曲同工之妙的調整。想要快速輕鬆把這幾字帶過的時候，一定是以嘴巴開合幅度最小的方式來表達，可以省時又省力，你會聽見語音語調的高音位置是在 like，以及 check in 的位置，而開頭 I 的聲音時間長度不僅變得很短，而且雙母音 [aɪ] 的尾音也不會很明顯，整個語速自然比起前一句咬字清晰的範例加快很多。

Ch 1

延伸聽寫 | Exercise A

解答參見第 31 頁

Track 0103

1. A Have you ①__________ __________ online already?

   B Yes, but I was wondering is that possible that I change my seat? I have a window seat but ②__________ __________ __________ __________ __________ __________.

   A May I have your passport, please? Let me check whether there's an aisle seat available... I'm sorry. It's a ③__________ __________ flight.

   B Alright, it's fine.

   A How ④__________ __________ __________ __________ do you want to check in?

   B No, I only have a ⑤__________ __________.

翻譯

A：您已經有辦理線上報到了嗎？

B：是的，不過我想要知道我是否可以換座位？我現在是靠窗的座位，但我想要換到走道的位置。

A：可以看一下您的護照嗎？我確認一下還有沒有走道的位置……很抱歉，這班飛機是滿座的。

B：好吧，沒關係。

A：有幾件要托運的行李呢？

B：不用，我就一件手提行李而已。

Track 0104 P = Passenger 乘客 G = Ground crew 地勤人員

2. P I missed my ⑥__________ __________ because ⑦__________ __________ __________ of my flight was delayed due to bad weather. Can you please tell me what I should do now?

G Don't worry. We can help you **find an alternate flight**.

P Thank you. I really need to be in Paris tomorrow night.

G Let me see what we can do. Okay sir, **the next available flight** to Paris is leaving tomorrow morning. **It leaves at 10:30 am and arrives at 2 pm**.

P That will be great. Thanks… Oh… and… can I… uh ⑧__________ __________ **for my missed connection**?

G Yes, please go to **the customer service desk**, and you also can claim a ⑨__________ for a hotel near the airport and meals for tonight.

翻譯

P：我錯過了轉機航班，我的第一趟航班因為天候狀況而延誤了。你可以告訴我現在該怎麼辦嗎？

G：不用擔心，我們會協助您找到其他的航班。

P：謝謝，我明天晚上一定要抵達巴黎。

G：讓我看看有什麼是我們能幫上忙的，好，先生，下一個飛往巴黎的航班是明天早上出發，上午 10:30 起飛，下午 2 點抵達。

P：那太好了，謝謝你。對了，我可以申請錯過轉機的補償嗎？

G：可以，請到客戶服務台那邊，您還可以索取機場附近酒店的折價券和今晚的餐券。

Track 0105 C = Custom officer 海關 M = Man 男士

3. C **How long will you be staying in the US?**

M Two weeks.

C **What is the purpose of your visit?**

M Visiting friends.

C **Where will you be staying?**

M I'll be staying with my friend and his family.

C **Do you have anything to ⑩__________?**

M No, I don't.

C Okay, **here's your passport**. Good day.

M Thank you very much.

翻譯

C：你會在美國停留多長時間呢？

M：兩週。

C：請問來美國的目的是什麼呢？

M：看我的朋友。

C：你會住在哪裡呢？

M：我會住在朋友家跟他的家人一起。

C：你有什麼東西要申報的嗎？

M：沒有。

C：好，護照還你，再見。

M：非常感謝你。

Ch 1

Track 0106

4. Would you like to ⑪__________ to business or first class?
   請問您有需要升等到商務艙或是頭等艙嗎？

5. Your flight has been delayed due to bad weather. Please check the departure boards for updated ⑫__________ times.
   由於天氣惡劣，您的航班已延誤。請參照佈告版來得知最新的登機時間。

6. Could you tell me how to ⑬__________ __________ the other terminal?
   可以請你告訴我要怎麼到另外一個航廈嗎？

實用字詞補充

1. **Here you go** 給你 ＊用於對方請你提供某物，而你給予他的當下可說的話。
2. **luggage / baggage**（不可數名詞）行李
   例 Never leave your luggage unattended. 請看管好隨身行李。
3. **leg** 段、階段
   例 If you have booked a return flight and the outbound leg is canceled, you can

get the cost of the return ticket from your airline. 如果您已經預訂了回程航班，而去程已取消，則可以從航空公司那裡獲得回程機票的退費。

4. **outbound** **去程** *inbound 回程

例 The airline has canceled all outbound flights due to the pandemic.
由於疫情，該航空公司取消了所有出境航班。

5. **voucher** **代金券、兌換券** *coupon 折價券

例 The voucher is valid between August and October.
這個兌換券從八月到十月之間有效。

情境會話 A／翻譯

地勤人員：午安，女士。

費利西亞：午安，我想辦理登機手續。

地勤人員：您的護照，謝謝。

費利西亞：好的（這是我的護照）。

地勤人員：您要托運幾件行李呢？

費利西亞：只有這一件。

地勤人員：謝謝，請把它放在秤上，您想要靠窗還是靠走道的座位？

費利西亞：靠窗的座位，麻煩您，您能把這個袋子標記為易碎嗎？

地勤人員：沒問題，但是女士，對不起，您的行李超重，限制是 20 公斤。您要把一些東西拿出來呢，還是要付行李超重的費用呢？

費利西亞：哦，我應該付多少錢？

地勤人員：130 美元。

費利西亞：好啊，可以刷信用卡嗎？

地勤人員：可以，請稍等……請在這裡簽名。

地勤人員：您會在華盛頓轉機，但您的行李會直接送到您最終目的地。這是您的登機證跟護照，13:45 在 C8 登機口登機。一路順風。

費利西亞：非常感謝。

情境會話 B 搭公車

聆聽重點

購買公車票時的「對話亮點」→ 公車購票相關單字

例如：目的地、幾人搭乘、票價總價、車程、找零錢。

Track 0107　M = Man　W = Woman　★ 請特別注意粗體字的部分 ★

M Excuse me?

W **How can I help you?**

M **Two tickets to** London Heathrow Airport, please.

W Okay, **will that be two adults**?

M Yes, please.

W Okay, two adults to London Heathrow Airport, **your total is** £29.92.

M **Here you go**. [1]**Um**, how long does the journey take?

W It takes usually about 2 hours, but it really depends on the traffic.

M Oh, I see.

W **Here's your change and your bus tickets**.

M [2]**Thank you**.

聽力提點

1. **Um**

類似中文的「嗯、那個、那、欸」之類的語氣詞，功能通常都是填補語氣的空白，當事人可能是猶豫、還在想要怎麼表達，或是用這種填空語氣詞來提醒對方注意等等。

2. **Thank**

[θæŋk] 的母音 [æ] 後面因為有 [ŋ]，實際口語美式發音不會把這個蝴蝶音 [æ] 發得那麼完整，聽起來比較像是 [eɪ]，而這個音檔中的說話者是英式發音，母音 [æ] 就比較明顯。

延伸聽寫 Exercise B

解答參見第 31 頁

Track 0108

1. A Does this bus ①__________ __________ Edinburgh Castle? Do I need to ②__________?

   B No, you don't. I think you take Bus 30 to…to…Wester…yeah…Wester Hailes and the Castle is in ③__________ __________.

翻譯

A：這班公車有到愛丁堡城堡嗎？我需要轉車嗎？

B：你不用轉車，就直接搭 30 路公車到……到……Wester……對，坐到 Wester Hailes 下車之後，城堡走路一下就到了。

Track 0109

2. A Does this bus go direct to the Veteran's Museum?

   B No, you'll have to ④__________.

   A Where can I do that?

   B Cross the road and change to Bus No.10.

翻譯

A：這班公車有到退伍軍人博物館嗎？

B：沒有喔，你要轉其他班公車。

A：我要在哪裡轉車呢？

B：過馬路到對面，改搭 10 號公車。

Track 0110

3. A Which bus should I take if I want to go to the Waterloo train station?

   B ⑤__________ bus X60 to the end of the line.

翻譯

A：如果我想要去滑鐵盧火車站，我要搭哪一班公車呢？

B：搭 X60 路線到終點站。

實用字詞補充

1. **transport hub 交通樞紐** *transportation hub

像是機場或是台北火車站這樣大型的交通樞紐都可以稱作 transport hub。這個 hub（中心）裡面通常會有多種運輸方式的轉運交會，像是火車站 (train stations)、轉運站 (transit stations) 或是公車站 (bus stops)，方便大批人潮通往不同目的地。

2. **cross the road 過馬路（到對向）**

Ch 1

情境會話 B／翻譯

男士：打擾一下？

女士：請問需要什麼嗎？

男士：我要買兩張車票到倫敦希思羅機場。

女士：好的，兩張全票嗎？

男士：是的，麻煩你。

女士：好的，兩張全票到倫敦希思羅機場，一共是 29.92 英鎊。

男士：好，嗯，請問車程要多久？

女士：通常大約需要 2 小時，但還是要看路況如何才能確定。

男士：我明白了。

女士：這是找您的零錢和車票。

男士：謝謝你。

情境會話 C 搭火車

聆聽重點

在火車站購票及乘車時的「對話亮點」→ 火車購票相關單字

例如：目的地與時間、客滿、最早一班火車、特快車、商務車廂或一般車廂、臥鋪列車。

Track 0111 W = Woman C = Clerk ★ 請特別注意粗體字的部分 ★

W Hello, I want to buy **a one-way ticket to Budapest**, please?

C **When would you like to leave**?

W Umm… anytime tonight… if there's…

C One moment, please. I'm sorry, ma'am. **The earliest I have** is the express leaving tomorrow at 6 am.

W No… really…[1]**oh… gee…** I need something right away… [2]**is it… isn't there** anything leaving tonight? **Pretty please**?

C **Tomorrow is the earliest I have**. I'm sorry. **It's fully booked** so there's nothing I can do.

W I… fine… I'll take it.

C Okay, **would you like to travel first class or second class**?

W Second class, please.

C Okay, the ticket is 136 Euros… Oh, wait, I have a [3]**couchette** leaving tonight at 21:00, but **the cheapest available one-way ticket costs** 210 Euros.

W Wow, **that's quite expensive**.

C Yes, it's first class.

W Um… well… okay, **do you take credit cards**?

聽力提點

1. **Oh... gee...**

   感嘆語助詞，如同中文用語的「天哪，不會吧」這類情緒表達詞彙。

2. **is it... isn't there...**

   更正自己本來說的用語，這在口語當中很常見，我們可能開了一個頭，發現想要換一個方式說。

3. **couchette**

   （有可折疊式臥鋪）臥鋪列車 ＊歐洲的夜車 (overnight trains) 有兩種，一種是 couchettes，另一種則是比較舒服一點的 sleepers。

Ch 1

延伸聽寫 | Exercise C

解答參見第 31 頁

Track 0112

1. A ①__________ __________ __________ Taipei Main Train Station, please.

   B ②__________ __________ __________?

   A Return, please.

   B That's 720 NT dollars.

   B Here are your tickets.

   翻譯

   A：一張到台北火車站的車票，謝謝。

   B：單程還是來回呢？

   A：來回，謝謝。

   B：總共台幣 720 元。

   B：這邊是你的車票

2. How much does an ③__________ ticket to Manchester cost?

   請問到曼徹斯特的特快車票價多少？

3. When is ④__________ __________ __________ to Washington?

   請問到華盛頓的下一班火車是幾點？

4. Does the train have a ⑤__________ __________?

   這班火車有餐車車廂嗎？

實用字詞補充

1. **pretty please**（比較撒嬌的口氣）拜託你

   例 Could you please check another destination again, please, pretty please? I just need to get to Europe tomorrow.

   能拜託你再查一次其他地點嗎？拜託，拜託拜託你。我明天真的一定要到歐洲去。

2. **one way / single** 單程

   例 How much is a one-way ticket to London? 到倫敦的單程車票多少錢？

3. **round trip** 來回

   例 It's usually an hour-long round trip by train.

   通常需要一個小時的火車往返車程。

4. **day pass** 一日暢遊票券

情境會話 C／翻譯

乘客：您好，我要買一張去布達佩斯的單程票。

職員：好的，你想搭什麼時候的火車？

乘客：嗯……今晚晚上出發的都可以。

職員：請稍等一下喔，抱歉，最早的一班是明天早上六點出發的特快車。

乘客：真的嗎……天哪，可是我一定要今天晚上出發耶，有沒有……就真的沒有一班今天晚上出發的列車嗎？拜託你。

職員：明天早上這班車就是最早的一班了，在那之前沒有別的列車有位子，很抱歉，我也愛莫能助。

乘客：那……那好吧，我買這班。

職員：請問要搭商務艙還是一班車廂呢？

乘客：請給我一般的車廂，謝謝。

職員：好的，車票是 136 歐元……噢，等一下，還有一張臥鋪列車的車票，今天晚上九點發車，但是最便宜的單程票售價 210 歐元。

乘客：哇，好貴喔。

職員：是的，因為是商務車廂。

乘客：嗯 ……那……那好吧，可以用信用卡付款嗎？

情境會話 D

搭乘捷運

聆聽重點

在捷運地鐵問路的「對話亮點」→ 捷運轉乘相關單字

例如：搭乘什麼路線、列車開往什麼方向、在哪裡轉車、在哪裡到站下車。

Track 0113　T = Tourist　P = Philip　★ 請特別注意粗體字的部分 ★

T **Excuse me, could you tell me how to get to** Diwa Street?

P Diwa Street? Diwa?

T Yes, Diwa Street, Taipei's [1]**oldest** street.

P Um, I don't… wait, **do you mean** Dihua Street, do you want to go to Dadaocheng?

T Yes, yes, Dadaocheng!

P [2]**Okay**, so… first, you **take the Blue Line bound for Nangang Exhibition Center**… and **get off** at Ximen. Then **transfer to** the Green Line bound for Songshan and take that to Beimen.

T Wow, thank you.

P [3]**Thank You**, I didn't even know that Dihua Street is the oldest street in Taipei.

T Well, I always do my homework before traveling abroad.

P Welcome to Taipei. I hope you [4]**enjoy** your stay.

聽力提點

1. **Old**

   雙母音有兩段聲音，例如 old [ould] 的雙母音 [ou]，下顎會先往下發出 [o] 的聲音然後緊接著嘴型聚合回到 [u] 的位置，只是要注意雙母音的第一個聲音 [o] 是比較高且長的聲音，然後往下降音到第二個聲音 [u] 較短收尾，類似中文裡面的「ㄡㄨ」，old 這個字會很清楚的聽到雙母音 [ou] 的聲音。請比較第二個提點。

2. **Okay**

音檔中的說話者把重音放在第一音節 [ˋoukeɪ]，可以聽到清楚的雙母音 [ou]，但是如果 okay 的雙母音 [ou] 是在非重音的音節，因為發音時間較短，不會把兩段聲音發完，即使音標一樣寫著 [ou]，實際上只會聽見短短的一個音。

3. **Thank you.**
這裡的音調重音（高音）在 you，用來表示強調「是我才要謝謝你呢」這樣的意思。可以比較一下 Tourist 先說的 Thank you 的 you 是尾音下降的。

4. **Enjoy 跟 Viewpoint**
雙母音 [ɔɪ] 在重音節與非重音節一樣會有差別。在重音節例如 enjoy [ɪn'dʒɔɪ]，會聽到很清楚的兩段連續的聲音，對比 viewpoint ['vjupɔɪnt] 的 [ɔɪ] 在非重音節，就會以稍微扁平且快速一點的發音呈現。

延伸聽寫 | Exercise D

➔ 解答參見第 31 頁

Track 0114

1. A Excuse me, do you know if there is a bookstore nearby?
B Oh, there's one right around the block ①__________ __________Wellcome Supermarket… wait… no… um… it's ②__________ today… there's a second-hand bookstore though. I'm not sure if you…
A Sure, where is the second-hand bookstore?
B Okay, that's easy. You just ③__________ __________ __________ and keep walking, keep walking for about 10 to 15 minutes and you will see a bronze statue. That's the bookstore.

翻譯

A：不好意思請問一下，附近有書店嗎？

B：哦，威爾康超市對面的轉角就有一家書店啊……等一下……不……那個 ... 那家今天沒有開耶……是還有另外一家，不過是二手書店，我不確定你有沒有……

A：好啊，請問那家二手書店在哪裡呢？

B：好喔，蠻好找的，你就往這個方向直直走，一直走下去，走大概 10 到 15 分鐘吧，然後你會看到一個銅像，那就是那家書店了。

Track 0115

2. A Could you tell me ④__________ __________ __________ __________ the

Taipei Zoo?

B No problem. You can easily ⑤__________ __________ __________ __________ to Zhongxiao Fuxing and then ⑥__________ __________ __________ __________ __________ and that goes all the way to the Taipei Zoo.

翻譯

A：可以請你告訴我台北市立動物園要怎麼去嗎？

B：沒問題喔，你就搭藍線到忠孝復興站，然後轉乘棕線，一路坐到底，就是台北市立動物園了。

Ch 1

實用字詞補充

1. **bound for...**（出發）前往……

例 The ship is bound for Spain. 這艘船開往西班牙。

2. **get off something** 下飛機、下車

例 Get off the bus at NorthWest High School. 要在西北高中那一站下車喔。

3. **around the block** 在下一個街口

例 She lives around the block. 她就住在前面轉過去下一條街上。

4. **across from...** 在……的對面

例 The restaurant is just across from the YumYum Bakery.
那家餐廳就在好喫烘焙坊的對面。

情境會話 D／翻譯

遊　客：對不起，你能告訴我怎麼去迪瓦街嗎？

菲利普：迪瓦？迪瓦？

遊　客：對，台北市最古老的街道，迪瓦街。

菲利普：嗯，我不知……等一下，你是說迪化街吧，你想去大稻埕嗎？

遊　客：對，對，大稻埕！

菲利普：好，所以……首先，你要搭藍線往南港展覽中心的方向……然後呢在西門下車，再轉乘開往松山的綠線，一路坐到北門就可以了。

遊　客：哇，謝謝你。

菲利普：謝謝你，我不知道迪化街是台北最古老的街道。

遊　客：那是因為我出國旅遊之前，都會很認真做功課喔！

菲利普：歡迎來到台北，希望你玩得愉快。

情境會話 E 搭乘計程車

聆聽重點

搭乘計程車時的「對話亮點」→ 計程車相關單字

例如：上車之後告知明確目的地、詢問車程預估時間、路況、走最快的捷徑、安全第一、結帳。

Track 0116 D = Driver P = Passenger ★ 請特別注意粗體字的部分 ★

D Yes, ma'am. Where are you going?

P **Hyde Park**, please.

D No problem!

P **How long does it take to get there**?

D Well, **it really depends**. If we're lucky,… [1]**you know what I mean**… it usually takes forty minutes.

P Okay, I'm in a bit of hurry… so **can you take the quickest route please**?

D Sure, count on me, ma'am.

P …um… **but safety first**.

D Of course.

D Oh… no… I think there's been an accident. Ma'am, I'm sorry but **you'll get there faster if you walk from here**.

P I'm afraid so… Alright, I'll walk. Can I [2]**pay by credit card**?

D Yes, of course.

聽力提點

1. **you know what I mean**

插入式的短語。如果不習慣這種短語，會覺得一下子來不及在心裡轉譯上下文。這種插入式的短語有時候也會因為語調的不同而有不同的語意情境，像這邊有點在開玩笑暗示「幸運」就是「沒塞車」的意思，聲音語調是輕鬆微笑的。但也有可能是比較嚴肅的口氣，變得像是在叮嚀或囑咐「你是有沒有懂，最好有懂喔」！因此，面對這種口語上的短語，若能在情境上下文當中去多聽、多練習，不僅會加強聽力的理解，更可以幫助口說的表達。

2. **pay 和 celebrate**

雙母音 [eɪ] 在 pay [peɪ] 跟 celebrate ['seləbreɪt] 兩個字之間的差別：celebrate 的 [eɪ] 在非重音的位置，雙母音兩段聲音變得較短，[eɪ] 的尾音 [ɪ] 在口語聽力當中是沒有的。

延伸聽寫 | Exercise E

解答參見第 31 頁

Track 0117

1. Would you ①__________ __________ __________ __________ __________?
   能請你走最快的路線嗎？
2. If the traffic isn't ②__________, can we ③__________ __________ the Longshan Temple on the way?
   如果不塞車的話，我們中途可以順便經過龍山寺嗎？
3. I'll put your luggage ④__________ __________ __________.
   我來幫你把行李放到後車廂。

實用字詞補充

1. **I'm afraid so.**（情況或結果）恐怕就是這樣子
   例 A: Do we really have to leave now? 我們一定要現在離開嗎？
   B: I'm afraid so. 恐怕是這樣沒錯。
2. **I'm afraid not.**（情況或結果）恐怕不是如此喔
   例 A: What did he say? He agreed, right! 他怎麼說？他同意了，對吧！
   B: I'm afraid not. 恐怕並非如此。

情境會話 E／翻譯

司機：女士，請問去哪裡呢？
乘客：海德公園，麻煩您。
司機：沒問題！
乘客：請問車程要多久？
司機：嗯，這就要看情況了，如果說我們很幸運的話，通常差不多 40 分鐘，你懂我的意思吧。
乘客：好的，我有點趕時間，可以走最快的路線嗎？
司機：好的，包在我身上。
乘客：那個，當然是安全第一。
司機：當然。
司機：噢……不……我想前面應該有發生車禍，女士，很抱歉，我想你可能從這邊用走路的會比較快喔。
乘客：恐怕是這樣沒錯啊！那好吧，我用走的，車錢可以刷卡嗎？
司機：當然可以。

租車

聆聽重點

找出與汽車租賃業務對話的「對話亮點」→ 租賃汽車相關單字
例如：租車、哪一種車型、詢價、租賃天數、總租金。

Track 0118 D = David C = Clerk ★ 請特別注意粗體字的部分 ★

D Hi, **I'd like to rent a car**.

C No problem, **what type of car would you like**, economy, compact, premium or van?

D **I'd like a premium**.

C Sure, we have a Nissan Maxima and a Toyota Avalon…

D **How much would it cost to** rent the Nissan?

C **How many days would you like to rent it for**?

D **For a** [1]**week**.

C Uh… then… **it will be** [2]fi..uh… four… four hundred dollars.

聽力提點

1. **week 和 it**
母音 [i]（例如 week [wik]）跟母音 [ɪ]（例如 it [ɪt]）兩者之間的差異困擾很多非母語人士，其實這兩者的差別並不在於聲音的長短，而是發音位置稍有不同，發 week 的 [i] 舌頭是稍微往前伸，有點類似中文的一的聲音，嘴形會稍微往前突出，但是 it 的 [ɪ] 則是嘴形微收扁，舌頭放鬆懸在口腔中間的位置，這個舌頭的位置比較接近中文注音符號的 ㄝ。

2. **fi..uh… four… hundred dollars**
更正重說。

情境會話 F／翻譯

大衛：您好，我要租車。

職員：沒問題，您想要多大的車款呢？經濟型、小型車、豪華轎車、還是休旅車之類的？

大衛：我想要豪華型的車款。

職員：沒問題，我們有日產千里馬和豐田阿瓦隆…

大衛：如果租日產這台費用是多少呢？

職員：您想租幾天呢？

大衛：一個星期。

職員：那就是……五……嗯，不對，是四百，四百美元。

情境會話 G 加油站

聆聽重點

找出在加油站與加油站員工的「對話亮點」→ 汽車加油相關單字

例如：油快沒了、油箱、加油、油加滿、總金額、付款方式。

Track 0119 G = Gas attendant C = Customer ★ 請特別注意粗體字的部分 ★

G How are you?

C I'm good, thanks.

G **What can I do for you today**?

C **Can you fill up the car, please**?

G Sure… and **that will come to 40 dollars**. **Will you be paying with cash or by card today**?

C Cash, here you go.

G Thanks.

實用字詞補充

1. **run out of** 用光

   例 I was running out of gas. 汽油快要用完了。

2. **gas tank** 油箱

   例 I need to make a stop to fill up my gas tank. 我要停一下，要加油。

3. **fill up** 填滿

   例 Please fill it up. 請把油加滿。

4. **pump the gas** 加油

   例 We usually pump our own gas. 我們通常都是自助加油。

情境會話 G／翻譯

加油站員：你好嗎？

顧　　客：很好，謝謝。

加油站員：今天需要什麼服務嗎？

顧　　客：幫我加滿油，謝謝！

加油站員：沒問題……總共是 40 美元，您今天要用現金還是信用卡付款呢？

顧　　客：現金。

加油站員：謝謝。

延伸聽寫 Answer Keys

Exercise A

① checked in、② I would like an aisle seat、③ fully booked、④ many pieces of luggage
⑤ carry-on、⑥ connecting flight、⑦ the first leg、⑧ claim compensation
⑨ voucher、⑩ declare、⑪ upgrade、⑫ boarding、⑬ get to

Exercise B

① go to、② transfer、③ walking distance、④ transfer、⑤ Take

Exercise C

① A ticket to、② Single or return、③ express、④ the next train、⑤ dining car

Exercise D

① across from、② closed、③ go this way、④ how to get to、⑤ take the Blue Line
⑥ transfer to the Brown Line

Exercise E

① take the most direct route、② heavy、③ drive past、④ in the trunk

加值學更多！

「路人問路，左轉右轉、直走到底、在左手邊還是右手邊 ......」超實用情境對話聽力練習內容，線上下載，隨時想聽就聽！

Unit 02

郵局寄包裹 · 銀行開戶及存匯款

美髮店 · 美甲店 · SPA 美容會館

情境會話 A 郵局寄包裹

聆聽重點

在郵局辦理郵寄包裹業務時的「對話亮點」→包裹相關單字

例如：秤重、包裹大小、包裹內容與價值、是否含有易碎物品、寄送方式的價格差異、追蹤郵件等。

Track 0201　C = Clerk　T = Theodore　★ 請特別注意粗體字的部分 ★

C Good morning, **how can I help you**?

T Hi, I need to **send this parcel to** Japan, please.

C Okay, let's see **how much it weighs**… It's less than 2 kilograms. **It's a small parcel**! Okay, um, does your package contain **valuable or fragile goods**?

T Not really, just some chocolates and T-shirts for my [1]father. It's for his birthday.

C That's nice. **How would you like to send it**?

T What are the **options**?

C Oh, there are several… um… here is the list. **Worldwide delivery often takes [1]about 7 working days**, and you also can choose International Tracked and Signed for extra peace of mind.

T Uh… sorry… this one, International Signed, **it's a lot cheaper**. **What's the difference**?

C The items can be **tracked** until they leave the UK.

T Oh… I see… so if I want to… [2]like… **monitor my parcels' whereabouts**, I have to choose the Tracked and Signed.

C Correct.

T Well, uh… a bit expensive… okay, okay… Tracked and Signed then.

C No problem.

T Oh, and how do I track my parcel?

C **You can easily check the progress of your delivery online** by entering your **tracking number**.

T Got it.

C Would you fill in the **shipping details**, please?

T Sure.

C Okay, your total comes to £ 6.85.

聽力提點

1. **about 跟 father**

[ə] 這個母音又叫作 schwa sound 或是輕聲的母音，會在非重音節，例如 about [ə`baut] 這個字，[ə] 的發音聽起來很短很輕。要發這個聲音很簡單，只要嘴巴微開，放鬆你的舌頭不要動，輕輕把氣送出口腔外，就會發出 [ə] 這樣的聲音。不過，當 [ə] 這個母音後面跟著子音 [r] 的時候，[ə] 聽起來就像被後面的 [r] 吸收過去，只是一個捲舌音而已，例如 father [`fɑðər] 聽起來其實是 [`fɑðɚ]。不過須注意，這是美式發音，若換成英式發音則不同了，英式發音的 schwa sound [ə] + r 的時候，很多時候是 [ə] 的聲音很清楚而已，例如英式發音的 father 聽起來會是 [`fɑðə]、teacher 聽起來是 [`titʃə]，而 understand 聽起來則是 [ʌndə`stænd]（美式 [ʌndɚ`stænd]）。

2. **If I want to... like... monitor my parcels' whereabouts, I have to choose the Tracked and Signed.**

like 是常見的填空詞語，通常是說話者語頓片刻的時候會說出來的詞語，並沒有特別的意義，比如說這裡換成中文來理解，我們可能會說「那要是我如果……就是說……我想要完全掌握我的包裹的行蹤的話……」，這個比喻並不是把「like」這個字翻出一個對應的中文，而是要呈現我們實際中文口語對話當中，每個人都可能說出這種填空詞語，沒有實際上的重要文意，只是在我們邊說話邊思考的過程當中很自然出現的輔助詞彙而已。

延伸聽寫 | Exercise A

➜解答參見第 48 頁

Track 0202

1. A I would like to ①__________ __________ __________.

   B **Where is it going?**

   A It's going to Coventry.

   B **How would you like to send it?** ②__________ __________ __________?

A Express, please.

翻譯

A：我想要寄包裹。

B：要寄到哪裡呢？

A：要寄到考文郡。

B：寄送方式是？快捷郵件或是一般郵件？

A：快捷，麻煩你。

Track 0203

2. Where do you want to ③__________ __________?
   你想要寄到哪個地方呢？

3. Can I ④__________ my regular mail?
   我可以追蹤一般郵件嗎？

4. Express post has ⑤________________ __________.
   快捷郵件是保證送達。

5. If you want to protect your goods ⑥__________ __________, you can wrap them in ⑦__________ __________.
   如果你想要保護你的物品不要受損，可以用這個氣泡袋把它們包起來。

6. Do you want to ⑧__________ your package against loss or damage?
   你有要幫你的包裹保險以防包裹遺失或是受損嗎？

實用字詞補充

1. **package / parcel** 包裹（美式／英式用法）
2. **recipient's address** 收件者地址
3. **peace of mind** 安心
   例 Installing a nanny cam will give you greater peace of mind.
   安裝隱藏式攝影機會讓你更加放心。
4. **overseas** 海外
   例 Check our website to find the best international service to send your parcel overseas. 請瀏覽我們的網站，尋找將包裹寄往海外的最佳國際服務。
5. **whereabouts** 下落、去向、行蹤
   例 His family's present whereabouts are a secret.
   他的家人至今的下落仍是一個祕密。

情境會話 A／翻譯

職　員：早安，請問需要什麼服務嗎？

西奧多：嗨，我要把這個包裹寄到日本。

職　員：好，讓我們先秤重……不到 2 公斤，是一個小包裹！好的，您的包裹中是否裝有貴重或易碎的物品？

西奧多：沒有耶，就是裝一些要送給我爸爸的巧克力和衣服，他的生日要到了。

職　員：真貼心，您想怎麼寄送呢？

西奧多：我有哪些選擇啊？

職　員：哦，有好幾種……嗯……來，這邊有細項可以看。通常國際包裹寄送需要大約 7 個工作天，那如果您選擇「國際包裹追蹤貨運進度及簽收」這個方式的話，您會更安心喔。

西奧多：那這一個，「國際包裹簽收」的方式便宜很多，它們有什麼區別呢？

職　員：您可以追蹤包裹進度到離開英國為止。

西奧多：喔，我明白了……所以，如果我希望可以像是監控我的包裹的下落的話，我就要選擇這個「追蹤貨運進度及簽收」的方式。

職　員：對的。

西奧多：有點貴……好的，那就「追蹤貨運進度及簽收」吧！

職　員：沒問題。

西奧多：哦，請問我要怎麼追蹤我的包裹？

職　員：您只要輸入追蹤包裹的序號，在網路上就可以輕鬆查詢交貨進度。

西奧多：了解。

職　員：麻煩您填寫運送的資料。

西奧多：好的。

職　員：好的，您的總金額為 6.85 英鎊。

情境會話 B 銀行開戶及存匯款

聆聽重點

在銀行辦理開戶相關業務時的「對話亮點」→ 開戶相關單字

例如：開戶、不同的帳戶種類、相關文件、開戶首存款、提款、填寫表格、金融卡、密碼。

Track 0204　S = Student　B = Bank clerk　★ 請特別注意粗體字的部分 ★

S Good morning! I'm a student from Taiwan and I'd like to **open a bank account**.

B No problem, sir. **What kind of account would you like to open**?

S I need both **a savings account and a current account**.

B Okay. Did you bring all the documents with you? **Your passport, your letter of introduction for the UK Banking Facilities and your CAS confirmation letter**. Also, to open these accounts, you need to **deposit a minimum of £100**.

S Here are the documents and I will be depositing £800 today and these traveler's checks as well.

B Thank you. I'll take care of it and **here is your application form**. **Please fill it out**.

S Of course.

B Take your time, and I'll be right back. Alright, Mr. Chen, normally it takes some days to **process your application** and we will **run a credit check**. Well, since you are an international student, it will be simpler. It means that, if everything goes fine, you will receive a letter from Bank of Scotland with your **debit card** in about 7-10 working days. **And your PIN will be sent separately**.

S Thank you for your help.

B My pleasure.

*CAS: Confirmation of Acceptance for Studies

英國學校發給國際學生的錄取正式信函

延伸聽寫 | Exercise B

解答參見第 48 頁

Track 0205

1. I would like to open a ①__________ __________.
   我要開一個活存帳戶。

2. I'd like to ②__________ £1,000 into my ③__________ __________.
   我想要存一千英鎊到我的儲蓄帳戶裡面。

3. In what ④________________ would you like the money?
   現鈔的面額想要哪種呢？

Track 0206

4. A I'd like to ⑤__________ £150, please.

   B **Please enter your PIN**.

   A Okay.

   B And **how do you want your money**?

   A Four twenties and the ⑥__________ __________ tens, please.

   B One moment, please. **Here's your cash**.

   A Thank you very much.

翻譯

A：我要提款 150 英鎊謝謝。
B：請輸入您的 PIN 密碼。
A：好。
B：請問你想要什麼面額呢？
A：四張面額 20 磅，其他都 10 磅。
B：請稍候，來，這是您的現金。
A：非常感謝你。

Track 0207

5. A I need to ⑦__________ __________ __________.

   B Please **write your account number here and sign your name on the back of the check**. And I also need to see a piece of ⑧_______________.

   A **Will a student card do?**

   B That would be fine.

翻譯

A：我要兌現這張支票。
B: 請在這邊填寫你的帳戶號碼，並在支票後面簽名，然後我還需要看一下您的證件。

A：學生證可以嗎？

B：沒問題

實用字詞補充

1. **checking account / current account** 活存帳戶（美式／英式的差別）
2. **Take your time.** 不急，慢慢來。

   例 You don't need to hurry. Take your time. 你不用著急，慢慢來沒關係。

情境會話 B／翻譯

學生：早安！我是從台灣來的留學生，我想開戶。

行員：沒問題，先生，請問您想開設哪一種帳戶？

學生：我要開儲蓄帳戶，還有活存帳戶。

行員：好的，您有帶所有需要的文件嗎？您的護照，英國銀行介紹信以及學校錄取的確認信。另外，要開設這些帳戶，您今天至少需要存入 100 英鎊。

學生：這裡是所有的文件，今天我要存 800 英鎊，還有這些旅行支票。

行員：謝謝，我來處理，然後這是申請表，請幫我填寫一下。

學生：當然。

行員：您可以慢慢寫，我等一下就回來。好的，陳先生，通常開設帳戶會需要幾天的時間來審核您的申請表，還會進行您的信用檢查，不過呢，由於您是國際學生，這個部分會蠻簡單的，這就是說呢，如果一切順利的話，大約 7 到 10 個工作日之內您會收到由銀行寄發的信，裡面會有您的簽帳金融卡，另外，您的 PIN 碼是會另外單獨寄送的。

學生：謝謝您的幫助。

行員：我的榮幸。

美髮店

聆聽重點

一般在美髮店會有的「對話亮點」→ 剪髮相關單字

例如：如何預約、如何跟髮型師溝通、髮型的名稱、襯托臉型、瀏海、修髮尾、分岔。

Track 0208 S = Stylist W = Woman ★ 請特別注意粗體字的部分 ★

S How are you doing today? You look fabulous in that dress.

W Oh, thank you.

S **How would you like your hair done today**?

W Umm… I always wanted to get an undercut but I don't know… just, I… I've never tried it. I think it … of course, it would be super cool, but I'm not sure whether it **suits my face shape**. Anyway, I'd like to know what you think. Maybe today is the today!

S **Let's take a look**… um… **your hair is naturally curly** and your jawline is very sexy,… I think an **undercut hairstyle suits you perfectly**. I think today is the day.

W Nice!

S Oh, but I would like to keep your **bangs**, and maybe add a **gentle curve**, I want you to show off your astonishing eyes.

W That's great! I love my bangs by the way.

S Good.

延伸聽寫 | Exercise C

➔ 解答參見第 48 頁

Track 0209

1. A How do you want it?

   B I think I'll **keep the same hairstyle**, but **I have a lot of** ① __________ __________, pretty annoying.

   A No problem. **Let's give it a** ② __________ **first** cause… I think it seems to be a bit long. Short hair makes you younger. What do you think?

B Fine. Go ahead. Do whatever you like!

A Wow, thank you for trusting me.

翻譯

A：今天想要怎麼剪呢？

B：我應該就是維持差不多這個造型就可以，但是我有好多分岔，蠻惱人的說。

A：沒問題，我們先修一下吧，因為我覺得現在看起來太長了，短髮讓你看起來比較年輕耶，你覺得呢？

B：都好啊，就照你的意思，怎麼樣都可以！

A：哇，謝謝你那麼相信我耶！

Track 0210

2. A Hi, **I would like to** ③__________ __________ __________ **for a haircut for tomorrow**.

B No problem. Would you like a **senior stylist or a junior one**? The price difference is 65 euros.

A Oh… there is price difference…

B Yes, we have different levels of pricing based on the experience of the stylists, but no matter what level you choose, you are promised absolutely exceptional service.

A um… **I'll have a senior stylist**, thanks.

B Okay, then I recommend Hitomi. She is really good.

A That's perfect. Can I come tomorrow morning?

B Let me check… yes, of course, I have 10:30 a.m.. ④__________ __________ __________ __________ __________?

A Yes, it does. Thank you.

B See you tomorrow.

翻譯

A：嗨，我想預約明天的理髮。

B：沒問題。您想要資深設計師還是年輕設計師？差價為 65 歐元。

A：哦……有價差……

B：是的，根據設計師的經驗，我們有不同的價格，但是無論您選擇哪一種，您放心我們保證為您提供絕對優質的服務。

A：嗯，那我選資深設計師好了，謝謝。

B：好的，那我推薦瞳，她超棒的。

A：那太好了，我明天早上來，可以嗎？

B：讓我確認一下喔……可以，沒問題的，有一個上午 10:30 的時間，您方便嗎？

A：可以喔，謝謝你。

B：明天見。

實用字詞補充

Ch 1

1. **trim 修剪**

例 Just give the ends a trim, thank you.

就幫我髮尾修一下就好，謝謝。

2. **go ahead 放手去做、著手開始做**

例 We have received permission to go ahead with the year end celebration party.

我們已獲准可以著手進行年終慶祝活動。

情境會話 C／翻譯

設計師：哈囉你好！你穿這條裙子真是好看。

女　士：謝謝。

髮型師：今天想要怎樣剪呢？

女　士：嗯……我一直想剪那種把兩邊全部都剃掉的造型，但我也不知道耶，就是我都一直還沒有真的剪過，我就是覺得那種髮型很酷，但是我不確定它會不會適合我的臉型，反正，我想知道你怎麼看，搞不好就是今天來把它們都剃掉吧！

髮型師：我看看喔……嗯……你的頭髮是微微自然捲，而且下巴非常性感……我覺得把雙邊推高的髮型非常適合妳，我覺得就是今天了！

女　士：真的嗎，太好了！

髮型師：對了，但是我想保留瀏海的部分，或許稍微讓它捲一點，我想要你大肆炫耀你美麗的雙眼。

女　士：太好了！順便說一句，我愛我的瀏海。

設計師：好呦。

情境會話 D 美甲店

聆聽重點

在美甲店常出現的「對話亮點」→ 美甲相關單字

例如：手部指甲美容、腳指甲美容、修剪指甲、指甲油顏色、襯托膚色、法式指甲。

Track 0211 R = Receptionist C = Ms Chen L = Lisa ★ 請特別注意粗體字的部分 ★

R **Welcome back to Posh Salon**! It's great to see you again! Ms Chen!

C Good to see you too. **I have an appointment for a manicure**.

R Yes, Ms Chen, **Lisa will be with you in a moment**.

C Okay.

R It's a [1]beautiful day, isn't it! May I get you something to drink? or magazines?

C No, I'm fine. Thank you.

L Ms Chen, welcome. This way, please.

L **What kind of nails would you like today?**

C The usual, **just make it square with round corners**.

L No problem… and **what nail polish color would you like**?

C Wow, they all look so pretty… um… it's a tough decision.

L It is. Spring is coming. These are our [2]new nail polish colors. Some of them are very fresh and will look good on you. It brightens your **skin tone**. If you want, I can pick two or three for you and you can pick from those.

C That will be a lot easier. Please do that.

L **Sure thing**. Well, I think this sakura pink and this salmon pink all **suit you**, and since you are unsure of the color today, my suggestion would be a **French Manicure**. You know, it's elegant, absolutely classic and subtle. You can't go wrong with a French Manicure.

C Oh, you are good. Lisa.

聽力提點

1. **beautiful** [ˋbjutəfəl]
雙母音 [ju] 很像 ㄧㄨ 兩個中文注音接連發音的聲音。

2. **new**
如果是英式發音，你會聽見 [nju]，但美式口音裡通常是 [nu]。關於這個 [u] 母音的更多介紹詳見 Unit 04 情境會話 C（P73.）。

Ch 1

延伸聽寫 | Exercise D

解答參見第 48 頁

Track 0212

1. The holidays are ①__________ __________ Dream Salon, this is Ashley, how can I help you?
佳節氣息在我們夢幻沙龍正濃呢，我是艾許莉，請問有什麼我能為您服務的嗎？

2. I have an appointment for a ②__________.
我有預約腳指甲美容。

3. Do you like ③__________ __________ __________ shape nails?
您喜歡方型還是圓型的指甲呢？

4. I would like my nails ④__________.
我想要指甲彩繪。

5. Would you like a ⑤__________ for your nails?
有想要做彩繪指甲嗎？

6. Have a look at the ⑥__________. 參考一下這些圖樣。

實用字詞補充

1. **manicure** 美甲手部護理
2. **pedicure** 腳指甲足部護理
3. **sure thing**（口語）表示同意、沒問題
例 A: Could you help me lift it up? 你能幫我把這個抬起來嗎？
B: Sure thing! 沒問題！
4. **you can't go wrong with...** 表達選擇某件事物一定不會有什麼閃失
例 If you want delicious street foods, you can't go wrong with Taiwan.
要是你想吃美味的小吃，選擇台灣絕對不會錯的。

情境會話 D／翻譯

接待員：歡迎您再度來到時尚沙龍！很高興再次見到您！陳女士

陳女士：我也很高興見到你。我有預約修指甲。

接待員：是的，陳女士，麗莎馬上就過來。

陳女士：好的。

接待員：今天天氣真好對吧！需要幫您準備一點喝的嗎？還是要給您雜誌呢？

陳女士：不用，我這樣就可以。謝謝。

麗　莎：陳女士，歡迎您。這邊請。

麗　莎：今天指甲想要怎麼修？

陳女士：和往常一樣，把它修成方圓型的。

麗　莎：沒問題……那您想要什麼顏色的指甲油呢？

陳女士：哇，它們看起來都那麼漂亮……嗯……好難抉擇啊。

麗　莎：真的。春天腳步近了，這些都是我們的新色，其中有一些非常清爽也很適合您，還會襯您的膚色。要是您願意的話，我可以替您先選出兩三款，然後您可以再從中選擇。

陳女士：那會容易得多，麻煩你了。

麗　莎：沒問題。嗯，我覺得這種櫻花粉和鮭魚粉都很適合您，那因為您今天不太確定想做的顏色，我的建議是做法式指甲，既優雅又絕對經典，還很低調，法式指甲無論什麼情況都絕對不會錯的。

陳女士：哇，你太厲害了，麗莎。

SPA 美容會館

聆聽重點

在 SPA 會出現的「對話亮點」→ 護膚美容相關單字

例如：美容課程、做臉、活膚、保濕、磨砂、去角質、蒸氣浴

Track 0213 C = Christine A = Abby ★ 請特別注意粗體字的部分 ★

Ch 1

C Nice to see you again, ma'am.

A How are you? Christine. It's been a busy week, and finally I got time to **treat myself to a facial massage**. So happy!

C You deserve it! Please follow me.

A **What packages would you recommend to me today?**

C Would you like to try our Spring **Rejuvenation Massage Package**?

A Rejuvenation! Oh my… that's what I need for sure.

C Especially, after this past year, we're all in need of a special renewal. This package includes an 80-minute Swedish massage, super **hydrating** Diva Body Butter Wrap, Honey Sugar **scrub** for your feet and full *<u>**body**</u> **exfoliation**.

A Wow, the total time would be…

C About 2 hours and it only costs 200 dollars today.

A Okay, I want this one. Oh, and I'm gonna try your **new sauna** as well.

C Good choice, ma'am.

聽力提點

***body**

body [bɑdi] 的母音 [ɑ] 很像中文的注音 ㄚ，本情境會話主題 SPA [spɑ], massage [məˋsɑʒ] 的重音（高音）以及 follow [ˋfɑloʊ] 的重音都是 [ɑ] 母音。

情境會話 E／翻譯

克里斯汀：很高興再次見到你，女士。

艾　　比：你好嗎，克里斯汀，這真是忙碌的一週，我今天總算有時間可以來做臉，太開心了！

克里斯汀：你值得好好休息一下的！請跟我來。

艾　　比：今天你會推薦我什麼套裝組合呢？

克里斯汀：你想不想嘗試我們的春季肌膚復活按摩組合？

艾　　比：肌膚復活，天哪，那就是我現在需要的啦！

克里斯汀：真的，尤其是過去一年來，我們大家都很需要復活過來才行，這個套餐包含 80 分鐘的瑞典式按摩，超保濕的 Diva 身體乳油護膚，雙腳的蜂蜜糖磨砂膏，以及全身的去角質。

艾　　比：哇，總時間是……

克里斯汀：大約 2 個小時，今天只花 200 美元。

艾　　比：好啊，我想要這個。哦，我也要嘗試你們的新蒸氣浴。

克里斯汀：這是個明智的選擇，女士。

延伸聽寫 Answer Keys

Exercise A

① send this package、② Express or normal、③ send it、④ track、⑤ guaranteed delivery、⑥ against damage、⑦ bubble wrap、⑧ insure

Exercise B

① checking account、② deposit、③ savings account、④ denominations、⑤ withdraw、⑥ rest in、⑦ cash the check、⑧ identification

Exercise C

① split ends、② trim、③ make an appointment、④ Does that work for you

Exercise D

① coming at、② pedicure、③ square or round、④ painted、⑤ design、⑥ pattern

Unit 03

藥局 · 電話預約看診 · 刺青店 · 健身房

藥局

聆聽重點

在藥局會出現的「對話亮點」→ 藥局相關單字

例如：處方箋、服藥指示、空腹、營養品、藥物交互作用、藥物諮詢、偏頭痛、止痛藥。

Track 0301 P = Pharmacist C = Client ★ 請特別注意粗體字的部分 ★

P Good morning, how may I help you?

C Hi, **I have this prescription**.

P Let me see… okay, one moment please… here you go, and don't forget, **you have to take these pills twice a day. Take one in the morning and one in the evening**.

C **Are there any special directions for using this?**

P Don't **take** your medication **on an empty stomach** and you should be aware of **drug interactions**. Are you taking two or more prescription drugs?

C No. But I **take** [1]**supplements**, like vitamins and… Is that okay?

P If it's vitamin C, then it's fine, but seriously, **mixing medications and supplements** can be really dangerous.

C I [1]understand. Thank you very much… um… How much?

P That will be 42 dollars. Do you need anything else?

C Yeah, **do you have something for a headache**?

P Yes, when did your pain start?

C Oh, actually **it's a migraine**, you know, the crushing, pounding, and throbbing pain. Annoying crazy thing living in people's head…

P **Would you be sensitive to light and sound sometimes?**

C Yes, it's really painful and depressing. I usually take **pain killers**, but it doesn't work recently. Don't know why… it's just… um… I… I am a lawyer, and I have to work for long hours… anyway…

P **You need prescription medicine.**

C To get stronger pain killers?

P No, actually, to deal with migraines, **there is no cure for a migraine**, umm… but there are effective approaches. Normally, when people have an ordinary headache, they might reach for an **over-the-counter pain reliever** like Advil, or simply drink herbal tea maybe. However, this is not enough to deal with migraines.

C So I have been doing it wrong for years… [2]that is… that is… wow…

P I'm afraid so. That's why I recommend that you talk to your doctor about your migraine. **It's a preventive treatment**.

C Thank you for your suggestion. It's very helpful. I will talk to my doctor.

Ch 1

聽力提點

1. **supplement 跟 understand**

這兩個字都有母音 [ʌ]，剛好 supplement 的 [ʌ] 是在重音節位置 [ˋsʌplɪmənt]，而 understand 的 [ʌ] 則在非重音節位置 [ʌndəˋstænd]。重音節位置會聽到明顯較長的由高音往下墜的 [ʌ]，而在非重音位置的 understand 則是很短的、較輕的聲音，因為聲音時間比較短，所以不會把往下墜的聲音發完。

2. **that is… that is…**

重複、重說。有時在口語對話中，說話者會一直重複幾個詞彙，這可能是尚未找到確切要表達的詞彙所產生的情緒上的延長，通常並沒有實際的語意。

延伸聽寫 | Exercise A

➔ 解答參見第 63 頁

Track 0302

1. My doctor ①____________ me stronger pain killers.
   我的醫生開給我這種比較強效的止痛藥。

2. It's illegal to give you this medicine ②__________ __________ __________.
   你沒有處方箋，我不能提供藥品給你，那是違法的。

3. Can you give me something for a ③__________?
   你可以給我一些感冒藥嗎？

4. What kind of reaction did you have? Did your throat ④__________ __________? Did you ⑤__________ __________ __________?
   你有什麼症狀反應呢？喉嚨有腫起來嗎？有出疹子嗎？

5. I feel ⑥__________ all over, especially my eyes, can you give me some allergy ⑦__________ __________?

我全身都好癢，尤其是我的眼睛，你可以給我過敏眼藥水嗎？

6. A Can I drink alcohol while taking the medications?

B It is not ⑧__________. Actually, alcohol can make these medications toxic to your body.

翻譯

A：我吃這些藥，還可以喝酒嗎？

B：不建議喔，事實上，酒精會讓這些藥物在你的身體裡面產生毒素。

實用字詞補充

1. **pharmacist 藥劑師**

例 Pharmacists can offer valuable information about your prescription drugs.

藥師可以針對你的處方藥提供很有幫助的資訊。

2. **prescribe 醫生開藥**

例 Doctor, is there anything stronger you can prescribe?

醫生，有沒有更強效的藥可以開給我呢？

3. **prescription 處方箋**

例 This kind of drug is only available on prescription. If you think you need it, you should talk to your doctor.

這種藥只能憑處方箋購買。如果你覺得你很需要，應該跟你的醫生討論。

4. **supplement 營養補充品**

例 They take vitamin supplements on a daily basis.

他們每天都會吃維他命的營養補充品。

5. **cough syrup 咳嗽糖漿**

例 Before you take the cough syrup, you should read the medicine label to know more about its uses and side effects.

在你服用這個咳嗽糖漿之前，應該還是要讀一下藥物標示以了解使用方式跟副作用。

6. **over-the-counter 不用處方箋就可以購買的成藥**

例 People can purchase most cold remedies over-the-counter.

大多數的感冒用藥是不用處方箋就可以買到的。

7. **allergic reaction 過敏反應**

例 I've had allergic reactions to the medicines.

我對這些藥物產生了過敏反應。

8. **eye drops** 眼藥水

例 These allergy eye drops can help relieve symptoms of red eyes.
這些抗過敏的眼藥水可以幫助減緩紅眼的症狀。

情境會話 A／翻譯

藥劑師：早安，請問需要什麼呢？

客　戶：您好，我有處方箋要拿藥。

藥劑師：讓我看一下……好喔，請稍等……來，藥在這邊，別忘了，藥一天吃兩次，早上一次，晚上再一次。

客　戶：請問一下用藥有沒有什麼要特別小心的地方呢？

藥劑師：不要空腹吃藥，然後你也要注意藥物交互作用的問題，你同時還有服用其他藥物嗎？

客　戶：沒有耶，不過我有吃保健食品，就像是維他命之類的，那沒關係吧？

藥劑師：如果就是維他命 C 是沒關係，但是嚴格說來，把藥物跟一般的營養補充品混用其實是非常危險的。

客　戶：好，我懂了，非常感謝。這樣多少錢？

藥劑師：42 塊（美金）。您還有需要其他東西嗎？

客　戶：是的，有頭痛藥嗎？

藥劑師：有，您的疼痛是從什麼時候開始的呢？

客　戶：哦，其實是偏頭痛啦，你知道，那種讓你感覺到重擊、刺痛、抽痛的偏頭痛，簡直是住在人們腦海中煩人的瘋狂東西…….

藥劑師：會不會有時候還對光線和聲音感到敏感？

客　戶：會啊，這真的是超痛苦也超令人沮喪。我通常會吃止痛藥，但最近都沒有效耶，不知道為什麼……這真的很……嗯……我是律師，必須工作很長時間，反正……

藥劑師：您需要處方箋的偏頭痛藥物。

客　戶：可以拿到更強效的止痛藥？

藥劑師：不是，實際上，偏頭痛不算是有所謂治癒的方法……但是有一些有效應對的方式。通常啊，當人們一覺得頭痛，他們可能會馬上去買一般藥妝店的非處方箋止痛藥，例如 Advil，或者就喝點花草茶之類。但是，這都不足以對付偏頭痛。

客　戶：所以我這麼多年來都做錯囉……

藥劑師：恐怕是這樣。因此，我建議您與您的醫生談談，有關於偏頭痛的處方箋用藥，那是一種預防性的治療。

客　戶：謝謝你的建議，這非常有幫助。我會和我的醫生談談。

B 電話預約看診

聆聽重點

請留意打電話預約掛號的「對話亮點」→看病相關單字

例如：約診、請求通融插隊、描述症狀、一般感冒、嘔吐、高燒不退、急診、診所。

Track 0303　R = Receptionist　P = Patient　★ 請特別注意粗體字的部分 ★

R Dr. Grey's office. Paul speaking. How may I help you?

P Hi, I'm Rachel Kao, and I'm calling to **make an appointment with Dr. Grey**. **I haven't been feeling very well.**

R Do you need urgent care? Ms Kao?

P um... I'm... I don't think so... but **I'd like to see Dr. Grey soon.**

R Sure, how about next Tuesday? **Dr. Grey can see you at 11 am.**

P Is it possible that you could **squeeze me in anytime today**? I'm... um...

R I'm sorry. **If there are any cancellations, I'll call you...** but I wouldn't count on it if I were you... If you aren't feeling well right now, you should consider going to an **urgent care clinic**.

P Oh... um... I **had a really bad headache** last week and **a fever** days ago. I thought it's just a **common cold** so I drank plenty of fluids. But **last night I started vomiting and I feel itchy all over**. I don't know why? I never... and this morning **I started to run a high fever and it didn't go down so...**

R Ms Kao, I suggest that you **go to an urgent care center or an emergency department** right away. Do you know where to go? And can you walk or drive?

P My roommate can drive me, thanks. Umm, there's **a walk-in center** at the corner of Oxford and Victoria Streets. Can they help me?

R **Let me check for you**... bear with me... Yes, it's St George Clinic. It's open 7.00 am to 7.30 pm.

P Thank you.

R Do you need anything else?

P That's all. Thanks for all your help.

R Glad that I can help. Be careful.

延伸聽寫 | Exercise B

➲ 解答參見第 63 頁

Track 0304

1. A Hi, I'm Dr. Huang. **What seems to be the problem?**

   B I crashed my bike and I think I ①__________ __________ __________. It's really… ouch…

   A Painful, don't worry. You're ②__________ __________ __________. **Can you move it at all**, your right arm?

   B No, I can't… ouch…

   A **Are you** ③__________ __________ __________ __________?

   B No… ow…

   A Okay, take these. You will need to **have an X-ray** ④__________ **first**.

   翻譯

   A：你好，我是黃醫師，哪裡不舒服？

   B：我騎腳踏車摔車，我想我應該是摔斷手臂了，真的好……啊……

   A：好痛！別擔心，我們會好好照顧你的，你的右手臂還能動嗎？

   B：沒辦法動……好痛……

   A：你有對任何藥物過敏嗎？

   B：沒有……好痛……

   A：好，拿著這些，你要先去照一下 X 光。

2. Doctor Grey is away. Dr. Yang will ⑤__________ __________ now.

   格蕾醫生今天不在，是楊醫師幫你看診喔。

3. A Have you been in before?

   B Yes, I had a ⑥____________ exam two months ago.

   翻譯

   A：請問有來看診過嗎？

   B：有，我兩個月前有去做過身體檢查。

實用字詞補充

1. **in good hands** 會被照顧的很好

例 You'll be in good hands with him—he is a great doctor.
你會被照顧得很好的，他是一個很棒的醫生。

2. **Bear with me.** 請耐心等我一下

例 Sorry, it will take a while. Please bear with me.
不好意思，這要花一點時間，請耐心稍等我一下。

3. **vitals (vital signs)** 生命跡象

例 The patient's vitals are stable. 病人的生命跡象穩定。

4. **physical** 體檢 *Physical Examination

情境會話 B／翻譯

接待：格蕾醫生辦公室，我是保羅，請問您需要什麼協助呢？

病人：嗨，我是高瑞秋，我想跟格蕾醫生約診。我身體不太舒服。

接待：是急症嗎？高小姐？

病人：嗯，我也，應該不算吧，但是我想快點見到格蕾醫生。

接待：當然，下週二如何呢？格蕾醫生可以早上 11 點幫你看診。

病人：不知道您有沒有可能幫我看看怎麼擠進去今天的約診呢？我真的……嗯……

接待：不好意思，如果有人取消，我可以打給你，但是如果我是你，我就不會等，因為機率很低，如果你現在真的很不舒服，你可以去緊急救護中心。

病人：歐……嗯……我上週頭痛很嚴重，前幾天也有發燒，我以為只是普通感冒，所以就喝了很多水。但是昨天晚上我開始嘔吐，然後我現在全身都發癢，我不知道為什麼，我沒有這樣過，而且今天早上，我又開始發燒，一直沒辦法退燒。

接待：高小姐，我會建議你直接去不用預約的急症診所，或是醫院的急診。你知道有哪些選擇嗎？你能走路或是自己開車嗎？

病人：我的室友可以載我沒問題，嗯，就在牛津路跟維多莉亞路的轉角那邊有一家不用預約的診所對不對，他們可以幫我嗎？

接待：我先幫你確認，你稍等我一下喔……有，那邊有一家聖喬治診所，早上七點到晚上七點有開。

病人：謝謝你。

接待：你還需要什麼嗎？

病人：這樣就可以了，謝謝你的幫忙。

接待：很高興我能幫上忙，路上小心。

刺青店

聆聽重點

請留意在刺青店裡會有的「對話亮點」→ 刺青相關單字

例如：刺青師傅、刺青圖案設計、草圖、刺青大小、預付訂金、刺青位置、去除刺青。

Track 0305 T = Terese W = Walton ★ 請特別注意粗體字的部分 ★

T Hi, I'm Terese. We spoke over the phone yesterday.

W Hi, Terese. I'm Walton.

T It's really nice to meet you. I've reviewed your work on your website. Your work is so unique and incredible.

W Thanks. You said that you want a tiger, but not sure whether you should go for just a head or a whole tiger jumping or something else.

T Yeah… umm… and I also want a rose. I'm sorry. Is it weird? I mean, rose and tiger.

W Not at all. But what is the idea behind? It will help me understand the style you really want.

T Actually, I have a drawing, well, a **sketch**, no… it's really bad, it's just a **doodle**…

W No, it's pretty great! I mean, I get it. You want a feeling like… like… wait… I'm trying to find the right words… aha… that's it! Marvel Studio's Black Widow. Do you like the movie? Natasha Romanoff?

T I love her. That's amazing. You know exactly what I want.

W Good. **But you have to book another time next week** 'cause **I'll get to work on your new design**, which of course I will send to you three days before your appointment. You can make any small changes, if you want.

T I see. **Do I need to pay a deposit for this**?

W Yes, if it's okay.

T How much is it?

W It depends. **You can expect to pay anything between £30–£200 as a deposit**

on your appointment and it goes towards the total price of the tattoo. Anyway, I need to know more details about the tattoo you want… **How big do you want your tattoo**?

T Umm… like a pack of cigarettes?

W You probably have to be more specific, saying something like a 15×20 tattoo **on your inner shoulder**.

T Oh, I get it now. It's my very first time getting a tattoo.

W Well, thank you for choosing me… and where do you want the tattoo?

T **I was thinking… along my waistline**?

延伸聽寫 | Exercise C

解答參見第 63 頁

Track 0306

1. Do you have a ①__________ __________ __________?
   你有刺青或是穿洞嗎？

2. If you end up ②__________ __________ __________, you'll have to go through the process of ③__________ __________.
   如果你最後覺得後悔刺青了，你就得經歷除掉刺青的過程。

3. My tattoo artist's hands are really ④__________. This was way ⑤__________ my expectations.
   我的刺青師傅的手真的好有才華，這個刺青真的是超越我的期待太多了！

4. How long do I have to keep the ⑥__________ __________?
   這個繃帶我要多久之後才能拆掉呢？

實用字詞補充

1. **disposable tattoo needles** 拋棄式刺青針頭
   例 Nowadays, tattoo artists all work with disposable tattoo needles, and they open every needle in front of their clients.
   現在刺青師傅都用拋棄式的刺青針頭，而且他們會在客人面前拆開每一個針頭。

2. **infection** 感染
   例 It lowers your risk of infection and complications.
   這會降低感染跟併發症的風險。

3. **over the phone** 透過電話……（溝通討論等）
   on the phone（正在）電話中

情境會話 C／翻譯

泰瑞斯：您好，我是泰瑞斯，昨天我們通過電話。

沃爾頓：嗨，泰瑞斯，我是沃爾頓。

泰瑞斯：很高興認識您，我看完你網站上所有的作品，你的作品真的是好特別，很讓人驚艷。

沃爾頓：謝謝。你說你想要一隻老虎，但不確定只是要老虎的頭還是說要整隻跳躍的老虎之類的。

泰瑞斯：對啊，嗯，我還想要一朵玫瑰，不好意思喔，會不會很怪，我的意思是說，玫瑰跟老虎耶。

沃爾頓：完全不會阿！但是這個圖案背後的想法是什麼呢？這會幫助我了解你真正想要的樣式。

泰瑞斯：其實我有畫一張圖，應該是說一個草圖啦，哎呀……我畫的真的很爛，就一個塗鴉……

沃爾頓：不會啊，很棒耶！我的意思是，我明白了！你是想要那一種……嗯……等等……我正在試圖找到合適的詞……啊哈……對了，就是那個！漫威電影裡面的黑寡婦，你喜歡黑寡婦嗎？娜塔莎．羅曼諾夫 (Natasha Romanoff)？

泰瑞斯：我超愛她，這簡直太酷了，你完全知道我想要什麼耶。

沃爾頓：很好啊，不過，你得下週再預約一次了，因為我要重新著手這個新設計，當然，會在你的預約時間之前三天給你草圖，你如果有什麼想要修改的小地方也可以。

泰瑞斯：我知道了，那我需要付押金嗎？

沃爾頓：對，如果可以的話先付押金。

泰瑞斯：多少錢呢？

泰瑞斯：要看情況耶，大概可以預期從 30 英鎊到 200 英鎊之間的都有可能，當然，押金就會合併計入到時候刺青的總價，無論如何，我需要了解更多關於你想要的刺青的細節……你想要多大的刺青呢？

泰瑞斯：嗯……大概是一包香煙的大小？

沃爾頓：你可能得再具體一點喔，比如說在你的內肩，一個 15×20 大小圖案的刺青。

泰瑞斯：哦，這樣我懂了，這是我第一次刺青。

沃爾頓：恩，那謝謝您選擇我……你希望刺在身體上哪一個位置呢？

泰瑞斯：我在想說……我的腰上。

情境會話 D 健身房

聆聽重點

在健身房裡會出現的「對話亮點」→ 健身相關單字

例如：健身教練、背部痠痛、伸展運動、健康體態、久坐、長肌肉、熱身運動、重訓。

Track 0307 P = Personal trainer B = Beatrice ★ 請特別注意粗體字的部分 ★

P Hi, Beatrice. How's your weekend?

B My weekend? So uneventful!

P You didn't go anywhere? What did you do? Watching TV, or spending time on the web?

B Well, you know, being a freelancer, I'm not free at all. Basically, I just sat in front of my computer all day.

P How are you feeling today? You must be exhausted.

B You got me. **I woke up this morning with back pain**.

P Oh no… but don't worry, we will show you some **stretching exercises** that you can easily do at home. Oh, and you haven't told me what your goal is. I asked you last week, remember?

B Haha, I know, okay, I thought about it. Well, I won't tell you that I want to look like Gal Gadot, **but I really want to get in shape**.

P Got you. People like you, forced to **spend prolonged periods of time sitting** at home, really need to **build muscle** first.

B Okay, let's get started.

延伸聽寫 | Exercise D

➔ 解答參見第 63 頁

Track 0308 M = Man W = Woman

M ①__________ ____________ **all right**?

W Oh yes. I just joined the gym days ago. I am pretty much trying everything out but I don't know… I think I must be doing something wrong.

M Did you do some ② __________ __________?

W Oh… no… I thought… it was…

M I know, a lot of people would think that ③ __________ __________ is not like a **cardio workout and not doing a warmup should be fine**. They are wrong.

W You've got me there. I usually do a ④ __________ __________ **on a treadmill or stationary bike**, so yap that's what I thought.

M If you don't mind, maybe I can help you. I've been working out on these machines for a year. I'm used to them. But I have to say, **for a beginner, getting a personal trainer is really helpful**. When I joined, I ⑤ __________ __________ for a personal trainer for about twelve sessions. My trainer helped me set long-term realistic goals, and she **offered nutritional guidance** and kept me on track to start healthy habits. The most amazing part is she challenged me in a way that no one could. I learned a lot from her.

W Thank you for your suggestion. It's a really good idea.

M I'm Aiden, by the way.

W I'm Adrian. Nice to meet you.

翻譯

M：你還好嗎？

W：哦，是的，我幾天前才剛加入健身房的，我就是在嘗試每一種機器，但我也不太確定……我想我一定有做錯什麼動作之類的。

M：你剛剛有做熱身動作嗎？

W：哦……不……我以為……

M：我知道，很多人會認為重訓不像有氧運動，好像不用做熱身運動也可以。他們錯了。

W：被你發現了啊！我通常都在跑步機或飛輪上運動，沒錯，我就是這麼想的。

M：如果你不介意，也許我可以幫忙。我用這些機器做訓練也用了一年了，已經很習慣它們了，但是我不得不說，對於初學者來說，請私人教練真的很有幫助。當初我加入這個健身房的時候，有報私人教練差不多十二堂課，我的教練幫助我訂定長期且實際的目標，她還提供了營養膳食的建議，還教我保持良好健康的習慣，最令人驚訝的是她以一種沒人能挑戰我的方式激勵了我，我從她那裡學到了很多東西。

W：謝謝你的建議，這是一個非常好的主意。

M：順道提一下，我是艾登。

W：我是雅德莉安。很高興認識你。

實用字詞補充

1. **uneventful** 平淡無奇的

   例 I thought it would be an uneventful journey, but it turned out to be amazing.

   我本來以為這會是一趟超平淡的旅程，結果沒想到超級令人驚艷的。

2. **You've got me.**（口語）被你發現了、你考倒我了

3. **get in shape / keep in shape** 保持身體健康狀態、保持身材

4. **Got you!**（口語）我明白了、我知道你的意思 *I got you.

情境會話 D／翻譯

健身教練：嗨，碧翠絲。週末過得如何？

碧 翠 絲：我的週末嗎？平淡無奇啊！

健身教練：沒去哪兒嗎？你都做了什麼啊？看電視還是上網？

碧 翠 絲：嗯，作為自由職業者，我一點都不自由。基本上，我整天都坐在電腦前面啊。

健身教練：你今天身體感覺還好嗎？一定精疲力盡吧。

碧 翠 絲：被你發現啦！我今天早上醒來時腰痠背痛。

健身教練：哦，不，但是你不用擔心，我們等一下教你一些伸展運動，你可以在家輕鬆做。哦對了，你還沒有告訴我你的目標是什麼？記得嗎？我上週問過你的。

碧 翠 絲：哈哈，我知道，好啦，我有想過了，嗯，我不會跟你說我要長得像蓋兒．加朵，但我當然是會想要保持身心健康的狀態啊。

健身教練：我明白了。像你這樣工作型態的人，被迫長時間坐在家裡，真的需要先鍛鍊你的肌肉。

碧 翠 絲：好啊，那我們開始吧。

延伸聽寫 Answer Keys

Exercise A

① prescribed、② without a prescription、③ cold、④ swell up、⑤ have a rash、⑥ itchy、⑦ eye drops、⑧ advisable

Exercise B

① broke my arm、② in good hands、③ allergic to any drugs、④ taken、⑤ see you、⑥ physical

Exercise C

① tattoo or piercing、② regretting the tattoo、③ tattoo removal、④ gifted、⑤ beyond
⑥ bandage on

Exercise D

① Is everything、② warmup moves、③ strength-training、④ cardio workout
⑤ signed up

加值學更多！

衣服送乾洗、咖啡漬、當天取件可以嗎？衣服褪色怎麼說？超實用情境對話聽力練習內容，線上下載，隨時想聽就聽！

NOTE

Unit 04

餐廳訂位 · 餐廳點菜 ·
餐廳點菜特殊需求 · 結帳與小費

情境會話 A 餐廳訂位

聆聽重點

打電話向餐廳訂位時的「對話亮點」→ 訂位相關單字

例如：訂位人數、時間及需要與餐廳人員溝通的特殊需求。

Track 0401 C = Clerk L = Lily ★ 請特別注意粗體字的部分 ★

C Good afternoon, Uncle Jon's Italian Kitchen. **How may I help you?**

L Hi, **I'd like to book a table for** eight for tomorrow night.

C Sure, and **what time would you like**?

L About six thirty or seven maybe?

C Let me see… um… yes, **we have a seven**. **Your name, please?**

L Lily Huang.

C No problem, Ms Huang. **That's a table for eight** at seven tomorrow evening.

L Yes, thank you… Oh, sorry, I almost forgot. **Can we have a table by the window**?

C I'm sorry that **we can't guarantee** a window table.

L Umm, it's for my granny's birthday and your pizza is her favorite in town. We really hope that the night can be really unforgettable for her. **We would appreciate it if** you could make it happen.

C I see, ma'am. **I'll see what I can do and of course I'll note your preference**.

L Thank you so much.

C **See you tomorrow**, Ms Huang.

延伸聽寫 | Exercise A

➡ 解答參見第 78 頁

Track 0402

1. A I'd like to ①__________ __________ __________ for tomorrow night, please?

   B **How many guests is it for?**

   A ②__________ __________ __________ four of us.

B What name is it?

A Jones, Philip Jones.

翻譯

A：我想要訂明天晚上的位子。

B：請為幾位貴賓用餐呢？

A：我們總共四位。

B：訂位大名是？

A：瓊斯，菲力普・瓊斯。

Track 0403

2. A **This is** George's Deli.

   B Hello, I'd like to **make a dinner reservation** for this Friday.

   A **What time would you like the reservation for?**

   B Eight o'clock or perhaps eight thirty?

   A Both are ③__________, **which one do you prefer**?

   B That's nice, then eight, please.

翻譯

A：喬治餐館您好。

B：嗨，我想訂這個禮拜五晚餐的位子。

A：請問要訂幾點的位子呢？

B：八點或是八點半之類？

A：兩個都還可以訂喔，請問您比較偏好哪一個時間呢？

B：真好，那就訂八點吧！

Track 0404

3. A Hello, **do you have any availability for a party of five at 8 pm on Saturday?**

   B **Let me check**… um… sorry, **it looks like we don't have 8 pm. Is 9 pm okay**?

   A Wow… then do you have six thirty or six… or…

   B No, **I'm afraid not**. Usually, ④__________ __________ __________ on Saturday.

   A Oh… let me talk to my friend and I'll call back.

   B Sure, no problem.

翻譯

A：嗨，請問禮拜六晚上八點還有五人聚餐的位子嗎？

B：我看一下喔，嗯，抱歉，看來我們沒有八點的時段，九點好嗎？

A：哇……還是有沒有六點半或是六點或是……

B：沒有耶，很抱歉，通常我們禮拜六都會是訂位全滿的狀態。

A：喔，那我跟我朋友說一下，我再撥電話進來好了。

B：當然，沒有問題。

實用字詞補充

1. **Let me see. 讓我想想看，讓我想一想**　* Let me think. 或是 Let's see.

   例 Let's see, what did I give to her? 我想想喔，我是給了她什麼東西呀？
2. **book a table（餐廳）訂位**
3. **make a reservation（餐廳）訂位**
4. **be booked (up) 訂位全滿**
5. **I'll see what I can do. 委婉表達會盡力幫忙，但是不保證能夠做到**
6. **I'm afraid there is nothing I can do. 委婉表示拒絕的意思**

情境會話 A／翻譯

店員：午安您好，喬恩叔叔的義大利廚房，請問需要什麼服務呢？

莉莉：您好，我想訂明天晚上八個人的位子。

店員：好的，您想要訂幾點呢？

莉莉：也許六點半，或是七點，可以嗎？

店員：讓我看一下喔……嗯……可以，七點可以，請問訂位大名？

莉莉：黃莉莉。

店員：沒問題，黃女士，那就是明天晚上七點，八位。

莉莉：是的，謝謝……哦，對不起，我差點忘了，我們的位置可以安排在窗邊嗎？

店員：對不起，我們沒有辦法跟您保證位置一定會在窗邊。

莉莉：嗯，這是我奶奶的生日，你們店裡的披薩是她在城裡最喜歡的，我們真的希望這個夜晚對她來說會是很難忘的，如果您能幫忙我們安排，我們不勝感激。

店員：我瞭解了，黃女士，我會盡力安排，當然我也會註記您的需求。

莉莉：非常感謝你。

店員：黃女士，那我們明天見囉。

Ch 1

聆聽重點

請留意在餐廳用餐會出現的「對話亮點」→ 餐廳相關單字
例如：介紹菜單、今日特餐、點餐流程、開胃菜、主餐、牛排幾分熟、配菜、飯後甜點等。

Track 0405 W = Waiter A = Woman A B = Woman B ★ 請特別注意粗體字的部分 ★

W Good evening. Welcome to Lucy's. I am Kenny. **Here's the menu and today's special is grilled seafood**.

A Thank you.

W **Can I get you anything to drink?**

A **Can I have** a lemonade please?

B **I'll have** a coke, **please**.

W A lemonade and coke **right away, ma'am.**

W **Here's your lemonade and here's your coke. Are you ready to order, ma'am?**

B Yes, we are. **For appetizers, could we have** stuffed clams, shrimp cocktail, maple bacon and smoked cheese stuffed mushrooms, **please**?

W Yes, of course, **what would you like for your main course**?

A **I'd like** the fish and chips.

B **I'll have** the steak.

W **How would you like your steak?**

B **Medium rare, thanks.**

W It's a good choice. **Any side dishes?**

B **I'll have** buttered corn and grilled zucchini.

W Excellent, **I'll be right back**.

W Did you enjoy your meal?

A Yes, everything is so delicious. Thank you.

W **Would you like something for dessert?**

B **What would you recommend?**

W Our chocolate fudge cake is **a must-try**, and my favorite is red velvet cake.

A Then we'll have both. Thanks.

W No problem.

延伸聽寫 | Exercise B

➡ 解答參見第 78 頁

Track 0406

1. Are you ready to ①__________, or do you need a few more minutes?
   您準備好要點餐了嗎？還是要再看一下呢？
2. What would you like to ②__________ __________? 想要先來點什麼呢？
3. Would you like anything to ③__________? 要不要先來點喝的呢？

Track 0407 W = Waiter C = Customer

4. W Have you decided ④__________ __________ __________ to order?

   C Yes, I'll have a garden salad and buffalo wings.

   W And what kind of ⑤__________ would you like?

   C **What do you have?**

   W We have Balsamic vinaigrette, ⑥__________ __________ __________ __________, and we also have avocado lime, honey mustard and greek yogurt ranch.

   C Wow, then… greek yogurt ranch, please.

翻譯

W：您有決定好想要吃什麼了嗎？
C：我想要花園沙拉跟水牛城雞翅。
W：沙拉醬汁要哪一種呢？
C：有哪些可以選呢？
W：我們有巴薩米哥油醋醬，非常清爽，還有酪梨萊姆醬汁，蜂蜜芥末醬汁，跟希臘優格沙拉醬。
C：哇，那就希臘優格沙拉醬好了。

5. W ⑦__________ do you like your eggs?

   C Scrambled, please.

   W **Anything else?**

   C No, **that's all**. Thanks.

翻譯

W：您的蛋想要怎麼做呢？

C ：炒蛋謝謝。

W：還需要其他的嗎？

C ：不用，這樣就好，謝謝喔。

6. W **Can I bring you anything else?**

C No, thank you. Just the ⑧__________, please.

翻譯

W：需要再來點什麼嗎？

C ：不用，謝謝你，麻煩給我帳單。

Ch 1

7. W **Can I get you anything else?**

C **Can you bring me** some more ketchup, **please**?

W Sure. **I'll be** ⑨__________ __________.

翻譯

W：需要幫您點什麼嗎？

C ：可以麻煩你再給我番茄醬嗎？

W：當然，我馬上來。

Track 0408

8. Excuse me, I seem to have ⑩__________ my fork.
不好意思，我的叉子掉到地上了。

9. **Could you please bring me** ⑪__________ fork?
可以再給我一隻叉子嗎？

10. **May I** ⑫__________ __________ spoon please? 可以給我湯匙嗎？

11. **Could we have** ⑬__________ **bill, please?** 我們想要結帳，麻煩你。

12. ⑭__________ **the change.** 零錢不用找了。

實用字詞補充

1. **appetizer 前菜、開胃菜** *starter

例 The appetizer includes shrimp cocktail, deviled eggs and chili cheese dip.
開胃菜包括蝦雞尾酒，芥末蛋和起司辣肉醬。

2. **Zucchini 櫛瓜** *courgette

例 Our zucchini bread is classic. Would you like some?
我們的櫛瓜麵包非常經典，您想要嚐嚐看嗎？

3. **side dish 配菜**

*通常是小份量搭配主餐的配菜，常見的有起司通心粉 (macaroni and cheese)、烤麵包、

各種沙拉或是烤蔬菜等等

4. **cutlery（刀、叉、匙等）餐具（不可數）** *eating utensil 用餐用具（可數）

   例 Bring Your Own Cutlery movement can help solve the plastic crisis.

   自備餐具運動可幫助解決塑膠製品帶來的危機。

情境會話 B／翻譯

服務生：您好，歡迎來到露西餐廳，我是肯尼。這是菜單，今天的特餐是烤海鮮。

女人 A：謝謝你。

服務生：要先來點喝的嗎？

女人 A：我要檸檬水。

女人 B：我要可樂。

服務生：檸檬水和可樂馬上來，女士。

服務生：這是您的檸檬水，這是您的可樂，女士們，準備好點餐了嗎？

女人 B：可以。開胃菜的話，我們想要點鑲嵌蛤蜊、雞尾酒蝦、楓糖培根以及煙燻起司釀蘑菇。

服務生：好的，您的主菜呢？

女人 A：我要炸魚薯條。

女人 B：我要牛排。

服務生：您的牛排要幾分熟呢？

女人 B：三分熟，謝謝。

服務生：選的好，牛排的配菜要什麼呢？

女人 B：我要加奶油玉米和烤櫛瓜。

服務生：太棒了，我馬上回來。

服務生：請問今天晚上的餐點都還滿意嗎？

女人 A：是的，每一樣都很美味，謝謝你。

服務生：你們想要來點飯後甜點嗎？

女人 B：你有推薦的嗎？

服務生：我們的巧克力軟蛋糕是您一定要試試看的，那我自己最喜歡的是紅絲絨蛋糕。

女人 A：那我們兩個都要，謝謝喔。

服務生：沒問題。

餐廳點菜特殊需求

Ch 1

聆聽重點

請仔細聆聽在餐廳會出現哪些關於特殊需求的相關單字。例如：素食者、飲食忌諱、食物的辣度、清眞食物、符合猶太教規的食物、對特定的食物過敏。

Track 0409　W = Waiter　C = Customer　★ 請特別注意粗體字的部分 ★

W How are you doing today? **Can I take your order?**

C Um… **I am vegetarian, do you have any vegan dishes**?

W Of course. We have a grilled veggie combo, and you can [1]**choose** two side dishes and two dressings. Also, **I recommend** our pumpkin soup if you like something a bit spicy. It's very special.

C **How spicy is it?**

W Do you like jalapeños?

C I love it!

W Then I think you'll love our pumpkin soup.

C Okay, I'll have the pumpkin soup and grilled veggie combo with the sesame ginger and ranch dressing on the side.

W **You also can choose side dishes. What would you like?**

C Oh, [2]**right**, I forgot…um…Can I have french fries and buttery green beans?

W No problem. **Do you have any food allergies or other dietary restrictions** that we should know about?

C No. Thank you.

聽力提點

1. **choose**

choose 這個字聽起來是 [tʃuz]，發 [u] 這個母音的訣竅在於不能一開始就想把嘴型噘成一個圓形，因為 [u] 並不是直接發中文注音符號「ㄨ」的聲音，否則 choose 這個字聽起來會像「處斯」，很奇怪。[u] 的正確發音方式是利用雙唇先微微張開放鬆，往前方推動到最後變成一個噘起唇型的發音，請想像中文的「速度」這兩個字，注音符號都有「ㄨ」，但是 ㄙㄨ ㄟ 的母音 ㄨ

跟ㄉㄨ丶的母音ㄨ其實聲音是有點不同，發「速」的音時，嘴巴兩側會放鬆而微微張開，然後才能往前推動送氣而發出「速」的音，要把 [u] 的聲音發得好聽也是類似的道理。本篇中一樣母音的字還有 food [fud]、two [tu]、soup [sup]、doing [duiŋ] 等，可以一起念以掌握母音 [u]。

2. **right**

感嘆語助詞。用在同意、認同或是聽懂對方的意思時，類似中文的「對喔、好、可以」等。

延伸聽寫 | Exercise C

➜ 解答參見第 78 頁

Track 0410

1. **Does this dish** ①__________ nuts? 這道菜裡面有堅果類的東西嗎。
2. **Which soup is** ②__________? 這些湯裡面哪一種是沒有乳製品的？
3. **Could I have** grilled vegetables instead of the French fries?
   炸薯條我可以換成烤蔬菜嗎？
4. **I can't eat wheat, can you** ③____________ **something for me?**
   我不能吃小麥，你能幫我推薦我可以吃的料理嗎？
5. **Is this** ④__________? 這道菜是素的嗎？
6. **Could you make it less spicy?** 你可以調整辣度讓它不要那麼辣嗎？
7. Would it be possible to have mashed potatoes ⑤__________ __________ fries?
   可以把薯條換成薯泥嗎？
8. What are today's ⑥__________? 你們今日的特餐是什麼？

Track 0411 C = Customer W = Waiter

9. C Excuse me? I think the soup might have cheese in it. I ⑦__________ __________ __________ cheese.

   W I'm sorry, ma'am. Let me replace it.

   C Wait, I'm… I'm not asking you to ⑧__________ __________ __________. I am just confused… I mean… I particularly asked the other waiter and I was told that it didn't have cheese in it… and now… I'm not feeling well. I would like to ⑨__________ __________ __________ __________.

翻譯

C：不好意思，我覺得這個湯裡面應該有起司吧，我對起司過敏。

W：很抱歉，女士，我幫你換一份。

C：等一下，我不是要你把這個退回去廚房，我只是不懂，我是說，我剛剛特別有問那位服務生，然後他告訴我這個湯裡面是沒有加起司的，那現在，我身體覺得不太舒服。我想要直接跟經理反應這件事情。

實用字詞補充

1. **Kosher food 符合猶太教規的食物**

例 "Kosher" is not a style of cooking. The food that complies with the dietary standards of traditional Jewish law can be called kosher food.

「猶太食品」不是一種烹飪方式，符合傳統猶太法律飲食標準的食物才可以稱為猶太食品。

2. **Halal food 清真食物**

例 If you want to look for Halal food in Taiwan, it is not a problem.

如果你想在台灣找清真食物，那是沒有問題的。

3. **food allergy 食物過敏**

例 It's easy to confuse a food allergy with food intolerance.

食物過敏很容易跟食物不耐症混為一談。

情境會話 C／翻譯

服務員：你們好。可以點餐了嗎？

顧　客：嗯……我吃素，你們這邊有素食料理嗎？

服務員：當然，我們有這個烤蔬菜組合，您可以選擇兩個配菜和兩種沾醬，另外，如果您喜歡辛辣一點的口味，我也推薦南瓜湯。非常特別。

顧　客：有多辣呢？

服務員：你喜歡墨西哥辣椒嗎？

顧　客：我喜歡啊！

服務員：那我想您會喜歡我們的南瓜湯的。

顧　客：好的，我要南瓜湯和烤蔬菜組合，再加芝麻薑汁沙拉醬和牧場沙拉醬。

服務員：還可以選擇配菜喔，想要來點什麼呢？

顧　客：哦，對喔，我都忘了……那我可以來點薯條和奶油青豆嗎？

服務員：沒問題！想請問您是否有對任何食物過敏或是還有其他的飲食限制呢？

顧　客：沒有。謝謝你。

情境會話 D 結帳與小費

情境概說

到餐廳慶祝週年紀念日的 Kerrie 和 Lance 對於該餐廳餐點及服務感到非常滿意，決定給予豐厚的小費……。

Track 0412　K = Kerrie　W = Waiter　L = Lance　★ 請特別注意粗體字的部分 ★

K Excuse me, **can we have the bill please**?

W Sure, **I'll get it for you**.

L Wow… **the food is really great**. We should come back again.

K I think so. I'd like to try their pesto ravioli next time, oh and the tiramisu, next time I won't share.

L Hahaha, fine… definitely next time, I couldn't eat another bite. Should we walk home?

K That's a good idea.

L **And their service is quite exceptional**. We didn't tell them we were here to celebrate our anniversary, but they still figured it out. [1]How did they… how did they… it's really surprising.

K It's really sweet that they started the meal with that wonderful amuse bouche. I'm really surprised, [2]really.

L The waiters must be all carefully listening and observing, you know, trying very hard to make us feel special.

K How much should we tip?

L How happy are you right now?

K Hahaha, umm, I think tonight is perfect.

L Well, then I say 30 percent.

K Okay.

聽力提點

1. **How did they... how did they...**
   重複或是連續的詞語，就像中文口語也會因為興致一來說「到底、到底」一樣，但是這片段的重複也不一定會接完整一句話，聽取時其實只要抓住情緒繼續往下聆聽即可。

2. **really**
   第 2 個 really 音調提高，表示強調。

Ch 1

實用字詞補充

1. **I couldn't eat another bite.（已經吃很飽而）再也吃不下別的食物了**
2. **amuse bouche 開胃小點**
   * 跟 appetizer 不一樣，是法國料理的主廚特別製作的小點，用意在讓客人品味主餐之前先刺激味蕾，提升用餐整體色香味的感官體驗。分量很少，通常也不會出現在菜單上。

情境會話 D／翻譯

凱　莉：不好意思，請給我們帳單好嗎。
服務生：好的，我幫您拿過來。
藍　斯：哇……這裡的食物真的很棒。我們應該下次再來。
凱　莉：我也這麼想耶，下次我想嚐嚐他們的青醬義大利餃，喔，對，還有提拉米蘇，下次，我不要跟你分著吃喔。
藍　斯：哈哈哈，好……肯定是下次，我現在一口都吃不下了。我們走路回家好嗎？
凱　莉：好主意喔。
藍　斯：他們的服務真的非常出色。我們沒有告訴他們我們是來慶祝我們的週年紀念日，但是他們還是發現了。這到底……到底 ... 哎，真的很令人驚訝耶！
凱　莉：他送給我們那個開胃小點，我很意外耶，真的。
藍　斯：服務生們一定都很認真地傾聽和觀察客人，拚命要讓我們感到備受重視啊。
凱　莉：我們今天應該給多少小費呢？
藍　斯：你現在有多高興？
凱　莉：哈哈哈，嗯，我覺得今晚非常完美。
藍　斯：好吧，那百分之三十。
凱　莉：好啊。

延伸聽寫 Answer Keys

Exercise A

① make a reservation、② There will be、③ available、④ we're fully booked

Exercise B

① order、② start with、③ drink、④ what you'd like、⑤ dressing、⑥ very light and fresh
⑦ How、⑧ bill、⑨ right back、⑩ dropped、⑪ another、⑫ have a、⑬ the、⑭ Keep

Exercise C

① have、② dairy-free、③ recommend、④ vegan、⑤ instead of、⑥ specials
⑦ am allergic to、⑧ send it back、⑨ speak to the manager

加值學更多！

對服務不佳之處提出反應、上菜有錯、肉沒有熟怎麼表達？如何跟餐廳經理反應？超實用情境對話聽力練習內容，線上下載，隨時想聽就聽！

Unit 05

- 修理水電
- 鄰居噪音
- 垃圾分類
- 辦理旅館入住

修理水電

家中水管爆裂，找專業技師求救

聆聽重點

特別留意家中管線報修時，與專業技師對話可能會出現的相關單字。
例如：修水管技師、淹水、關掉總開關、物業修繕管理中心、停電、暖氣壞掉、水管爆裂、天花板。

Track 0501 P = Plumber K = Kira ★ 請特別注意粗體字的部分 ★

P Hello, Dalton **Plumbing Service**.

K Hi, I just got home and found that **my kitchen is flooded**. Water is everywhere. I don't know what to do.

P Have you **turned the water off**? There's **a stop valve**. Do you know?

K Oh, I don't… **can you tell me where it is exactly**?

P Umm, normally the **control valve should be next to the water meter**. Can you go look now?

K Yeah, but please don't hang up, I'm using my cell phone… I've called my **complex's emergency maintenance line** maybe seven times, but no one answered… okay, done. I **turned it off**… **I turned it off**. What should I do now?

P I'm afraid there's nothing else you can do now. Do you have **temporary accommodation**? 'Cause I can't go fix the pipes for you until this Friday. That… I'm sorry…

K Oh… no…, **blackouts,…** [1]and… and… **my heating broke**… and now what… **burst pipes**… great! So what's next, do I wait for the **ceiling to cave in**… this is ridiculous. I just heard that we're still without power tonight… What a day, [2]huh!

P Ma'am, the situation can be dangerous and families all over our area are all dealing with **frozen pipes that are bursting**… so… we've been moving around quite a bit. It's… we're trying our best to help.

K I know. You… I'm sorry, too. Thank you, really.

P Look, umm… the… the earliest I can be there is at ten o'clock on Friday morning. Is that okay?

K [3]Yeah, yeah… sure… thanks for your help.

聽力提點

1. **and... and...**

   重複某個語詞在有情緒起伏的對話當中很容易出現，說話者可能在尋找恰當的表達文字，而會有重複呢喃似的表達，有時候也有可能聽起來比較瑣碎，甚至含糊不清。

2. **huh**（感嘆詞）

   多用於句尾，欲尋求他人的贊同時，很像中文的「對吧、是齁、嗯」。有時也可用於一種諷刺似的表達不贊同之意，很像中文的「哼」「最好是這樣」的語氣。

3. **Yeah, yeah...**

   重複、重述。

延伸聽寫 | Exercise A

解答參見第 91 頁

Track 0502

1. I called my complex's emergency maintenance line maybe ten times, but ①__________ __________ __________. What can I do now? How do I find temporary homes with electricity? Almost every hotel is fully booked.
   我打電話給社區的緊急維修人員大概十次了吧，但是都沒人接聽，現在我要怎麼辦呢？我要怎麼找到臨時的有正常供電的住宿，幾乎所有的旅館都被訂滿了。

2. ②__________ __________ __________ __________ __________ __________ and I used a ③__________ to ④__________ the pipes, but it doesn't work. I don't … I am not sure what I'm doing, sorry. Can you send someone to ⑤__________ __________ __________ at it, please?
   水槽在漏水，我有用板手試試看把水管轉緊一點，但是沒有用，我也不知道，我不確定我做的是不是對的，能請你派人來幫我看一下嗎？

實用字詞補充

complex 綜合大樓

例 My cousins live in a very big apartment complex.

我的表兄妹們都住在一個很大型的綜合公寓社區裡。

情境會話 A／翻譯

水管工：你好，道爾頓水管公司。

凱　拉：嗨，我剛到家，發現我的廚房整個被水淹得到處都是，我現在不知道該怎麼辦。

水管工：你有把水關起來嗎？有一個把水關掉的總開關，你知道嗎？

凱　拉：哦，我不知道……你能告訴我那個開關確切的位置嗎？

水管工：嗯，通常那個開關應該就在水表旁邊，你現在可以去看看嗎？

凱　拉：好，但是請不要掛斷電話好嗎，我用手機……我剛剛打了大概七次社區緊急維修專線，但都沒人接……好了，弄好了，我關掉了……關了，那我現在應該怎麼辦呢？

水管工：恐怕沒有什麼是你現在可以做的了，你有臨時住所嗎？因為這個星期五以前我都沒辦法去幫你修水管，抱歉……

凱　拉：哦……不是啊……那……先是停電，然後呢，然後暖氣壞了……現在水管爆開……真的是好極了！那麼接下來是怎樣，我要等天花板塌下來嗎……這一切太荒謬了。我還聽說今天晚上我們還是沒有電……啊這樣……

水管工：女士，其實這個情況是有危險性的，這個地區的所有家庭都忙著在處理水管因為冰凍而裂開的問題……所以我們一直到處奔走，我們正盡力協助大家。

凱　拉：我知道，我也很抱歉。謝謝你，真的。

水管工：那個……嗯……最早最早我可以在星期五早上十點鐘到，好嗎？

凱　拉：好的，謝謝您的幫助。

情境會話 B

鄰居噪音

向鄰居反應及溝通噪音問題

聆聽重點

向鄰居反應噪音的音量時，相關單字包括：噪音持續多久、跟房東反應、鄰居的說法、溝通結果等等。

Track 0503　L = Lana　S = Sloan　N = Neighbor　★ 請特別注意粗體字的部分 ★

L Oh my gosh… not again…

S What's that noise? Is someone hitting the wall?

L It's my neighbor. I don't know what he's trying to do in his apartment. **It's been a whole week and he just keeps hitting the wall**.

S **Did you talk to him?**

L No, I don't like that kind of conversation, you know… to complain about something. It's really embarrassing.

S You don't need to feel embarrassed. I mean, yes, complaining is definitely not something enjoyable, but **you just gotta do what you gotta do**, right, I mean, **at least you try to talk to him before you tell the landlord**.

L You're right. Wanna go with me?

S Haha, … alright, why not. Let's go.

[*knocking the door*]

N Hi! Lana, your friend?

L Ya, he's… um… my friend… anyway…

N **Can I help you with something?**

L …uh… the thing is…

S Hi, we haven't met before, I'm Sloan. **Here's the thing**… um… what my friend Lana is trying to say is that **the noise you have been making this whole week is seriously disturbing**. We all work from home so… you know…

N Oh… that… wow… I am very sorry… uh… In fact, it's my first DIY project. I thought redoing kitchen cabinets should be easy, you know, just adding some refreshing touches. How hard could it be? I was wrong. **It turned out that it [1]took more days than I thought… uh… the noise, I am really sorry… sorry…**

L um, it's okay.... [2]I'm... I understand.

S **Do you think you could finish it soon?**

N Uh... well...

S Maybe I can help! I am quite good at DIY stuff.

N Are you sure? Wow... **it would be great if you could give me a hand**. I think we could finish it today. And dinner is on me.

S Cool.

聽力提點

1. **took / book**

   took [tʊk] 跟 book [bʊk] 的母音 [ʊ] 是很多人沒有辦法發好的聲音。[ʊ] 比較難的是舌頭的位置，舌根會稍微向後抬起，前半舌尖則往下墜，但是不會碰觸到下顎齒，有一點類似我們中文要發兒子的「兒」的那個聲音的舌頭動作，只是這裡的 [ʊ] 並不需要真的卷舌，而只要把舌頭放在正確的位置，嘴巴微微張開，就可以發出 [ʊ] 這個聲音，你會發現如果能正確發出 [ʊ] 這個聲音，facebook 這個字就絕對不可能會唸成「face 不可」了。

2. **I'm... I understand**

   更正重說。

延伸聽寫 | Exercise B

解答參見第 91 頁

Track 0504

1. A Excuse me, sir. **You are speaking loudly and it's the** ①__________ __________.

   B Oh, ②__________ __________. Sorry.

   翻譯

   A：不好意思，先生，你講話太大聲了，而且這邊是保持安靜的區域。

   B：噢，我跟你道歉，對不起喔。

2. Hey, mate, **everybody here** ③__________ __________ __________. **Would you mind keeping your voice down?**

   嘿，這裡大家都可以聽到你的聲音了，你能小聲一點嗎？

3. Sorry, mate, **your** ④__________ **are too loud**. 抱歉，你的耳機聲音太大聲了。

實用字詞補充

1. **You gotta do what you gotta do. 該做什麼就去做**

   ＊有多說無益，該面對就是去面對的意思。

2. **Here's the thing.（口語）重點是**

   在溝通過程中，想要強調以下資訊是說話者特別想要表達的文意內容。

情境會話 B／翻譯

拉娜：哦，天哪……又來了……

史隆：那是什麼聲音？有人在敲撞牆壁嗎？

拉娜：是我的鄰居啦，我真的不知道他到底在他的公寓裡做什麼，整整一個星期，他一直在敲牆壁。

史隆：你有跟他談過了嗎？

拉娜：沒有，我不喜歡那種對話，你知道……去跟人家抱怨這種事情，哎呦，很尷尬耶。

史隆：你沒必要覺得尷尬啊，我的意思是，對啦，抱怨絕對不是什麼令人感到愉快的事情，但是有事情該怎麼做就要怎麼做啊，對吧，所以說，至少你在告訴房東之前得試著跟他溝通吧。

拉娜：對，想和我一起去嗎？

史隆：哈，好啦，也沒什麼不可以。

〔敲門〕

鄰居：嗨！拉娜，這是你的朋友嗎？

拉娜：對啊，我朋友。

鄰居：我能幫你什麼嗎？

拉娜：是……呃……事情是……

史隆：嗨，初次見面，我是史隆。我的朋友拉娜是想要跟你說，這一整個禮拜你一直製造出的那個噪音讓人很不舒服，我們都在家工作，所以……

鄰居：哦……那個……哇……我很抱歉……呃……事實上，這是我第一次弄 DIY，我還想說重做廚櫃應該很容易吧，我的意思是，不就加一些新的零件而已啊，能有多難！結果我錯了，事實證明，這超出我預期的時間好多……呃……那個噪音，我真的感到很抱歉……對不起……

拉娜：嗯，也沒關係啦……

史隆：那你覺得你可以盡快完成嗎？

鄰居：呃……

史隆：也許我可以幫忙喔！我蠻擅長 DIY 的東西。

鄰居：你確定嗎？如果你能幫助我，那就太棒了。我想我們今天可以完成，晚餐包在我身上。

史隆：好啊。

情境會話 C

垃圾分類

跟新搬來的鄰居解釋垃圾分類

聆聽重點

與垃圾分類相關的單字：垃圾桶、資源回收、回收桶、分類（玻璃瓶罐、塑膠類、金屬類、紙類）、環保永續。

Track 0505 S = Stanley N = Nora ★ 請特別注意粗體字的部分 ★

S Hey, excuse me, what are you doing?

N Uh… sorry, do I know you?

S I'm sorry. I'm Stanley, living in 3B and you are?

N Nora, I just moved in yesterday. Nice to meet you.

S Welcome, Nora, but **you just threw your garbage into the bin. Don't you recycle**?

N Oh… I see… um… I have been unpacking for hours and I got tired. I just… Okay, I'm sorry. The place I lived before, they didn't recycle, so I used to **throw them away**. I do feel guilty about it… I do… I really do, especially right now…

S Relax. I'm sorry if my attitude is a bit… anyway! **Don't take it the wrong way**. Well, **let me introduce you to three different recycle bins in our community**. **The green one is for glass bottles and plastic bags, the yellow one is for aluminum cans and other metals, and the white bin is for paper. Aside from those, everything else goes in to the red "trash" bin**.

N Thank you very much. I will recycle right. Promise.

S **When we all recycle right, we not only reduce our waste but also live more sustainably**.

延伸聽寫 | Exercise C

解答參見第 91 頁

Track 0506

1. These containers are made from ①____________________ materials.
這些保鮮盒都是用可生物分解的原料做成的。

2. We have to ②__________ __________ __________ __________.

我們得停止使用一次性的產品。

3. These ③__________ __________ __________ should be recycled. Could you help me ④__________ __________ __________ the recycling bin?

這些塑膠瓶都應該要回收啊，你能幫我一起把這些瓶子丟到回收箱裡面嗎？

實用字詞補充

1. **disposable 拋棄式的、用完即丟的**

例 The impact of using disposable products on the environment is serious.

使用拋棄式產品對環境的影響是很嚴重的。

2. **recycling symbol 可回收標示**

例 Recycling symbols appearing on many everyday items help people to identify how different types of packaging can be recycled correctly.

許多日常用品上出現的回收標誌可幫助人們了解如何正確回收不同材質的外包裝。

3. **toss 丟、投、擲**

例 The old man just glanced at the flyer and then tossed it into the bin.

老先生只瞄了一眼那張傳單就把它扔進垃圾桶。

情境會話 C／翻譯

史丹利：嘿，對不起，你在做什麼？

諾　拉：呃……我認識你嗎？

史丹利：抱歉，我是史丹利，我住在 3B，你呢？

諾　拉：我是諾拉，我昨天才搬來，很高興認識你。

史丹利：歡迎你，諾拉，但你剛剛把垃圾全部丟進垃圾箱對吧，你都不回收的嗎？

諾　拉：哦，原來是為了這個，嗯，我已經整理了好幾個小時的行李，因為真的很累所以……我只是……哎，好啦，實在對不起，我以前住的地方，他們都沒有在做回收，所以我習慣就把垃圾通通丟掉，我感到很抱歉……我真的……我真的覺得很抱歉，尤其是現在……

史丹利：沒事啦，不好意思喔，如果我的態度有點……哎呀，你千萬不要誤會我的意思，來，讓我跟您介紹一下我們社區呢，這三個不同功能的回收桶。綠色的這一個是裝玻璃瓶和塑膠袋的，黃色的這個裝鋁罐和其他金屬，那白色的就裝紙類，除此之外呢，就全部都可以丟進紅色那個垃圾箱囉。

諾　拉：非常謝謝你，我會正確做回收的，我答應你。

史丹利：當我們大家都正確做好回收，我們不僅可以垃圾減量，而且也能夠邁向永續的生活。

辦理旅館入住

聆聽重點

辦理旅館入住時，客人與櫃臺人員的「對話亮點」→ 辦理旅館入住手續的相關單字。例如：招呼、確認身份、確認預定房型及人數、資料填寫、費用、信用卡預授權等。

Track 0507 C = Clerk G = Guest ★ 請特別注意粗體字的部分 ★

C Good morning, welcome to Rose Resort. How may I help you?

G Hi, **I have a reservation**.

C May I have your name, sir?

G YenChun Chin, from Taiwan.

C **May I have your passport?**

G Sure.

C Thank you. **Just one moment, please…** Yes, Mr. Chin, **we have your reservation. It's for a deluxe double for five nights, is that correct?**

G Yes.

C **Could you fill out this form, please? And May I have your credit card, please? We will place an authorization hold on your card for any balance due on the reservation**. Of course you will only be charged for what you actually spend.

G No problem. Here you are.

C Thank you.

C Okay, Mr. Chin. **Here are your keys. You'll be staying in Room 718**. Enjoy your stay, sir.

G Thank you.

延伸聽寫 | Exercise D

解答參見第 91 頁

Track 0508

1. I'd like to ①__________ __________ __________ __________ for three nights from July 2nd to July fifth. Do you have any vacancies? 我想要預訂七月二號到

七月五號三個晚上的住宿，包含衛浴設備的一間雙人房，你們還有空房嗎？

2. A **How long will you be ② __________?**

   B **I'll be staying for three nights.**

   A **How many people is the reservation for?**

   B There will be my wife and I.

翻譯

A：請問住宿準備停留多長時間呢？

B：我會住三個晚上。

A：請問是幾個人預定入住呢？

B：我老婆跟我兩個人。

3. A **Do you ③ __________ the room with the lake or mountain view?**

   B **I'd like** a room facing the lake.

翻譯

A：您比較偏好湖景還是山景的房間呢？

B：我想要湖景的房間。

4. A Could you please ④ __________ __________ __________ __________ for me?

   B Sure, it's K-I-M.

翻譯

A：能請您拼一下您的姓氏嗎？

B：當然，是 K-I-M。

5. We have an ⑤ __________ swimming pool and sauna.
   我們有室內游泳池跟三溫暖。

6. **Would you prefer** a smoking or ⑥ __________ room?
   您會偏好吸菸的房間還是非吸菸的房間呢？

7. A Room service.

   B Hi, this is room 718. I'd like to order breakfast.

   A What would you like to order, Mr. Chin?

   B I want English breakfast and black coffee.

   A Yes, sir. It will ⑦ __________ __________ fifteen minutes. It that okay?

   B Yeah, it's fine.

翻譯

A：客房服務。

B：嗨，我是 718 房，我想要點早餐。

A：秦先生，請問您想要點什麼呢？

B：我想要英式早餐跟黑咖啡。

A：是的沒問題，會需要 15 分鐘的時間，這樣可以嗎？

B：好啊，沒問題。

實用字詞補充

1. **a single room 單人房**

   例 I'd like a single room, please. 我想要一間單人房，謝謝。

2. **a double room 雙人房** ＊通常會是一大床的房型。
3. **a twin room 標準雙人房** ＊有兩張雙人床的房間。
4. **adjoining room 房間相連的房間**
5. **authorization hold 授權保留**

   ＊台灣飯店會用「過卡」或是「預授權」來表示，先預刷一個額度，確保客人退房後不會因為信用卡額度或是任何問題而無法成功扣款。

情境會話 D／翻譯

接待員：早安您好，歡迎光臨玫瑰度假村，請問有什麼我能為您效勞嗎？

客　人：您好，我有訂房。

接待員：先生，請問您的大名？

客　人：秦彥君，從台灣來的。

接待員：可以看一下您的護照嗎？

客　人：好的。

接待員：謝謝，請稍等一下，沒錯，秦先生，我們有您的訂房資料，是預定五個晚上的豪華雙人房，對嗎？

客　人：沒錯。

接待員：可以請您填寫這些表格嗎？然後能給我您的信用卡嗎？我們會在您的信用卡上面取一個授權金額過卡，當然，最後只會依照您退房之後結算的實際花費來刷卡。

客　人：沒問題。這裡是信用卡。

接待員：謝謝您。

接待員：秦先生，這是您的鑰匙，您的房間是 718，祝您入住愉快。

客　人：謝謝。

延伸聽寫 Answer Keys

Exercise A
① no one answered、② There's a leak under the sink、③ wrench、④ tighten
⑤ take a look

Exercise B
① Quiet Zone、② I apologize、③ can hear you、④ headphones

Exercise C
① biodegradable、② stop using disposable products、③ plastic water bottles
④ toss them into

Exercise D
① book a double room、② staying、③ prefer、④ spell your last name
⑤ indoor、⑥ non-smoking、⑦ be about

NOTE

Chapter 2
學會英語的發音變化原理

聽力重點：連音／消音／省音／變音／同化音／弱讀／削弱音

在日常生活口語中聽到的英語不會像課本 CD 那樣速度穩定且字正腔圓，每一個單字在字典中標注的音標，放到實境生活口語當中都會有所調整或改變，本章將更進一步介紹各種常見的發音變化。

Track 0600

1. 連音

★ **字尾為子音的單字後面接的是母音開頭的字，需要連音。**

像是 in a room 的 in a 就會連音，口語上不會念 [ɪn] [ə] 兩個分開的音，因為母音 [ə] 在後，需與前方連音，所以尾音 [n] 會跟 [ə] 合在一起，聽起來是 [ɪ nə]，很像中文「飲ㄋ」的聲音，你會發現一時之間並不好念，如果你單獨發 [ɪ] 然後再發 [nə] 聽起來也不像母語人士的發音，主要原因是必須連音，要把它想成一個連貫不換氣的聲音，我們舉「飲ㄋ」的例子中「飲」的母音有「ㄣ」這個鼻音的聲音，跟 in a 連音的型態比較接近，可以試著揣摩看看，再跟著內文對話的各種範例音檔多做練習即可進步。

Example 1: in a room, in a book, in a dream

★ **英文單字後面接的是子音開頭的字，不需要連音。**

但是需注意 [p] [t] [k] [b] [d] [g] 這六個子音又被稱為「塞音」(stop

sound) 或「聲門閉鎖音」，可分為有聲及無聲兩類。塞音會因為其後延續音之子音或母音，或是存在於單字的字首、字中、字尾而有不同的變化。

[p] [t] [k] 為無聲塞音，當字尾是無聲塞音的時候，要用一種「頓一下」（塞音 stop）的方式來念，才能接下一個字，有點像想要打嗝但是沒有打出嗝來那一個短暫瞬間，口腔中的氣流是梗塞住的，不會把氣流送出口腔外，或是用閩南語數數字的一（念做 chit），這個數字的尾音也會把口腔氣流塞住，像是一瞬間一小口氣在嘴巴裡憋著的感覺。差別在於 [p] [t] [k] 是無聲，所以只需要做到憋一下口腔的氣流即可。例如 stop that、it will、make me 這三組詞中 [p] [t] [k] 的發音變化都是一個短暫阻斷氣流的停頓。此外，很多人會把這樣的字在字尾尾音加上一個 [ə]，念起來變成很奇怪的 [stɑpə]（斯大 P ㄜ）[ɪtə]（一ㄒㄜ）或是 [meɪkə]（妹 k ㄜ），這些都是錯誤的念法。請跟著內文更多實用範例音檔練習正確發音。

[b]、[d]、[g] 為有聲塞音，在實際口說發音上與無聲塞音有些微差異，這三個有聲塞音在口語上停頓音 (stop) 的長度會比無聲塞音要來得短促，像是 laptop 跟 lab safety，無聲塞音 [p] 在 top 之前會有一個明顯的停頓，但是有聲塞音 [b] 在 safety 之前的停頓就更為短促。此外，你會發現這兩個例子裡面的母音長度不一樣，無聲塞音 p 之前的母音 (lap) 較短，有聲塞音 b 之前的母音 (lab) 是比較長的。

Example 2: stop that、make me

Example 3: laptop、lab safety

★ Glottal Stop T ＋ 母音 ＋ n

在上述六個塞音中的 t 比較特別，當其後出現了＋母音＋ n 的時候，像是 button, cotton, kitten，美式發音通常會把這個夾在 t 跟 n 之間的母音吸收掉，連帶 stop T 的憋氣效果，整個字念起來會變成 [ˋbʌtn̩]、[ˋkɑtn̩]、[ˋkɪtn̩]，這樣的變化會發生在非重音節的位置。在美式發音的實境口語表達過程中，這樣的發音變化十分普遍，若不了解則會影響聽力理解。

Example 4: bu*tt*on, co*tt*on, ki*tt*en

2. 消音／省音

消音或省音也是在實境口語當中很常見的發音變化，會發生這樣變化的原因同樣是為了讓連續口語的發音可以流暢滑順不費力。舉例來說，I don't know 很多時候會變成 [ɪ duno]，又或像是 the first person 在口語中會把卡在中間的 [t] 省略。

Example 5: I don't know、the first person

3. 變音／同化音

impossible、imbalance 都是字根加上代表否定的字首 in- 所組成的字，但是拼音卻不是 inpossible 或 inbalance，這就是聲音同化的例子。由於 p 跟 b 的聲音需要雙唇緊閉，因此 n 受到後面雙唇音的影響變成 m，這樣一來，這些單字在發音上就會更加流暢滑順。這類變化有很多種，例如 [t] [d] [s] [z] 後面如果接 [j] 就會變成以下四組不同的聲音 [tʃ]、[dʒ]、[ʃ]、[ʒ]。像是 Did you do it? 這句話裡面的 [d] + [j] 就會變成 [dʒ] 的音，did you 聽起來就會變成 [dɪ dʒu]。

Example 6: Did you do it?

4. 弱讀音／削弱音

口語當中的弱讀音變化非常多，也會因為說話者的語速而有不同的情況。在美式口語發音變化當中，很多像是連接詞 and、助動詞 can 等字都是次要資訊，在語速加快的輕鬆對話過程中，都會被弱讀，其母音通常會被弱讀為 schwa sound（輕聲母音），也就是母音 [ə]，因此 I can do it 的 can 聽起來不會是 [kæn]，母音 [æ] 會弱讀成 [ə]，變成 [kən]，[ə] 的嘴型只有微張，聲音輕且短，方便說話者在說話過程中迅速把音一下子帶過去。本章的大量對話內容包含了各種常見的弱讀音，只要跟著音檔有耐心的反覆聆聽加深印象，並且搭配口語跟讀的模仿練習，聽力跟口說的能力必能同步提升。

Example 7:（can 沒有弱讀）**I can do it.**

Example 8:（can 弱讀）**I can do it.**

NOTE

Unit 06

校園新鮮人 ① 與指導教授面談

校園新鮮人 ② 與同學討論選課問題

校園新鮮人 ①

與指導教授面談

情境概說

學期剛開始，今天是 Jane 跟指導教授 Jack Smith 第一次見面。雙方就選課事宜作了一些討論。請仔細聆聽以下三段對話。

Track 0601　J = Jane　P = Professor　★ 請特別注意粗體字的部分 ★

Conversation A-1

J Hi, Professor Smith. I'm Jane Lee.

P Hi, [1]**it's nice to** [2]**meet you**. [3]**Sit down please.**

J Thanks.

P Have you settled into your dorm? [4]**Is everything okay with you?**

J Thanks for asking. To be honest, [5]**it's been a tough week.** [6]**The orientation** is quite informative, but I haven't decided how many courses **I should sign up for**.

P I see. Well, why don't we **go through your course schedule now**!

J **That would be great.**

聽力提點

1. **It's nice to...**

   it's 是由 it is 縮寫而來，但是縮寫和縮讀是不一樣的，縮寫只是文字書寫上的簡化，但是縮讀有不同的發音變化。例如 it's 在口語發音上，不只是從 [ɪt] [ɪs] 的發音縮短成 [ɪts]，有時候你會聽到很快的 [ts] 的聲音，因為說話者把前面母音 [ɪ] 省略掉了。it's 在輕鬆隨性的對話情境中聽起來像是只有 [ts] 的現象是常見的。

2. **meet you**

   t [t] + y [j] 連音會產生同化現象，變音為 [tʃ]，聽起來不是分開的 [mit] [ju] 兩個字，而是 [mitʃu]。後面段落還有更多的 [t] + [j] 的例子，請仔細聽聽看。

3. **Sit down please.**

   Sit 後面接的字首 [d] 並不是母音，不需要連音，但是 Sit 尾音這個 t，是塞音

stop T，發音的時候，舌頭抵住上顎但是不把原本要發出 [t] 這個聲音氣流釋放出去，很像突然憋住零點一秒一樣，然後再馬上發下一個字首 [d] 的聲音，因此，sit down 聽起來會是 [sɪt| daʊn]。

4. **Is everything okay with you?**

Is 後面是母音字首，必須連音。Is everything 兩個字聽起來是 [ɪzevriθɪŋ]。

5. **It's been a tough week.**

連音在句子中出現得很頻繁，如果不了解這些實際口語上的發音規則，當語速一加快，非母語人士很容易一下子適應不過來而聽不清楚。been a 連音聽起來像是 [bɪnə]，整句話其實是一氣呵成連續的聲音，聽起來是 [tsbɪnə]。另外，你會發現 tough week 一樣是連續滑順不中斷的聲音，前方字尾子音 [f] 與後方字首子音 [w] 之間嘴形接續而不中斷換氣，聽起來會很像是 [tʌfwik] 一個單字而已，這種連續滑順不中斷的發音現象是美式英語當中很重要的特色，當然，如果句子拉長，不可能在句點之前完全不換氣，至於什麼時候是換氣的位置，我們會在後面的章節作介紹。

6. **The orientation**

the 的發音有時候是 [ðə]，有時候是 [ði]，規則是當後面接續的字首是母音或雙母音的時候，會發 [ði] 的聲音，因此這裡聽起來是 [ðiorɪən`teʃən]。

Track 0602　J = Jane　P = Professor　★ 請特別注意粗體字的部分 ★

Conversation A-2

P [1]**Let's see**... you've [2]**signed up for** Ancient Egyptian History, 18th Century English Poets, Feminism, and Social Research Method. [3]**Wait**, if my memory **serves me right**, you should take Statistics, [4]**isn't it the required course**?

J Yeah, umm… **my exemption request was approved**, because I've already taken the course during my undergraduate studies, and actually I'm not that [5]**interested in** Statistics… so…

P I understand, but I recommend that you take [6]**at least** the SPSS tutorial course, given that your research topic probably **won't involve** quantitive methods.

聽力提點

1. **Let's see...**

   兩個無聲子音 s 接續出現的時候，如果要連續發兩次 [s] 的音會有 Gemination 輔音延長的發音變化讓滑順的連續發音因而中斷，因此遇到像是這樣兩個一樣的子音，只需要當作一個稍微長一點的 [s] 即可，聽起來是 [lɛtsi]。

2. **signed up for**

   d 跟 u 子母連音，聽起來像 [dʌp]。後面的 up for 這兩個字，[p] 是塞音，要短暫 stop，聽起來不會有 [p] 的氣音，而只有嘴唇緊閉，然後緊接著不中斷地接續發出 [fɔr] 的聲音。

3. **Wait**

   字尾 t 是塞音 stop T。

4. **isn't it**

   英文裡的 n't 否定縮寫在口語發音上，isn't 尾音的 [t] 是塞音，要 stop。有些人可能覺得那乾脆只要發 [n] 的聲音，當作後面的 t 是不存在的，但這樣念起來其實並不正確，這個鼻音 [n] 後面還有一個 stop T，也就是需要稍微憋一下氣，聽起來才是道地的美式發音，不過這裡不只是 isn't，後面還有 it 這個字，母音字首的 [ɪ] 會連音，isn't it 聽起來是 [ɪzə`nɪt|]。

5. **interested in**

   子母連音，聽起來像 [dɪn]。

6. **at least**

   介系詞 at 在句子當中通常會弱讀來讓語句更流暢快速，這裡的發音不是 [æt] 而是 [ət]，此外，at 的尾音 [t] 發塞音，需要非常短暫的 stop，因此 at least 兩個字在句子當中聽起來是 [ət| list]。

Track 0603 J = Jane P = Professor ★ 請特別注意粗體字的部分 ★

Conversation A-3

J Okay… but my friend Susan told me days before that the class is full, so… **I guess I just** [1]**wait and see** if anyone **drops** the course.

P Let me think... why [2]**don't you** [3]**send an email** to the tutorial TA and ask [4]them to [5]**put you on a waiting list**.

J [6]**That's a good idea**, thanks professor.

P Just let me know **how things are going**, and I'll see what I can do for you. I think you're in good shape. Any questions?

J No, that would be all.

P Wonderful! **Just so you know**, if you have any other questions, feel free to [7]**drop by** during my office hours.

聽力提點

1. **I just wait and see**

   and 在句子裡為了語速順暢滑溜，常常會弱讀成 [ən]，再加上跟前面 [t] 的子母連音，wait and see 這三個字連在一起，聽起來就變成 [weɪdənsi]，wait 的尾音 [t] 在這裡因為後面是母音的關係，不發 stop T，而是會變成 flap T，也稱為彈舌音的 T，這個 T 聽起來很像是 [d]，但是其實並不是真的要發一個清楚的 [d]，這個 flap T 只需要輕輕的點一下上顎然後接續發後面的 [ən] 就可以。

2. **why don't you...**

   t 碰到 y 會結合變化出一個新的發音 [tʃ]（就是 church 的 [tʃ]）。

3. **send an email**

   子母連音，聽起來像 [sendə nimeɪl]。

4. **them**

   them 這個字，本來的發音是 [ðem]，但是在句子裡常常會被弱讀成 [ðəm]。

5. **put you on a waiting list**

   t [t] 碰到 y [j] 產生連音變化成 [tʃ] 的音，聽起來是 [putʃu]。on a 兩個字連音，聽起來像 [nə]。此外，waiting 這個字的 [t] 發 flap T（彈舌音 T），第一點介紹的規則不只出現在句子連音中，在單字中也會有這個發音現象，因為後面是母音而要做發音的變化，這是美式英語的特色。

6. **That's a good idea.**

   子音、母音連音。

Ch 2

7. **drop by**

塞音 [p] 後面遇到子音為首的發音要 stop，聽起來幾乎像是 [drɑbaɪ]，但是若要發音正確，必須要 stop，很短促的頓一下。下一個「情境對話 B」的延伸聽寫會碰到的 drop my course 的發音也是同樣的例子。

延伸聽寫 | Exercise A

解答參見第 112 頁

Track 0604

1. A Hello, __________ really nice __________ __________ __________.

   B It's nice to meet you too.

   翻譯

   A：真開心見到你。

   B：我也很開心見到你。

2. __________ __________ __________, please.

   請坐。

3. You look tired. __________ __________ __________ with you?

   你看起來好累呀，一切還好嗎？

4. A You should take my Feminism Seminar. Since it's a small class, you'll have a great opportunity to discuss your ideas with other people.

   B I'd like to but I've already __________ __________ __________ twelve **courses**.

   翻譯

   A：你應該修我的女性主義研討課。那個班很小，你會有很棒的機會可以討論你的想法。

   B：我很想啊，但是我已經修了 12 門課了。

5. A Are you going to take Statistics __________ __________?

   B I wish I could, but it requires **tutorial sessions** and they're on Saturday.

   翻譯

   A：你這學期有打算修量化嗎？

   B：我真希望我可以，可是那門課還要求要上額外的輔導課程，時間都在禮拜六。

Track 0605

6. A Why __________ __________ take Professor Smith's class? His class is

always interesting!

B I'd like to, but they're all full.

翻譯

A：你要不要就去修 Smith 教授的哪堂課啊？他的課一向都是很有趣的。

B：我想啊，但是它們都額滿了。

7. A Hi, Professor, __________ __________ __________ you some questions about the class you're teaching, the course on Japanese Literature, I was thinking of taking it.

B Oh, that's an advanced course. Do you speak Japanese well?

A __________ __________ __________, to be honest.

B Well, then I suggest that you take Japanese Culture. The class discussion will be in English, so it won't be too difficult to follow.

A __________ __________ be great. Thanks for your help.

翻譯

A：嗨，教授，我可以問您一些有關於課程的問題嗎？您教的那門日本文學課，我在考慮要不要修。

B：那門課是進階課程，你日文說的流利嗎？

A：坦白講，沒有很好耶。

B：那我會建議你修日本文化這門課，這門課程的討論都是英文，對你來說要跟上才不會太困難。

A：那太棒了，謝謝您的幫忙。

實用字詞補充

1. **required course 必修課**

例 You have to pass all required courses with a grade of B or above.

你必須以 B 或優於 B 的成績通過所有必修課程。

2. **supervisor（工作上的）管理者，（學術上的）指導教授**

例 Sammy's supervisor is constantly giving her feedback on how to improve her writing.

森美的指導教授持續地針對她的寫作給予回饋。

3. **sign up for（報名）參加（有組織的活動）**

例 Tim has signed up for cooking class at the community college.

提姆已經報名社區大學的烹飪課。

4. **exempt** **免除、豁免（責任或款項等）**

例 The company has been exempted from the tax increase.

這間公司可豁免增稅。

5. **drop a course** **退選一門課**

例 Dropping a class after October 10th is considered a withdrawal.

10 月 10 日之後退選將被視為停修。

6. **office hours** **（教授）辦公時間**

例 Professor Smith has office hours Wednesday and Friday mornings from 09:00 to 11:00.

史密斯教授的辦公時間為週三和週五的上午 09:00 至 11:00。

7. **if my memory serves me right** **如果我沒記錯的話**

例 If my memory serves me right, it was a sunny day and you dropped by.

如果我記的沒錯的話，那天是晴天，你順道來拜訪。

情境會話 A／翻譯

Conversation A-1

珍　：史密斯教授，我是李珍。

教授：嗨，很開心見到你，來，請坐。

珍　：謝謝。

教授：你安頓好了嗎？一切都順利吧？

珍　：謝謝您的關心，這一週真的太累了，新生訓練的訊息是蠻豐富的，不過我還沒決定好我要選修多少課程。

教授：了解，那不如我們現在一起看一下你目前的課表吧！

珍　：那太好了。

Conversation A-2

教授：我看看歐，你已經有選古代埃及歷史、十八世紀的英國詩人、女性主義，還有社會研究方法，慢著，如果我沒記錯的話，你應該還要修統計學吧，那不是必修科目嗎？

珍　：對，可是，我可以免修，因為我大學的時候已經有修過統計學了，而且我對統計其實沒什麼興趣啦……

教授：我了解，基於你目前的研究主題大概之後也不會用到量化方法，但是我還是建議你至少上一門 SPSS（社會科學統計軟體）吧！

Conversation A-3

珍　：好，可是我朋友蘇珊幾天前告訴我說那門課已經滿了，我想我就是等等看有沒有人會退選那門課……

教授：我想想，那你要不要寄信給助教，請他們看能不能把你放到候補名單裡。

珍　：這是個好主意，謝謝教授。

教授：讓我知道之後情況如何，我看看還能怎麼協助你。現在看起來都挺好的，還有什麼問題嗎？

珍　：沒有其他問題了。

教授：那太好了，歐，對了，如果你有任何其他問題，我在辦公室的時間隨時可過來。

情境會話 B

校園新鮮人 ②

與同學討論選課問題

情境概說

新學期開始時，最重要的事情之一就是確定自己整個學年的學習計畫，畢竟每個人一天只有 24 小時，時間和精力都有限，一定得做好妥善規畫。來聽聽看剛與 supervisor 面談過的 Jane，如何跟她在校園巡禮 (Campus Tour) 時認識的新朋友 Ben 討論彼此的選課方向和課表安排。

Track 0606　J = Jane　B = Ben　★ 請特別注意粗體字的部分 ★

Conversation B-1

J Hey, Ben, [1]**are you going to** attend the department information session tomorrow?

B Tomorrow… maybe not. I planned to attend the archeology seminar. The guest speaker is so great. I have literally read all his books and papers, and its a whole day session, so… **I don't think I can [2]make it**.

J Oh, I can't go either, but I heard that they will be discussing some changes to the major requirements.

B Don't worry. We'll just go ask the secretary of the department afterwards. We will be fine.

J Yeah, [3]**we can do that**, but **don't you think** the whole orientation program is [4]**a bit confusing**.

B Why? I find it's quite informative and helpful.

J No, I mean… umm… there are so many **things on our plates**, right, and we are only granted five days to [5]**sort it out**. [6]**What if** I suddenly change my mind next week after I read through the syllabus of an elected course, not to mention that I am not sure whether there are any **pre-requisites** for some courses?

聽力提點

1. **Hey, Ben, are you going to...**

   are 的發音是 [ɑr]，但是在句子裡面有可能會想要輕巧帶過而弱讀，聽起來變成 [ər]。

2. **make it**

   連音，[k] 受到後面母音的影響，聽起來像 [meɪgɪt]，但並不是要去發一個像是 good 的 [g]，而是原本要發 [k] 的時候吐出嘴巴的氣流減弱而跟後面的母音交疊在一起，可以試著把這兩個字的發音放慢動作，但是不要中斷換氣，試試看揣摩音檔裡面的發音。* 無聲子音因為子母連音而產生的變化。

3. **Yeah, we can do that.**

   can 弱讀 [kən]。

4. **a bit confusing**

   a 弱讀 [ə]。bit 的尾音 [t] 因為後面接的是子音，所以發 stop T。

5. **sort it out**

   兩個 [t] 都一樣受到後面母音的影響，要發 flap T，聽起來很像中間有兩個 [d] 的聲音，[sorṭɪṭɑu]。

6. **What if**

   同上，[t] 發 flap T，聽起來很像 [hwʌdɪf]。

Track 0607 J = Jane B = Ben ★ 請特別注意粗體字的部分 ★

Conversation B-2

B Calm down, Jane, it's not [1]**the end of the world**! Let's take one thing [2]**at a time**. For the pre-reqs, [3]**you do know** that we can simply check the course catalog and [4]**all the information** you need is there.

J Didn't know that, thanks a lot!

B No problem. As for how to choose the "right" courses with no regrets, I [5]**must say**, **you'll** never know.

J I guess you're right, and I am **a bit overthinking the whole thing**.

B **And don't forget**, although the deadline to register for classes online is the

25th, you still can do it in person at the registrar's office after that.

J Indeed, thank you, Ben, you've [6]**been a great help**.

B Alright, [7]**I'd better get going**. I'm going to check if I am **eligible** for any grants. Wish me luck!

聽力提點

1. **the end of the world**

   第一個 the 跟第二個 the 發音不同。the 在句子裡面會受到後面單字的字首母音影響而發 [ði]，如果後面接的單字字首為子音，則發弱讀音 [ðə]，再加上 end of 的連音 [dʌ]，這整句聽起來會是 [ðiendʌfðəwɜld]。在本段對話中還有其他 the 在句中發音變化的例子，請仔細聽聽看。

2. **at a time**（弱讀 at）

   [t] 與後面母音連音，發 flap T。聽起來是 [ədətaɪm]。

3. **you do know...**

   do 是句子中被強調的關鍵字，音調會被拉高。

4. **all the information**

   the 發音 [ði]。

5. **must say**

   must 在句子當中常常會有弱讀音的選擇，發音清楚咬字的時候聽起來是 [mʌst]，弱讀則是 [məst] 或是 [məs]，在這個例子中，連音聽起來是 [məseɪ]。

6. **been a**

   子音母音連音，聽起來像 [nə]。

7. **I'd better**

   I'd 是 I would 的縮寫，這個 [d] 不管是在 I would like to 或是 I'd like to 的發音都不是 dog, dam 或是 door 的 [d]，這裡的 [d] 後面跟著子音 [l]，[d] 在這裡是塞音 (stop sound)，發音的時候只要記得舌頭擺在本來要發字母 D 的位置，但是要把氣流堵在嘴巴裡面，念起來很像非常短促的停頓，並且迅速接著發 [b]。

延伸聽寫 | Exercise B

解答參見第 112 頁

Track 0608 ★ 弱讀的字詞以斜體表示 ★

1. A *Excuse* me, **do you have a minute**? Can I ask you some questions about course 120?

   B Sure, *how* can I help?

   A I wonder if there're any **pre-reqs** for this course.

   B No, __________ __________ **introductory course**.

   翻譯

   A：不好意思耽誤您一下，我能問一些關於 120 這堂課的問題嗎？

   B：當然，請問什麼問題呢？

   A：我是在想說不知道這門課有沒有什麼修課門檻。

   B：沒有，這是入門基礎課程喔。

2. A __________ __________ __________!

   B ***I'll* keep my fingers crossed for you.**

   翻譯

   A：祝我好運吧！

   B：我會幫你祈禱一切順利的！

3. __________ __________, you only can register for classes online before the 25th. After that, you have to do it in person at the **registrar's office**.

   別忘了，25 號之前可以網路選課，超過時間，你就得親自到註冊組辦理。

4. A What do you plan to __________ __________?

   B I think I'll do psychology, *but I'm* also interested in literature.

   翻譯

   A：你打算主修什麼？

   B：我想主修心理學，不過我對文學也蠻有興趣的。

5. A __________ __________ __________ **drop my** Psychology class.

   B Oh, I'm sorry, but the deadline for dropping classes has passed. If you don't want to take the course, *you* have to **withdraw** from it.

   翻譯

   A：我想要退選心理學這門課。

   B：不好意思喔，退選的截止日已經過了，如果你不想修這門課，你只能停修。

實用字詞補充

1. **Do you have a minute?**
   這句話不能直翻，真正意思就如同中文的「請問你現在有空嗎？（我方便耽誤你一點時間嗎？）」。
2. **You do know..., right?**
   在動詞前面加上 do，表示說話者加強語氣，這裡的意思變成「你真的知道吧（不可能不知道吧？！）」，或者像是 I do love you，中文語意就是「我是真的愛你。」。
3. **I'll keep my fingers crossed for you.**
   或是簡短版本 "fingers crossed"，都是表達祝福對方好運，祈願成真的意思。
4. **information session 說明會**
   例 Will you attend the information session tonight?
   你會去參加晚上的說明會嗎？
5. **major requirement 主修要求**
   例 Students with questions about major requirements should speak with their supervisors. 對於主修的要求有問題的學生請與指導教授討論。
6. **Prerequisites 先決條件／門檻（簡稱 pre-reqs）**
   例 Are there any prerequisites for Psychology 201?
   心理學 201 這門課有沒有修課的門檻呢？
7. **course catalog 課程目錄**
   例 Please go check the course catalog online if you have questions.
   如果你有問題，請參考網上的課程目錄。
8. **registrar's office 註冊組**
   例 The registrar's office is committed to ensuring the integrity, accuracy, and security of student academic records.
   註冊組致力於確保學生成績紀錄的完整性、準確性和安全性。
9. **eligible 符合資格的**
   例 It is advised to look at the information provided online to find scholarships you **are eligible for**. 建議查看網路上提供的資訊來尋找你有資格申請的獎學金。

情境會話 B／翻譯

Conversation B-1

珍：嗨！班，你明天會去系上的說明會嗎？

班：明天啊，應該不會，我打算去參加一個考古學的研討會，客座講者超棒的，我幾乎可以算是拜讀過他全部的書籍跟期刊論文了，主要是研討會是一整天的，所以，我覺得我應該是來不及回來參加說明會了。

珍：歐，我也沒辦法去參加說明會，但是我聽說他們會討論關於主修的要求，好像有些地方有修改。

班：不用擔心啦，我們就之後再去系辦問祕書就好啦，沒事的。

珍：對歐，說的也是，但是你不覺得這整個新生週實在是有點讓人搞得團團轉嗎？

班：會嗎？我倒覺得提供的資訊很豐富也都蠻有幫助的啊！

珍：不是啦，我的意思是說，你看我們手邊有那麼多事情要處理，然後我們卻只有五天可以把一切弄清楚，如果一週之後我讀完某門選修課的課程大綱才突然改變主意不想修了怎麼辦？更不要說我都還沒搞清楚某幾門課到底有沒有修課門檻。

Conversation B-2

班：珍，冷靜一點，情況沒那麼可怕啦，我們一樣一樣來，首先，關於修課門檻，你該不會不知道我們直接查課程目錄就都一清二楚了？

珍：我還真不知道耶，太謝謝你了！

班：小事情！那至於到底要怎樣才能選到「對的」課程，坦白講，誰知道呢！

珍：你說的也對啦！我對這整件事情的確是有點過度焦慮了。

班：而且別忘了，就算網路選課截止日是 25 日，你之後還是可以直接到註冊組辦理啊。

珍：沒錯！謝啦，班，你真的是幫了我一個大忙呀！

班：好啦，我要趕快出發了，我要去看看我有沒有符合的獎學金可以申請的，祝我好運啊！

延伸聽寫 Answer Keys

Exercise A

（請參考以下答案及解說，可弱讀的字詞以斜體表示。）

1. *it's* really nice *to* meet you.（t+y 的變音在實際口語中會有因人而異的差異，例如此處及第 6 題都是不變音而把 [t] 發塞音 stop。）
2. Have a seat, please.
3. *Is* everything okay with you?
4. sign up for（連音，n u 相連聽起來是 [nʌp]。）
5. this semester
6. don't you
7. can I ask / Not very well / That will

Exercise B

1. it's an（子音母音連音，聽起來是 [zən]。）
2. Wish me luck
3. Don't forget
4. major in
5. I'd like to

Unit 07

生活新鮮人 ① 租屋洽談

生活新鮮人 ② 入住宿舍

生活新鮮人 ③ 與室友溝通

情境會話 A 生活新鮮人 ①

租屋洽談

情境概說

Jim 是博士研究生，剛到英國，正在跟房東詢問租屋的細節。例如：環境、租金、押金、其他房間的分租狀況等。

Track 0701 J = Jim L = Landlord ★ 請特別注意粗體字的部分 ★

Conversation A-1

J Hi, I am Jim, **we [1]spoke on the phone this morning**!

L Hi Jim. **Nice to meet you**. I'm Samatha Hopkins. Let me give you a tour of the house.

J Thanks, **[2]it's a quiet neighborhood**.

L **Isn't it! It's a great place** to concentrate on your work. That's why many grad students live here. Okay, here's the cozy living room and the kitchen is **[3]back there**. You're very lucky! **The area [4]has been** renovated so **it's all brand new and shiny**.

J Yeah, it's very modern and posh.

L Here we are! This is your double en-suite bedroom.

聽力提點

1. **spoke/ spoon / speed / spin**

   [p] 是無聲子音，發這個聲音的時候會有氣流送出嘴巴外，但是像 spoke 這樣的例子，因為受後面母音的影響，[p] 的發音會稍微改變，送出嘴巴外的氣流不那麼強烈，反而變成比較輕短的雙唇音，聽起來很像輕弱的 [b]。其他常見的例子有 spoon、speed、spin 等等。

2. **it's a**

   a 弱讀變成 [ə]，子母連音，聽起來是 [ɪzə]。本段有好幾個同樣的連音，請仔細聽聽看。

3. **back there**

   [k] 遇到後面字首是子音的時候，發音是塞音 stop，聽起來像是很短促的頓

一下，[bæk| ðer]，流行歌曲 “How you like that” 的 like that 也是一樣的道理，你會聽見 [laɪk| ðæt]。

4. **has been...**

has 發音是 [hæz]，但是在句子當中弱讀的時候會變成 [həz]，語速更快時有可能只會聽見 [əz]。這裡的 has been 聽起來是 [əzbɪn]。

Track 0702 J = Jim L = Landlord ★ 請特別注意粗體字的部分 ★

Conversation A-2

J Are the utilities **included in the rent**?

L No, I'm afraid not... you'll have to [1]**split bills** with the housemates.

J I see, and **I have to sign a one-year lease**, am I right?

L [2]**That's right**, and there **is a** security deposit of two month's rent, which of course will be returned to you at the end of your lease if everything is fine.

J How many [3]**bedrooms** are upstairs?

L Oh, there're two... umm... A PhD student from Korea lives in the single bedroom, and two graduate students share the other double bedroom.

J **That sounds nice**. When [4]**can** I move in?

聽力提點

1. **split bills**

無聲子音 [t] 後面是子音 [b]，因此要發塞音 stop T，舌頭擺到要準備發出 [t] 的位置，但是不要發出聲音，聽起來是 [splɪt| bɪls]。

2. **That's right**

子音字尾接續下一個字的字首是子音時，依然要把兩個聲音滑順的帶過去，可以先放慢語速但是不要在字跟字之間中斷換氣，然後逐漸練習加快語速，that's right 聽起來是 [ðætsraɪt]。

3. **bedroom**

[d] 跟 [r] 兩個字音連在一起，耳朵尖的人可能會覺得 [bɛdrum] 中間夾了一個很像中文字「準」的聲音，那個聲音就是兩個子音 [d][r] 一起的聲音，不習慣的人一樣可以透過把 [bɛd_rum] 中間刻意拉長，念慢一點但是不要換氣，

Ch 2

然後再加快速度多練習幾次就能熟練了。

4. **When can I move in?**

can 弱讀成 [kən]。

延伸聽寫 | Exercise A 解答參見第 126 頁

Track 0703

1. A Hey, ①__________ you okay?

B I've been house-hunting for months and ②__________ __________ nightmare.

A How come?

B You know ③__________ I'm looking for a flat **off-campus** since my budget ④__________ __________ bit tight. I went to see so many flats but they're either too small or too expensive.

翻譯

A：嘿，你還好嗎？

B：我已經找了好幾個月房子了，簡直是場惡夢。

A：怎麼會這樣呢？

B：我最近不是在找校外的單層公寓嗎？畢竟我預算有限啊，我看了好多間，不是太小就是太貴。

2. A Hi, this is Jane Smith. The 4B kitchen's microwave isn't working. Can you send someone to **fix** it?

B Sure, but our technician isn't available ⑤__________ __________ moment. They ⑥__________ go check until Wednesday, is that okay?

A That's fine… well… I guess we can just use the oven instead.

B Okay, thank you for calling.

翻譯

A：嗨，我是珍．史密斯。4B 廚房的微波爐壞掉了耶，你能找人來修理嗎？

B：沒問題啊，但是我們的維修人員現在都不在，要等到禮拜三之後，可以嗎？

A：好吧……那……我想我們就只能先用烤箱囉。

B：謝謝你〔電話上的禮貌結尾〕。

實用字詞補充

1. **security deposit** 押金／保證金

   例 Security deposits can be either refundable or nonrefundable, depending on the terms. 保證金可退還或不可退還，具體取決於條款怎麼約定。

2. **one-bedroom apartment** 一房一廳的公寓
3. **studio apartment** 套房型的（小）公寓

   * 除了浴室還會有小廚房、小客廳等等，跟 one-bedroom 的差別就是沒有隔間。

4. **flat** 單層公寓（英式用法）

   例 Is the flat furnished or unfurnished?

   這間公寓是有附傢俱還是沒有附傢俱呢？

5. **air-conditioning** 冷氣、空調

   例 How do you manage to study in this heat without air conditioning?

   你是怎麼辦到的？在沒有冷氣這麼熱的環境下讀書？

6. **landlord** 房東

   例 My landlord is a teacher.

   我的房東是一名教師。

7. **en-suite** （附帶）浴室的

   例 All bedrooms in the mansion are en-suite.

   這棟豪宅的所有臥室都有浴室。

8. **Off-campus** 校外 *on-campus 校內
9. **Do something instead** 不做本來的選擇，選擇了另外一個

   例 There were no double rooms so I booked two single rooms instead.

   雙人房都沒有了，所以我就訂了兩間單人房。

情境會話 A／翻譯

Conversation A-1

吉姆：嗨，我是吉姆，我們早上有通過電話！

房東：嗨，吉姆，很高興見到你，我是薩曼莎 · 霍普金斯，我來帶你參觀一下房子。

吉姆：謝謝，這一帶還蠻安靜的。

房東：對吧！很多研究生住在這一帶，你會發現這是個可以安心工作的很棒的地方。這裡是舒適的客廳，然後廚房在後面。你很幸運！這一區都重新整修過了，所以非常新。

吉姆：恩，看起來非常時髦和豪華。

房東：這邊就是啦！來看看你的雙人套房。

Conversation A-2

吉姆：租金有包含水電嗎？

房東：很抱歉沒有喔，你要跟樓友們一起分攤。

吉姆：我了解，那這邊是要簽一年約的，對嗎？

房東：沒錯，然後還需要收取兩個月的租金作為押金，當然等你退租之後如果一切無恙就會退還給你。

吉姆：樓上還有幾間房間呢？

房東：樓上還有兩間。有一個韓國來的博士班學生住在單人雅房，然後有兩個研究生住在另外一間雙人房。

吉姆：聽起來還不錯，請問我什麼時候可以搬進來？

生活新鮮人 ②

入住宿舍

情境概說

Jessy 正準備搬進學校宿舍，今天是她跟新室友 Angela 第一次見面。兩人一起協調了房間使用的分配問題。

Track 0704　A = Angela　J = Jessy　★ 請特別注意粗體字的部分 ★

Conversation B-1

A Hi, you must be Jessy. [1]**You** [2]**look great in that dress**!

J Thank you, and you must be Angela. It's nice to finally [3]**meet you**.

A Well, after [4]**like a** whole month following you [5]**on instagram**, it's really nice to talk [6]**face-to-face**!

J I know! Wow, the room [7]**looks so much bigger** than in the picture on the website.

A It's great, **isn't it**! And everything is brand new.

J We are so lucky.

聽力提點

1. **you**

   [ju] 弱讀，聽起來是 [jə]。

2. **look great in**

   [k] 塞音 stop，聽起來是 [lʊk| gret]，不過，great 字尾還要跟 in 連音，[t] 後面接的是母音字首所以要發 flap T 彈舌音，三個字聽起來是 [lʊk| gre ţɪn]。

3. **meet you**

   t [t] 碰到 y [j] 變音 [tʃ]，meet you 聽起來是 [ˋmi tʃu]。

4. **like a**

   子音母音連音。無聲子音 [k] 後面連接母音，[k] 送出嘴巴外的氣流變弱而成為比較輕短的聲音，聽起來很像是 [ˋlaɪ gə]，會讓你覺得中間有一個很像 [g] 的聲音，但是不需要真的刻意去發出 [g] 的聲音。

5. **on instagram**

子音母音連音，聽起來是 [ɑnɪn stəgræm]。

6. **face *to* face**

to 弱讀成 [tə]。

7. **looks so much bigger**

兩個相同的無聲子音 [s] 在一起時有省音變化，聽起來像是 [lʊkso]。

Track 0705　A = Angela　J = Jessy　★ 請特別注意粗體字的部分 ★

Conversation B-2

A I hope you don't mind, but I [1]**took the bed** by the window.

J That's fine. [2]**How about** these drawers? Do you [3]**mind if I take the top two**?

A [4]**Not at all**, then I'll take the [5]**bottom** two.

J I think I should unpack first.

A Did you bring **lots of clothes**?

J Not really, why?

A Well, the **hanger space** is not enough so if you need s-hooks, I have spare ones. Feel free to use them.

J Cool, thanks.

聽力提點

1. **took the bed**

k 後面是子音，所以要發塞音 stop，聽起來像是 [ðə] 之前有一個非常短促的停頓 [tʊk| ðə]。後面還有一樣的例子，可多留意。

2. **How about these drawers?**

單字的最後一個音是 [u]、[aʊ] 或 [oʊ]，而要與下一個母音連音的時候，要把 [w] 作為下一個字的起始聲音，這個發音規則稱為「滑音」(glide)，因此 how about 兩個字連在一起聽起來是 [haʊ wə`baʊt]，當然這個插入的 [w] 聲音是非常輕微的，目的只是為了讓母音跟母音之間的連音聲音聽起來更加滑順而已。

3. **mind if I take the top two**

連音，聽起來是 [maɪn dɪfaɪ]。

4. **Not at all**（美式）/ **Not at all**（英式）

母音子音連音，[t] 後面是母音，會發 flap T 彈舌音，聽起來是 [nɑ ṭə ṭɔl]。如果是英式發音，t 一樣發無聲子音 [t]，即使三個字連著講，還是會聽到很明顯的 [t] 的聲音 [nɑ tæ tɔl]。

5. **bottom / pretty / party**（美式）

前面舉過很多尾音 [t] 的單字因為與後面字首的母音連音而改為發出彈舌音 [ṭ]，在單字的發音中也會有一樣的現象。當 [t] 夾在兩個母音之間，會發聽起來像 [d] 的彈舌音 [ṭ]，例如 pretty [prɪṭi] 或是 party [pɑrṭi]，這樣的發音現象是美式口音的特色，如果是英式口音則會聽起來是 pretty [prɪti] 或是 party [pɑrti]。

Ch 2

延伸聽寫 | Exercise B

解答參見第 126 頁

Track 0706

1. A The shared kitchen has two stoves, a refrigerator, two microwaves, and two electric kettles. Please remember to ①__________ __________ back **after you finish with them**.

   B ②__________ __________ the **appliances are broken**?

   A You ③__________ go to the first floor and find either a resident assistant or a staff member.

翻譯

A：共用廚房有兩個爐台，一台冰箱，兩個微波爐和兩個電熱水壺。用完後請記得將其放回原處。

B：那如果電器有壞掉呢？

A：你可以去一樓然後跟舍監或是我們的職員說一聲。

2. A My roommate is a ④__________ __________, and she leaves a lot of bottles and empty food containers in the kitchen every Friday night.

   B Have you talked to her?

   A No, I don't know how to.

   B Well, you just have to **tell her how you feel** and ask her to clean her stuff, oh, and you can always talk to your resident assistant.

翻譯

A：我的室友超愛派對，她每週五都在廚房留下一堆酒瓶跟空的食物盒。

B：你有跟她談過了嗎？

A：沒有啊，我不知道怎麼說。

B：哎，你就跟她說你的感受，然後要她把自己的東西收拾乾淨啊，歐，然後你也可以去找你的舍監反應一下。

情境會話 B／翻譯

Conversation B-1

安琪拉：嗨，你一定就是潔西吧！你穿那件洋裝真好看。

潔　西：謝謝，你是安琪拉對吧！真高興終於見到你了。

安琪拉：經過整個月都在 IG 上面追蹤你，能夠見到本尊真的是太好了呀！

潔　西：可不是嗎！哇，房間看起來比網站上的照片大很多耶。

安琪拉：真的超讚啊！而且一切都是新的。

潔　西：我們好幸運喔。

Conversation B-2

安琪拉：希望你不會介意喔，我已經先選窗邊的床鋪了。

潔　西：沒關係啊，那這些抽屜呢？你介意我用上面兩層嗎？

安琪拉：不介意啊，那我就用下面兩層囉！

潔　西：我覺得我應該先來整理行李。

安琪拉：你有帶很多衣服嗎？

潔　西：還好，怎麼了嗎？

安琪拉：因為掛衣服的空間不太夠，所以如果你有需要 s 掛鉤，我有多的歐，你想用就拿去用沒關係。

潔　西：酷！謝啦！

情境會話 C

生活新鮮人 ③

與室友溝通

情境概說

每個人的生活習慣不同，在宿舍生活一定會遇到許多需要與室友互相溝通協調的情況。來聽聽以下發生了什麼事。

Track 0707 J = Jessy B = Brian ★ 請特別注意粗體字的部分 ★

J Hey, Brian, **do you** [1]**have a minute**?

B Sure, **what's going on**?

J It's just… I'm sorry to [2]**bring it up**, but I need to concentrate on my reading, [3]**you know**, I have a test tomorrow and I try to **cram for the test**… so **would you mind**?

B Oh, sorry, I'll [4]**turn it off**.

J No… no… just… it would be great if you could [5]**turn it down** a little.

B Of course, and Jessy, don't worry about the test, [6]**you got this**!

Ch 2

聽力提點

1. **have a**

   have 弱讀為 [həv]，a 弱讀為 [ə]，子音母音連音，聽起來是 [həvə]。

2. **bring it up** 連音。

3. **you know**

   you 弱讀，聽起來是 [jəno]。

4. **turn it off**

   子音母音連音，聽起來是 [tɜ nɪ tɔf]。比較一下第五點中 it 的發音。

5. **turn it down**

   it 後面的字首是子音，所以 t 要發塞音 stop，聽起來是 [tɜ nɪt| daʊn]。

6. **You got this!**

   塞音 stop，聽起來是 [gɑt| ðɪs]。

延伸聽寫 | Exercise C ➔ 解答參見第 126 頁

Track 0708

1. A I don't mind if you **borrow my utensils** and other kitchen stuff, but please ①__________ __________ after you use it.

   B Oh, I'm so sorry. I will, **I promise**.

   翻譯

   A：我不介意你借用我的餐具和其他廚房用品，但是麻煩要在使用後洗乾淨。

   B：歐，真抱歉，我保證，我之後會洗乾淨的。

2. A Do you know where I can buy a hair dryer?

   B Just go to Wal-Mart. They have ②__________, **no kidding**.

   翻譯

   A：你知道我可以在哪裡買到吹風機嗎？

   B：去 Wal-Mart 就對啦！他們什麼都賣，真的！

3. A **Don't take this the wrong way**, **but** the music is too loud and it's ③__________. You can have a party if you want but it's not okay to bother other people.

   B Right, sorry, **I didn't realize that**.

   翻譯

   A：我這麼說你不要往心裡去歐，可是講真的，音樂聲音真的太大聲了，而且現在是半夜。你想開派對當然是可以沒錯，但是如果打擾到別人那就是不應該的啊。

   B：你說的對，抱歉，是我沒有注意到。

4. A The resident tutor was here earlier and she complained that our kitchen floor is really dirty. I think we all should have a meeting, you know, to sort things out!

   B The party ④__________ __________ was crazy. What were we thinking?

   A I'm sure ⑤__________ __________ __________ was thinking about the floor.

   B Okay, why don't we go ⑥__________ __________ mop and soap and let's clean it!

   A Should we call Jane since she was the one who came up with the idea of "let's drink them all"?

B Yeah-huh!

翻譯

A：舍監剛剛有來，她抱怨我們的廚房地板真的很髒。我覺得我們所有人應該開個會，來解決一下這個問題。

B：昨天晚上的派對真的太瘋狂了，我們那時候到底在想什麼啊？

A：我確定我們沒有人在管地板啦！

B：何不去找一支拖把跟肥皂，然後我們來清理一下。

A：我們應該叫珍一起嗎？畢竟她是那個說"我們把酒全喝光吧"的人啊。

B：當然一定要叫她啊！

實用字詞補充

1. **No kidding**

口語意思就是表達說話者剛剛說的話是千真萬確的 (honestly)。

2. **Don't take it the wrong way, but...**

這句話類似中文的要說醜話之前先打個預防針，先打聲招呼提醒對方，接下來的對話可能不太好聽（或許冒犯），但是你不是惡意要造成對方不舒服的感受。

例 Don't take it the wrong way, but we all think you really need to try to be in other people's shoes. 希望（我這麼說）你不要有疙瘩誤會啦，但是我們都覺得你真的應該要試著站在別人的立場想一想。

3. **You got this! 鼓勵對方他一定可以克服困難戰勝一切！**

例 I know you will pass it. You got this! 我知道你一定會通過的，你一定沒問題的！

* 也可以說 You've got this!

情境會話 C／翻譯

潔　西：嘿，布萊恩，你有空嗎？

布萊恩：當然啊，怎麼了嗎？

潔　西：就是……那個……我也不想去講這件事情，但是我真的需要專心讀書，就是我明天要考試，我正在努力把東西塞進我的腦袋，所以，你介意嗎（把電視關小一點）？

布萊恩：噢，對不起，我把電視關掉。

潔　西：不用不用，只是就是說，如果可以的話，你關小聲一點好嗎？

布萊恩：當然，還有，潔西，你不要太擔心考試啦，你沒問題的！

延伸聽寫 Answer Keys

Exercise A（請參考以下答案及解說，可弱讀的字詞以斜體表示。）

① Are you okay? / Are you okay? / Are you okay?

Are you okay? 實際對話場合其實可能有各種細微變化，看說話者想要強調哪一個字。（套色為強調的字）

Are you okay? [ər jə oˋke]（前面兩個字都弱讀）

Are you okay? [ər ju oˋke]（只有 are 弱讀）

② it's a　③ that　④ is a

⑤ at the（[t] 連後面有聲子音 [ð]，塞音 stop，聽起來是 [æt| ðə]。）

⑥ can't go check（美式）/ can't go check（英式）

can't 尾音 [t] 是塞音 stop。如果是英式口音，這個 can't 聽起來是 [kɑnt]，但是在句子當中 [kɑnt] 的尾音 t 會被消掉，因為前後都是子音的關係，要連續發三個子音比較費力，因此像是這邊的 can't go check，英式口音聽起來會是 [kɑn(t) go tʃek]。

Exercise B（請參考以下答案及解說。）

① put things（[t] 發塞音 stop，聽起來是 [pʊt| θɪŋs]。）

② What if（母音為首的字要跟前面連音，聽起來是 [wɑ tɪf]。）

③ can（弱讀成 [kən]。）

④ party animal

Exercise C（請參考以下答案及解說。）

① clean it（子音母音連音，聽起來是 [klinɪt]。）

② EVERYTHING（如果說話的時候想要強調某一個字，除了語氣音調提高之外，也可能把每個音節刻意發音清楚，[ev ri θɪŋ]。）

③ midnight（[d] 的聲音有很多種，在這個單字裡面，你會發現沒有聽見 dog 的 [d]，這裡的聲音就如同我們前面提過的塞音 stop，舌頭擺放到 [d] 要發音的位置，但是並不把氣送出口腔之外，頓了一下，聽起來是 [mɪd|naɪt]。）

④ last night（為了發音方便，[t] 有時候會有消音的現象，像是 first time 聽起來好像是變成 firs(t) time，last night 聽起來也像是 las(t) night。）

⑤ none of us（子音母音連音。）

⑥ find a（子音母音連音，聽起來是 [faɪndə]。）

加值學更多！

線上下載關於校園打工機會的情境聽力練習，隨時想聽就聽！

Unit 08

課後討論・向教授提問

情境會話 A 課後討論

情境概說

Victor 跟 Natasha 約好要在圖書館討論報告，結果 Victor 遲到了……。

Track 0801　V = Victor　N = Natasha　★ 請特別注意粗體字的部分 ★

Conversation A-1

V **So sorry I'm late.**

N **It's no big deal**, but you look terrible, [1]**is everything alright?**

V [2]**I stayed up late last night** for my psychology [3]**mid-term paper**, and the citations are killing me.

N [4]**That makes two of us**! Writing papers is always like… like a nightmare for me.

V Tell me about it. Hey, where should we sit?

N How about the table by the window?

V Lovely, **wait**… umm… I'm going to get some [5]**chips and coffee** from the vending machine first? Want anything?

N **Can you get me black coffee**, thanks.

聽力提點

1. **is everything alright?**
   這個句子的開頭 is 弱讀，本來發音是 [ɪz]，弱讀的聲音是 [z] 或 [s]。

2. **I stayed up**
   [d] 跟 [ʌp] 連音，聽起來像是 [dʌp] 一個聲音。

3. **mid-term paper**
   兩個字念起來變成 [mitɜm]，[d] 跟 [t] 兩個聲音連在一起的時候，通常會省略前面的 [d] 發音，這個發音現象在美式英語很常見，例如 I'm glad to see you. 的 glad to 聽起來也會變成 [glætu]。

4. **That makes two of us**

two 的最後一個音是 [u]，與下一個母音連音的時候，要把 [w] 作為下一個字的起始聲音，這個發音規則稱為「滑音」(glide)，因此 two of 兩個字連在一起聽起來是 [tu wəvəs]，當然這個插入的 [w] 聲音非常輕微，目的只是為了讓母音跟母音之間的連音聽起來更加滑順而已。

5. **chips and coffee**

   這句除了 chips 的尾音 [s] 跟後面的母音 [ɔ] 連音，and 這個字也弱讀，從 [ænd] 變成 [ən]，因此實際聽起來是 [tʃɪpsən kɔfi]。

Track 0802　V = Victor　N = Natasha　★ 請特別注意粗體字的部分 ★

Conversation A-2

V [1]**You know what**… I'm really glad we meet up **at the library**. Whenever I feel so tired, studying in the library **always can do** [2]**some magic**. Anyway, **I'm gonna** [3]**stick around after we're done here**.

N **Really**?! It is too quiet for me to concentrate, especially the silent floors. Actually, **I prefer to stay in** [4]**a bit noisy environment, like a coffeehouse**. That kind of vibes somehow **keeps me doing what I'm trying to do**!

聽力提點

1. **You know what**

   You [ju] 弱讀音變成 [jə]，what 的尾音 [t] 則是塞音 stop。

2. **some magic**

   前後兩個 [m] 子音相連發音，只會聽見一個稍微長一點的 m，[səmædʒɪk]。

3. **stick around**

   子音 [k] 受到後面母音影響，[k] 發氣音比較弱而輕短的聲音，聽起來會像是 [g]。

4. **a bit**

   [t] 是尾音塞音 stop。

Ch 2

Track 0803 V = Victor N = Natasha ★ 請特別注意粗體字的部分 ★

Conversation A-3

V Well, **I can't imagine I** [1]**would ever study** [2]**in a coffeehouse**. I mean, I don't think **I have ever tried to do that**. [3]**When it comes to** cramming for exams or writing essays, I go to the library [4]**without a second thought**.

N *It wouldn't hurt* to try something different, right?

V I bet.

N **Tell you what**, you should go to the Varsity with me after we finish this. Who knows? Maybe you will get some reading done today in a less quiet place.

V Yeah, why not! Let's do it!

聽力提點

1. **would ever**

   強調 ever（從來沒想過會有一天），音調提高。

2. **in a**

   連音，子音 [n] 與母音 [ə] 相連時會有類似中文「呢」的發音出現，聽起來是 [ɪnə]。

3. **When it**

   連音，聽起來是 [wenɪt]。

4. **without a**

   這個 a 一樣為了句子的流暢快速帶過，弱讀為 [ə]，與前面的字尾 [t] 連音，[t] 要發彈舌音 [t̬]。

情境聽寫 | Exercise A

解答參見第 138 頁

Track 0804

1. ______ ______ ______ ______ ______ ______ ______ ______ ______?

   你能幫我帶杯黑咖啡嗎？

2. ______ ______ ______ ______!

   沒關係啦！

3. ______ ______ ______ ______ ______ ______
______.
我還要在這兒待一會。

4. ______ ______ ______ ______ ______ ______
______ ______ ______ ______ ______, ______
______ ______.
我比較喜歡待在有點吵雜的環境，像咖啡店。

5. ______ ______ ______ ______!
沒錯啊！

6. ______ ______ ______?
你知道嗎？

7. ______ ______ ______ ______ ______?
我們要在哪裡碰面比較好呀？

8. ______ ______ ______ ______ ______ ______.
它總是有神奇的效果。

9. ______ ______ ______ ______ ______ ______
______ ______.
那種氛圍莫名的就是讓我感到開心。

Ch 2

實用字詞補充

1. **same here** **表達同意對方的意思。**

   跟對話 A 裡面的 "That makes two of us!" 以及 "Tell me about it!" 是同樣的表達方式。

   例 A: Today's event kind of sucks.

   今天的活動真的有點遜耶！

   B: Same here.

   我也有同感啊！

2. **You know what!**

   就跟中文口語對話時常常聽到的「你知道嗎！」一樣，當我們說出這句話的時候，並不是真的在問對方知道或不知道，而是作為自己即將要開啓的話題的一個「快速開場白」而已，用來提醒對方要仔細聽我們接下來說的內容。

3. **Tell you what!** **用來表達建議，類似中文的「不如我們這麼做」。**

   例 I'll tell you what–let's split it.

   不如我們就平分如何！

情境會話 A／翻譯

Conversation A-1

維　克：不好意思我遲到了。

娜塔莎：小事情沒關係啊，可是你看起來好慘，還好嗎？

維　克：我昨天晚上熬夜寫我的心理學期中報告，引用參考文件那些東西真的要折磨死人了。

娜塔莎：我懂，寫報告根本就像惡夢一樣。

維　克：你說的沒錯！你覺得我們要坐哪個位置啊？

娜塔莎：靠窗的那張桌子好嗎？

維　克：當然好啊！對了，我要先去販賣機買點薯片跟咖啡？你有想要什麼嗎？

娜塔莎：能幫我帶杯黑咖啡嗎，謝啦。

Conversation A-2

維　克：我很開心我們選在圖書館討論。每當我感到很累時，圖書館總能產生一些魔力。等一下跟你討論完，我就要繼續在這邊讀點書。

娜塔莎：真假？我都覺得圖書館實在是太安靜到我根本無法專心耶，尤其是在禁音樓層。事實上，我還是比較喜歡待在像是咖啡店這種吵鬧一點的環境讀書，那種活躍的氣氛就會讓我很有幹勁繼續處理手邊的事情。

Conversation A-3

維　克：哎，我還真無法想像我有辦法在咖啡店這種地方讀書耶，印象中我應該是從來沒有這麼做過，每次要考前衝刺或是寫報告，我就是去圖書館，毫不猶豫耶。

娜塔莎：嘗試看看不一樣的，也沒有什麼損失啊，對不對？

維　克：你說的也對啦！

娜塔莎：不如我們等一下討論完，你就跟我一起去 Varsity 如何？誰知道你今天可能就在一個沒那麼安靜的地方讀了些書呢！

維　克：好啊，那我們就去吧！

向教授提問

情境概說

在 office hour 時間找教授詢問報告的修改建議。

Track 0805　N = Nathan　P = Professor　★ 請特別注意粗體字的部分 ★

Conversation B-1

N [1]**Thank you for meeting with me**, Professor Smith. I've received your comments on my essay and [2]**I wanted to talk to you about it, if it's okay.**

P Sure, how can I help?

N Humm, I [3]**got a B**, but I really think [4]**I can perform better**. If you don't mind, can you give me some advice and then I can rewrite it?

P That's the positive attitude I always value, but I have to warn you that this essay will need a lot of revision. I hope you're ready for a quite long, tiring process.

N To be honest, I am really interested in the topic so what can I say, [5]**I can't wait**!

P **Good to hear that! Quick question**, after you submitted your essay, have you ever read it?

N No, why?

聽力提點

1. **Thank *you for* meeting with me.**

   Thank you 的連音聽起來像是 [kju]。此外，這個句子裡面的 you 跟 for 都是弱讀，for 本來是 [fɔr]，口語速度影響下母音弱化變成 [fɚ]，而 you 聽起來也不是 [ju]，而是 [jə]。

2. **I wanted *to* talk *to you about* it.**

   語速很快的時候句子中弱讀的字會比較多，要多跟著音檔練習開口跟讀，才能加強聽力的反應。

Ch 2

3. **I got a B**

連音，t 受到後面母音的影響，聽起來不會是氣音 [t]，而會變成 flap T，彈舌音 [ţ] 聽起來很像是 [d]，加上 a 弱讀成 [ə]，所以連著一起說的時候聽起來是 [gɑţə]。

4. **I *can* perform better.**

can 弱讀為 [kən]（像是 drunken 的 [kən]）。

5. **I can't wait!**

對比第 4 點 I can perform better 的弱讀音 [kən]，can't 通常在口語中會語調上揚強調「無法、不能」的感受，單字發音是 [kænt]，在句子裡的 [t] 尾音會以塞音 stop 表現。但是，如果是英式發音，這個 a 會發 [ɑ]（像是 not [nɑt]、dot [dɑt]），can't 聽起來是 [kɑnt]。就如同 aunt 這個字，美式發音是 [ænt]，英式發音則是 [ɑnt]。

Track 0806 N = Nathan P = Professor ★ 請特別注意粗體字的部分 ★

Conversation B-2

P See, [1]**lots of students** think that after they [2]**hand in** their homework, it's done. You know what?! They're wrong. A few days after you finish your work, you just have to sit down and read your paper, like you're reading someone else's work.

N Wow, **I've never thought about that before**, so **what you're saying is** we should be our own critics.

P Yes, of course, **you have to be objective, but it's more than that**.

N I guess… hum… we can do more than just editing or a grammar check!

P [3]**Absolutely**! In fact, you do have a very interesting idea to work with, and **do remember** to **cut out anything** that doesn't support your thesis statement. In other words, you have to [4]**tighten everything up**!

聽力提點

1. **lots of students**

連音，聽起來是 [lɑtsəv]。

2. **hand in**

子音 [d] 和母音 [ɪ] 相連，聽起來是 [dɪn]。

3. **Absolutely**

因為在 t 的後面有一個字母 e，很多人在發音的時候會情不自禁加一個母音 [ə]，念成 ab-so-lu-te-ly，其實應該要念成 [æbsəˋlutli] 才是正確的，其他副詞像是 definitely, 的最後 -tely 也是同樣的發音原理。

4. **tighten**

這個字中的兩個 t 發音不同。字首 t 發 [t] 音，第二個 t 因為受到後面 en 的影響，雖然音標寫起來是 [taɪtən]，但是通常是英式口音會把這個音標裡面的第二個 [t] sound 清晰發出來，而美式發音則會把這個夾在 t 跟 n 之間的母音吸收掉，連帶 stop T 的憋氣效果（舌頭要同時抵著上齒齦），整個字聽起來就很像 [taɪ- 嗯] 的聲音。確實掌握這類字的發音要訣，對於想要說出道地美式英語的學習者來說是重要的關鍵之一。

延伸聽寫 Exercise B

➡ 解答參見第 138 頁

Track 0807

1. Hello, Professor Norman, __________ __________ __________ meeting with __________. I'm writing my mid-term paper, and I was hoping that you could __________ __________ some advice.

   謝謝您跟我見面，諾曼教授。我正在寫期中報告，我想說不知道您能不能給我一點意見。

2. How are you, Professor Newbury? I'm afraid I don't quite understand what you were saying yesterday. __________ I ask you __________ __________ questions?

   紐伯理教授您好嗎？關於您昨天的上課內容我有點不太懂，有些問題想請教您可以嗎？

3. __________ __________ __________? You __________ __________ __________ objective.

   你知道嗎？你得要保持客觀。

4. __________ __________! __________ __________.

   別擔心！沒事的！

5. Good morning, Professor Lawson. __________ __________ __________ __________, but I'm really swamped with essay writing and my field work. I was wondering if I could get an extension?
早安，勞森教授，不好意思跟您提這件事情，但是我真的很忙於論文寫作和現場工作。我想知道我是不是可以請求延期繳交報告呢？

6. I believe that __________ __________ __________ better, if I can have a couple more days.
我相信我可以表現得更好，如果我有多幾天時間的話。

7. __________ __________ __________ __________.
很高興聽到你這麼說。

8. Hey, __________ __________, what's your favorite color?
問你喔，你最喜歡什麼顏色？

9. Do you have a minute, Professor Macy? I have some quick questions about how to __________ __________ a research project.
梅西教授，不好意思方便耽誤您幾分鐘時間嗎？我有幾個關於如何寫好一份研究計畫的小問題想問您。

實用字詞補充

1. **so what you're saying is...**
在對話當中出現的用意是確認自己沒有誤解對方的意思，如同中文的「所以你剛剛的意思是說……」。

2. **I was hoping that...**
was + Ving 表達禮貌詢問的意思，如同中文的「我是在想說不知道你願不願意……」，其他類似的表達像是 I was wondering that...，這種句型在書信跟口語都很常見。

3. **advice**
這個字是不可數名詞，some advice or a piece of advice，但是沒有 advices，切記不要用錯囉！可搭配的動詞有 take 和 give。

例 Can you give me some advice?
你能幫我指點迷津嗎？

例 I think I will take your advice, thanks!
我想我會接受你的建議的，謝謝。

4. **Tighten everything up.**
在情境對話 B 當中，教授用來提醒 Nathan 要把報告理出一個更精簡有力的架構。

情境會話 B／翻譯

Conversation B-1

納森：史密斯教授，謝謝您跟我見面，我已經收到您對於我的報告的回饋，如果方便的話，我想跟您討論一下。

教授：好啊，是什麼樣的問題呢？

納森：那個……你給我 B，但是我真的覺得我可以做得更好，如果您不介意的話，能不能提供我一點建議，讓我可以重寫一次呢？

教授：這種態度是我一直很讚賞的喔，但是我得提醒你，這份報告將需要大幅度修改，這可是一段又長又累的旅程，你做好心理準備了嗎？

納森：坦白說，這個題目我非常有興趣，所以，我只能說，我等不及要著手修改啦！

教授：聽你這麼說真是太好了，我先問你喔，在你遞交你的作業之後，你有讀過你的報告嗎？

納森：沒有啊，為什麼這樣問呢？

Conversation B-2

教授：我跟你說，很多學生都會覺得，報告交了就交了，無事一身輕，他們錯了。其實在你繳交作業之後幾天，你應該要坐下來好好的讀你自己的作品，就好像你在讀別人的作品那樣。

納森：哇，我從來沒有這樣想過耶，所以，教授您剛剛的意思是說，我們應該作為自己作品的評論者。

教授：是啊，你必須保持客觀的去閱讀，但是還不只有這樣而已喔。

納森：我猜……嗯……除了校稿跟找出文法錯誤之外，我們其實可以做更多囉？

教授：正是這樣沒錯！其實你這個主題相當有趣的，一定要記得把那些沒有支持你的主論點的東西都刪掉，也就是說，你得力求簡潔有效。

延伸聽寫 Answer Keys

Exercise A

（請參考以下答案及解說，可弱讀的字詞以斜體表示。）

1. *Can* you get me a cup of black coffee?（black 的尾音 [k] 跟後面的子音 c 相近，前面的 [k] 消音。）
2. It's no big deal!（big 的尾音 [g] stop。）
3. I'm gonna stick around a bit longer.
4. I prefer to stay in an environment that's a bit noisy, like a coffeehouse.
5. Tell me about it!
6. *You* know what!
7. Where should we meet up?（美式口音念 meet up 的 [t] 受到後面母音的影響，發 flapT 的聲音，聽起來像是 [mi`ţʌp]，本句是英式口音的不同變化。）
8. It always *can* do some magic（本來 can 的發音是 [kæn]，在句子當中弱讀變成 [kən]，加快語句流暢速度。）
9. That kind of vibes somehow make me happy.（這個句子中的 that kind 和 make me 都是子音跟子音相連，而個別前方的 [t] 以及 [k] 都是塞音 stop。）

Exercise B

（請參考以下答案及解說，可弱讀的字詞以斜體表示。）

1. thank *you for* meeting with me / give me some advice
2. Can I ask you a few questions?
3. You know what? / *You have to* be objective.

   （英文口語常常會因說話者的心情及表達的語意不同而只強調句子中幾個重要的字，其他字就會以連音、弱讀等方式很快速順暢的帶過，像是唱歌一樣順滑 (smooth)，抑揚頓挫不會像中文那麼頻繁變化。從這個句子更可以看出來，說話者在 objective（客觀的）這個字之前的 you have to 連在一起並且很輕的快速帶過，你聽到的聲音並不是 [ju] [hæv] [to]，而比較像是 [jəvtə]。當然，同樣這一句話，不同人在不同的情況下說，或許會有不同的抑揚頓挫。例如父母在嚴正的告訴小孩某件事情真的很重要，那麼他們會想要強調 "you"，而 you have to 也許聽起來就會像是 [ju] [hævtə] 了。這種變化只要多聽多說，自然可以領略其中的變化。）

4. Don't worry! It's okay.（Don't worry 聽起來是 [dont| wɜi]。而 It's 的母音 [i] 因為語速及隨性的表達被省略掉，聽起來是 [tsoʊˋkeɪ]。）
5. I hate to ask.
6. *I* believe that *I can* perform better.
（better 的雙 t 發音如果在英式發音中，你會聽見清晰的氣音 [t]，但是在美式發音中，你會聽見這個雙 t 實際上的發音變成彈舌音 [ţ]。在美式英語當中 t 這樣的轉變發音都是為了要讓語句發音起來更加流暢。）
7. Good to hear that!
8. quick question（子音 k、q 相連，不需要連發出兩次子音，就如同 Ask question 一樣。）
9. write up

Ch 2

Unit 09

校園日常・圖書館・課堂討論

情境會話 A 校園日常

情境概說

三五好友聚在一起聊天是校園生活的日常，來聽聽 Jonathan 和 Amy 這天在圖書館咖啡廳裡聊些什麼吧！

Track 0901　J = Jonathan　A = Amy　★ 請特別注意粗體字的部分 ★

J Seriously, [1]**I've never enjoy the cafeteria's coffee**.

A Really? I don't really care about coffee's taste, as long as it can **boost my energy** and **kick-start my brain**, it's good coffee.

J What? I can't believe you just said that. **You're missing** [2]**out on the joys of life**, how about this, I'm going to renew some books first, and let's go to the mall. [3]**There's a cafe**,… um… it's called Jamie's. Oh they serve the best pour-over coffee, [4]**the best in town**!

A Sounds expensive… but okay…

J Great! Do you need me to [5]**check out** some books for you? Have you got the books on your reading list?

A No, I haven't. Some books I need are supposed to be on reserve, **but they're not there**.

J Why **don't** [6]**you ask** the library to **recall them**, although it may **take a few days** or [7]**even a** week to get them.

A Good idea!

聽力提點

1. **I've** 聽起來是 [aɪf]。
2. **out on the joys of life** 連音，聽起來分別是 [t̬ɑn]、[səf]。
3. **There's a** 連音，聽起來是 [ðɛr sə]。
4. **the best in town** 連音，[t̬ɪn]。
5. **check out** 連音。
6. **you ask** 在句子中母音和母音連音的時候，會在中間多一個很細微的音，以這個例子來說，you 的最後一個音是母音 [u]，連著下一個音要有 [w] 的聲音做為滑順的連結，聽起來是 [ju wæsk]，其他像 You are 也是一樣念成 [ju wɑr]。(這個發音現象又稱為滑音 glide，當單字最後一個音是母音 [u]、[aʊ] 或 [oʊ]，在連接下一個字的中間會先有一個滑音 [w]，這也是為了語音的滑順所產生的變化)。

7. **even a** 連音，[ivə nə]。(n、a 連音的時候聽起來會很像中文裡很輕微的ㄋ的聲音。)

延伸聽寫 | Exercise A

解答參見第 154 頁

Track 0902

1. A Don't forget to return those books… you wouldn't want to pay the overdue fine, would you?

   B Ya, thank you… wait, oh no! The ①__________ __________ was two days ago!

   翻譯

   A：別忘了還書喔，你不會想要付罰金吧？對吧？

   B：對耶，謝謝你，等一下，不……兩天前就過期了。

2. A **Excuse me**, where do I return my books?

   B You see the circulation desk?… The red sign over there? You can either leave your books there or ②__________ __________ in the ③__________ __________ slot on **the outside of** ④__________ **library**.

   翻譯

   A：請問，我要在哪裡還書呢？

   B：你看到借還書櫃台了嗎？那邊那個紅色的標示？你可以把書放在那裡或是把書放在圖書館外面的還書箱裡。

實用字詞補充

1. **kick-start** 促使開始

   例 He shared some tips about how to kick-start our brain in the morning.

   他分享如何一早醒來就能讓大腦「開機運作」的祕訣。

2. **How about something?** 提出某個建議

   例 How about ordering some pizza for dinner?

   晚餐訂披薩如何？

3. **miss out on something** 錯失、錯過某事

例 Don't miss out on our winter sale. 別錯過我們的冬季特賣。

4. **return** 還書
5. **renew** 續借
6. **on reserve** 保留預約
7. **recall** 催還
8. **due date** 到期日
9. **Collection** 館藏
10. **Rare collection** 珍稀館藏
11. **Archive** 檔案室
12. **Bulletin board** 布告欄
13. **Circulation desk** 借還書櫃台
14. **Digital media lab** 數位媒體室
15. **Periodical** 期刊
16. **Microform** 微縮膠片（資料）
17. **Reference** 參考書目

情境會話 A／翻譯

強納森：講真的，我從來都不愛學校咖啡廳的咖啡。

艾　米：真的喔，我好像從來都沒在管咖啡好不好喝耶，反正只要喝了可以有精神，整個人醒來，就是好咖啡啦！

強納森：天哪，我不敢相信你竟然這樣說，你根本錯過人生一大樂事耶！不如這樣，我現在要先去續借我的書，我們等一下去購物中心，有一間咖啡，叫做 Jamie's，天哪，他們有最好的手沖咖啡，全鎮最棒的！

艾　米：聽起來很貴……但是好喔……

強納森：太好了！你有需要我幫你借什麼書嗎？你拿到必讀書目所有的書了沒？

艾　米：還沒啊，有些我需要的書明明就應該在預約架上面，但是根本沒有啊。

強納森：你怎麼不去請圖書館幫你催還書呀，雖然可能你也是要等幾天或是一個禮拜才拿得到啦！

艾　米：好主意。

情境會話 B 圖書館

情境概說

圖書館資源豐富，想找資料卻不知從何找起時，向圖書館員尋求協助或許是最直接有效的方式喔！

Track 0903 J = Justine L = Librarian ★ 請特別注意粗體字的部分 ★

J Sorry, I'm [1]**having a hard time** finding sources for my **mid-term** paper, and um…, I really hope you can help me.

L Sure, that's why I'm here. Is there a specific article, or a book that you can't find? or…

J I'm supposed to do a literature review first, but I don't even know where to [2]**start looking**.

L Oh, **don't panic**! Do you know **that most** of our materials are available electronically? And all of the library's electronic sources can be easily accessed through any computer connected to the university network.

J Yes, actually I did try it [3]**last night** at home and I accessed the database… and…

L And?

J It's kind of embarrassing, the thing is, I searched by title with some key words, and too many articles came up… I was wondering whether… umm… I can save some time by doing…

L I see, and that's easy. There's an abstract **at the top of the first page of every article**, right? What you need to do is skim those to decide whether you want to read the whole article or not.

J Wow, **I didn't** [4]**think of that**… thank you so much… that's very helpful.

L Anytime, and hey, collecting sources for a research paper can sometimes be a daunting task, but you'll be fine.

聽力提點

1. **having *a* hard time** a 弱讀為 [ə]。
2. **start looking** 跟後面的 don't panic，兩個 t 都是發 stop T。
3. **last night** 在句子中語速加快聽起來會像是 las(t) night，就像 last summer（去年夏天）在口語發音中聽起來是 las(t) summer，這是子音 [t] 的消音現象（通常在連續的子音之間會有消音現象），當我們說 next please（下一位），聽起來會是 [neks(t) pliz]。
4. **think of** 母音和子音連音，[k] 受到後面母音影響發出像輕短的 [g] 的聲音。

延伸聽寫 | Exercise B

➜ 解答參見第 154 頁

Track 0904

1. A Hello, I'm looking for ①__________ __________ American literature.

   B I ②__________ __________ you search for relevant books first. You will find our **online catalog** very useful.

   翻譯

   A：哈囉，我想找有關於美國文學的資料。

   B：我建議你可以先去找相關的書目，你會發現我們的線上館藏目錄非常好用。

2. A Excuse me, can you tell me how to use the photocopier?

   B Sure, first you need to press any button to exit the machine's Energy saver mode, swipe your University card on the card reader, and then press the "Copy" button. ③__________ __________, pretty simple, huh! Oh, right, ④__________ __________ __________ press the button beneath the key symbol in order to log out.

   翻譯

   A：不好意思，可以請你告訴我怎麼使用這台影印機嗎？

   B：當然，先按任何一個按鈕讓機器離開休眠模式，然後在感應器上刷你的學生證，再按下「影印」的按鈕就可以啦，很簡單吧，歐，對了，別忘記要按那個鑰匙形狀下面的按鈕才可以登出喔。

3. A How do I ⑤__________ __________ my printing balance?

   B You can do it online or use the machines on the first floor just next to the catalogue computers and South Wing corridor.

   翻譯

A：我要怎麼加值我的影印卡呢？

B：你可以上網或是用機器加值，機器在一樓，就在檢索電腦旁邊，或是在南翼走廊那邊也有一台。（＊小提醒：first floor 在英國跟美國不一樣，因為英國還有一層叫做 ground floor「地面層」，也就是一樓的意思，因此在英國的 first floor 反而是指二樓。）

實用字詞補充

1. **Anytime** 不客氣（隨時都很樂意再提供協助）

   例 A: Thanks for your help. 謝謝你的幫忙。 B: Anytime. 不客氣。

2. **daunting** 很令人氣餒的

   例 We were so sure that he would do well, even though it's a daunting task.
   我們非常確信他能做的很好，即使這是一項艱鉅的任務。

3. **skim and scan** 略讀與快速瀏覽

   例 Generally, skimming helps you grasp the general idea within a section while scanning helps you locate a specific factual information. 通常，略讀可以幫助你掌握一個段落裡面的基本概念，而瀏覽文章則幫助你找到特定的訊息。

4. **I'm supposed to do...** 我應該要去做某事

   例 We are supposed to be there for her. 我們理當要去支持她的。

5. **Have a hard time doing something** 做某件事情遇到困難

   例 Many college students are having a hard time living within their budget.
   許多大學生很難寬裕（有餘裕）的過生活。

情境會話 B／翻譯

賈 絲 丁：不好意思，我在找期中報告需要的資料時遇到一些問題，希望你可以幫忙我好嗎？

圖書館員：當然啊，我很樂意的。所以你是有哪篇文章或是哪本書想找找不到嗎？還是……

賈 絲 丁：我應該要先做一份文獻回顧，但是我不知道我要從哪裡著手。

圖書館員：噢，別緊張，你知道我們的資料大部分都已經可以上網查詢了，而且你只要連到學校網絡，任何地方都可以連上我們圖書館的電子資源。

賈 絲 丁：對，其實我昨天晚上在家裡有試著使用，我連上了資料庫，然後……

圖書館員：然後？

賈 絲 丁：這有點難為情，事情是這樣的，我用標題搜尋了幾個關鍵字，然後一下子出現了非常多的檢索文章，我只是在想說，嗯，有沒有什麼是我可以節省一點時間的作法……

圖書館員：原來是這樣，那很簡單啊，每篇文章的第一頁一開始不是有摘要嗎？你需要做的就是迅速的略讀所有的摘要，來決定哪一篇文章是你需要的。

賈 絲 丁：哇，我都沒想到……真的很感謝你，這個建議真的太受用了。

圖書館員：不客氣，還有，做報告找資料有時候真的是一件很艱鉅的任務，但是你會沒事的！

情境會話 C

課堂討論

情境概說

許多教授在課堂上會安排分組討論的時間，讓學生在討論的過程中，學習溝通與思考的能力。一起來聽聽看以下會話中的討論內容。

Track 0905　K = Kim　A = Albert　★ 請特別注意粗體字的部分 ★

Conversation C-1

K I just [1]**finished the reading about reinforcement theory** and I think it's quite interesting.

A But I think it's a bit like common sense, don't you think… I mean…well, we've all been there, we know **we** [2]**gotta do something**, like **getting up** early in the morning, but we are reluctant to [3]**do it**. What else can we do [4]**about it**? We just have to figure out ways to stimulate ourselves, **no matter what**!

K I don't understand… so you think the article is like about something you've already known?

A Yeah, but no… I think the theory does explain in detail how an individual encourages themselves to change their behavior, and for that part **I would say**, the process of shaping a human's behavior by controlling the **consequences of it**, wow, it's like I had the eerie feeling of déjà vu.

K **I see your point**, but we are talking about psychology here. If you think that way, I guess **tons of articles** could give you goosebumps.

聽力提點

1. **finished the reading**

finished 動詞的過去式字尾 ed 應該要發 [t]，但是在句中如果跟後面以子音為首的字連音的時候，常常會把 [t] 聲音省略，聽起來就像是現在式一樣，finish the reading，這是實境口語當中比較隨性的時候會發生的省音現象。

* 補充說明：ed 結尾的讀音分為三種，[t] [d] 和 [ɪd]。

① 當動詞字尾是無聲子音，加了 ed 之後字尾一樣是無聲 [t]，例如 liked [laɪkt]。

② 當動詞字尾是有聲子音，例如 open，加了 ed 要發 [d] 的音。

③ 當 ed 之前是字母 d 或 t，則 ed 要發 [ɪd] 的音，例如 needed 要念成 [nidɪd]。

2. **gotta**

[t] 的發音受到第二個音節母音的影響，發 [d] 的音，聽起來是 [gɑdə]。本段落還有好幾個一樣的發音變化，仔細聽聽看。

3. **do it**

當單字最後一個音是母音 [u]、[aʊ] 或 [oʊ]，跟後面的母音之間要加入很輕的一聲滑音 [w]，連起來是 [duwɪt]。

4. **about it**

如果是美式發音，母音子音連音聽起來會是 [dɪt]，而這裡是英式口音的例子，連音的時候 [t] 的聲音沒有趨近 [d] 的變化，聽起來是 [tɪt]。

Ch 2

Track 0906　K = Kim　A = Albert　★ 請特別注意粗體字的部分 ★

Conversation C-2

A That's my point. We are told that we have to identify our biases, right? But who knows, maybe we just [1]**stop seeking** any alternative explanation without being aware of it?

K Well, I have to say, it's a bit philosophical! And **you** [2]**do know** that we still have to **come up with** the topic of our group work!

A I know, okay, and I am also curious about that after we read through these articles, know all the secrets of motivation, how far can we literally change our behavior in our lives?

K Wow, I think you just **hit the nail on the head**.

A [3]**I did**?

K Yes, I think that's a perceptive point, Albert. I guess maybe we can focus on the influence of reading these articles toward students who major in psychology and …

A K and other departments!

A It sounds like a very interesting topic for our group presentation!

聽力提點

1. **stop seeking**

   stop 的字尾是無聲子音 [p]，當後面接的單字字首為子音時，要把舌頭擺在 [p] 的發音位置，但不真的把氣流送出嘴巴外，聽起來是 [stɑp| sikɪŋ]。這個段落還有一樣的例子，仔細聽聽看。

2. You **do** know that…

   do 在句子中的作用是強調語意的時候，會是該句子的重音（音調上揚）位置。

3. I **did**?

   did 的音調上揚，作為疑問的表示，「是嗎？真的嗎？」。

延伸聽寫 | Exercise C

解答參見第 154 頁

Track 0907

1. A We're ①__________ __________ give a presentation about Beyond Meat, but have you guys even tried it before? Well, I haven't.

   B I almost ate it ②__________ __________ but I just…

   A What do you mean "you almost ate it"?

   B Haha, it's nothing. My girlfriend and I had a fight the other night and she kind of forced me to eat that… but anyway, I didn't because… I don't know… I just couldn't eat that.

   翻譯

   A：我們要做一個關於未來肉 (Beyond Meat) 的介紹，但是你們有誰吃過嗎？我是還沒有啦。

   B：我上個月差一點吃了，但是我就是⋯⋯

   A：什麼意思啊，你說你差一點吃了？

   B：哈哈，沒有啦，我有一天晚上跟我女朋友吵架，她就逼我吃那個素食肉啊，但是反正我後來是沒有吃啦，我不知道耶，我就覺得那個東西我真的吃不下去。

2. A Yeah, I find it really interesting, but the title, Beyond Meat, is way too broad.

   B I agree. Why don't we ③__________ __________ college students in Taiwan only?

   A Sounds good.

翻譯

A：對啊，我覺得這個主題很有趣，但是標題，Beyond Meat 有點太廣了。

B：我同意，那我們何不聚焦在台灣的大學生的觀點就好。

A：聽起來不錯喔！

3. A ④__________ __________ think sometimes Sammy **can be** really stubborn.

B Yeah, it makes me feel like she only wants to do things her way.

翻譯

A：你不覺得有時候珊米真的是非常固執。

B：對啊，讓我覺得她根本就只是想按照她的方式做事情。

4. A I don't ⑤__________ __________ most of the research, but the truth is I'm doing everything. It's not fair.

B I am sorry that you feel this way, but there must be some misunderstanding.

翻譯

A：我其實不介意做大部分的研究工作，但事實上是我根本做了全部的事情耶。這不公平。

B：我很抱歉讓你感受不好，但是我覺得是不是有什麼誤會。

實用字詞補充

1. **I don't know**（不只是表達我不知道某事）也可以在對話當中用來表示有點懷疑或是不確定）

例 A: Nancy's new boyfriend is a nice guy. 南希的新男友是個不錯的男生耶。

B: *I don't know*, he seems a bit arrogant, don't you think?

會嗎？你不覺得他有點太自負了嗎？

2. **We've all been there** 我們都曾經歷過（我能了解你的感受）

例 We've all been there. It happens to everyone **at some point**.

我們都曾經歷過，每個人在生命中的某些時機點都會遇到這樣的事情。

3. **gotta do something** 必須去做某事（gotta 是 have got to 的省略縮寫）

例 You gotta stop. 你得停止。

You've gotta be kidding me. 你一定是在跟我開玩笑吧！

4. **no matter what / when / why** 不管什麼原因或是什麼時候

* 用來強調某件事情是千真萬確的，或是必須去做到某事等等。

例 We have to be there on time, no matter what.

不管如何我們就是得準時抵達就是了。

5. **eerie** 奇怪的、怪異的

例 We all had the eerie feeling that we met this man before.
我們都有種怪異的感覺，覺得我們以前見過這個男人。

6. **déjà vu 既視感（似曾經歷過的感覺、似曾相識的感覺）**

例 When I first met him, I had an eerie feeling of *déjà vu*.
我第一次遇見他的時候，我有種似曾相識的怪異感覺。

7. **I would say（如果你問我的意見的話）我覺得**

* 用來作為比較客氣的開場白

例 I would say, you really should pull yourself together.
我覺得，你真的應該要振作起來了。

8. **I have to say 我必須要說**

* 與第七點同樣作為開場白，作為後續表達的一個比較和緩委婉的鋪陳

例 I have to say, even though it sounds nice but I don't think it's gonna work.
我不得不說，就算表面聽起來還不錯，但我認為它起不了什麼作用的。

9. **hit the nail on the head 說中要害、說到重點處**

例 He thought he hit the nail on the head but unfortunately it's not even close.
他以為自己說到重點了，可惜還差得遠。

10. **come up with something 提出、想到、想出（計畫或是主意）**

例 We have come up with a really amazing plan to impress them.
我們想出了一個非常讚的計畫來打動他們。

11. **perceptive 感知能力強的、觀察敏銳的、有洞察力**

例 The article is full of perceptive insights into flaws of human beings.
這篇文章有許多對人類缺點的深入洞見。

情境會話 C／翻譯

Conversation C-1

金　姆：我剛讀完有關增強理論的文章，我認為很有趣。

艾伯特：但是我認為這比較像常識，不是嗎……我的意思是……好吧，我們都有過這種經驗吧，我們知道我們必須做某些事情，像是早起好了，不過我們內心不情願這麼做，我們還能怎麼辦啊！無論如何，我們就是需要找出刺激自己改變行為的方法啊！

金　姆：我不明白耶……所以說你是覺得這篇文章說的其實你早就已經知道了嗎？

艾伯特：也不完全是這樣啦，我認為這個理論確實詳細解釋了個體如何鼓勵自己去改變行為，就這一部分而言，我想說的是，通過控制行為的後果來塑造人的行為的過程，哇，讓我有一種令人毛骨悚然的既視感耶。

金　姆：我懂你的意思了，但是我們現在是在討論心理學耶，如果你要這樣想，那不就一大堆文章都會讓你讀了起雞皮疙瘩嗎？

Conversation C-2

艾伯特：這就是我的意思啊！我們被灌輸說我們應該要去判別自己的偏見，對吧？但是我們怎麼知道，也許我們只是在不知不覺中就停止尋求其他解釋？

金　姆：好吧，我不得不說，這有點太哲學了！而且你知道我們還是要想出分組報告的主題喔！

艾伯特：我知道啊，好啦，而且我也很好奇，在閱讀完這些文章之後，我們知道了所有關於動機的祕密，那老實講到底我們又可以在真實生活裡改變自己的行為嗎？

金　姆：哇，我覺得你講到重點了耶！

艾伯特：有嗎？

金　姆：是的，我認為這是一個很有洞察力的點耶，艾伯特。我想也許我們可以將重點放在閱讀這些文章對心理學專業的學生來說，跟……

艾伯特 & 金：跟其他專業的學生來說有什麼不一樣的影響！

艾伯特：看來我們的小組報告有個非常有趣的主題了！

Ch 2

延伸聽寫 Answer Keys

Exercise A（請參考以下答案及解說。）

① due date

② drop them（[p] 發塞音 stop，drop them 聽起來是 [drap| ðəm]，同樣的發音現象例子如 drop by「順道」聽起來是 [drap|baɪ]。比較一下第三題。）

③ book return（[k] 塞音 stop。）

④ the（在 the outside of the library 這一小段句子中的兩個 the 剛好是不同的發音，第一個 the 受到後面字首為母音的影響，要發 [ði]，而後面的 the library 則發 [ðə]。）

Exercise B（請參考以下答案及解說。）

① sources about（連音。）

② suggest that（[t] 省略，聽起來是 sugges(t) that。因為字尾和字首都是子音 [t]，若都清楚發音會拖慢速度且無法滑順帶過。）

③ That's it!（連音。）

④ don't forget to（第一個 [t] 是 stop T，第二個 [t] 消音，聽起來是 [dont| fəgɛ to]。）

⑤ top up（[p] 受到後面母音影響，氣音會減弱變短，輕聲的 [p] 在與後方母音連音之後聽起來像是輕聲的 [b]。）

Exercise C（請參考以下答案及解說。）

① supposed to（ed 字尾的 [t] sound 省音。）

② last month

③ focus on（母音子音連音，聽起來是 [fokə zan]。）

④ Don't you（t + y 發 [tʃ]。）

⑤ mind doing

加值學更多！

線上下載更多聽力技巧練習，「遠距教學的多人討論情境」，隨時想聽就聽！

Unit 10

社交活動：生日派對 ①

社交活動：生日派對 ②

社交活動：聖誕節

社交活動：生日派對 ①

情境概說

留學生活除了課業學習之外，多彩多姿的社交活動肯定是不容錯過的。首先來聽聽 Andrew 受邀參加生日派對時，和壽星 Lisa 的對話。

Track 1001　A = Andrew　L = Lisa　★ 請特別注意粗體字的部分 ★

A Happy Birthday!

L Wow, [1]**glad you made it**!

A **Look at you**, birthday girl! You look stunning today!

L Aww, you're so sweet. Can I **get you** a drink?

A Ya, what do you have?

L Oh, we have everything! Here are different [2]**kinds of beers in the cooler, and we also have a bunch of soda and juices**. We've also got red wine, white wine and so many mixed drinks in the kitchen.

A Amazing, I'll **have** a Guinness first.

L There you go, and **a bag of** chips.

A Thanks! You're the best host, aren't you!

聽力提點

1. **glad you made it!**
   d [d] 碰到 y [j] 會產生發音變化，連音發 [dʒ] 的音（[dʒ] 就跟 judge [dʒʌdʒ] 一樣。）這句聽起來是 [glæ dʒu]。
2. **kinds of beers in the cooler, and we also have a bunch of soda and juices**
   接續連音，[zəf] [zɪn] [və] [tʃə]。

延伸聽寫 | Exercise A

➡ 解答參見第 165 頁

Track 1002

1. A Easter is coming, do you have any plans for the long weekend?

   B Na, my ①__________ __________ going to Paris so I won't go back home.

   A I'm not going home either. Hey, let's ②__________ __________ potluck party, what do you say?

   B Sounds fun! ③__________ __________!

   翻譯

   A：快要復活節了，你長假有什麼計畫嗎？

   B：沒啊，我爸媽要去巴黎，所以我不會回家。

   A：我也沒有要回家耶，嘿，要不我們來辦一個大家出一道菜的派對，你覺得如何？

   B：聽起來不錯啊，我要參加！

2. A I'm going to Japan for winter break. What about you?

   B I probably just go to some friends' for dinner. I'm going to ④__________ __________ on some reading for my PhD application.

   翻譯

   A：寒假我要去日本耶，你勒？

   B：我可能就去幾個朋友家吃吃飯而已吧，我得加緊腳步趕一下我博士班申請的閱讀進度。

Ch 2

實用字詞補充

1. **Aww（狀聲詞）噢** ＊常常會用在覺得某事物很可愛、很感人、很貼心等時候。

   例 Aww, aren't you the best?

   噢，最棒的不是你還有誰啊！

2. **There you go 給你**

   ① **如果對話語意是要表達「(東西) 給你囉！」，則 There you go 和 Here you go 的意思差不多，都是用於給對方東西的時候。**

   例 A: Can I have a glass of red wine? 我想要一杯紅酒好嗎？

   B: Sure, here you go/there you go! 好啊，給你！

   ② **但是如果對話語意是要表達「看吧」(帶揶揄諷刺意味)，就不會用 here you go 囉！**

   例 A: Hey everyone, I'm sorry. I forgot my password again.

   大家不好意思喔，我又忘記我的密碼了。

   B: There you go. 看吧 (就知道你會這樣)。

③ **there you go** 也可以表達「就是這樣囉」(尤其在對話情境中，你在解說某一件感覺很複雜，但其實只要做完步驟就可以完成任務的狀態，話語末尾可以加這句。)

例 A: I don't know how to do this. 我不知道這個怎麼弄。

B: Let me show you. Just pull this and press the green button. There you go.
來我示範給你看，只要拉一下這邊，然後按那個綠色按鈕，這樣就好啦！

3. **You're the best, aren't you? 你是最棒的，對吧！**

句尾的 aren't you 在英文中稱作 question tags（附加疑問句），像是 isn't it?、can you? 或是 didn't they? 這種 question tags 在對話當中的作用是「希望對方也認同我們所說的話，或是期望對方確認我們的感受」。常見於口語對話當中，少見於寫作。

例 You love me, don't you?
你是愛我的吧？（你愛我，對嗎？）

4. **I'm in（口語）我要加入／參加**

5. **Look at you! 看看你！**

這句話會因為音調語氣不同搭配上下文而含有恭維或貶義。

情境會話 A／翻譯

安德魯：生日快樂！

麗　莎：哇，太開心你還是趕來了！

安德魯：看看你，大壽星！你今天美得令人讚嘆呀！

麗　莎：你嘴巴好甜，拿杯飲料給你？你想喝什麼？

安德魯：好啊，有哪些喝的啊？

麗　莎：哦，什麼都有喔！這邊冷藏箱裡面有各種啤酒，還有一堆汽水和果汁。我們在廚房裡也還有紅酒，白葡萄酒跟超多可以做雞尾酒的東西。

安德魯：太讚了，我先來一瓶 Ginness（一種啤酒）吧！

麗　莎：給你，還有一袋薯片。

安德魯：謝啦！你真的是最棒的女主人了，不是嗎？！

社交活動：生日派對 ②

情境概說

Sandy 跟室友 Maggie 一起去參加班上同學的生日派對，但是 Maggie 喝醉了，醉得不省人事。Sandy 和好朋友 Jon 正在商量該怎麼辦。

Track 1003　J = Jon　S = Sandy　★ 請特別注意粗體字的部分 ★

J Hey, where's Maggie?

S [1]**She's so** wasted tonight. About 10 minutes ago, she told me she's gonna throw up. Maybe [2]**she's in** the bathroom.

J I just used the bathroom.

S No… oh, she's there, on the couch, under the pile of coats.

J And snoring.

S Well, didn't know that Maggie planned to turn her **birthday party** into a **sleepover** onc.

J Haha, joking aside, what do we do now?

S Do you want go home now? Or you can stay and I'll [3]**take care of** her. I am her roommate, what can I say?

J I can go with you. Jason and Donald, they are leaving too.

S umm… I'll tell you what, let's call a cab and [4]**get her out here**. And we have some pizza and beer at home. We can hang out if you want.

J Love the idea. I'll go get my coat.

聽力提點

1. **She's so...**
   兩個相同的子音連音，聽起來像是只有發後面子音的聲音 [ʃi so]。比較下一個提點。
2. **she's in** 母音子音連音，聽起來是 [ʃi zɪn]。
3. **take care of** [k] 後面是子音，要發塞音 stop。
4. **get her out here**
   英式口音的 er 發音會聽到清楚的母音 [ə]，[r] 則不會捲舌，不同於美式的 [ɜ] 或是 [ɚ]。

Ch 2

延伸聽寫 | Exercise B

解答參見第 165 頁

Track 1004

1. A ①__________ __________ supposed to garnish the drink with some fruits?

   B ②__________ __________ I don't understand. See, if we never eat those fruits, why bother?

   翻譯

   A：你不是應該要在酒上面擺一些水果裝飾嗎？

   B：那就是我不懂的地方了，你想，如果我們從來都不吃那些裝飾的水果，那我們何必那麼麻煩啊！

2. A Oh no, we forgot to ③__________ __________ corkscrew!

   B ④__________ __________, we still have a pack of Heineken.

   翻譯

   A：不會吧，我們忘記帶我們的螺旋開瓶器了。

   B：好險我們還有六瓶海尼根啤酒。

實用字詞補充

1. **Tell you what**（用於提出建議之前）我們不如這麼做好了

   例 A: We are running out of time. 我們要來不及了啦。

   B: Yeah, (I'll) tell you what, you go get the Chinese food and I go get the tickets and I'll see you at home. 對耶，不然這樣好不好，你去買中國菜，然後我去拿票，那我們等一下在家裡碰面囉。

2. **wasted**（口語）爛醉的

   例 Jon was too wasted to drive home.

   喬恩喝得爛醉，無法開車回家。

3. **be about to do something** 剛要……、就要……

   例 They were about to leave when I arrived.

   我到的時候他們才剛準備要走。

4. **sleepover** 留宿派對（類似 **slumber party** 睡衣派對）

   例 What kinds of activities and food will our guests enjoy at the sleepover party?

   哪些活動和食物會讓我們的客人在留宿派對可以放鬆享受呀？

5. **Joking aside/apart**（先不說笑）言歸正傳

   例 Joking apart, will you help me tomorrow? I really need your help.

   言歸正傳，你明天能幫忙我嗎？我真的很需要你的幫忙。

6. **what do you say**（口語上做為在提出建議的時候潤飾語意之用）好嗎？你覺得如何呢？

例 Let's throw a party for Jason? What do you say?

我們幫杰森辦個派對吧，妳覺得勒？

7. **Why bother?** 何必（多此一舉）呢？

情境會話 B／翻譯

強　：嘿，你有看到瑪姬嗎？

姍蒂：她今晚整個超醉，大約十分鐘前她跟我說她差不多要去吐了，我猜她應該在廁所吧。

強　：我才剛從廁所出來。

姍蒂：喔不，她在那邊啦，躺在沙發上，身上蓋一堆外套。

強　：還在打呼呢！

姍蒂：哎呀，我不知道瑪姬原來打算把生日派對變成過夜派對勒！

強　：哈哈，好啦，說真的，那我們現在要怎麼辦啊？

姍蒂：你有想現在回家嗎？還是不然你可以繼續待著啊，我照顧她就好，反正我是她的室友啊，我還能說什麼呢！

強　：我可以跟你們一起啊，傑森跟唐納他們也要走了。

姍蒂：嗯，那不然這樣好不好，我們叫車，然後帶瑪姬回去，我們家還有一點披薩跟啤酒，如果你還不想回家就在我們家玩好了。

強　：這個好耶，我去拿我的外套。

社交活動：聖誕節

情境概說

Jessie 是從台灣到美國讀書的留學生，她接受好友 Eason 的邀請到他家共度了傳統又溫馨的聖誕節。

Track 1005　J = Jessie　E = Eason　M = Eason's Mom　★ 請特別注意粗體字的部分 ★

J　Thank you for **having me over** for Christmas.

E　We all are very happy to have you. My grandma even forced me to teach her how to say "hello" and "you are so beautiful" in Chinese last night!

J　**Aww**, [1]**that's so sweet**. **Can't wait to meet her.**

E　Mom, Jessis's here. Hey, have you ever had Christmas dinner before?

J　Not really, you know, Taiwanese people love Christmas and lots of restaurants would have Christmas Specials, but to be invited to a traditional Christmas dinner, this is my very first time.

E　Wow, I hope you have a good appetite because **there's a lot of food**. I mean **A LOT**.

M　Hi, Jessie, right! I've heard so much **about you** from Eason and **it's so nice** that I finally **get to meet you**. Make yourself [2]**comfortable**, okay!

J　Can I help?

M　Of course, sweet heart, can you… umm… let me think… can you put the stuffing and these biscuits on the table please?

J　Sure, wow, **it smells so good**.

E　Doesn't it! When I was little, every [3]**Christmas** I threw a tantrum because I couldn't eat more.

聽力提點

1. **That's so sweet.**
   這裡的 so 母音拉長音，是說話者的情緒變化，就像中文會說，我真的「超～～～喜歡」。

2. **comfortable**

有一個口語當中的發音現象稱為 elision of schwa sound（元音／母音的省略），comfortable 的讀音為 [ˋkʌmfətəbəl]，但是在實際口語中卻常常會聽到 [ˋkʌmftəbəl]，類似的例子還有 vegetable 聽起來是 [vedʒ.tə.bəl]，而不是 [vedʒə.tə.bəl]。（其他還有像是 chocolate, camera 等等也有類似情況）。

3. **Christmas**

當 [t][d] 出現在子音之間，要連發三個子音會很拗口，很多時候會省略。因此這個字會念 Chris(t)mas，其他常見例子如 san(d)wich。

延伸聽寫 | Exercise C

解答參見第 165 頁

Track 1006

1. A I went to my uncle's for an __________ __________ hunt. It was fun.
   B I've never done that before.

   翻譯

   A：我去我叔叔家玩復活節蛋的尋寶遊戲，很好玩耶。

   B：我從來沒有玩過。

2. A Are you going back to Taiwan for the summer?
   B No, my __________ __________ __________ will go to Europe this summer.

   翻譯

   A：你這個暑假有要回去台灣嗎？

   B：沒有耶，我跟我朋友們這個暑假要去歐洲。

實用字詞補充

1. **for the very first time**

   加 very 的意思只是作為強調之意。有點像是中文的「我還真的從來都沒有這樣過」或是「這真的是我第一次這樣子耶」的語氣。

2. **make yourself comfortable** 不要拘束喔！（同 **make yourself at home**）

3. **throw / have a tantrum** （小孩）鬧脾氣，或指大人像小孩子般鬧脾氣

   例 When Tim doesn't get his own way, he always throws a tantrum.

   當提姆不能（讓別人）按照自己的意思行事的時候，他總是要大發脾氣。

情境會話 C／翻譯

潔西　　　：謝謝你們邀請我來過聖誕節。

伊森　　　：我們也很開心你來啊，我奶奶昨天晚上還逼我教她中文的「你好」跟「你很漂亮」怎麼講。

潔西　　　：噢，太溫馨了啦，我等不及要見她了。

伊森　　　：媽，潔西到囉！嘿，你以前有吃過聖誕晚餐嗎？

潔西　　　：不算真的有吃過，雖然說台灣人很愛聖誕節，很多餐廳還會推出聖誕特餐，但是，被邀請來參加這樣傳統溫馨的聖誕晚餐，還是我第一次。

伊森　　　：哇，那我希望你今天晚上胃口大開，因為有超多食物的，我是說，超！級！多！

伊森的媽媽：哈囉，潔西對吧！我聽 Eason 說過好多你的事情耶，終於見到你本人真是太好了。當自己家，不要拘束喔！

潔西　　　：我可以幫忙嗎？

伊森的媽媽：當然了親愛的，你幫我……嗯……我想想喔……啊請你幫我把餡料跟小餅乾放到桌子上好嗎？

潔西　　　：當然，哇，聞起來超香的。

伊森　　　：對吧，小時候，每年聖誕節我都要發一次脾氣，因為我吃不下更多東西了。

延伸聽寫 Answer Keys

Exercise A

（請參考以下答案及解說。）

① parents are（連音 [zɑ]）

② have a（連音 [və]）

③ I'm in（連音 [mɪn]）

④ catch up

Exercise B

① Aren't you（變音，t 跟 y 連在一起發 [tʃ]。）

② That's something（相同子音一起，發後面的子音，聽起來是 [ðæ sʌmθɪŋ]。）

③ bring our（母音跟子音連音，[brɪ ŋaʊr]，聽起來很像中間有一個中文ㄋㄠ 的聲音。）

④ Thank god（聽起來像 than_god，是因為 [k] 後面是子音的關係，會發塞音〔保持該聲音嘴型 [k] 以及舌頭在口腔內該有的位置，但是會稍停頓而不把氣送出口〕）。

Exercise C

1. Easter egg
2. friends *and* I

加值學更多！

「表達自己意見以及溝通討論的實用句型」，立馬下載、收藏！

NOTE

Unit 11

- 表達謝意

表達謝意 ①

情境概說

工作出現問題，得到同事的熱心幫助之後眞誠地向對方道謝。

Track 1101 S = Sam L = Lily ★ 請特別注意粗體字的部分 ★

S Thank you so much, Lily. You literally [1]**saved my life**.

L No problem! **I'm glad that I can help**.

S To be honest, I can't imagine [2]**what would happen** [3]**if it weren't for you**. **I owe you** [4]**big time**.

L **No worries**. I know you would do the same for me. We are a team, and that's what a teammate is for, right!

S Seriously, you are the best colleague that [5]everyone can ever have.

L Wow, **I am** [6]**flattered**.

S **Let me know if and when I can return the favor**.

聽力提點

1. **saved**

   動詞的過去式／過去分詞一般是在字尾加上 ed，其發音有三種可能 [t] [d] 或 [ɪd]。當動詞的結尾是有聲子音的時候，這個 ed 發 [d]，所以 saved 聽起來是 [seɪvd]，注意，不要在字尾多一個 [ə] 而變成了像是中文「ㄉㄜ」的聲音，這是不正確的。

2. **What would happen**

   單字字尾是 [t] [d] [p] [b] [k] [g]，後面接的單字字首是子音的時候，這些音都會發塞音 stop，這邊剛好連續出現，聽起來是 [wɑt| wəd| hæpən]。(would 在這裡為了語速順暢及發音輕鬆而弱讀 [wəd]。)

3. **if it** 母音子音連音，聽起來是 [ɪfɪt]。

4. **big time** 同第 2 點。[g] 是塞音 stop。

5. **everyone**

   elision of schwa sound (元／母音的省略)，第二個音節的 [ə] 音省略，聽起來是 [ˋevrēwən]。

6. **flattered**

當 [t] 音不在重音的位置而需要與母音連音時，會發彈舌音 flap T [ţ]。

延伸聽寫 | Exercise A

解答參見第 177 頁

Track 1102

1. A ①__________ __________ the right track. So, don't worry okay?

B Thanks, I really appreciate ②__________ __________ __________ for me. Your ③______________ __________ very helpful.

A Well, you know me, **I'm always happy to help.**

B It's very thoughtful of you. Thanks for being in our shoes.

A It's my pleasure.

翻譯

A：你正朝著正確的方向前進，所以，別擔心喔！

B：謝謝你，我真的很感謝你做的一切，你的建議都非常有幫助。

A：嘿，你知道的啊，我一向都很樂於幫助大家的。

B：你真的好貼心。謝謝你替我們設身處地著想。

A：我很樂意這麼做的。

Track 1103

2. A Yeah, that's everything you need. If you have any questions, feel free to call me any time.

B Thank you very much.

A ④__________ mention it. Oh, I gotta go now, or I'll miss the train.

B I can give you a lift if you want, Taipei Train Station, right?

A ⑤__________ would be great! Thanks.

翻譯

A：好，應該這樣就差不多沒問題了。如果你還有什麼問題，不要客氣隨時打電話給我。

B：真的很感謝你。

A：小事情而已啦！噢，天哪，我現在得先走，不然我要錯過火車了。

B：如果你想的話我可以順道送你一程，台北火車站對吧！

A：那太棒了，謝謝喔。

實用字詞補充

1. **in someone's shoes** 站在他人的立場，設身處地理解他人的感受。

   例 I'd appreciate it if you could put yourself in my shoes.

   如果你願意站在我的立場想一想，我會很感謝的。

2. **No problem** 沒問題；（用於回答對方的感謝）沒什麼，小事情而已！

   例 A: Thanks for the ride. 謝謝你讓我搭便車

   B: No problem.

   這裡的 no problem 不要翻成沒有問題，而是回應別人的感謝的口語用法，意思就是小事一樁而已。

3. **Can't thank you enough!** 字面上理解是「不能再謝你更多了」，其實就是「非常感謝你」的意思。

4. **would have + 過去分詞**（假設語氣）表示當時本來會做某事

   例 I don't know what I would have done without your help.

   如果沒有你的幫忙，我真不知道當時我還能怎麼辦。

5. **It's very kind of you** 你人真好

   例 It's very kind of you to have spent time doing this for me.

   你願意花時間為我做這些事情，你真的很好。

6. **You would do the same for me.**（如果易地而處）你也會這麼做的。

7. **return the favor** 回報

   例 I gave Mr. Anderson a ride when his mini cooper broke down and now he is returning the favor.

   那天安德森先生的 mini cooper 拋錨時我順路載了他一程，他現在來報答我。

情境會話 A／翻譯

山姆：太感謝你了，莉莉，你真的救了我一命。

莉莉：我很高興我有機會幫上忙。

山姆：講真的，我完全不敢想像今天要不是你，後果會如何，我欠你一個大人情。

莉莉：沒事的，我相信如果易地而處，你也會這麼做的。我們是一個團隊啊，身為隊友，這是應該的啊。

山姆：我跟你說真的，你簡直就是人人夢寐以求的好同事。

莉莉：哇，你這麼說我受寵若驚。

山姆：要給我機會回報你喔。

表達謝意 ②

情境概說

致電感謝友人的盛情款待。

Track 1104 [S] = Serena [A] = Amy ★ 請特別注意粗體字的部分 ★

[S] Hi, Amy, this is Serena.

[A] Hi, Serena, have you returned home safely?

[S] Yeah, [1]**safe and sound!**

[A] That's wonderful.

[S] I just want to thank you again for your loving [2]**hospitality and generosity**.

[A] Don't mention it and I **had a** great time.

[S] You're the best **host ever**! I'm so lucky to [3]**have a friend** who spoils me [4]**rotten**.

[A] Anytime, my friend! And thank you for your lovely gifts. They are perfect for my desk decorations.

[S] [5]**Glad you like it!** I **bought them** in the National Palace Museum.

[A] I can't wait to show them to my colleagues. By the way, how's the weather in Taiwan? We [6]**had our** first snowfall **last night** and the broadcast said that **there's a storm coming**!

[S] Stay safe, Amy.

[A] Haha, don't worry! That's called "winter", Serena.

[S] How much [7]**am I** gonna miss your **sense of humor**?

[A] Well. What can I say? Winter is super long here. You gotta find something to amuse yourself.

聽力提點

1. **safe and sound**

   and 作為連接詞通常會弱讀為 [ənd] 或 [ən]，目的是讓語速更加輕快順暢，safe and sound 三個字聽起來是 [seɪ fən saund]。

Ch 2

2. **hospitality and generosity**

在單字當中非重音節的這兩個 [t] 都受到後面母音的影響，美式口音會發彈舌音 [ţ]，而這裡英式口音則不會有這個變化，還是發 [t]。

3. **have a friend** 連音。

4. **rotten**

前面章節對話當中曾提到，flattered, better, butter 的 [t] 在該單字中非重音節位置，受到後面母音之影響，會發彈舌音 [ţ]，要注意的是，當 t 後面接的是 en 的時候，像是 lighten, kitten, bitten，[t] 後面的母音 e 會被省略掉，[t] stop T，整個字念起來就會變成 [ˋrɑtn̩]，這個聲音對於很多非英語母語人士來說很不好揣摩，記得要讓舌頭輕輕抵住上齒齦，但是不要把原本發 [t] 的氣流送出口中，在這個憋住的瞬間接著發一個聽起來像是中文輕聲「嗯」的聲音，這是美式發音的特色，實際口語聽力上面，要習慣會有這樣的發音變化。這是美式發音的特色，而這句英式口音則會聽見清楚的 [t]。

5. **Glad you like it!**

d + y 變音產生 [dʒ] 的聲音，glad you 連音之後聽起來是 [glæ dʒu]。

6. **had our** 子母連音。

7. **am I gonna**

連音的位置聽起來是 [maɪ]。

延伸聽寫 | Exercise B

解答參見第 177 頁

Track 1105

A Louise, I can never thank you enough for your generosity. I hope you will spend some days of your winter vacation ①__________ __________.

B Yeah, it would be great. Oh, John and I ②__________ __________ talking about your ③________________ cake for like months.

A Oh, you're making me embarrassed. Who is the ④__________ __________ in town? The lamb last night was cooked to perfection. **It was so good!**

B Well, practice makes perfect.

翻譯

A：路易絲，我永遠感謝你的慷慨。希望你能和我們一起度過幾天的寒假。

B：是啊，那會很棒。哦，約翰和我幾個月來一直在談論你的巧克力蛋糕。

A：哦，你讓我很尷尬。誰是鎮上最好的廚師？昨晚的羊肉煮得恰到好處。太好吃了！

B：嗯，熟能生巧。

實用字詞補充

1. **Don't mention it!** 哪裡（舉手之勞的小事而已，不用介意）。
2. **spoil someone rotten** 寵壞某人

   例 George is spoiled rotten by his grandparents.

   喬治被爺爺奶奶給寵壞了。

情境會話 B／翻譯

瑟琳娜：嗨，艾米，是我啦，瑟琳娜。

艾　米：嗨，瑟琳娜，你安全回到家了嗎？

瑟琳娜：對啊，安然無恙的。

艾　米：太好了。

瑟琳娜：我是要再次感謝你的盛情款待和慷慨。

艾　米：哎喲，小事情啦，我也玩得很開心啊。

瑟琳娜：你是最棒的女主人了，我真的是太幸運了，有你這樣會寵壞我的朋友。

艾　米：親愛的，隨時來沒問題喔！還有謝謝你可愛的禮物，他們用來裝飾我的桌子簡直完美。

瑟琳娜：真開心你喜歡他們，我是在故宮博物院買的喔。

艾　米：我等不及要給我的同事們看了，對了，台灣天氣如何，我們昨天晚上下雪了，而且天氣預報說，有暴風雪要來了。

瑟琳娜：艾米要小心安全耶。

艾　米：哈哈，不用緊張啦，這不過就是我們的冬天日常而已啊，瑟琳娜。

瑟琳娜：都不知道我會有多想念你的幽默感呀！

艾　米：哈，還能怎麼說呢？這裡的冬天超級長，你總得想點法子來逗樂自己啊！

情境會話 C 表達謝意 ③

情境概說

剛到新單位的 Peter 對很多事情不熟悉，因爲得到同事大力協助而想表達感謝之意。

Track 1106 P = Peter J = Jane ★ 請特別注意粗體字的部分 ★

P Hello Jane, **this is** Peter.

J [1]**It's good to hear from you**. How are you doing?

P [2]**Couldn't be better**, and it's all [3]**because of you**. Thank you so much for showing me the ropes. **If it weren't for you**, I wouldn't be able to handle this project well. I appreciate the time you've taken from your own work.

J Thanks for saying that, but you know, it's nothing. I'm happy to help.

P Hey, I also have some good news. I will meet with the potential buyer this Friday, and they seem to be very [4]**interested in our** project.

J **Good for you**, Peter.

聽力提點

1. **It's good to hear from you.** good 的尾音 [d] 發塞音 stop。
2. **Couldn't be better.**
   n't 的縮寫像是 shouldn't, won't, isn't 的尾音 [t] 都要發塞音 stop T。注意，因為 could 的尾音 [d] 也是會在句子當中發塞音 stop，所以 couldn't 聽起來是 [kʊd| ənt|]。
3. **because of you** 連音，聽起來是 [bɪˋkɑzəfju]。
4. **interested in our** 連音，聽起來是 [dɪnaʊr]。

延伸聽寫 | Exercise C

➔ 解答參見第 177 頁

Track 1107

1. Thank you for __________ with me.
   謝謝你與我會面。

2. Thank you very much ________ your referral.
非常感謝你的轉介。

3. We ________ thank you enough for referring your friend to our firm.
我們真的非常感謝你介紹你的朋友到我們的公司。

4. Your ________ ________ very helpful.
你的建議真的非常有幫助。

5. Thanks for ________ ________.
謝謝你從中斡旋。

6. ________ so lucky to have you.
我們有你真的是太幸運了。

7. Thank you for taking the time to share your experience ________ ________ team.
感謝你花時間跟我們的團隊分享你的經驗。

8. Thank you very much for your ________ and help.
非常感謝你的善意與協助。

9. Thank you very much for your willingness to ________ ________ the project.
非常感謝您願意加入這個計畫。

Ch 2

實用字詞補充

1. **show someone the ropes 指導某人該怎麼進行某事**
   *ropes 在這裡是指規則、準則或是技巧程序等等。

2. **know the ropes 對某事物很了解、相當有經驗**
   例 Go ask the manager. She knows the ropes.
   去問經理，她的經驗非常豐富。

3. **step in 插手；介入；居中斡旋**
   例 The lawyer's father has stepped in to save the law firm from going out of business. 律師的父親介入，使得事務所免於破產。

4. **be willing to do something 願意去做某事**
   例 It is unfortunate that he is not willing to understand other people's points of view. 不幸的是，他不願意去理解別人的觀點。

5. **Couldn't be better 非常好**
   例 A: How have you been? 你最近過得好嗎？
   B: Couldn't be better. 很棒啊！

6. **If it weren't for**（假設語氣）如果不是……的話

例 If it weren't for you, I wouldn't be here.

如果不是你，我不會在這裡。

7. **It's nothing.**（口語）沒什麼（不足掛齒）

例 A: Thank you for stepping in. 謝謝你居中斡旋。

B: It's nothing. 小事情而已。

情境會話 C／翻譯

彼得：哈囉，珍，我是彼得。

珍　：很開心聽到你的聲音，你好嗎？

彼得：非常好啊，而且都是因為你的關係啊，非常謝謝你幫助我進入狀況，如果不是你，我沒辦法把這個專案做的這麼好，你願意抽空來幫助我，我真的很感激。

珍　：謝謝你這麼說，但是你知道的，這是小事啦，我很樂意幫忙的啊。

彼得：而且我還有好消息耶，我這禮拜五會跟潛在客戶見面，而且他們似乎對我們的專案非常感興趣。

珍　：彼得，你真是太棒了！

延伸聽寫 Answer Keys

Exercise A

（請參考以下答案及解說。）

① You're on

r 的發音在單字中不管是 [ɑr] 或是弱讀 [ər]，常是許多人說英文時易忽略或是無法克服的地方。而如果放在句子當中與後面母音連音的時候，發音起來可能就沒有那麼清楚或道地了。r 這個字母的發音是 [ɑr]，如果用中文發音來比喻，比較像是ㄚ＋ㄦ兩個聲音黏在一起的聲音。而在 you're on 的發音當中，還要跟後方的 on 字首母音連音，聽起來是 [jurɑn]，讓人可能會誤以為聽見了 "run" 這個聲音，請仔細重聽看看，試著把速度放慢，自己跟著多練習幾次由 [ɑr] 到 [ɑn]，就會比較熟練。

② what you did

t + y 發 [tʃ]。另外可以特別仔細聽 did 的發音，開頭的 d 跟字尾的 d 聽起來發音並不相同，這是塞音（[p]、[b]、[t]、[d]、[k] 、[g]）的特色，這些音會因為出現在字首、字中或是字尾而可能有不同的變化，字首的 d 就像 door 或 dog 一樣，但是尾音的 [d] 就是發 stop，要短暫憋一下口中的氣流。

③ suggestions are

④ Don't mention it（[t] 發塞音 stop，n 跟後面的母音連音，發 [nɪ]。）

⑤ That

Exercise B

（請參考以下答案及解說，可弱讀的字詞以斜體表示。）

① with us（連音 [wɪ ðəs]。）

② John and I *have been* talking about

③ chocolate（消音，聽起來是 choc_late [`tʃɑklət]。）

④ best chef（消音。）

Exercise C

（請參考以下答案及解說。 ）

1. meeting（[t] 在非重音音節，受後面有母音影響，發彈舌音 [ţ]。）
2. for（弱讀 [fɚ]，而不是 [fɔr]。）
3. can't
4. suggestions are（連音，聽起來是 [zər]。）
5. stepping in
6. We're（聽起來是 [wɪr]。）
7. with our

Ch 2

8. kindness（發音聽起來不像是 [ˋkaɪndnəs]，因為你不會聽到 [d] 音的氣流送出嘴巴的痕跡，這個 [d] 夾在兩個子音之間，若要刻意發 [d] 的聲音會比較不順暢，因此聽起來是 [ˋkaɪn(d)nəs]。）

9. participate in（子音母音連音，聽起來像是 [dɪn]。）

⊕加值學更多！

「朋友來電相互表達關心的生活情境聽力」

線上下載，隨時想聽就聽！

Unit 12

· 表達歉意

表達歉意 ①

情境概說

Andrew 準備要跟廠商代表 Jasmine 開會。因為在等小孩的老師來電，所以他無法將電話關靜音，為了這個舉動以及可能造成的不便而向對方表達歉意。

Track 1201　A = Andrew　J = Jasmine　★ 請特別注意粗體字的部分 ★

A I'm going to **put my phone on** vibrate [1]**because I** expect a call from my child's teacher. [2]**Would you mind?**

J **Not at all**.

A We all are very **interested in** your new product. The winter **collection is amazing**.

J That's great. I **got** some samples here. **Would you** like to **take a look** first? Or should we start from the campaign?

(*Cellphone vibrate sound*)

A Sorry, I need to take this. **Would you excuse me for a moment?**

J Sure.

(*Ten minutes later*)

A Hi, so sorry to have [3]**kept you waiting**.

J **It's all right.**

聽力提點

1. **because I**

   because 在句子中有時候會縮讀成 `cause，若再跟後面母音 I 連音，聽起來就會像是 [kəzaɪ]。
2. **Would you mind?** d + y 連音會變成 [dʒ] 的音。
3. **kept you** t + y 變成發 [tʃ] 的音。

延伸聽寫 | Exercise A

解答參見第 187 頁

Track 1202

1. Sorry, I have to ①__________ __________ call. 不好意思，我必須接這通電話。
2. I'm sorry I ②__________ __________ call. I ③__________ __________ a meeting and I put my ④__________ __________ silent.
   不好意思沒接到你的電話，我在開會，我的電話轉靜音。
3. Voice mail: Hi. This is Cynthia Lee. I'm sorry I'm not able to take your call. Please **leave a** message, and I'll ⑤__________ __________ __________ you ⑥__________ __________ __________ possible. **Have a** nice day.
   嗨，我是 Cynthia Lee，很抱歉現在沒辦法接你的電話，請留言，我會盡快回電給你，祝你有美好的一天。

Ch 2

實用字詞補充

1. **So sorry to have kept you waiting. 或是 So sorry to keep you waiting.**
   用完成式 have kept 是表達剛剛過去一段時間對方都在等待你的語意，而口語上也會有直接用現在式 keep you waiting 來表達。
2. **Put your phone on silent 或是 mute your phone**
   例 The meeting is about to start. Please mute your phone.
   會議要開始了，請將你的手機轉為靜音。
   類似用法：*Please silence your mobile phone. / *Please keep your phone in silence mode.
3. **Get back to somebody 回電或是回覆資訊給某人**
   例 I'll get back to you later. 我晚點回覆（回電）給你。

情境會話 A／翻譯

安德魯：我需要把手機調為震動，因為我在等我小孩的老師來電，您會介意嗎？

潔思敏：沒關係！

安德魯：我們大家都對你們公司的新產品感到非常有興趣，這次的冬季系列真是太棒了。

潔思敏：那太好了，我帶了樣品來，你想要現在先看一下嗎？還是我們要先從活動開始討論？

（手機震動聲）

安德魯：抱歉，我得接一下電話，請容我失陪一下。

潔思敏：好的。（十分鐘之後）

安德魯：嗨，真的很抱歉讓您等了那麼久。

潔思敏：還好啦，沒事的。

表達歉意 ②

情境概說

在派對上與朋友發生不愉快的事情，事後致電以表達歉意。

Track 1203　J = Jack　L = Lisa　★ 請特別注意粗體字的部分 ★

J　Lisa? Umm, hi, [1]**how're you doing today?**

L　[2]**I'm alright.** Hey, Jack, [3]**about last night**… I'm sorry that I spilled wine on you. It was…

J　Lisa, no, I am sorry. [4]**I truly am.** Look, I was drunk and… anyway, I **shouldn't** have **lost my temper in front of everyone**. [5]**That's awful.**

L　Well, [6]**I did** ruin your white shirt and I feel so bad. Please let me pay for the dry cleaning, or let me buy you a new one.

J　Oh, sweet heart, you are making me feel even more embarrassed.

L　Am I?

J　Come on, what you did happens all the time. It's a party, and we're friends. **No big deal.** But my behavior was really unacceptable. It's me, not you, who ruined Frank's birthday **party**.

聽力提點

1. **how're you doing today?**
   how are 的縮寫 how're，聽起來是 [haʊɚ]。
2. **I'm alright.**
   母音和子音連音，聽起來是 [mɔl]。
3. **about last night**
   第一個 [t] 是 stop，第二個 [t] 是省略發音，仔細聆聽音檔會發現兩個位置的時間長度有些微不同。
4. **I truly am.**
   由於 be 動詞 (am, is, are) 在句子當中都不是語意重點，通常會縮讀或弱讀，但在這一句中的 am 卻是 Jack 要強調的關鍵，表示他真的感到很抱歉，所以不弱讀，發 [æm] 的音。

5. **That's awful.**

母音和子音連音，聽起來是 [ðæzɔfəl]。

6. **I did ruin your white shirt.**

為了強調「的的確確」的意思，就像這個例句裡面的 [dɪd]，音量跟語調都會稍微提高。

延伸聽寫 | Exercise B

解答參見第 187 頁

Track 1204

1. A I'm sorry ①__________ __________ the wine.

   B You ②__________ be.

   翻譯

   A：我很抱歉把酒打翻了。　B：你是應該如此。

2. It's very ③__________ __________ me.

   我真是笨手笨腳的。

3. I feel really awful ④__________ __________. I ⑤____________ have lost my temper in front of everyone.

   我對此事感到非常糟糕。我不應該在大家面前發脾氣。

4. I didn't mean to ⑥__________ __________ your foot.

   我不是故意踩你的腳的。

5. We are ⑦__________ __________, and I ⑧____________ done better for you. We were both to blame.

   我們是好朋友，我應該為你做得更好。我們都有責任。

實用字詞補充

1. **I didn't mean it** 我不是有意的

   例 Please forgive me. I really didn't mean to say that.

   請原諒我，我並不是故意要那麼說的。

2. **meant to (be/do something)** 注定要如何

   例 If it's meant to be, it will happen anyway.

   如果那是注定要發生的事情，無論如何它就是會發生。

3. **I shouldn't have done it.** 我不該那麼做的（但是已經做了，為此感到懊悔）

Ch 2

例 I feel so sad. I shouldn't have done it.

我覺得好難過，早知道我根本就不該那麼做的。

4. **ruin 毀壞、糟蹋**

例 The bad weather ruined Sammy's birthday party.

壞天氣毀了珊米的生日派對。

5. **No big deal 或 It's no big deal 沒什麼大不了的**

例 A: Sorry, I thought you left. I ate your cake.

不好意思，我想說你先離開了，我吃了你的蛋糕。

B: Haha, no big deal.

哈哈，沒關係啦，小事情。

6. **Keep someone's temper under control 克制住脾氣**

例 You really have to try to keep your temper under control. Otherwise, you will make everyone, including yourself, feel embarrassed. 你真的應該要好好的試著控制自己的脾氣，不然，你會讓所有人，當然包括你自己在內，感到尷尬丟臉。

情境會話 B／翻譯

傑克：麗莎，嗯……那個，你今天還好嗎？

麗莎：我還好啊，那個，傑克，昨天晚上……不好意思我把酒灑到你身上了，那真的是……

傑克：麗莎，是我很抱歉，真的。聽著，我醉了，而且……不管怎麼樣，我根本不應該在大家面前那樣失控，那簡直糟透了。

麗莎：哎，可是我就是毀了你的白上衣啊，我覺得很抱歉。讓我幫你付乾洗的錢吧，或是我買一件新的給你。

傑克：噢，親愛的，你這樣不就讓我覺得更尷尬了。

麗莎：會嗎？

傑克：拜託，(你不過就打翻了酒) 那是難免的事情，派對上不就這樣嗎？而且我們是朋友耶，沒什麼大不了的。但是我的行為是真的不應該的。是我，而不是你，毀了法蘭克的生日派對啊！

表達歉意③

情境概說

因爲自己的失約而造成朋友的不便，向朋友道歉。

Track 1205 N = Noah C = Charlotte ★ 請特別注意粗體字的部分 ★

N I want to apologize for [1]**what I** have done yesterday. [2]**It's all** my fault.

C **You know what!** I [3]**kind of don't wanna talk about it**, really.

N Oh… I… I understand how disappointed you must be. I shouldn't… I **promised you** I would be there for you, but I [4]**didn't** deliver. I wish I could have… Charlotte, I'm sorry.

C Do you know how embarrassed I was? Everybody was asking me where you were and I just **stood there like an idiot**.

N I'm really truly sorry.

C I don't know. I am still so **mad**. Noah, [5]you **promised**… how could you…

N I know, let me [6]**fix it**, please. If you let me, I would do anything, anything, to make it up to you.

聽力提點

1. **what I**
   [t] 受到後面母音的影響，會發彈舌音 [t̬]（很像是比較輕聲的 [d]），聽起來是 [wɑt̬aɪ]。
2. **It's all** 母音和子音連音念成 [ɪtsɑl]。
3. **I kind of don't wanna talk about it.**
   連續的連音，kind of [kaɪndəv]、talk about it [tɔgə`baʊdɪt]。
4. **didn't**
   口語情境中說話流利快速的情況下，didn't 這個否定字尾的念法如同 couldn't, shouldn't, wouldn't 也是一樣的發音規則。
5. **You promised**
   ed 結尾的字，[d] 若沒有受到後面連音的影響，就可以聽到比較短促且微弱的 [t]。

6. **fix it** 連音，[fɪksɪt]。

延伸聽寫 Exercise C

解答參見第 188 頁

Track 1206

1. I ①__________ understand why you don't ②__________ __________ __________ __________ me, and maybe you don't even want see me anymore.
   我完全可以理解為什麼你不想再跟我說話，而且你大概也不想再見到我了。

2. I know ③__________ __________ __________ I say or what I do, you probably will never forgive me. But I still want to apologize. I am so sorry.
   我知道不管我說什麼或做什麼，你或許永遠都不會原諒我，但是我還是想要跟你道歉，我真的很抱歉。

3. I promised you, but I didn't deliver. I ④__________ __________ suffer.
   我答應過你的事情卻沒有做到，我讓你受苦了。

實用字詞補充

1. **I want to apologize for... 我要為了某事跟您道歉**
   若再更正式一點可以說 I would like to apologize for...

2. **It wasn't your fault. 這不是你的錯**
   例 Don't say that. Actually, it wasn't your fault. I should be more careful.
   別那麼說，這其實不是你的錯，我應該要更小心一點的。

3. **I wanna 是 I want to 的口語縮讀，念起來是** [aɪwɑnə]。

情境會話 C／翻譯

諾　亞：我要為了我昨天的所作所為跟你道歉，一切都是我不好。

夏綠蒂：你知道嗎？我不太想講這件事情，真的。

諾　亞：我知道你一定非常失望，我答應你我會去支持你，但是我沒做到，我希望一切可以重來……夏綠蒂，我很抱歉。

夏綠蒂：你知道我有多尷尬嗎？大家都在問我你到哪裡去了，然後我就站在那邊跟笨蛋一樣。

諾　亞：我真的非常非常抱歉 .

夏綠蒂：我不知道啦，我就是很氣，諾亞，你答應過我的，你怎麼可以這樣。

諾　亞：我知道，讓我補償你好嗎？如果你給我機會，我願意做任何事情，真的任何事情，來彌補你。

延伸聽寫 Answer Keys

Exercise A

（請參考以下答案及解說。）

① take this（[k] 後面是子音，發塞音 stop，聽起來是 [teɪk| ðɪs]。）

② missed your（[d] 後面是 [j]，連音會變成 [dʒ]。[dʒ] 就像是 join [dʒɔɪn] 的字首音。）

③ was in（was 弱讀為 [wəz]，跟 in 連音聽起來是 [wəzɪn]。）

④ phone on（連音聽起來是 [fonɑn]。）

⑤ get back to（連續塞音。get 和 back 的兩個尾音都是塞音 stop，聽起來是 [get| bæk| to]。）

⑥ as soon as（as 弱讀及連音，as soon as 聽起來是 [əsunəz]。）

Exercise B

（請參考以下答案及解說，可弱讀的字詞以斜體表示。）

① about spilling（仔細聽尾音 t 是 stop T。〈跟第 3 題做比較〉）

② should（仔細聽尾音的 d，同第 5 題的 good friend。〈可跟第 5 點一起比較〉）

③ clumsy of

像 [klʌmzi] 這個單字的尾音是 [i]，且後面接的字首也是母音時，母音和母音連音之間要增加一個滑音 [j]，這就很像中文的「好啊（ㄏㄠˇ ㄚ）」，口語上很多人在語速加快且連著不中斷發音的時候，聽起來是「ㄏㄠˇ（ㄨ）ㄚ」，很接近真正的「好哇（ㄏㄠˇ ㄨㄚ）」，差別就是「好啊」的滑順口語所增添的那個 ㄨ 是很輕、很細微的一個過渡的聲音而已。

④ about it

仔細聽兩個尾音 t 的變化〈可以跟第 1 句話的 about 比較〉，第一個 t 因受後方母音影響，要發彈舌音，連起來是 [t̬ɪt|]。

⑤ shouldn't

⑥ step on

⑦ good friends

這邊有兩個 [d] 的發音變化，接在第一個 [d] 後面的字首為子音，所以要發塞音 stop，第二個 [d] 是尾音且後面有複數 s，這種情況下的 [d] 會被省略掉，同樣的例子像是 hands, sounds 跟 minds 等等。

⑧ should've

should've 是由 should have 省略而來，縮讀的時候會聽到很短促的弱化母音 [ə]，整個字念起來是 [ʃʊdəv]。

Ch 2

Exercise C

（請參考以下答案及解說。）

1. totally（第 2 個 t 在兩個母音之間，又是非重音節，會發一個輕短微弱近似 [d] 的聲音，念成 [touṭəli]）
2. want to talk to（第一個 to 比起第二個 to 還要弱讀音，聽起來是一個很快速的 [tə] 的聲音。）
3. no matter what I（tt 在單字中非重音節的位置且受到後面母音影響，發彈舌音念成 [mæṭə]，what 的尾音 [t] 與後面母音連音，也是發彈舌音 [ṭ]。）
4. made you（d+y 發 [dʒ]，如同 promised you 的連音一樣。）

加值學更多！

「委婉打斷對方談話的對話內容」

線上下載更多聽力技巧練習，隨時想聽就聽！

Unit 13

· 表達同情和慰問

表達同情和慰問 ①

情境概說

Alexander 帶著小點心去安慰因某事而陷入困境的 Sophia。

Track 1301　A = Alexander　S = Sophia　★ 請特別注意粗體字的部分 ★

Conversation A-1

A Sophia, I brought you some cookies, [1]**just out of the oven**!

S Oh, aren't you the sweetest? They smell so good.

A [2]**How are you feeling today?**

S Um…[3]**I don't know**. I guess… um… I'm still shocked. [4]**You know**, I just… [5]**I can't believe it.** I never thought that **it could happen** [6]**to me**.

A It's so depressing and unfair, really.

S So not fair, but **I don't know** what I can do. I even thought about selling this house last night.

A [7]**Don't!** I mean… it's tough, but I think we shouldn't make any decisions when we are still upset, right!

聽力提點

1. **just out of** 連續連音。
2. **How are you feeling today?**
   單字 how 的最後一個音是雙母音 [aʊ]，且下一個字首為母音，連音的時候會多一個輕微的滑音 [w]，聽起來會像是 [haʊwɑr]。
3. **I don't know**
   這句聽起來像是 I dunno，日常口語對話當中經常會有這種聽起來不太像單字原本發音的現象。I don't know 如果因為說話者當時的情緒表達是屬於義正嚴辭，或是沒有想要含糊地把句子快速帶過去的話，那麼通常會聽見這樣的發音 [aɪ doʊnt| noʊ]。
4. **You know**
   you 弱讀，聽起來是 [jə]，know 尾音上揚。
5. **I can't believe it**

can't 的尾音 [t] 發 stop T sound。而 believe it 母音子音連音，聽起來像 [vɪt]。(請仔細聽第 7 點的 don't，以及下一段的第一句)。

6. **it could happen to me**
   to 弱讀，聽起來不是 [tu]，而是 [tə]。
7. **Don't!**
   這個 Don't 單獨存在，因為是在對話當中一來一往，Don't ~~do that~~ 的後半句子被省略了。

Track 1302　A = Alexander　S = Sophia　★ 請特別注意粗體字的部分 ★

Conversation A-2

A **It can't be easy for sure**, but it's not [1]the **end of** the world.

S [2]**I'm not sure about that.**

A **Okay**, [3]**that's why I am here.** I couldn't fall asleep last night and I couldn't stop thinking that you would sit there all day and cry.

S [4]**Come on**, [5]I **do** feel wretched, but I'm not crazy alright.

A What I am saying is that I am here for you. I want you to remember you are not alone, okay? Wanna have some cookies?

S Okay, why not! I heard that sugar can improve our mood when we're feeling down.

Ch 2

聽力提點

1. **the end of the world** 連音，聽起來是 [dəv]。
2. **I'm not sure about that.**
   I'm 作為句子的開頭，在口語情境中若是比較隨性的話，很容易只剩下 [m] 的聲音。
3. **that's why I am here**
   that's 開頭發音快速，短促到 [z] 的聲音比較明顯。
4. **Come on!** 連音，聽起來是 [kʌmɔn]。
5. **I do feel wretched.**
   說話時若有像 do 這樣強調的用法，通常會成為句子的重音位置（音調略高）。

延伸聽寫 | Exercise A

➔ 解答參見第 200 頁

Track 1303

1. These __________ __________ just out of the oven! 這些餅乾才剛出爐呢！
2. I __________ believe it. 我不敢相信！
3. It's __________ __________ __________ __________ the world.
   這不是世界末日。

實用字詞補充

1. **Aren't you sweet? 否定疑問句 (negative questions)**
   這種問句在口語中通常有兩種功能：
   ① 表達質疑（責備）或是表達難道不是這樣嗎？
   例 Aren't you supposed to be there?
   你不是應該人要在那邊嗎？
   ② 表達驚訝驚喜等等
   例 Aren't you the cutest!
   你真的是最可愛呀！（難道不是嗎？）
2. **depressing 令人沮喪的**
   例 The situation is so depressing.
   這整件事情真的超令人沮喪的。
   例 It is very depressing hearing the news last night.
   昨天晚上知道這事情，真的是令人感到難受。
3. **depressed 憂鬱的、消沉的**
   例 He is deeply depressed about the situation.
   他對於整個情況感到相當沮喪。
4. **unfair 不公平的、不正當的**
   例 It's totally unfair to judge a book by its cover.
   以貌取人非常不公平。
5. **shocked 感到震驚、不可置信的**
   例 They were all shocked when they heard the sad news.
   當他們聽到這個不幸的消息時，都很震驚。
6. **wretched 不愉快的、生病的**
   例 I've been feeling wretched for two days.
   我連著兩天都好不舒服

例 What happened? You look wretched.

發生什麼事情了？你看起來好慘。

7. **boost 提振**

例 Chocolate always can boost our mood.

巧克力總是能提振我們的心情。

例 When you are down, have some chocolate. It's a mood booster.

當你覺得沮喪，來點巧克力吧，這可是能激勵人心的東西。

8. **the end of the world 世界末日（糟糕至極的情況）**

例 It is not the end of the world.

天還沒塌下來！

情境會話 A／翻譯

Conversation A-1

亞歷山大：嗨，蘇菲亞，我帶了些餅乾給你，是剛出爐的喔。

蘇菲亞　：歐，你好貼心喔，餅乾聞起來好香。

亞歷山大：你今天感覺怎麼樣？

蘇菲亞　：哎，我也不知道耶，我大概還在驚嚇狀態中吧，我真的無法接受這是真的。我從來沒想過這種事情會發生在我身上。

亞歷山大：這真的很令人沮喪而且很不公平。

蘇菲亞　：超不公平啊，我真的不知道我能怎麼辦，我昨晚甚至想說乾脆把房子賣掉好了。

亞歷山大：不可以！我是說……這很難，但我覺得我們不應該在難過沮喪的時候去做任何決定，對吧！

Conversation A-2

亞歷山大：這肯定不容易，但是這不是世界末日。

蘇菲亞　：是嗎？我不知道。

亞歷山大：嘿，這就是為什麼我今天要來看你，我昨天晚上根本睡不著，我無法不去想像你就那樣一個人坐在那兒一整天，然後一直哭。

蘇菲亞　：拜託，我是真的感覺很糟，但是我沒瘋好嗎？

亞歷山大：我要跟你說的是，我會陪你，我要你記得你並不是孤單一個人。要吃點餅乾嗎？

蘇菲亞　：好哇！聽說當我們低潮的時候，糖可以改善我們的心情啊。

表達同情和慰問 ②

情境概說

朋友間相約要幫另一位因爲被公司解雇而失意的朋友加油打氣。

Track 1304 M = Man W = Woman ★ 請特別注意粗體字的部分 ★

M [1]**Have you heard** the news about Mila?

W Yeah, that's shocking. Can you believe it? Mila has been working so hard. She must have no idea how come it would happen.

M You're right. I went to see her yesterday. You should see those teary eyes.

W **It's so depressing**. My company fired [2]**a lot of** people too. To be honest, I am a bit worried about my job.

M It's been a **tough year** for [3]**all of us**. I guess we all feel gloomy **about the future**.

W **Tell me about it**. Still, poor Mila, she must feel lonely and depressed now. I think we should do something for her.

M Couldn't agree with you more! Hey, why don't we have a zoom date tonight?

W Sure, during the lockdown, we still have to find our way to get together and be there for our friends.

聽力提點

1. **Have you**
   have 作為句子的開頭有時候會因實境當中隨性、語速、情緒而產生變化，速度最短的是弱讀為 [əv]，因為 [əv] 的聲音已經足夠讓對方了解這個字是 have。
2. **a lot of** 連音，lot 的尾音 t 要發彈舌音 [t̬]。
3. **all of us** 連音，聽起來是 [ɔləvəs]。

延伸聽寫 | Exercise B

解答參見第 200 頁

Track 1305

1. Have you ①__________ __________ what happened to Sandy?
你有聽說珊蒂的事情嗎？

2. There are ②__________ __________ __________ people. 超多人的！

3. ③__________ agree with you more. ④__________ __________ a ⑤__________ __________ for all of us.
你說的非常正確！這一年對大家來說真的是很艱苦的一年。

實用字詞補充

1. **Shocking** 令人震驚的，令人驚訝的

例 The news is extremely shocking for all of us.
這個消息對我們來說是個很大的打擊。

2. **Gloomy** 沮喪的，鬱悶憂愁的，天氣灰濛的

例 We've had a month of gloomy weather. 整個月都是灰濛濛的天氣。

3. **Couldn't agree with you more!**

用否定句型來表達肯定以及強調之意在英文當中是很常見的運用。聆聽時只要聽到後面的動詞 agree，那就是非常同意的意思。這句話也可以簡化為 couldn't agree more，就是 strongly agree 之意，就像 I couldn't care less. 實際上的意思就是非常不在乎 (care less)，如果希望在口語表達時也能運用自如，則需要整句多念誦到相當熟習，才能在與人對談的時候也能直覺反應。

4. **Look on the bright side.**（鼓勵別人）往好的方面想

例 Don't be so disappointed. Look on the bright side—no one was hurt.
不要沮喪了，往好的方面想，沒有人受傷啊。

情境會話 B／翻譯

男：你有聽說蜜拉的事情嗎？

女：有啊，真的很令人震驚。你能相信嗎？像蜜拉工作這麼認真的人，她一定完全無法理解到底怎麼會發生這樣的事情。

男：沒錯，我昨天去看她，你真該看看她那雙淚汪汪的眼睛。

女：這真的太令人洩氣了，我公司也開除了很多人，講真的，我其實也蠻擔心我自己的工作的。

男：我想大家想到未來都覺得很悲觀吧，畢竟這一年來真的不容易。

女：那還用說嗎！總之，可憐的蜜拉，她現在一定又孤單又沮喪，我覺得我們應該為她做點什麼。

男：超級同意。我們何不今天晚上大家來個 zoom 約會？

女：當然好啊，在這種封城的時候，我們還是得找到我們的方法跟朋友聚在一起互相加油打氣呀。

表達同情和慰問 ③

情境概說

向突然接到父親過世噩耗的公司同事致哀慰問。

Track 1306 W = Woman M = Man ★ 請特別注意粗體字的部分 ★

W Hi, Simon, this is Sammy. We are so sorry to hear about the [1]**heartbreaking** news. Please allow me, on behalf of **all of us** at Kind Company, to extend the sincerest sympathies to you.

M **Thank you.** I appreciate that.

W And knowing that [2]**this is a** difficult time for you and your family, I **would like** to **let you know** that you **don't** need to worry **about** your cases. [3]I'll have it covered.

M Thank you for saying that. I must say, I do worry about that.

W [4]**I am here to help**, Simon. Miss Huang, my secretary, will be contacting you [5]**shortly** to see what we can do for you, especially like additional [6]**time off** or flexible schedules.

M It's very helpful.

W Please [7]**take care**. You are **in our** thoughts.

聽力提點

1. **heartbreaking** t 消音，聽起來會像 [ˋhɑr͵brekiŋ]。
2. **this is a** 連續兩個母音和子音的連音，聽起來是 [ðɪ sɪ sə]。
3. **I will have it covered**
   have it covered 連音聽起來會像 [hɑvit| ˋkʌvəd]。
4. **I am here to help** to 弱讀，聽起來像 [tə]。
5. **shortly** 請比較第 1 點，一樣是單字當中 [t] 消音。
6. **time off** 子音母音連音，[taɪ mɔf]。
7. **take care** 子音與子音並列，發後面的子音，聽起來是 [te ker]。

延伸聽寫 | Exercise C

解答參見第 200 頁

Track 1307

1. I feel ①__________ for him. 我為他感到難過。
2. I'm so sorry. I'm going to ②__________ __________, too. Please ③__________ __________ of yourself!
   真的很遺憾，我也好想念她啊，請你一定要好好保重。
3. Healing takes time, and you're doing the ④__________ __________ can.
   療傷需要時間的，你已經做得很棒了。

實用字詞補充

1. **I am/feel so sorry that...**

   「我深感遺憾」，用英文來說就是 I am so sorry.。這個 sorry，並不是跟對方致歉，而是對某人某事感到哀傷並且表達自己的慰問同情之意 (feeling sorrow or sympathy)，例如：I am so *sorry* for your loss，可以用來表達對於他人痛失珍惜的人事物的慰問之情，這個句子可以把動詞改為 feel 來稍微做一個小變化，I *feel* sorry for him，對於他面臨的「處境」「問題」「失去」等等感到同情而表達關切。

2. **sadden 使悲傷、使難過**

   例 I am deeply saddened by the sad tragedy.
   這個令人感傷的悲劇讓我沉浸在深深的悲痛之中。

3. **grief（尤指某人之死引起的）悲痛與悲傷**

   例 We were worried that he wouldn't be able to recover from his grief at his father's death. 我們很擔心他無法從父親亡故的悲痛中走出來。

4. **You are in our thoughts. 我們惦記著你（我們會為你禱告祈福）**

   *You are in our prayers.

5. **pity（覺得可憐而感到）同情憐憫**

   * 跟 sympathy 或是 empathy 不太一樣，很多情境當中使用 pity 是要表達因為鄙視而產生的同情感受

   例 If you really want to help them, don't make them feel that you just feel pity for them. 如果你真的想幫助他們，就不要讓他們覺得你只是可憐人家。

情境會話 C／翻譯

女：嗨 Simon，我是 Sammy，聽到這個不幸的消息我們都感到非常遺憾。在此時此刻，你經歷巨大的哀傷的同時，請容我，代表整個公司，致上我們最深的哀悼之意。

男：謝謝，你們的心意我收到了。

女：此刻對你跟你的家人來說都是很艱難的，我想讓你知道，你不需要擔心你手上的那些專案，我會安排人處理。

男：你這麼說真的是太好了，其實，我正擔心那些事情呢。

女：我就是來幫你解決這些煩惱的，所以我的助理黃小姐很快會聯繫你，看看還有什麼是我們能協助你的，像是你需要延長休假或是彈性調整工時等等。

男：這真的對我很有幫助。

女：請照顧好自己，我們都惦記著你。

表達同情慰問實用句型

慰問、悼念、致哀

① Our deepest condolences sympathies go out to you and your family.
給予您與您的家人，我們致上深切的慰問。

② Our heartfelt condolences to your family 向您的家人致哀

③ All of us are deeply saddened by the sudden passing of your father. Please accept our deepest condolences.
獲悉您父親驟然離世的消息，全體上下都感到非常難過。請接收我們最深切／誠摯的慰問。

④ Although words seem woefully inadequate/empty/ superfluous in this difficult time, please know that you and your family are in our thoughts.
雖然此刻或許多說無益（不足／徒勞／多餘），我還是想讓你知道，我們掛念著您與您的家人。

鼓舞人心萬用短句

① I am here for you whenever you need me.
無論何時，你需要我，我都在。

② Don't forget that we are just a phone call away.
別忘了，我隨 call 隨到的。

③ What doesn't kill you will make you stronger.
凡事殺不死你的，必會使你更強壯。

④ Nothing can hurt you unless you let them.
沒有你的同意，誰都傷不了你。

⑤ When life gives you lemons, make lemonade.
生活不如意之事，轉個念頭，正向面對它吧！

⑥ We can't sit and wait for the storm to be over. We have to learn to dance in the rain.
面對困難與其坐以待斃，不如順應而為。

延伸聽寫 Answer Keys

Exercise A

（請參考以下答案及解說。）

1. These cookies are just out of the oven!（are [ɑr] 弱讀變成 [ɚ] 的聲音〈就像 What are you doing? 的 are 也是 [ɚ]〉，然後再跟前面的 s 連音。聽起來是 [kʊkizɚ]。）
2. can't（如果是英式發音，can't 的母音 a 會聽起來很明顯的與美式口音不同。英式 [kɑnt]、美式 [kænt]）。
3. It's not the end of the world.（這個句子的重音通常會落在 not 這個字，表達鼓勵對方「其實還很有希望，要往好處想」之意。）

Exercise B

（請參考以下答案及解說。）

① heard of（這裡的 heard 是 hear 的動詞過去分詞，如果比較少開口練習過去分詞的發音，再加上 [d] 跟後面的母音連音，在聆聽時很可能一下子反應不過來，因此在加強聽力的同時，別忘了可同時跟著音檔跟讀模仿發音，這樣必能有效提升聽力當下的迅速理解反應。）

② a lot of

③ Couldn't

④ It is（[t] 因為後面是母音，發彈舌音 [t̬]，it is 聽起來會是 [ɪt̬s]。）

⑤ tough year / tough fight（tough 的字尾 gh 發音 [f] 跟 year 母音字首 [j] 連音聽起來像 [təfjir]，這個是母音和子音連音的例子。但如果是 tough fight，tough 的字尾 [f] 音則會被省略，因為後面有相同的 f 子音，因此兩個字聽起來變成 [təfaɪt]。）

Exercise C

（請參考以下答案及解說。 ）

① sorry

② miss her

③ take care

④ best you（t+y 連音變成 [tʃ] 的聲音，[bestʃu]。）

加值學更多！

「慰問受傷的朋友，關於加油打氣的情境聽力」

線上下載，隨時想聽就聽！

Unit 14

· 表達恭維或祝賀

表達恭維或祝賀 ①

情境概說

誇獎朋友的才華與能力。

Track 1401　C = Cole　M = Miranda　★ 請特別注意粗體字的部分 ★

C　Wow, did you [2]**make these** by yourself? The patio [1]**chairs are** so beautiful.

M　Yeah, I've been working from home for [2]**like months** and I [3]**gotta** find something different, you know… anyway, [4]I found my **old toolkit** the other day and one thing [5]**led to another**… well, [2]**do you really think** [6]**they are good?** I thought…

C　Yes, they are terrific!

M　Aww, you are just being nice.

C　No, [7]**I mean it.** You seem to have a real gift for this sort of work.

聽力提點

1. **The patio chairs are so beautiful.** 母音子音連音，[sɑr]。
2. **did you make these, for like months, do you really think they**
   [k] 塞音 stop。
3. **I gotta find something**
   tt 在非重音音節及兩個母音之間，發彈舌音 [gɑtə]。
4. **I found my old toolkit.**
   兩個 [d] 都在字尾，而其後的字首為子音，發塞音 stop。
5. **One thing led to another** 同上。
6. **They are good** 口語中會用尾音上揚來表示問句。
7. **I mean it** 連音，讀成 [minɪt]。

延伸聽寫 | Exercise A

解答參見第 210 頁

Track 1402

1. A　I really ①__________ you. If I were you, I ②__________ __________ to do that.

B It's very nice of you to say so.

翻譯

A：我真的很欣賞你，如果我是你，我才不敢去做那件事情呢。

B：你這麼說真的很貼心。

2. We're pleased that you ③__________ __________ the main projects perfectly, but we're even more pleased that you finished them in only two weeks. We're quite impressed by your performance.

我們很滿意你完美的完成了這些主要的案子，但是我們更加激賞你只花了兩週就完成了，我們對於你的表現感到驚艷。

3. It's the most delicate ④__________ card I have ever seen.

這是我看過最精緻的手工卡片了。

Ch 2

實用字詞補充

1. **terrific（口語）極好的**

例 A: Guess what, I passed my exam. 猜猜怎麼著，我考試過關啦！

B: That's terrific! Let's celebrate! 棒呆了！我們來慶祝一下吧。

2. **I mean it.（用來強調）我是說真的**

例 Don't do it again. I mean it.

不要再這樣了，我是說真的喔！

3. **one thing leads to another 一件事情接著一件事情環環相扣發生**

例 At first, we were just talking about his problems, but one thing led to another, and he called his boss and quit. 一開始我們只是在討論他的問題，但是一件事情接著另一件事情，最後他就打給他的老闆並辭職了。

情境會話 A／翻譯

柯　爾：哇，這些都是你自己做的嗎？這些露台椅子好漂亮喔。

米蘭達：對啊，我已經居家辦公好幾個月了，我得找些不一樣的事情來做，你懂的，總之，我找到我的舊工具箱啊，然後一件事接著另外一件事情發展下去就變成你現在看到的這樣啦，話說回來，你真的覺得它們很不錯嗎？我以為……

柯　爾：真的，它們棒透了！

米蘭達：噢，你只是好意才這麼說吧！

柯　爾：沒有好嗎，我是講真的，你其實在這種事情上很有天賦耶。

表達恭維或祝賀 ②

情境概說

拜訪新朋友，找話題進行攀談、拉近距離。

Track 1403　M = Mark　L = Lexi　★ 請特別注意粗體字的部分 ★

M Hi, I'm Mark, Jessie's brother. She asked me to bring you these children's books and toys.

L Hi Mark, thank you so much. My son will be so excited. [1]**Come on in**. **Would you** [2]**like something to drink**?

M Water is fine, thanks. Your place **is so lovely**.

L We just **spent a lot of money** redoing the kitchen. It's kind of [3]**worth it**, huh!

M [4]**Totally!** It's very posh and modern. Jessie told me that your husband built the house, and you designed it. It's amazing. I wish I had **bought a** house **like this**.

L Oh, then Jessie probably **didn't** tell you how disastrous the house **was all** because of my **helpless obsession** with details.

M Haha, Jessie **said nothing** but good things about you.

聽力提點

1. **come on in** 連音，聽起來是 [kʌmonɪn]。
2. **Would you like something to drink?** like 在句中 [k] 發塞音 stop，而 drink 在句尾可以聽見 [k] 的聲音。
3. **worth it** 連音 [wɜθɪt]。
4. **totally** t 在非重音節，夾在兩個母音間，發彈舌音 [toʊt̬əli]。

延伸聽寫 | Exercise B

➜ 解答參見第 210 頁

Track 1404

A I believe we haven't met before, I am Sam. ①__________ __________ __________ you.

B Nice to meet you too. I'm Julia. We ②__________ __________ met but I'll be working with you on this project, and I've ③__________ __________ __________ __________ __________.

A All good I hope.

翻譯

A：我們還沒見過吧，我是 Sam，很高興認識你。

B：我也很高興認識你，我是 Julia，我們雖然還沒正式見過面，但是我將會跟你一起合作這個專案，而且我已經聽說過你了喔。

A：希望都是關於好事。

實用字詞補充

1. **Come on in!**（對熟客、朋友等）招呼「請進」

   * 與 Come in 不太相同，若是在辦公室有人敲門，我們不知道門外是誰，會用 Come in 的「請進」，比較中規中矩、正式一點，而 Come on in 有招呼的意味，有點類似中文的「快進來坐」。

2. **redo 重新粉刷／裝修**

   例 We plan to redo the living room. 我們打算重新粉刷客廳。

3. **Say nothing but good things about someone**

   都只說某人的好話（稱讚的意思）

情境會話 B／翻譯

馬克：嗨，我是馬克，潔希的哥哥，她請我帶這些小朋友的書跟玩具給你。

蕾西：嗨，馬克，真是太感謝你了，我兒子一定會很開心的。快點進來坐，你要喝點什麼嗎？

馬克：水就好了，謝謝，你家好漂亮喔！

蕾西：我們才剛花一大筆錢整修廚房呢！看來還蠻值得喲！

馬克：超級值得啊！看起來非常時尚摩登。潔希有跟我說過你丈夫自己建造這棟房子，然後你負責設計，這太棒了，我真希望我買了一間像你們這樣的房子就太好了。

蕾西：噢，那潔希大概沒跟你說過這間房子之前有多慘，都是因為我對於細節過於偏執的無可救藥啊！

馬克：哈哈，我可從來沒聽潔希跟我說過什麼你不好的事情喔。

表達恭維或祝賀 ③

情境概說

朋友之間互相祝賀好事發生。

Track 1405 A = April M = Melody ★ 請特別注意粗體字的部分 ★

A Okay, ladies, [1]**drinks are on me tonight**. **Let's celebrate**!

M April, I **couldn't be** happier for you. You have been working so hard for your dream and you've done **such a remarkable job**. You **deserve it**.

A **That's so sweet**, Mel. Cheers!

M Oh, sweetie, **drink one for me**.

A What?…Wait… no… you're not kidding, are you?

M No, I'm not. I [2]**AM** [3]**pregnant**!

A Congratulations, my dear dear friend! I am so happy for you.

M April, I hope you don't think I'm stealing your thunder. It's your night, and I…

A No, I would never… I am so excited. I think I'm gonna cry…

聽力提點

1. **drinks are on me tonight!**
   are 弱讀 [ər]，前後連音，語速加快之後聽起來是 [drɪŋksərɑn]。
2. **I AM pregnant.**
   這裡的 am 沒有弱讀，因為是語意上的強調重點，會念 [æm]。
3. **pregnant** pregnant 這個 g 不是發像 good 的 [g]，而是很快速的頓一下（塞音 stop）再接續後面的 [nənt]。

延伸聽寫 | Exercise C

➔ 解答參見第 210 頁

Track 1406

1. A I wanna tell you something. Jim ①__________ __________ me ②__________ __________.

   B Congratulations! You guys will be so happy.

翻譯

A：我要跟你說一件事情，Jim 昨天晚上跟我求婚了。

B：恭喜！你們會很幸福的。

2. May happiness, health and ③______________ be with you through the years to come. 祝福你們往後的每一天都健康、快樂又富足。

實用字詞補充

1. **drinks are on me!（口語省略）酒錢我請客**

例 Hey, friends, I just got promoted, so drinks are on me tonight!
朋友們，我剛升遷啦，所以今天晚上酒錢都算我的。

2. **Couldn't be happier 非常高興**

例 A: How have you been? You look glowing. 你好嗎？你整個人看起來容光煥發耶！
B: Well, I finally quit and I'm a freelancer now. Couldn't be happier.
我終於辭掉工作了，現在是自由接案者，真的非常開心。

3. **so sweet 很貼心**

例 A: I bought you flowers. 我買了花給你。
B: You are so sweet. 你好貼心喔。

4. **Sweetie（口語）親愛的** *sweetheart

5. **Steal someone's thunder 搶了某人的風頭**

例 Lily stole my thunder when she announced that she was engaged at my birthday party. Lily 在我的生日派對上宣布她訂婚，搶了我的風頭。

情境會話 C／翻譯

艾　波：大家，今天晚上酒都算我的喔，我們來慶祝吧！

美樂蒂：艾波，我真的是為你感到超開心的，一直以來你為了夢想拚了命努力，而且做的那麼棒，這一切你當之無愧。

艾　波：你太感人了啦，美樂蒂，來乾杯！

美樂蒂：噢，親愛的，你得幫我喝了。

艾　波：什麼意思？等一下……不會吧，你是認真的還是開玩笑的啊？

美樂蒂：我沒有開玩笑，我真的懷孕了。

艾　波：哇！恭喜你，我最親愛的朋友。我好為你開心喔！

美樂蒂：艾波，希望你不會覺得我搶了你的風采，今天你是主角……

艾　波：我才不會那樣想，我好興奮喔，我要哭了啦……

表達恭維或祝賀 ④

情境概說

祝賀朋友新居落成。

Track 1407 W = Wyatt Z = Zoey ★ 請特別注意粗體字的部分 ★

W Did you know Vincent and Debra bought a new house?

Z [1]**They did!**

W Yeah, I **just talked** to Vincent this morning. **He's surprisingly calm**. If I were him, the **first house** in my life, I would be like over the moon. Anyway, [2]we **should buy** them a present!

Z Of course, how about the painting they have been talking about for [3]**like a** month?

W [4]**Sounds good**!

Z Wait, what if they have already [5]**bought it**? We should go to the gallery to **figure it out** now!

W Now, you mean right now! I haven't finished my cake.

聽力提點

1. **They did!** did 語氣上揚，代表驚訝的疑問。
2. **We should buy them a present!**
   當 [b] 作為 [d] 的延續音時，會產生語音同化現象 (assimilation)，你會聽見 shoul(d)buy。
3. **like a month** 連音。
4. **Sounds good!**
   當 [d] 前面有 [n] 後面有 [s]，這個 [d] 在口語發音上會被省略，其他類似的例子像是 friends，minds。
5. **bought it** [t] 跟後面的母音連音，會發彈舌音，[bɔt̬ɪt]。

延伸聽寫 | Exercise D

解答參見第 210 頁

Track 1408

1. Here's to the ___________ ___________ a wonderful adventure.
   我們來為此後一段美好的旅程乾杯。
2. You've ___________ ___________ keys! I'm so thrilled for you.
   你拿到房子鑰匙了！我好為你開心。
3. High five! You ___________ ___________! Now it's time to celebrate.
   擊掌！你做到了！現在是慶祝的時候啦。
4. You bought your first house. We're so incredibly ___________ ___________ ___________. 你買下人生第一間房子，我們為你感到驕傲。

實用字詞補充

1. **over the moon 非常高興**
   例 Mr. Smith was over the moon about his new convertible.
   Smith 先生對於他的嶄新敞篷車感到非常開心。
2. **What if（如果發生……事情的話）要怎麼辦呢？**
   例 What if the train is late? 要是火車誤點的話怎麼辦呢？
3. **Here's to 為了……乾杯**
   例 Here's to the beautiful couple! 祝福這美麗的一對。
4. **thrilled 極度開心的**
   例 I was thrilled that so many people came to support the event.
   看到這麼多人出席來支持這個活動，我感到超級開心的。

情境會話 D／翻譯

懷特：你知道文森跟黛博拉買了新房子嗎？

柔伊：他們買房子了？！

懷特：對啊，我早上有跟文森說話，很令人驚訝的是他很平靜耶，如果我是他，買了生平第一間房子，我應該會超級無敵高興吧！總之，我們應該要送他們新居落成禮物吧。

柔伊：當然要啊，要不要送那幅他們兩個講了快一個月的畫作？

懷特：不錯啊！

柔伊：慢著，要是他們已經買下那幅畫了怎麼辦？我們應該現在就去畫廊看看。

懷特：現在！你是說此刻馬上嗎？我都還沒吃完我的蛋糕耶。

延伸聽寫 Answer Keys

Exercise A（請參考以下答案及解說。）

① admire（[d] 在字中發 stop d 的聲音，要注意，有些人會在這個要頓一下的 stop d 後面加上一個 [ə]，變成 a-de-mire，這是錯誤的。而會犯這個錯誤是因為在這個單字中發出 [d] 這個塞音容易造成中斷、比較不好念，若不了解這個發音規則，就會不小心讓這個字從兩個音節變成三個音節。admire 正確流暢的發音是發 stop d 的聲音，迅速憋氣且不要中斷，直接延續後面 mire 的發音。）

② wouldn't dare

③ have finalized

④ handmade（[d] 消音。）

Exercise B（請參考以下答案及解說。）

① Nice *to* meet you

② haven't officially

③ heard a lot about you（heard a 連音 [də]，而下一組 lot about 的連音因為 t 受到後面母音影響，發音 [t̬ə]，[t]+[j] 變音 [tʃ]。）

Exercise C（請參考以下答案及解說。）

① proposed to（消音。）

② last night（消音。）

③ prosperity（[p] sound 在很多單字像是 pepper，spoon 聽起來都不像是 [p]，反而讓人以為是 [b]，以 prosperity 這個字來說，第 2 個 [p] 在口語上為了發音順暢，反而是比較微弱輕短的聲音，搭上後面的母音，聲音聽起來有 [b] 的錯覺，其實這樣的字只需要兩唇輕輕閉一下即可完成發音。）

Exercise D（請參考以下答案及解說。）

1. start of（連音，[stɑrdəv]。）
2. got the
3. did it（連音，[dɪdɪt]）
4. proud of you（連音。）

加值學更多！

「如何讚美朋友或同事的衣著打扮」

線上下載更多聽力技巧練習，隨時想聽就聽！

Unit 15

・邀請與請求幫助

邀請與請求幫助 ①

情境概說

請朋友幫忙掛一幅畫。

Track 1501 J = Josh A = Alice ★ 請特別注意粗體字的部分 ★

J Alice, **would you** [1]**mind giving me a hand**?

A No, [2]**what do you need?**

J Umm, can you help me hang this painting? **I need you** to [3]**hold it** straight while I mark the spot.

A Wow, **it's a** super-heavy piece. Have you used a [4]**stud-finder** first to locate a [5]**stud**?

J That's a [6]**good question**! I haven't and I think I [7]**should** [8]**do it**.

A Well, I don't do this often, so we can try your way. Just tell me what I should do.

J Haha, in fact, I've never done this before and I didn't think it through because **I thought it** shouldn't be that hard.

A You know, you can always just **lean it**! It's the laziest way to display art but I think it's very posh and modern.

J Yeah, that makes sense, and actually **I'm not up for** hammers and nails since I will be moving next year. However, it's kind of funny. Well, the painting is a gift from my boss and I'm having a party Saturday night for all my colleagues. You know, I just figured that he would want to see the painting on the wall.

A Okay, let's **do it** my way. First, we **need a** stud-finder!

聽力提點

1. **mind giving**

   [d] 發塞音 sotp，這個段落有非常多字尾是這樣的 [d]，請仔細聽聽看，並且嘗試發音。

2. **What do you need?**

這個 need 的尾音 [d] 因為是整句的尾音，舌頭會很短促且微弱的點一下上齒齦來發音，聽起來會跟第 1 點的 mind 有所不同。

3. **hold it**

這裡的 [d] 受到後面母音影響，又是與第 1、2 點都不同的變化，聽起來是 [houldɪt|]。最後一句的 need a 也是一樣的例子。

4. **stud-finder**
5. **stud** 第 4、5 點可以一起重聽比較。
6. **good question** 就像 good boy 一樣，[d] 發塞音 stop。
7. **I should do it** [d] 消音。
8. **do it**

單字尾音是 [u]，接續後面的母音之前要增加一個輕輕的滑音 [w]，所以這兩個字在口語中聽起來常常會是 [duwɪt]。

Ch 2

延伸聽寫 | Exercise A 解答參見第 224 頁

Track 1502

1. A Can you ①__________ __________ the hammer and those nails, please?

   B ②__________ __________ __________.

   翻譯

   A：可以請你遞給我鐵鎚跟釘子嗎？

   B：拿去。

2. A Could you spare a few minutes?

   B Sure, how ③__________ __________ help?

   翻譯

   A：能耽誤您一分鐘嗎？

   B：當然，我能幫你什麼忙嗎？

3. A ④__________ __________ __________ in such a hurry?

   B I'm rushing to the hospital to see my brother. I just got a phone call from the hospital telling me that he was hit by a car.

   A I'm so sorry. ⑤__________ __________ __________ do for you?

   B I was wondering if you could give me a lift.

A No problem! ⑥__________ __________.

翻譯

A：你怎麼那麼匆忙呢？

B：我趕著去醫院看我弟弟，我剛剛才接到醫院打來的電話說他出了車禍。

A：怎麼會這樣，我能幫你什麼忙嗎？

B：不知道你能不能載我去醫院呢？

A：當然沒問題，來吧！

實用字詞補充

1. **There you go**（在遞交東西給對方的時候說）給你

   例 A: Could you pass the salad? 能幫我把沙拉遞過來嗎？

   B: There you go. 來，給你。

2. **I was wondering if...** 表示委婉提問是否可能……

   例 I was wondering if you could buy a ticket for me.

   我在想說有沒有可能請你幫我買一張票。

3. **Could you spare a few minutes?** 能耽誤你幾分鐘時間嗎？

4. **Give someone a lift** 順道載某人一程

   例 Jim gave me a lift to school yesterday.

   Jim 昨天載我去學校。

5. **Would you mind doing...**（委婉提醒對方配合）請問你能夠做某件事情嗎？

   例 Would you mind putting out your cigarette? It's a non-smoking area.

   能夠麻煩你把香菸熄掉嗎？這邊是非吸菸區域。

6. **I figured that...** 我認為（思考過後判斷或是預期事情應該會如何發展）

   例 I figured you and Sam would want to take a break after the whole thing.

   我想說你跟山姆在這一切之後應該會想好好休息一下。

情境會話 A／翻譯

喬　許：愛麗絲，你會介意幫我一個忙嗎？

愛麗絲：當然不介意啊，你需要我幫什麼呢？

喬　許：嗯……你能幫我把這幅畫掛起來嗎？我需要你幫忙扶好它然後我可以標記位置。

愛麗絲：哇，這幅畫超重耶，你有用木頭支撐框架定位器先確認一下可以支撐的梁木位置嗎？

喬　許：你問得很好！我沒有，然後我現在覺得我應該要耶。

愛麗絲：哎，我其實也不是很常在掛這種東西，所以我們可以用你的方法做啦！你就跟我說要怎麼做就好了。

喬　許：哈哈，其實我從來沒掛過這種東西，我一開始也沒想太多，反正我覺得這應該也不會太難吧……

愛麗絲：不過，你知道你也可以就讓它斜靠在牆上就好啊！這是陳列藝術品最懶惰的方法，但是我覺得非常時髦新潮喔！

喬　許：是啊！這樣說也是有道理，而且我根本不想弄那些鐵鎚釘子的，我明年要搬家的耶，但是，這真的很好笑，這幅畫是我老闆送我的，而我這星期六晚上要辦聚會，同事都要來，我就覺得說我老闆應該會想看到他送我的禮物被掛在牆上吧！

愛麗絲：好吧，那我們就按照我的步驟來做，首先，我們需要一個木頭支撐框架定位器。

邀請與請求幫助 ②

情境概說

邀約朋友一起準備驚喜的生日派對活動。

Track 1503 J = John A = Ashley ★ 請特別注意粗體字的部分 ★

J Hey, Ashley, **what are** you doing this weekend?

A Nothing special. **Why**?

J I wanna throw a surprise birthday party for James. Do you [1]**want to** help me?

A That's cool. [2]**I'm in**. You know how much I love to scare people.

J Haha, okay, for food, should we have pizza and drinks or should we order Chinese food?

A Why don't we try Mexican food this time? There's a new one near us and I've got coupons!

J Nice!

A Oh, should we hire a live band?

J We're gonna pay for it, you know!

A Then maybe just food and some balloons!

J [3]**Good idea**!

聽力提點

1. **want to**
   這兩個字在口語上也會念成語速更快的 wanna [wʌnə]。不過要注意，若句子主詞變成 He wants to，這時候的 wants to 就算語速再快也不會變成 wanna，只有 want to 才會在口語上有 wanna 的語音變化。
2. **I'm in** 連音，[aɪmɪn]。
3. **Good idea** 連音，[gʊdaɪdiə]。

延伸聽寫 | Exercise B

➔ 解答參見第 224 頁

Track 1504

1. A Would you help me plan the farewell party?

   B ________ ________ ________! What would you like me to help you with?

   翻譯

   A：你能幫我一起籌辦歡送會嗎？

   B：我很樂意啊！你需要我幫你什麼呢？

2. If it's not too much trouble, could you ________ ________ ________ for the event?

   如果不會太麻煩的話，你能幫忙挑選歡送會的外燴嗎？

3. A Would you please ________ ________ ladder while I hang holiday decorations?

   B Happy to help!

   翻譯

   A：你能在我掛節日裝飾品的時候幫忙扶著這個梯子嗎？

   B：我很樂意幫忙！

4. A I was thinking it would be fun to have a pool party this Friday night. What do you think?

   B ________ me in.

   翻譯

   A：我在想說如果禮拜五晚上辦一個泳池派對應該會很好玩，你覺得呢？

   B：好啊，算我一份啊！

實用字詞補充

1. **farewell party** 歡送會／餞別會
2. **If it's not too much trouble,** 如果不是太麻煩的話（說在委婉請求對方幫忙之前）

   例 Sandy, if it's not too much trouble, could you help me organize these files?

   Sandy，如果不會太麻煩的話，能請你幫我整理一下這些檔案嗎？
3. **Happy to (help)**

   * 非常樂意應該是 I'm happy to help out 或是 I'd be happy to help.，口語上如果更輕鬆的對話也會簡化到 Happy to help。

例 A: Could you give me a hand? 你能幫我一個忙嗎？

B: Happy to (help). 樂意之至。

4. **be gonna do something 我會去做某事**

*gonna 就是 going to 的口語縮讀。

情境會話 B／翻譯

約　翰：艾許莉，你這個週末有要做什麼嗎？

艾許莉：沒什麼特別的啊，為什麼這麼問？

約　翰：我想要幫詹姆士辦一個驚喜的生日派對，你想幫我一起準備嗎？

艾許莉：那很棒啊，好啊我加入。你知道我有多喜歡嚇朋友吧！

約　翰：哈哈，好啦，關於吃的東西，你覺得我們應該要叫披薩跟酒水，還是要叫中國菜呢？

艾許莉：我們這次何不試試看墨西哥菜？我們附近有一家新的店耶，而且我有拿到折價卷。

約　翰：讚！

艾許莉：噢，我們要找個樂團來嗎？

約　翰：欸，是我們要付錢喔！

艾許莉：那不然就吃的跟一些氣球就好了。

約　翰：好主意。

邀請與請求幫助 ③

情境概說

關心朋友近況，並邀請她一同渡過週末假期。

Track 1505 H = Hank G = Grace ★ 請特別注意粗體字的部分 ★

H Grace, how have you been?

G Good! Everything is fine. **How about you?** I heard that you **got promoted** and became super busy.

H Yeah, I have a new boss, and a new set of peers, and I just **got a** feeling that I have something to prove…

G Well, don't push yourself too hard. You'll **get there**. You will.

H Thanks, **it's very nice of you**.

G Do you know what you need? A break from work! Hey, Jim and I are planning a weekend getaway to the mountains! You're more than welcome to join us! It should be fun.

H **Thank you for inviting me**, but I don't know. I should finish a proposal [1]**next week**, and it feels like **I am falling behind schedule**.

G Oh dear, you [2]**must come**. **I'm telling you**. [3]**Just a** weekend. **You deserve this**!

H I guess you're right! I am driving myself crazy. I should take a real break.

聽力提點

1. **next week**
   跟前面章節提過的 last night 一樣，[t] 消音以方便字與字之間的發音變得滑順不費力。
2. **must come** [t] 消音。
3. **Just a weekend** [t] 後面是母音需要連音，發彈舌音 [ṭ]。

Ch 2

延伸聽寫 | Exercise C

解答參見第 224 頁

Track 1506

1. A Excuse me, Mr. Smith, if you don't mind, please ①__________ __________ your cigarette. ②__________ __________ non-smoking area.

   B Oh, sorry. I didn't know.

   翻譯

   A：不好意思，Smith 先生，如果你不介意的話，請熄掉你的香菸好嗎？這邊是非吸菸區域。

   B：噢，抱歉，我不知道。

2. Would you be ③__________ __________ to send me those files since we are already two weeks ④__________ __________?

   能不能請你（好心一點）把這些檔案寄給我呢？畢竟我們的進度已經落後兩週了啊。

實用字詞補充

1. **have/get a feeling** 有一種感覺（不確定是真是假）

   例 I had the feeling that the security guy was watching me.

   我有種感覺，好像那個警衛一直盯著我看。

2. **Don't push yourself too hard** 不要太過強求或逼迫自己
   = Don't be too hard on yourself

3. **You'll get there.** 你最後會辦得到的

   例 Don't panic right now. Just go through the procedure step by step. You'll get there. It's not that difficult.

   現在先不要慌張，只要跟著步驟一步一步來，你最後就會做到了，沒有那麼困難。

4. **getaway** 逃跑，也被用來形容遠離塵囂的度假之旅

   例 The resort offers the ideal getaway to tiny cabins in the woods.

   這個度假村提供理想的森林小屋渡假行程。

5. **You're more than welcome to join us.** 非常歡迎你加入我們

   這裡的 welcome 不是翻成不客氣的意思，而是表示非常樂意。

6. **fall behind** 進度落後

   例 He is falling behind with his school work.

   他學校功課趕不上進度。

7. **I'm telling you**（用來強調所說的是真的）聽我說，我說的沒錯

   例 I'm telling you, Justine Chen is the best product manager in our company.

   我跟你說，Justine Chen 是我們公司最好的產品經理。

情境會話 C／翻譯

漢　克：葛蕾絲，你最近好嗎？

葛蕾絲：很好啊，一切順利！你呢？我聽說你升官了而且變得超忙碌的。

漢　克：對啊，有了新的老闆，一群新的同事，不知道為什麼我就有種感覺，好像自己一定要證明自己是值得的那樣。

葛蕾絲：不要太過勉強自己，你做得到的！一定可以的。

漢　克：謝謝，你真的很貼心。

葛蕾絲：你知道你現在需要的是什麼嗎？休息！欸，吉姆和我正計畫週末要去山上度假，非常歡迎你加入我們，一定會很好玩的。

漢　克：謝謝你邀請我，但是我也不知道耶，我下週應該要完成一份提案，然後我又一直覺得我好像進度落後耶。

葛蕾絲：親愛的，你一定得跟我們去，我跟你講的絕對沒錯，就是一個週末而已啊！這個休假是你應得的！

漢　克：我想你說的是！我已經要把自己給逼瘋了，我的確是該給自己放個假。

邀請與請求幫助 ④

情境概說

客氣並且委婉的請求別人配合。

Track 1507 C = Carter D = Debby ★ 請特別注意粗體字的部分 ★

C Debby, could you help me for a second?

D Sure, how can I help?

C It just [1]**occurred** to me that I am [2]**supposed** to [3]**meet a** client this afternoon. I **totally** forgot. It's **somewhat** urgent. Would it be too much trouble for you to **take a look at** this powerpoint?

D **Let me see**… umm, yeah, I think I can do it. **I got this.** Don't worry.

C Thank you so much. You're the best.

聽力提點

1. **occurred to me** ed 消音，to 弱讀為 [tə]。
2. **supposed to** 同上。
3. **meet a** 連音，a 弱讀為 [ə]，meet a 聽起來是 [mitə]。

延伸聽寫 | Exercise D

解答參見第 224 頁

Track 1508

1. Do you ①________ ________ ________? ②________ ________ ________ ________ some questions about the application?
你現在有空嗎？我能夠問你一些關於申請的問題嗎？

2. If you don't mind, I really ③________ ________ ________, please.
如果你不介意的話，我真的需要你幫忙，拜託。

3. ④________ ________ do me a favor? I'm moving tomorrow, and I am afraid that I couldn't **finish it on** my own.
你可以幫我個忙嗎？我明天要搬家了，我怕我沒辦法靠我自己弄完。

4. ⑤________ ________ any chance that we could reschedule our meeting

because I need more time to ⑥__________ __________ document?

不知道我們能不能改約別的時間呢？因為我需要多一點時間校對這份文件。

5. Is it possible ⑦__________ __________ __________ reschedule our meeting?

不知道你有沒有可能可以重新敲一個會議的日期呢？

6. A I have a really important presentation tomorrow, but **I've got a problem** and I ⑧__________ really use your help.

B Sure! What's the problem?

翻譯

A：我明天有一個很重要的簡報，但是我現在有點困難，我很需要你的幫忙。

B：好啊，我可以幫你啊，問題是什麼？

實用字詞補充

1. **Can you help me?**

跟 Could you help me? 的差別在於用過去式 Could 來請求或是要求會比較有禮貌一點。

2. **I could really use your help**（婉轉表達）我很需要你的幫忙

這裡的 use 不能翻作「使用」，整句話就是「我需要你，請你幫我好嗎」的意思。

3. **I got this** 交給我就好（不用擔心）

* 也可以是我來付帳的意思。

4. **occur to somebody**（想法或主意）出現在（某人）頭腦中

例 Does it ever occur to you that we are always late?

你難道從沒想過我們總是遲到嗎？

情境會話 D／翻譯

卡特：黛比，你現在有空嗎？可以幫我一下嗎？

黛比：沒問題啊！我要怎麼幫你呢？

卡特：我突然想到我今天下午應該要去見客戶的，但我完全忘記了，現在有點緊急，不知道如果我請你幫我看一下這份簡報檔案會不會太麻煩你呢？

黛比：我看一下喔，嗯，可以啊，我覺得我應該沒問題，交給我吧，不要擔心。

卡特：你最棒了，太感謝了。

延伸聽寫 Answer Keys

Exercise A

（請參考以下答案及解說，可弱讀的字詞以斜體表示。）

① hand me *the* hammer *and* those nails（[d] 消音。）

② There *you* go（you 弱讀 [jə]。）

③ *can* I（can 弱讀 [kən]。）

④ Why *are* you（are 弱讀 [ər]。）

⑤ What can I（[t] 在這裡是 stop T。）

⑥ Come on（連音，[kʌmɑn]。）

Exercise B

（請參考以下答案及解說。）

1. I'd love to（[d] 發塞音 stop d。）
2. choose a caterer
3. hold this（[d] 消音。）
4. Count me in（[t] 發塞音 stop t。）

Exercise C

（請參考以下答案及解說。 ）

① put out（[t] 跟延續的母音連音，發彈舌音 [t̬]，[pʊ t̬aʊt]。）

② It's a（連音。）

③ kind enough（連音 [kaɪndɪˋnʌf]。）

④ behind schedule（[d] 消音，behin(d) schedule。）

Exercise D

（請參考以下答案及解說，可弱讀的字詞以斜體表示。）

① have *a* minute

② Can I ask you

③ need your help

④ Could you

⑤ *Is* there（is 弱讀 [s]。）

⑥ proofread the

⑦ for you to（三個字都可以有弱讀的變化 [fər] [jə] [tə]。）

⑧ could（could 在句中想要快速帶過的時候，會弱讀 [kəd]。）

Chapter 3

習慣英語口語表達時的各種語調

聽力重點：了解並模仿基本的語音語調／重音位置為句子語意的重點

接續前幾個篇章我們介紹了母音的發音、實境口語當中常見的連音、變音、消音等發音變化，Chapter3 除了會複習前面篇章提點過的聽力重點之外，還增列許多容易搞混的子音發音規則，此部分在實際聆聽時的影響雖不如前述變化規則來得大，但是若想要能夠呈現更道地的美式發音，以下篇章的範例音檔也很值得反覆練習。

重音位置及說話過程中語音語調的改變是影響聽力理解程度的重要關鍵，外語學習者尤須特別留意對話過程當中的重音（聲音提高上揚）位置，其為語意的重點。在英文當中有實詞和虛詞的差別，實詞指名詞、動詞、形容詞、副詞等表達語意資訊的位置，虛詞（或者又稱為功能詞）則是指連接詞、介系詞、冠詞、助動詞等表示文法結構關係的位置，由此可知句子當中實詞的語音語調會是聽力時的重點。

在語句中的上升語調或說話語氣的抑揚頓挫雖然會因個人性格習慣而有所差異，但是每一種語言仍然有它基本的一個語音語調樣貌，了解並且能夠模仿這個樣貌，會是外語學習者的一大突破。本書越後面的對話段落會越長，加上語調提示的輔助標示，若能看著文本搭配音檔重複進行跟讀練習，不僅對於提升聽力理解能力有所幫助，更能強化口說時語音語調的表現。

Unit 16

・一對一面試・遠端視訊面試

・面試後續詢問

一對一面試

情境概說

原本在科技公司擔任行銷主管的 Anderson，爲了生涯規劃而去應徵一家有外派機會的公司，來聽聽他在面試過程中談了些什麼吧！

Track 1601 S = Sandra A = Anderson ★ 請特別注意粗體字的部分 ★

Conversation A-1

S **Good morning**, Mr. Wang. I am the **product manager from the key account team**, Sandra Yang.

A It's nice to meet you.

S [1]**Nice to meet you too.**

S Okay, so why don't you tell me [2]**a little** [3]**bit about yourself**?

A Sure, I am Anderson Wang and and I'm the marketing director at Aero Technology. We have been developing innovative marketing campaigns since 2017, and that's why I love chatting with people and learning more about [4]**their phone usage**.

S [5]**Thank you.**

聽力提點

1. **Nice to meet you too.**
   to 和 too 的讀音都是 [tu]，但是在句子中的介系詞 to 常會弱讀，變成 [tə]。
2. **little**
   [t] 在重音節之後，兩個母音之間，會發彈舌音 [lɪt̬əl]。其他生活常見的字像是 water，butter，都是一樣的發音現象。
3. **bit about yourself** 連音。
4. **their**
   th 會有 [θ] 或 [ð] 兩種發音，像是 their [ðer]、that [ðæt]、they [ðeɪ] 或 the [ðə] 這些字當中，th 都是發 [ð] 的音，要注意在發這個音的時候，舌尖一定要在上下兩排牙齒之間，若只是把舌尖擺到上齒齦後面，就只能發出 [d] 或 [t] 的聲音，這樣念出來的 their 聽起來會變成 deir，是不正確的。

5. **Thank** th 在此發 [θ] 的音 [θæŋk]，可以和第 4 點做比較。

Track 1602　S = Sandra　A = Anderson　★ 請特別注意粗體字的部分 ★

Conversation A-2

S **What are** your [1]**strengths** and weaknesses?

A Last year, I [2]**increased** my team's productivity and we reached the target profit goal. I appreciate the diverse perspectives that [3]**allowed** me to achieve more. I couldn't have done this without my team. So for my strengths, I would say that I'm very team-oriented.

S What about weaknesses?

A I can be too critical of everything and that has been the pattern [4]**throughout** my career. I've noticed that this kind of obsessions with details could lead to negative self-talk. Even worse, my colleagues would be influenced. [5]**Three** years ago, I decided to openly communicate with my team regarding my weakness. It was amazing that their understanding **helped me genuincly appreciate more** and recognize the value of teamwork. Gradually, I learned when to stop pushing myself too hard. We make a great team together.

Ch 3

聽力提點

1. **strength 跟 strengths**　Track 1603

   th 發 [θ] 的音時（像是 thank you），舌頭需伸出放在上下牙齒之間，發出氣音。但是當 [θ] 這個發音出現在字尾時（像是 strength [streŋθ]）就不會把舌頭伸出來發出氣音，反而是鬆鬆的放在微張的上下排牙齒之間，發出一個短的氣音，而當這個字尾後面出現 s 的時候，這個短的氣音就會快速到你以為沒有這個氣音，只會聽到尾音的 [s]。可以仔細聽一下 strength 跟 strengths 這兩個發音的細微變化。

2. **increased**

   當 ed 字尾的前面是無聲子音，像是 increased 的 [s]，ed 會發無聲子音 [t]，所以 increased 聽起來是 [ɪn`krist]，另外，實際口語也常發生 ed 被省略的現象，請留意對話中 Anderson 的回答。

3. **allowed**

當 ed 字尾前面是有聲母音或子音，ed 要發 [d] 的音，因此 allowed 聽起來是 [ə`laʊd]，但是在對話中一樣有 ed 尾音省略的現象。

4. **throughout**

thr 的發音是 [θr]，整個字是讀成 [θruaʊt]。

5. **three**

thr 對於很多人來說比較不容易揣摩發音，three [θri] 的 [θr] 發音方式其實是先讓舌尖放在上下牙齒之間，發出 [θ] 的聲音之後很快的把舌頭往後退，持續吐氣到發出 [r] 的位置發 [r] 的聲音。

Track 1604 S = Sandra A = Anderson ★ 請特別注意粗體字的部分 ★

Conversation A-3

S That's really nice. Umm, where do you see [1]**yourself** five **years from now**?

A I hope I will be [2]**working** abroad for at least three [3]**years** by then. That's not only my ideal [4]**career** path, but also why I'm here. I understand that this position is an expat job and I am [5]**prepared** for a challenging adventure.

S Glad to know that. Okay, do you have any [6]**questions** for me?

A No, thank you very much for your time.

S Thank you for coming.

聽力提點

1. **yourself**

非重音節裡面的這個 r 發 [ɚ] 的音，讀成 yourself [jɚ`sɛlf]，其他如 teacher [`titʃɚ]、paper [`pepɚ]、father [`fɑðɚ]、number [`nʌmbɚ]、other [`ʌðɚ] 也是相同發音，以都是捲舌音來比較，這個 [ɚ] 相較於第 2 點的 [ɝ]，是比較不強烈 (weak) 的捲舌音，舌頭會在口腔中間靠前的位置，放鬆的狀況下輕輕的發一個近似中文的「ㄜ」到「ㄦ」之間的聲音。

2. **working abroad**

在 working 這個單字重音節的 r 要發 [ɝ] 的音，這是清晰的捲舌音，像是中文的「而」或「兒」一樣，舌頭往口腔後方確實捲起才能發出清楚的 working [`wɝkɪŋ]，其他例子還有 her [hɝ]，girl [gɝl]、learning [`lɝnɪŋ]、person [`pɝsən]、first [fɝst]、circle [`sɝkəl] 等。

3. **year** 4. **career** 5. **prepare**

[r] 跟母音一起發音的例子，year [jɪr]、career [kə`rɪr]、prepare [prɪ`per]。

4. **question**

名詞字尾 -tion 的發音直覺上應該是念作 [ʃən]，例如 conversation [ˌkɑnvɚ`seɪʃən]，但是這裡聽起來卻是 [`kwestʃən]，發 [tʃ] 的音，其他例子像是 exhaustion [ɪg`zɑstʃən]，digestion [daɪ`dʒestʃən]，其發音規則是當 -tion 字尾前面是字母 s 的時候，會讀成 [tʃən]。請跟「延伸聽寫」的第 1 題一起比較練習。

延伸聽寫 | Exercise A

解答參見第 239 頁

Track 1605

1. I enjoyed our ①________________ about your new campaigns and ②____________ more about the **marketing** specialist ③______________.

我很喜歡我們關於您的新廣告系列的對話，並且樂於更深入了解有關行銷分析職位的訊息。

2. A Excuse me, I am Steven Chang and **I'm here to see** Samantha Kim for ④__________ interview.

B ⑤__________ __________ seat. Ms Kim will be with you ⑥__________ __________ __________.

A Thank you.

翻譯

A：不好意思，我是 Steven 張，我是來跟 Samantha 金面試的。

B：這邊坐，金小姐很快就會過來。

A：謝謝你。

3. A ⑦__________ __________ meet you. How was the traffic?

B It was good. I'm glad that the traffic was light this morning.

A Great! Why ⑧__________ __________ tell me why you are interested in changing positions?

翻譯

A：很高興見到你，一路上過來都還順利嗎，沒塞車吧？

B：都很好，我很慶幸今天早上車不多。

A：太好了！不如你先說說為什麼你想換職位呢？

實用字詞補充

1. **expat job 外派工作**

   例 The article shares tips about how to find expat jobs.

   這篇文章分享如何找外派的工作機會

2. **light traffic 交通通暢的（不堵塞的）** *heavy traffic 交通繁忙的

3. **gadgets 各種新奇的小玩意**

   例 How will gadgets change our lives in 2022 and beyond?

   各式各樣的電子新產品在 2022 年以及往後將會如何改變我們的生活？

4. **strengths and weaknesses 優缺點（優勢、劣勢）**

   例 What are your strengths and weaknesses?

   你的優點以及缺點是什麼？

5. **I'll be right with you. 我馬上就來**

   常見於職場上請對方稍等一下的禮貌招呼用語。

6. **(I'm) pleased to meet you!**

   （初次見面打招呼用語）很高興見到你，I'm 在口語上有時候會省略。

情境會話 A／翻譯

Conversation A-1

珊朵拉：早安，Anderson，我是主要客戶專案產品經理 Sandra 楊。

安德森：很開心見到你。

珊朵拉：我也很高興見到你。

珊朵拉：好，那你不如先簡單介紹一下你自己好嗎？

安德森：當然，我是 Anderson 王，我目前在 Aero 科技擔任行銷主管，我們自 2017 年以來一直在開發幾個創新的行銷項目，因而我很喜歡跟人談話，從中去了解他們日常生活中手機的使用情形。

珊朵拉：謝謝。

Conversation A-2

珊朵拉：你有什麼優缺點呢？

安德森：去年，我提升了我的團隊的工作效力，達成利潤目標，我很感謝團隊裡面不同的意見背景讓我可以有更好的表現，沒有我的團隊，我也做不到這樣的成績，所以我的優點呢，我會說，我是一個非常注重團隊合作的人。

珊朵拉：那缺點呢？

安德森：我有時候真的會對細節非常吹毛求疵，而且這個習慣在我開始工作以來就一直存在。

我自己有注意到這樣對於細節過於執著的個性是可能會導致負面的自我對話，更不好的是，我的同事也會被我的心情影響到，三年前，我決定要向我的團隊成員溝通我個性的這一部分，很令人讚嘆的是，他們的理解包容幫助我更加的重視團隊合作的價值，逐漸地，我學會如何控制自己、不要過度負面的檢討自己，團隊合作就是那麼有效的事情。

Conversation A-3

珊朵拉：那真的很好，嗯，那你覺得五年後的自己會在哪裡呢？

安德森：我希望我可以有至少三年的海外工作經驗，這不只是我理想的工作經歷，也是為什麼我今天會來這裡應徵這個職位，這個職位是一個外派的工作，我也準備好了要接受這個充滿挑戰的冒險旅程。

珊朵拉：太好了，對了，你有沒有什麼問題要問我呢？

安德森：沒有，謝謝你的時間。

珊朵拉：謝謝你來面談。

遠端視訊面試

情境概說

Leah 爲了應徵業務助理的工作而與業務主管 Jimmy 進行了遠距面試。

Track 1606 J = Jimmy L = Leah ★ 請特別注意粗體字的部分 ★

J Hi Leah, how are you?

L I'm doing great, [1]**thanks**!

J Great! Before we get started, I want to [2]**make sure** that we will be communicating effectively. So, can you see and hear me clearly?

L Yes.

J Lovely. Okay, I think Sam has told you about this job, right. It's basically an entry-level position and you will be working closely with the sales representatives in the marketing department. And you have two years experience working **in a** sales team. Umm, can you tell me about how you keep yourself motivated while supporting the whole team?

L I think that a sense of humor and being considerate are very helpful. No job is a [3]**cakewalk**. To put yourself in someone else's place actually [4]**makes a big difference**. If we all pull together, we can not only accomplish a task on time, but also do it enthusiastically.

J [5]**I like that.** It's exactly what we need here.

聽力提點

1. **Thanks**

   [k] sound 跟 [t] [p] [g] [b] [d] 為同一類塞音，但在實際口語發音上會有不同的變化。這裡的 [θæŋks] 可以聽到很輕的一個 [k]，試比較下面兩個提點中不一樣的 [k] sound。

2. **make sure**

   [k] 要跟後面的 sure 連音，但是 [k] 若要像第 1 個提點那樣發出氣音則必須中斷，無法做到跟 sure 連音。因此為了要連出滑順的聲音，[k] 在這裡會做 stop sound 的表現，聽起來像 ma(ke)sure，但其實不是真的完全刪除 [k]。

注意，若聽起來變成 masure，那就不正確了。

3. **cakewalk**

可比較兩個 [k] 的聲音。第二個 [k] 會聽到明顯的氣音。

4. **makes a big difference / make a big difference**

make 在這兩個例子中，[k] 的後面都有母音需要連音，差別在第三人稱動詞單數的 makes 是由 [s] 跟後面的 [ə] 連音變成 [meɪksə]，你會聽到輕輕的 [k] sound。但若是 make a 連音，[k] sound 的氣音會減弱縮短而跟後面延續的母音結合在一起，聽起來會有點像是 [meɪgə]，但請不要真的去發一個清晰的 [g] 的聲音。

5. **I like that.**

[k] [t] 發塞音 stop。

延伸聽寫 | Exercise B

➔ 解答參見第 239 頁

Track 1607

1. A I just graduated with a Bachelor's degree in Finance and I have been working part-time as a data analysis assistant for one year.

   B You do not mind ①__________ __________ __________, do you?

   翻譯

   A：我剛畢業，獲得了財金學士學位，我已經做了一年的兼職資料分析助理。

   B：你不介意長時間工作，是嗎？

2. A Good afternoon. Thank you for ②__________ __________ __________ to interview me.

   B Good afternoon. Have a seat, please. Did you have any trouble finding the place?

   A No, actually, I am quite familiar with this neighborhood.

   B Great! Would you ③__________ __________ introduce yourself first?

   翻譯

   A：午安，謝謝您給我這個機會來參加面試。

   B：午安啊，來，請坐，這個地方應該沒有很難找吧！

   A：其實我對這附近很熟悉。

   B：你想先介紹一下自己嗎？

實用字詞補充

1. **cakewalk**（口語）輕而易舉的事情

   例 It's no cakewalk. 這可不是什麼簡簡單單的事情。

2. **Make a big difference** 讓一切有很大的改觀，也可以用 **make all the difference**

   例 The manager's suggestions made a big difference in our proposal.

   經理給的建議讓我們的提案完全不一樣了。

3. **I'm doing great!**（禮貌回答對方的問候）我一切都好

情境會話 B／翻譯

吉米：嗨，莉亞，你好嗎？

莉亞：一切都很好，謝謝你。

吉米：很好！在我們開始之前，我想先確認一下我們等一下溝通順暢，你能清楚的看見以及聽見我嗎？

莉亞：可以。

吉米：太好了，好，我想山姆已經有告訴過你關於這份工作，這算是入門的職務，你會跟整個業務部門裡面的所有業務專員密切合作，那你有兩年在業務團隊的工作經驗，你可以跟我聊一下你是如何在支援整個業務部門的同時，還能保持自己的動力呢？

莉亞：我認為幽默感跟貼心是很重要的，沒有哪一份工作是家常便飯的簡單事情，嘗試著去站在別人的角度來思考事情其實真的會讓一切完全不同，那就是為什麼我可以幫助整個團隊團結在一起，非常有精神、有效率地完成每個任務。

吉米：我很喜歡這個說法，那恰好是我們這裡需要的特質啊！

面試後續詢問

情境概說

Samantha 在與 Mr. Cruise 面試完的隔天，打了一通 Follow up call。

🎧 **Track 1608** S = Samantha M = Mr. Cruise ★ 請特別注意粗體字的部分 ★

S Hi, [1]**Mr. Cruise**, [2]**this is** Samantha May.

C Hi, how are you, Miss May?

S I am great, thanks. I just want to say thank you for yesterday's interview. It **was** really a pleasure to meet with you. I really appreciate being considered for **this role**.

C Thanks. I enjoyed our conversation and I believe you're a cultural fit.

S Thank you. I am looking forward to hearing from you soon. **Have a great day**!

聽力提點

1. **Mr. Cruise**

   Cruise 的 s 發 [z] 的音，[kruz]。s 跟在母音或有聲子音之後常會念 [z]，可以比較一下第 2 點。

2. **This is** 兩個字連音聽起來是 [ðɪsɪz]。

延伸聽寫 | Exercise C

➜ 解答參見第 239 頁

🎧 **Track 1609**

1. I'm calling to follow up about my application to the product manager position. Thank you again for ①__________ the time to ②__________ __________ me about joining your team.

   我打電話來關心一下我之前應徵產品經理的進度，也謝謝您花時間跟我面談有關於加入您的團隊的相關細節。

2. I ③__________ __________ the hiring process can be time-consuming.

   我了解整個人員招聘過程可能是會非常耗時的。

Ch 3

3. I hope to have the opportunity to ④__________ __________ __________.

Thank you for seeing me.

我希望能有機會為您工作。感謝您與我見面。

實用字詞補充

1. **a cultural fit 與（公司的）文化契合、合拍**

例 I am sorry to say that she won't be a cultural fit.

我很遺憾的要這麼說，我想她不是跟我們公司文化那麼合拍的人選。

2. **follow up （口語）關心／追（事情發展的）進度與近況**

例 I wanted to follow up to express my interest in the position.

我想再跟您表達一下我對於這個職位的興趣。

例 The meeting is a follow-up to the one we had two weeks ago.

這個會議是我們兩週前那個會的後續會議。

情境會話 C／翻譯

莎曼莎　　：嗨，克魯斯先生，我是莎曼莎．梅。

克魯斯先生：嗨，你好嗎，梅小姐？

莎曼莎　　：我很好，謝謝您，我是為了昨天的面談跟您說聲謝謝，非常榮幸可以跟您見面並且聊聊，我非常感謝您有考慮我來擔任這個職位。

克魯斯先生：謝謝，我覺得我們的談話相當愉快，而我也覺得你跟我們公司文化是很合拍的。

莎曼莎　　：謝謝您，期待得到您那邊後續的消息，祝您有美好的一天。

延伸聽寫 Answer Keys

Exercise A

① conversation [kɑnvɚˋseɪʃən]、② learning、③ position

④ an 弱讀 [ən]、⑤ Have a、⑥ in a moment、⑦ Pleased *to*

⑧ don't you

Exercise B

① working long hours、② taking the time、③ like to

Exercise C

① taking、② talk to、③ understand that、④ work for you

Ch 3

Unit 17

辦公室社交

① 祝賀同事升遷

② 讚美同事的好表現

③ 同事間互相寒暄

④ 共進午餐

情境會話 A

辦公室社交 ①

祝賀同事升遷

情境概說

Andrew 升遷了，他的同事 Naomi 給予溫馨祝賀。

Track 1701 [N] = Naomi [A] = Andrew ★ 請特別注意粗體字的部分 ★

[N] Andrew, **congratulations on** your new appointment as product manager. **It's a** well-deserved promotion.

[A] Thanks, Naomi. I'm quite excited about it. I will be working closely with several department heads. It's a big challenge for sure.

[N] **It is**, but I think you will be doing a marvelous job.

[A] ***I appreciate it**.

[N] Hey, I mean it. What you have achieved in this department is quite something. You have made us all proud. Keep up the good work.

[A] I will! See you later.

聽力提點

***I appreciate it.**

I appreciate 是母音與母音連音的例子，當 I 這個雙母音 [aɪ] 要跟後面的母音 [ə] 連音，中間會增加一個很輕很快的滑音 [j]，聽起來就好像 I_yappreciate 一樣，這個變化是為了讓連音聽起來更滑順。此外，appreciate it 母音子音連音，[t] 要發 flap T 彈舌音。

延伸聽寫 | Exercise A

解答參見第 253 頁

Track 1702

1. ①__________ __________ your new position as product manager. All your hard work ②__________ __________ __________.
恭喜你榮升部門經理，你辛苦的耕耘終於受到肯定了。

2. I was thrilled when I ③__________ __________ your ④__________ __________ __________. ⑤__________ __________ the good work.
我得知你升遷的好消息之後，為你感到非常高興，繼續保持優異的表現喔！

3. ⑥__________ __________ your own ⑦__________!

繼續再創佳績吧！

實用字詞補充

1. **quite something** **相當傑出，令人刮目相看的**

例 He is quite something. You'll love him.

他是真的很了不起，你一定會喜歡他的。

2. **for sure** **肯定地、無疑地**

例 I know for sure that she is the one we can count on.

我很確定她就是那個我們可以倚靠的人。

3. **Keep up the good work!** **（做得很好）繼續加油**

4. **All your hard work has paid off.** **辛苦工作得到回報**

情境會話 A／翻譯

娜歐咪：安德魯，恭喜你榮升產品經理，完全實至名歸呀！

安德魯：謝謝你，娜歐咪。我自己也蠻興奮的，我之後要跟好幾個部門主管密切工作，這當然是一個很大的挑戰。

娜歐咪：是啊，但是我覺得你一定可以完全勝任沒問題的。

安德魯：很感謝你這麼說。

娜歐咪：我是認真的喔，你在這個部門做出來的成績真的是令人刮目相看的，你讓我們感到驕傲，繼續加油！

安德魯：我會的，回頭見喔。

情境會話 B

辦公室社交 ②

讚美同事的好表現

情境概說

Bella 做完簡報之後，Jay 對於她的好表現讚賞不已。

Track 1703 J = Jay B = Bella ★ 請特別注意粗體字的部分 ★

J **Bella, [1]you've certainly given us an impactful presentation.**

B (Do) you really think so? **[2]I thought it was a bit too long and I worried that you would get bored.**

J You are absolutely charismatic, you know?

B Oh, **I'm flattered**. Thank you for saying that.

J Also, I've been always interested in topics about effective transitions in a company and I particularly like the conclusion you made. Culture **does** play an important role.

B **Totally**, for some companies that I studied, it made reform more difficult than ever.

J Yeah, do you want to **grab a bite**?

B Sure.

聽力提點

Track 1704

1. Bella, you've **certainly** given us an impactful presentation.

   Bella, you've certainly given us an **impactful** presentation.

   在這個例句中，Jay 在呼喚 Bella 的名字之後，稍微停頓了一下，然後就一口氣說完 you've certainly given us an impactful presentation，這就像唱歌的換氣一樣，若我們想要提升英文聽力及口說，一定要習慣這樣的說話節奏。一個句子或是詞組 (thought group) 在停頓 (pause) 之前是不會中斷的，而這就要靠我們前面介紹過的連音、縮讀、弱讀、變音等發音技巧的發揮，才能做到一氣呵成。在這一氣呵成當中，你可以試試看先挑選一個字作為句子的重音（高音），就像爬山一樣，把這個字當作山頂，上山的聲音緩緩高升，過了山頭之後的聲音可以緩緩下滑。這裡有兩個例子，一個是以 certainly 為句子重點，下一句則是以 impactful 為句子重點，你可以跟著念念看，記得，不要中斷。

you've 縮讀

given us 子母連音 [gɪvə nəs]

us an an 弱讀 [ən]，再跟前面的 s 連音變成 [əsən]

an impactful 子母連音 [ənɪm`pæktfəl]

you've given us an impactful 整個句子聽起來是 [jəv gɪvə nəsənɪm`pæktfəl]

注意，要一氣呵成發出 impactful presentation 的技巧就是在舌頭往上齒齦頂著要發完 [l] sound 的時候不要中斷，直接把嘴唇閉上發出 [p] 的聲音，這樣就能接著把 presentation 這個字念完。

再重複練習幾次，記得沒說完這句話之前不要鬆口換氣。

2. **I thought it was a bit too long and I worried that you would get bored.**

   I thought it was a bit too long and … umm, I worried that you would get bored.

   延續第 1 點的練習，這裡的兩句話有不同的換氣位置，第一句可以一氣呵成，第二句可以因為語意上說話者有點遲疑或是在思考，and 的聲音聽起來就不一樣。第一句為了加快語速，and 弱讀成一個很輕的 [ən] sound，可以很快速的跟後面的 I 連音，聽起來是 [əndaɪ]，或者幾乎像是 [daɪ]，那個 [ən] sound 在 long 跟 I 之間變成一個輕微到幾乎讓你忘記它的存在的聲音。第二句的 and 在說話當中有了語氣延長的表現，接了語助詞「嗯」的聲音，短促停頓之後，重新開始的 I 沒有與前面連音，聽起來就是一個完整清楚的 I。試試看跟著音檔模仿練習。

Ch 3

延伸聽寫 | Exercise B

解答參見第 253 頁

Track 1705

1. ①__________ always ②__________ __________ from the crowd. I am so happy for your achievement.
   你總是那個脫穎而出的人，我為你的成就感到高興。

2. ③__________ __________ __________! I can't think of anyone else who **deserves this recognition** more than you do. Congratulations!
   做得太好了！我想不出除了你之外的任何人可以值得這份榮耀。

實用字詞補充

1. **impactful 相當有效的、有影響力的**

   例 He gave an absolutely impactful speech.

   他發表了一段絕對是非常有影響力的演說。

2. **charismatic 具有獨特個人魅力的**

   例 Few people can resist the charismatic CEO.

   很少人有辦法抵抗這個 CEO 的個人魅力。

3. **I'm flattered. 我感到受寵若驚**

   * 用在回答對方的稱讚之後，禮貌並且感謝的回應。

4. **than ever（強調）更加地**

   例 The place is dirtier than ever. 這個地方比以往還要髒。

5. **stand out from the crowd 在眾人之間脫穎而出**

   例 The delicacy of the art piece makes it stand out from the crowd.

   這件藝術品的精美使其在眾多作品中脫穎而出。

情境會話 B／翻譯

傑　：貝拉，你做了一次真的非常有力的簡報。

貝拉：你真的這樣認為嗎？我本來還想說這次簡報太長了，擔心會讓你們覺得太無聊。

傑　：你超有魅力的耶！

貝拉：你這麼說讓我受寵若驚耶，謝謝你。

傑　：還有，我其實一直都對關於組織怎麼有效轉型的主題很有興趣，而且我特別喜歡你做的結論，文化的的確確就在其中扮演了關鍵的角色。

貝拉：絕對是啊，在我研究的某些公司案例當中，文化這件事情讓改革變成難上加難。

傑　：對啊，你有想要去吃點東西嗎？

貝拉：好啊！

辦公室社交 ③

同事間互相寒暄

情境概說

Dylan 在活動聚會上巧遇公司同事，兩人輕鬆寒暄。

Track 1706 D = Dylan J = Jasmine ★ 請特別注意粗體字的部分 ★

D It's great to see you again, Jasmine.

J Hey, Dylan, happy to see you.

D How are things with you?

J I've been quite busy with our winter collection lately. How about you?

D I took a few days off and went to the mountains. [1]My **wife and I rent a lovely cabin in the woods**. No WiFi, no emails, no social media, just two of us. It's so soothing. We had some simple food, and finally read some great books.

J Wow, it sounds spiritual, but **no Wifi**? I don't know. I guess I would prefer free WiFi [2]**even if I go to the mountains for holidays**.

D Come on, you should try it sometime. Just ditch social media for a few days. [3]**Trust me, you won't regret it.**

J Alright, maybe I will!

D Um…would you like another drink?

J No, I'm fine thanks.

D Okay, I'm gonna go get myself another glass of wine.

聽力提點

1. **My wife and I**

   [f] 子音與後面的母音連音是相當好發音的，上排牙齒輕咬下唇發出 [f] sound，在吐氣的同時不要中斷，只要改變嘴型跟著發 [ənd] 即可完成滑順的連音，聽起來是 [maɪwaɪfəndaɪ]。

2. **Even if I**

   [f] sound 與不同的母音連音，一樣只要在吐氣發 [f] sound 的時候氣息不要中斷，改變嘴型發 [aɪ] sound，聽起來是 [ivənɪfaɪ]。

Ch 3

3. **Trust me, you won't regret it!**
這個例句裡面有四個 [t] sound，仔細聽聽看實際口語上的不同變化，並試著跟讀模仿。

延伸聽寫 | Exercise C

解答參見第 253 頁

Track 1707

1. ①__________ __________ __________ vacation until ②__________ __________ __________ __________ month.
他度假去了，要到月底才能回來。

2. A Oh, I ③__________ __________ to tell you. We're going to a bar tonight. (Do you) Wanna ④__________ __________?
B I wish ⑤__________ __________, but I ⑥__________ __________ work overtime to finish my proposal. Have fun!
A Okay! Well, see you next week then!
B Bye.

翻譯
A：歐，我差點忘記跟你說，我們晚上要去酒吧，你想來嗎？
B：我希望我可以啊，但是今天要加班弄完我的提案，祝你們玩得開心喔！
A：好，那我們就下週見囉！
B：掰。

實用字詞補充

1. **How are things (with you)?**
口語問候的用語，比 How are you 更隨興。

2. **ditch**（口語）甩開、丟棄
例 Did you know that Sam ditched his girlfriend?
Sam 把女朋友給甩了，你知道嗎？

3. **long weekend** 連假
例 I went camping for a long weekend.
我連假去露營。

4. **then** 在當時（過去或未來）

例 Tom was working in Taipei then.

Tom 那時候在台北工作。

5. **soothing** 放鬆舒緩的

例 It is said that classical music has a soothing effect on babies.

聽說古典樂對於小寶寶有舒緩放鬆的效果。

6. **You won't regret it!** 你不會後悔的（結果一定是像我說的這樣好的）

情境會話 C／翻譯

迪　倫：潔絲敏，很開心在這裡碰到你。

潔絲敏：嘿，迪倫，見到你真好。

迪　倫：你最近好嗎？

潔絲敏：最近都在忙我們的冬季目錄啊，你呢？都好嗎？

迪　倫：我休了幾天假，跑去山上，我跟我老婆租了一間可愛的森林小木屋，沒有無線網路，沒有電子郵件，沒有社群媒體，就是我們兩個人，超級舒心的。我們就吃很簡單的食物，然後終於可以好好的讀幾本好書。

潔絲敏：哇，聽起來很有感覺耶，但是沒有網路？我不知道耶，我猜要是我，就算去山上度假，應該還是比較想要有網路。

迪　倫：喂，你有機會要試試看把社群通通拋開，就幾天而已，相信我，你絕對不會後悔的！

潔絲敏：好吧，也許我會去試試看喔！

迪　倫：嗯，你要喝點什麼嗎？

潔絲敏：我不用喔，謝謝。

迪　倫：好啊，那我要再去拿一杯酒！

情境會話 D

辦公室社交 ④

共進午餐

情境概說

Lily 和 David 是同事，這天中午他們一起吃午餐並閒聊……。

Track 1708 L = Lily D = David ★ 請特別注意粗體字的部分 ★

L Wow, I'm full. The cheeseburger was so good.

D Yeah, I'm glad that we picked the right one.

L We should thank google. Those reviews are quite helpful, don't you think?

D Totally, but sometimes that can be really tricky.

L Why?

D Well… like a garden salad is always tasty for you but for me, it's just a salad.

L Haha, **got you**. By the way, are you looking forward to the party after work **tonight**?

D Oh, my boss told me that she would bring her [1]**chocolate** cake!

L Hooray! Her chocolate cake is the best I've ever had.

D Wow, [2]**I'll tell her that you love it!** She **will be** really pleased.

L Oh, no. I think I need a piece of chocolate cake right now. Hey, do you want to take a short walk?

D Sure! Um, there's a new Cafe on Vincent Street! My friend has tried their chocolate cake. I heard it was good. We should go!

L Wow, **it sounds nice!** Excuse me, **may I have the check, please**?

D Oh, **it's on me this time**, Lily.

L No, no, no. I got this.

D Hey, let's not argue about this, okay! You can buy me a coffee later.

L **Deal**! Thank you.

聽力提點

1. **chocolate**

   聽到的是 choc(o)late，而不是 [tʃɑkələt]，[ə] 這個 schwa sounds（非重讀的母音）被省略了，就像 camera 要念 cam(e)ra，而不是 [ˋkæmərə]。

2. **I'll tell her that you love it!**

   [h] sound 在口語當中常會因為連音而被省略，你在這裡聽到的不是 [tel] [hɝ]，而是 [telɚ]。

延伸聽寫 | Exercise D

解答參見第 253 頁

Track 1709

1. You don't need to pay. I'll ①__________ __________ __________ the bill.
   你不用付錢，我來付就好。

2. It's your birthday. I can't ②__________ __________ __________! ③__________ __________ __________. It's my treat!
   是你生日耶，怎麼能讓你出錢，我買單，這頓我請。

3. Please don't argue with me. Let me ④__________ __________ __________ __________ this time.
   別跟我爭啦，這次就讓我請客吧！

實用字詞補充

1. **hooray** 表達開心的語助詞

   例 Hip, hip, hooray!
   耶～耶～萬歲！

2. **I got this!**（口語）我來處理就好 * 或是 I've got this!

   例 A: Let me pay!
   我來付帳啊！
   B: Grandma, I got this!
   奶奶，我處理就好啦！

情境會話 D／翻譯

莉莉：哇，我吃超飽的，起司漢堡超好吃的。

大衛：對啊，我很慶幸我們選對了餐廳。

莉莉：我們該感謝 Google，那些評論真的是蠻有幫助的，你不覺得嗎？

大衛：我同意，但是有時候又可能有點尷尬！

莉莉：為什麼啊？

大衛：因為……，像是，花園沙拉，你怎麼吃都覺得很美味，但是我就真的覺得，不就是沙拉而已嗎。

莉莉：哈哈哈，懂。對了，晚上的派對，你會很期待嗎？

大衛：哦，我老闆跟我說，她會帶她的巧克力蛋糕來耶！

莉莉：太棒了！她的巧克力蛋糕是我吃過最好吃的。

大衛：哇，我會跟她說的，她知道了一定很開心。

莉莉：噢不，我覺得我現在就需要來一塊巧克力蛋糕了，嘿，你想要散個步嗎？

大衛：當然好啊！文森街上有一家新開的咖啡屋，我朋友吃過他們的巧克力蛋糕，聽說很不錯，我們就去吧！

莉莉：哇，聽起來很棒！不好意思，我們要買單！

大衛：莉莉，這次讓我請客吧！

莉莉：不用啦，我自己付我自己的啊。

大衛：我們不要爭這個啦，好嗎！那你等一下可以請我喝咖啡啊。

莉莉：一言為定，謝謝你啦。

延伸聽寫 Answer Keys

Exercise A（請參考以下答案及解說。）

① Congratulations on

② has paid off

③ heard about

④ well-deserved promotion（消音。）

⑤ Keep up the good work.（[p] 受到後面母音的影響，連音時會變成像是比較輕聲的 [b]。但並不是真的刻意很清楚的發出一個 [b] 的聲音。）

⑥ Keep breaking（[p] 跟 [b] 的發音嘴形相近，可以很輕鬆的連音，只要做好發 [p] 音的嘴型準備，但是不要把 [p] sound 的氣流送出口腔之外，稍微憋一下，非常短暫的一下，然後接著發 [b] 的音。）

⑦ records（[d] 消音。）

Exercise B（請參考以下答案及解說。）

① You 弱讀 [jə]。

② stand out（連音。）

③ Good for you（[d] 要發 stop sound，for 在這裡是弱讀 [fər]。）

Exercise C（請參考以下答案及解說。）

① He is on

② the end of the month（第一個 the 因為後面接母音而發 [ði]，第二個 the 因為後面是子音開頭所以弱讀成 [ðə]。）

③ almost forgot（跟句尾的 [t] 不一樣，第一個 [t] 消音。可以重聽幾次，跟著念念看。）

④ join us

⑤ I could

⑥ need to

Exercise D

① take care of、② let you pay、③ I got this、④ pick up the tab

Ch 3

加值學更多！

想知道在茶水間遇到同事該怎麼聊嗎？
線上下載更多聽力技巧練習，隨時想聽就聽！

Unit 18

- 會議開場：介紹貴賓
- 會議開場：說明議題
- 會議中的小插曲
- 會議的協商與溝通
- 會議總結與散會

會議開場：介紹貴賓

Track 1801 ★ 請特別注意粗體字的部分 ★

Alright, since everyone is here, **let's get started**. Good morning, ladies and gentlemen, on behalf of Aero Technology, I would like to welcome our guest, [1]**who** [2]came **all** the way from London. She is not only an award-winning writer, **best known** for her **work on** Netflix, A Secret Diary, but also a successful entrepreneur. Everyone, **please join me in welcoming**, Jane Lee.

聽力提點

1. **who**
   語速很快的時候會只聽見很輕短的氣音。
2. **came all the way from London**
   came all 母音和子音連音，聽起來是 [keɪmɑl]。

延伸聽寫 | Exercise A

解答參見第 268 頁

Track 1802

1. Glad to ①__________ __________ __________ today.
   很開心今天看到大家。
2. ②__________, we'd better start. ③__________ to our first monthly meeting of 2022.
   那麼，我們應該要開始囉！歡迎大家參加 2022 年的第一場月會。
3. Okay, let's begin. It's a pleasure to welcome everyone to our ④__________ meeting.
   好，那我們就開始吧！非常高興在此歡迎大家來參加我們的年會。
4. I ⑤__________ __________ __________ start by welcoming our new product manager, Smith Wang.
   我們先掌聲歡迎我們的新任產品經理 Smith Wang。
5. ⑥__________ __________ __________ for attending today. We have a lot to

cover today, so we really should begin.
謝謝大家今天出席會議，今天討論事項蠻多的，所以我們現在就開始吧！

實用字詞補充

1. **On behalf of someone 謹代表（某人、某公司、某組織等）**

   例 On behalf of the marketing department, I would like to thank you for your hard work. 我謹代表整個行銷部門，對於您的努力耕耘表示感謝。

2. **Come all the way from 從……遠道而來**

   例 The representative came all the way from New York.
   那位代表遠從紐約而來。

情境會話 A／翻譯

好的，既然大家都到了，那我們就開始吧。女士先生們，早安，我代表 Aero Technology 歡迎來自倫敦的貴賓，她不僅是一位屢獲殊榮的作家，在 Netflix 製作廣為人知的《祕密日記》，她還是一位相當成功的企業家。各位，請跟我一起歡迎 Jane Lee。

會議開場：說明議題

Track 1803 ★ 請特別注意粗體字的部分 ★

Let me begin by **welcoming you all** to the second meeting for this quarter. The purpose of this meeting is to review certain issues proposed by department **heads**. As you [1]**can** see on the agenda, we have four main topics today, and most importantly, we have to go over the financial figures released this morning. However, we only have forty minutes and we have [2]**a lot to** cover. So, let's begin with our first item.

聽力提點

1. **As you can see...**
   can 這個字當名詞時不會弱讀，例如在 a can of tuna（鮪魚罐頭）中，你會聽到清楚的母音 [æ]。但是 can 當助動詞時常會有弱讀的現象，比如說在這個句子當中 As you can see 的 can 聽起來不僅是弱讀成 [kən]，而且語速也比較快，聲音短促。
2. **We have a lot to cover.**
   兩個 [t] 子音相連，發後面的 [t]，此外，to 在這裡又是一個很常見的弱讀發音 [tə]，一連串聽起來是 [əlɑtə]。

延伸聽寫 | Exercise B

解答參見第 268 頁

Track 1804

1. A The meeting should have ended at 3:00. Where is Jack?
   B Umm, Jack is not here right now. ①__________ __________ __________ help you?
   A Can you help me to send these files to our clients?
   B Yes, ②__________ __________.

翻譯

A：那個會應該三點就要結束了啊，Jack 人到哪裡去了啊？

B：嗯，Jack 現在不在，那我能幫忙你什麼嗎？

A：你能幫我把這些檔案寄給我們的客戶嗎？
B：我可以，沒問題。

2. I have ③__________ __________ meeting in order to give us a chance to ④__________ __________ proposed campaigns. We will be discussing two main topics. 我召開這個會議是為了讓大家有機會可以逐一審視這些活動提案，我們將針對兩個主題進行討論。

3. The reason ⑤__________ __________ __________ tonight is to decide which candidate would be able to join our Asia project.
今天開會的主要目的是決定哪一位候選人可以加入我們的「亞洲企劃」。

4. Let's ⑥__________ __________ __________ at the production budgets on the agenda.
我們看一下議程表上的生產預算。

5. We are here today to ⑦__________ __________ decision on the winter campaign strategy.
我們今天是要拍板定案冬季活動的策略。

實用字詞補充

1. **Go over something 仔細審查、查看**
   例 We have to go over the details of the contract.
   我們必須把合約的細節都仔細看過一遍。

2. **Should have + 過去分詞的句型表示對於應該要發生卻沒有按照預期發生的情形**
   例 They should have arrived. Can anyone call them again to make sure they are alright? 他們應該早就要到了才對啊，誰可以打個電話給他們確認他們都安好嗎？

情境會話 B／翻譯

首先，歡迎大家參加本季第二次會議。本次會議的目的是商討部門負責人提出的幾個問題。正如您在議程上看到的那樣，我們今天有四個主要議題，最重要的是，我們必須審視今天上午發布的財務數據。但是，我們總共只有 40 分鐘，而且還有很多要討論的內容。因此，我們開始討論第一個議題。

會議中的小插曲

情境概說

Jim 在會議中想就前一個議題發表更多意見，但遭到主席和其他與會者阻止……。

Track 1805 [C] = Chair [J] = Jim [L] = Laura [S] = Sandy ★ 請特別注意粗體字的部分 ★

[C] Okay, let's **move on** to the next item.

[J] Excuse me, **can we get back to the previous item**? **I'd like to comment on the issue of customer complaint response**.

[C] Let's just deal with the commercial plans right now. We can further discuss other concerns later.

[J] **I understand**, but I believe no matter how fancy our commercial plan will be, the project cannot succeed if we don't hire additional staff. It seems to me that we focus too much on our marketing campaigns…

[L] Sorry, the way I see it…

[J] Excuse me, can I finish what [1]**I was saying**?

[L] To be honest, I don't think that optimizing customer calls and emails that account for 6% of our cost gives a fair representation of the…

[S] No offense, but I think you should let Jim finish first. Also, I'm not sure I see how this relates to our agenda.

[C] Ladies and gentlemen, let me stop you there for just a moment. Although what you're talking about is interesting, it isn't something we have time to delve into today. And I [2]**have to** remind you that we **have to** finish this in 20 minutes and we still have a lot to cover, so let's **leave it here**, okay?

聽力提點

1. **I was saying**

   was 在口語中常會被弱讀成 [wəz]，而不會讀 [wɑz]。這是母音 [ɑ] 變成 schwa sound 的現象。

2. **I have to**

have to 表示「必須」(must) 的意思時，通常不會弱讀 [ə]，這裡發音聽起來是 [aɪ hɑf tu]。

延伸聽寫 | Exercise C

解答參見第 268 頁

Track 1806

1. A **Does anyone else have ideas to add?** If not, **that** ① __________ __________ **to the end of the last item.**

   B Excuse me, can I say something here? We can't ② __________ __________ introduce another product line at this moment.

   翻譯

   A：有誰想要補充的嗎？沒有的話，那我們就進行到最後了。

   B：不好意思，我想說一下，我們這個時候無法負擔另外一個產品線。

2. A ③ __________ __________ for item four. And let's move on to the next topic.

   B Sorry, may I interrupt? I do agree with Mike that our department has spent too much money on advertisements. However, I just want to ④ __________ __________ __________ we don't have a **debt** problem and we have increased our revenue. I don't think the cost **should be an issue here**, right now.

   A Let me make sure ⑤ __________ ________________ what you're saying.

   翻譯

   A：第四項討論就進行到這邊，我們開始進行下一個主題的討論。

   B：抱歉，我打個岔！我同意麥可說的，我們部門的確花費太多錢在廣告上面，但是我只是覺得我們現在沒有債務問題，也增加了營收，我不覺得成本對於現在的我們來說會是一個需要拿出來討論的問題。

   A：先讓我確認一下我沒有誤會你的意思。

3. A Let's leave it there.

   B Excuse me, ⑥ __________ __________ __________ __________ __________ the topic of reducing the cost? I think we need to finish that first.

   翻譯

   A：我們就先討論到這邊。

   B：不好意思，我們可以回到降低成本的話題嗎？我覺得我們應該要把這個部分討論完。

4. I hate to interrupt but I wanted to let you know ⑦__________ __________ __________ leave the meeting early.
很不想打斷大家，但是我想說我必須要提早離開。

5. I'm so sorry to interrupt but ⑧__________ __________ __________ say something here.
我很抱歉打斷大家，但是我想插個話。

6. Sorry, I don't ⑨__________ __________ be rude but may I interrupt quickly?
抱歉，我無意冒犯，但是我能很快的插個話嗎？

實用字詞補充

1. **It seems to me that** 我認為
2. **the way I see it** 我認為
3. **I can't follow you** 我聽不懂你想表達的意思
4. **Let me stop you there**（非禮貌的用法）請停止發言
5. **Sorry, may I interrupt?** 抱歉我可以打個岔嗎？
6. **account for**（在數量上）佔

   例 Smartphones account for about 7% of web traffic now.
   智能手機目前約佔網絡流量的 7%。

情境會話 C／翻譯

主席：好的，讓我們繼續討論下一個議題。

吉姆：不好意思，我們可以回頭談談上一個議題嗎？我想就客戶投訴回覆這個部分發表一點意見。

主席：讓我們現在先聚焦在我們的商業計劃上。稍後可以進一步討論其他問題。

吉姆：我知道，但是我相信，無論我們的商業計劃多麼理想，如果不增加人力，我們這個專案無法成功。在我看來，我們過於專注於營銷活動……

蘿拉：對不起，我的看法是……

吉姆：不好意思，能先讓我講完嗎？

蘿拉：說實話，我認為優化占我們成本 6% 的客戶電話和電子郵件並不能代表……

珊蒂：我想您應該讓吉姆說完他要說的。此外，我不確定我是否知道這與我們的議程有何關係。

主席：女士先生們，我必須停止你們繼續發言。儘管你們正在談論的事情是很好的，不過我們今天沒有時間去深入討論。我要提醒你們，我們必須在 20 分鐘內結束這個會議，但我們還有很多事情要討論，所以這個部分我們先緩一下好嗎？

會議的協商與溝通

情境概說

針對公司該優先推出新產品還是將原來的產品升級，與會者展開了激烈的討論……。

Track 1807 S = Sandra A = Anderson V = Vivian L = Lucas ★ 請特別注意粗體字的部分 ★

S In my opinion, I think we should spend more time doing research before we jump to conclusions.

A I see your point, but I'm afraid to say that if we really want to remain competitive, we cannot wait for even two weeks. It's a critical moment for our company.

S According to my experience, if we rush into the market at this time, we would have a budget deficit next quarter.

A I follow you. However, I believe if we don't launch new products, we will lose our chance forever.

S I [1]**completely** disagree. **The most important thing** for us this quarter should be upgrading our products. And to do that, we [2]**definitely** need to do more research. There's…

A I'm so sorry for interrupting but I'd like to make sure I understand you [3]**correctly**. Do you mean that our priority is doing research **instead of** entering the U.S. market?

S I'm not sure what you mean.

V May I add something quickly? It seems to me that we are talking about an either-or situation here, which is not making sense at all.

L Excuse me, we need to finish this meeting in ten minutes. Can we move on to the last item?

聽力提點

1. **completely**

   發音是 [kəm`plitli]，聽起來像是 completly，t 後面的 e 沒有發音。
2. **definitely** 發音聽起來是 [defənetli]，後面的 e 沒有發音。
3. **correctly** 聽起來是 [kə`rek(t)li]，就像 correc(t)ly 一樣。

延伸聽寫 | Exercise D

➲ 解答參見第 268 頁

Track 1808

1. I'm ①__________ __________.

   我同意你說的。

2. ②__________ __________ __________ __________ __________, but could you explain more about the ③__________ __________ our budge deficit?

   我明白你的意思，但是你能針對預算赤字的問題再解釋詳細一點嗎？

3. ④__________ __________ rephrase that?

   你能換個方式重新闡述一次嗎？

4. We seem to be ⑤__________ __________ __________. I don't think we can **reach a deal** unless you agree to lower the price.

   我們似乎陷入僵局。我不認為我們有辦法做成這筆交易，除非你同意調降價格。

5. We can't ⑥__________ __________ condition. If I agree to lower the price, **would you make concessions**?

   我們無法滿足你開出來的條件。如果我降低價格，你能夠做出讓步嗎？

6. Can you ⑦__________ __________ reasonable offer? I will be able to place a large order if we can both be more flexible.

   你能提出一個比較合理的價格嗎？我會願意大量訂購，如果我們彼此都願意更有彈性一點。

實用字詞補充

1. **jump to conclusions** 貿然或是過早下定論

   例 Don't jump to conclusions. Let's give them some time.

   不要太早下決斷，我們給他們多一點時間吧！
2. **I see your point** 我明白你的意思
3. **either-or situation**（只能）二擇一的情況

例 It's unfortunately an either-or situation. It's so sad that we can't do both.
很遺憾這是一個二選一的狀況，真糟糕我們無法兩個都選。

情境會話 D／翻譯

珊卓拉：我認為，在得出結論之前，我們應該花更多的時間進行研究。

安德森：我明白您的意思，但是我要說的是，如果我們真的想保持競爭優勢，我們根本連兩個星期都不能等。現在對我們公司來說是關鍵時刻。

珊卓拉：以我的經驗來說，如果我們現在進入市場，下個季度將會出現預算赤字。

安德森：我懂您的意思。但是，我相信，如果我們不讓新產品上市，我們將永遠無法搶先商機。

珊卓拉：我完全不同意。對我們來說，本季最重要的事情應該是將我們的產品升級。為此，我們當然需要做更多的研究。有……

安德森：很抱歉打斷您，但我想確保我沒有誤解您的意思，您是說我們應該優先考慮研究這一塊而不是加緊打進美國市場嗎？

珊卓拉：我不確定您現在這麼說的用意為何？

薇薇安：我可以很快說一下嗎？在我看來，我們在這裡談論的是一種「二選一」的情況，這其實沒有什麼道理……

盧卡斯：對不起，我們需要在十分鐘內結束這次會議。我們可以討論最後一個議題了嗎？

會議總結與散會

Track 1809 ★ 請特別注意粗體字的部分 ★

Thanks for all your contributions today and thankfully we not only efficiently **came up with a couple of** solutions, but also [1]**reached the** consensus on the retirement plan. Does anyone have any questions? If not, let's [2]**call it a day**.

聽力提點

1. **reached the consensus**
   reached 如果單獨一個字，按照規則，在有聲子音字尾 [tʃ] 之後的過去式字尾 ed 會發 [d] 的聲音，但是這裡因為是在句子中連音，受到後面 the 的影響，非正式口語情境當中 ed 的聲音會省略掉。
2. **call it a day**
   對於非母語使用者來說，當母音、子音一組一組跟著連音的時候，會比較不容易模仿，建議放慢速度，不要中斷換氣來練習，等熟悉了之後再加快語速即可。

延伸聽寫 | Exercise E

➔ 解答參見第 268 頁

Track 1810

1. If there's no further suggestions, we'll __________ __________ for today. Thank you.
   如果沒有其他進一步的建議，我們今天就到這邊，謝謝大家。

2. Let's __________ __________ the main points again.
   我們把主要的討論問題走過一遍。

3. Let me just __________ briefly.
   我很快簡要地說明一下。

4. Thank you for your proposal. It sounds like our __________ __________. I'll take a closer look at this and let you know tomorrow. Thanks for coming.
   謝謝你跟我們介紹你的方案，聽起來似乎是我們最安全的選擇了。我會仔細研究一下，明天告訴你。感謝你的到來。

實用字詞補充

1. **Let's call it a day.**（結束活動、會議、工作等等的當下可以說的輕鬆句子）今天就到此為止吧）

   例 Okay, everybody is tired and I don't think we can finish it today. So, let's call it a day. See you tomorrow. 好吧，大家都累了，而且我想我們今天也無法完成它，那我們今天就先到這裡吧，明天見。

2. **best bet** 最安全可靠的辦法

   例 Believe me! Our best bet would be taking a bus.
   相信我，所們最好的選擇就是搭公車。

情境會話 E／翻譯

感謝大家今天的貢獻，值得高興的是，我們不僅有效地提出了一些解決方案，而且還就退休計劃達成了共識。有人還有其他問題嗎？如果沒有的話，那我們會議就進行到這裡。

延伸聽寫 Answer Keys

Exercise A（請參考以下答案及解說。）

① see you all、② Well、③ Welcome、④ annual

⑤ would like to（[l] sound 放在單字開頭時的發音比較簡單，只需要把舌頭擺放至上齒齦後方的位置，有點像是中文「ㄌ」的位置，但是舌頭並不需要像發「ㄌ」那麼用力，以 like 這個字為例，只需要輕輕地從上齒齦後方滑下來，跟著發母音 [aɪ] 就可以。）

⑥ Thank you all

Exercise B（請參考以下答案及解說。）

① How can I（can 弱讀 [kən]。）

② Yes, I can.（我們前面舉過幾個 can 弱讀為 [kən] 的例子，但是，如果 can 是用在 I can. 這個簡答的句子當中就不會被弱讀，而應讀成 [kæn]。）

③ called this、④ go through、⑤ we are here、⑥ have a look、⑦ make a

Exercise C（請參考以下答案及解說，可弱讀的字詞以斜體表示。）

① brings us、② afford to、③ That's all、④ point out that

⑤ I understand（母音 [aɪ]，後面會增加一個很輕的滑音 [j]，聽起來像是 I yunderstand。）

⑥ *can* we go back to、⑦ I have to、⑧ I'd like to、⑨ mean to

Exercise D（請參考以下答案及解說，可弱讀的字詞以斜體表示。）

① with you（若要表達聽不懂對方說的可用 I'm not with you.）

② I see what you *mean*、③ problem of、④ Could you

⑤ in a deadlock、⑥ meet your、⑦ make a

Exercise E（請參考以下答案及解說。）

1. stop here
2. go over（兩個母音相連，語氣不中斷的情況下，你會聽見 o 這個聲音稍微有點拉長。）
3. recap
4. best bet（best 的尾音 [t] 消音。）

加值學更多！

你知道視訊會議的 small talk 都聊些什麼？

線上下載更多聽力技巧練習，隨時想聽就聽！

Unit 19

- 撥出電話的開場白
- 接聽電話的開場白
- 轉接電話：對方忙線中
- 轉接電話：不知道確切的洽談對象
- 代接電話

撥出電話的開場白

Track 1901 W = Woman M = Man ★ 請特別注意粗體字的部分 ★

W Good morning, Titan Technology. How [1]**may I help you**?

M Hello. This is Joe Parson from Impact Company. May I speak to Ms Kim, please?

W I'm sorry. [2]**Ms Kim is on another** line. Is it okay with you if I put you through to her secretary?

M Yes, please.

W [3]**Just a moment**, please.

聽力提點

1. **may I help you?**
   may [meɪ] 的母音是 [eɪ]，口語連音的時候，在下一個單字字首的母音之前要增加一個輕短的滑音 [j]，所以 May I 兩個字聽起來會像是 May yI [meɪ jaɪ]。
2. **Ms Kim is on another line.**
   母音子音連續幾次連音的練習。這裡的 Ms Kim is 若只有連音而沒有縮讀，聽起來是 [mɪs kɪmɪz]，口語上也常常有縮讀的例子，聽起來就會是 [mɪs kɪmz]。此外，[z] 的音要繼續跟 on 及後面的 another 母音字首連音，聽起來是 [mɪs kɪmɪzɑnə`nʌðɚ laɪn]。
3. **Just a moment.** 子音和母音連音，[t] 發彈舌音。

延伸聽寫 | Exercise A

解答參見第 281 頁

Track 1902

1. A Hello, Jack Smith Design Vice President's office. ①__________ __________ __________ help you?

   B Hello. This is Jane Parson. ②__________ __________ __________ __________?

   A Yes. Just a moment, please.

翻譯

A：您好，傑克史密斯設計副總辦公室，有什麼我能為您效勞的嗎？

B：嗨，我是珍．帕森，李先生在嗎？

A：他在，請稍等一下。

2. A Volunteer For Taiwan. How may I ③__________ __________ __________?

B Hi, I would like to speak to David Brown, please.

翻譯

A：Volunteer For Taiwan，請問您電話要轉哪一位？

B：嗨，我想找大衛．布朗，麻煩你。

3. A Good morning. This is Steven Davis calling from Dream Salon. Could I speak to Lily Carson?

B She's on the phone right now. Can I ④__________ __________ __________ __________?

翻譯

A：早安，我是 Dream Salon 的史蒂芬 · 戴維斯，我找莉莉．卡森，她在嗎？

B：她現在正在電話中，您可以在線上稍等一下嗎？

4. A Marketing Department. This is Jessie Jones. How may I help you?

B Hi, this is Jack Miller. Is Alan available?

A Yes, let me ⑤__________ __________ through.

翻譯

A：市場行銷部，我是潔西．瓊斯，很高興為您服務。

B：嗨，我是傑克．米勒，請問艾倫在嗎？

A：他在，我幫您轉接。

5. A Golden Design. How may I assist you?

B Hello, is Shirley Wang in?

A I'm sorry, she is not in the office. Would you like to ⑥__________ __________ __________?

翻譯

A：Golden 設計，請問有什麼我能為您服務的嗎？

B：嗨，請問王雪莉在嗎？

A：抱歉，她現在不在辦公室，您要留言嗎？

Ch 3

6. [A] Thank you for calling Watson Industry. How may I direct your call?

[B] ⑦______________ 120, please.

[A] Please hold.

翻譯

A：謝謝您致電 Watson 企業，請問您要轉接哪一個分機號碼呢？

B：請幫我轉接分機 120。

A：幫您轉接，請不要掛斷。

實用字詞補充

1. **put someone through** 幫（來電的）人轉接電話

   例 Could you put me through to marketing department, please?

   請幫我轉行銷部好嗎？

2. **on hold**（不掛斷電話）等待

   例 Can I put you on hold? 你不要掛斷電話，等一下可以嗎？

   * 或是簡短一點的 Please hold.

3. **May/Could/Can I speak to ...**（打電話的時候開場問）我想找……

4. **extension** 分機

   例 When you call, ask for extension 120.

   你打過去的時候，請總機幫你轉分機 120。

5. **in the office** 在辦公室

   例 Jackie is not in the office at the moment.

   傑克現在不在辦公室。

情境會話 A／翻譯

女：早安，Titan 科技公司，請問需要什麼服務呢？

男：嗨，我是 Impact 公司的喬 · 帕森，麻煩請幫我轉接金女士。

女：很抱歉，金女士現在通話中，我幫您轉接給她的祕書好嗎？

男：好的，麻煩你。

女：請稍待一下。

接聽電話的開場白

Track 1903 B = Ben J = Jackie ★ 請特別注意粗體字的部分 ★

B Hi, Eagle Consultant. How can I help you?

J May I speak to Ben Simpson?

B Speaking.

J Hi, Mr. Simpson. This is Jackie Williams calling **about the order that you** *__placed last week__.

聽力提點

***placed last week**

placed 的過去式動詞字尾 ed 跟在無聲子音 [s] 後面發 [t]，但是在口語中加快語速的時候被省略，last 的尾音 [t] 是因為受到後面單字字首為子音的影響而消音。

延伸聽寫 | Exercise B

➔ 解答參見第 281 頁

Ch 3

Track 1904

1. A Hello, I'd ______ ______ ______ ______ Mr. Simpson.

   B This is he.

   翻譯

   A：嗨，我想找辛普森先生。 B：我就是。

2. A Good morning. Moonlake travel agency.

   B I'd like to speak to Bradley May.

   A I'm sorry. Nobody ______ ______ ______ works here. May I ask what number you were calling?

   B Umm, can I check the number I've got... is that not 22632288.

   A The number is right, but there's no one named Bradley here.

   B Sorry, I'll check the number again.

翻譯

A：Moonlake 旅行社，早安您好。

B：我想找布拉德利．梅。

A：抱歉，我們這邊沒有這個人喔，請問一下您撥的電話是幾號呢？

B：嗯，我找一下，電話號碼是 22632288 嗎？

A：電話號碼是對的，但是我們這邊沒有布拉德利這個人耶。

B：那抱歉，我再確認一下。

3. A Hello, is Jason Burg in?

B Yes, he's in. May I ________ ________ who's calling, please?

A This is Mike Cole from Fasto supermarket.

翻譯

A：哈囉，傑森．伯格在嗎？

B：他在，能請教您貴姓大名嗎？

A：我是 Fasto 超市的麥可．柯爾。

實用字詞補充

1. **speaking** 我就是（這是 **This is** 某人 **speaking** 的簡短說法）

例 This is Simpson speaking.

我就是 Simpson 先生。

2. **place an order** 下訂單

例 If you place an order today, we could give you 5% discount.

如果你今天就下訂，我們可以給你 5% 折扣。

情境會話 B／翻譯

班　：嗨，Eagle 顧問公司，請問有什麼我能為您效勞的嗎？

傑克：我想找班．辛普森。

班　：我就是。

傑克：嗨，辛普森先生，我是傑克．威廉斯，我打來是想告訴您有關於您上週下的訂單。

轉接電話

對方忙線中

Track 1905　W = Woman　M = Man　★ 請特別注意粗體字的部分 ★

W [1]**Good afternoon. Fox International**.

M Good afternoon. I'd like to speak to Lisa Johnson. This is James Miller of Mason Corporation.

W No problem, please hold and I'll put you through.

W Sorry, the extension is busy. Would you mind holding? Or, [2]**would you like to leave a message?**

M Yes, could you ask Ms Johnson to return my call?

W Sure. May I have your phone number?

聽力提點

1. **Good afternoon. Fox International.**
   在電話接待禮儀當中，為了營造企業的形象，電話上的抑揚頓挫常常會更加清晰明顯，這裡短短四個字，兩個重音位置落在 good afternoon 的第一個連音段落，第二個重音位置落在公司的名字 Fox，然後聲音緩緩降低直到 international 的尾音 [l]。當然，這種重音的位置會因為情境或是說話者的選擇而有不同。
2. **Would you like to leave a message?**
   Would you 如果在生活中與熟人對話、語速加快的時候可能會變得很短促且兩個都會弱讀、連音變成 [ədʒu] 這樣一個很短的聲音，但是在電話禮儀中，反而常會因刻意地咬字清晰而聽到 would [wʊd]。

延伸聽寫 | Exercise C

➔ 解答參見第 281 頁

Track 1906

1. A ①__________ __________ like to call back or be put on hold?
   B Umm, ②__________ __________, thanks.
   A Okay, I'll put you on hold.

Ch 3

翻譯

A：您要再來電還是要在線上等一下呢？

B：嗯，我等一下好了，謝謝。

A：好的，請稍待一下不要掛斷。

2. A Sorry, the line is busy. ③__________ __________ __________ she is not available right now.

B Can I leave a message for Ms Watson?

翻譯

A：抱歉，她正在忙線中，現在無法接聽您的電話。

B：那我可以留言給華森小姐嗎？

3. A Vice President ④__________ __________ __________ __________. Would you like to hold?

B I'd like to leave a message ⑤__________ __________ __________.

翻譯

A：副總電話中，請問您要在線上稍等一下嗎？ B：如果方便的話，我想留言。

4. A Sorry, she is out today. Would you like to leave a message?

B I'll ⑥__________ __________ again tomorrow morning. Thank you.

翻譯

A：抱歉，她今天外出喔，你要留言給她嗎？

B：我明天早上再打過來好了，謝謝你。

實用字詞補充

1. **on the phone** 通話中

例 Jimmy is on the phone all day. 吉米整天都在電話中。

2. **Someone is not available**（電話情境中表示）某人不在位置上或是無法接電話

3. **May I put you on hold?**（讓對方在線等待之前的禮貌提問）你介意稍等一下嗎？

情境會話 C／翻譯

女：午安您好，這裡是 Fox 國際。

男：午安，我想找麗沙．強森，我是 Mason 公司的詹姆斯．米勒。

女：沒有問題，我幫您轉接。

女：抱歉，她的分機忙線中，您介意在線上等待一下嗎？還是您要留言呢？

男：好，麻煩你轉告強森小姐，請她回撥電話給我。

女：好的，能請問您的電話號碼是幾號呢？

轉接電話

不知道確切的洽談對象

Track 1907 W = Woman M = Man ★ 請特別注意粗體字的部分 ★

W Hello. Eagle Consultant. **How can I help you**?

M Hi, umm, could I speak with the person **who takes care of** *<u>**advertisements**</u>, please?

W Sure. May I have your name, please?

M Yes. Tom, Tom Benson from Walker Magazine.

W Thank you, Mr. Benson. You'll be speaking to Cynthia Lee. If the call doesn't go through, you can reach her direction at 22345678.

聽力提點

***advertisements**

這個字很多人會念成 adevertisement，等於在 [d] 之後多了一個 schwa sound [ə]，聽起來像有個中文「的」的音，這樣是不正確的。這裡的 [d] 要 stop，不需要刻意發出聲音，而字首的 a 發 [æ]，重（高）音節在 tise。

Ch 3

延伸聽寫 | Exercise D

➔ 解答參見第 281 頁

Track 1908

1. A Good morning. Watson Company.

   B Could you put me through to the ____________ ____________, please?

   翻譯

   A：Watson 企業您早。

   B：可以幫我轉接業務部相關人員嗎？

2. Could you please connect me with the person __________ __________ __________ __________ organizing charity events?

   可以幫我轉接負責慈善活動的相關人員嗎？

3. I would like to transfer you to our ______________ ______________. Is that okay with you?

   我幫您轉接市場行銷部門好嗎？

4. Could you put me through to the ________ ________, please?
請幫我轉接公關辦公室好嗎？

情境會話 D／翻譯

女：哈囉，Eagle 顧問，請問需要什麼服務嗎？

男：嗨，我想找負責廣告業務的人洽談。

女：沒問題，請教您貴姓大名？

男：我是湯姆，Walker 雜誌的湯姆．班森。

女：謝謝你，班森先生，這邊幫您轉接辛西亞李，如果電話沒有接通，您可以撥 22345678 這個號碼。

代接電話

Track 1909 W = Woman M = Man ★ 請特別注意粗體字的部分 ★

W Good morning, Customer Service, this is Lucy Carlos. How may I help you?

M Hello. This is James Parson from Impact Company. May I speak to Mr. Lee, please?

W I'm sorry. **He's away from his desk at the moment**. [1]**Can I help?**

M Umm, no, I just need to talk to Mr. Lee.

W Can you call back later or can I take a message?

M Actually, umm, would you mind? Could you tell him that James Parson called and that I will be [2]**in my office** till five if he could call me back?

W May I take your number, please?

M Yes, it's 0911268268.

W Okay, is there anything else I can help you with?

M No, that's all for now. Thank you very much for your help. Bye.

W Have a nice day. Bye.

Ch 3

聽力提點

1. **Can I help?**
   [n] 跟後面的母音連音時會有很輕短的、類似中文「ㄋ」的聲音，[kə naɪhelp]。
2. **in my office**
   當母音跟母音連音，前方母音是 [aɪ] [ɪ] [eɪ] 的時候，中間要增加一個輕短的滑音 [j] 來作為下一個單字的開頭音，但不能過於突兀。例如這句聽起來會很像 in my yoffice [ɪn maɪ jɑfɪs]。

延伸聽寫 | Exercise E

解答參見第 281 頁

Track 1910

1. A Good afternoon, finance department.
   B I'd like to speak to Luna Adams. Is she available?
   A I'm sorry. Ms Adams ① __________ __________ __________. She will be

back next Friday. Can I ②__________ __________ __________?

B I need... (background noise)... if she can...(background noise)

A Excuse me, I am having a little difficulty hearing you. Can you ③__________ __________ __________?

翻譯

A：午安，財務部。

B：我找盧娜．亞當斯，請問她在嗎？

A：抱歉，亞當斯小姐休假中，她下週五才會進辦公室，要幫您留言嗎？

B：我需要……（雜音）如果她可以的話……（雜音）

A：不好意思，我聽不太清楚你的聲音，能麻煩您說大聲一點嗎？

2. I need to transfer your call to the consumer service department ④__________ __________ __________ __________ answer your question.

我必須先把你的電話轉給客服部門，這樣他們可以一一回答你的問題。

實用字詞補充

1. **in the office** 在辦公室

（介系詞 in 用於表示一個空間，in 表示在裡面、在其中。）

例 If you need me, I will be in my office. 如果你要找我，我會在我的辦公室裡。

2. **at the office** 在辦公室

（介系詞 at 用於表示一個地點、位置）

例 Let's meet at the office, what do you think? 不如我們就在辦公室碰頭吧？好嗎？

情境會話 E／翻譯

女：早安，顧客服務部，我是露西．卡洛斯，請問需要什麼服務嗎？

男：哈囉，我是 Impact 公司的詹姆士．帕森，麻煩請找李先生。

女：抱歉，他離開位置喔，有什麼我能替您效勞的嗎？

男：嗯，沒關係，我是需要跟李先生洽談一下。

女：那您要晚一點再撥過來，還是要幫您留言給李先生呢？

男：那就……麻煩您了，請您轉告他詹姆士．帕森打電話過來，然後我今天五點以前都在辦公室，如果他可以的話回電給我。

女：請教您的聯絡電話是？

男：喔，我的電話是 0911268268.

女：好的，還有什麼其他我能為您服務的嗎？

男：沒有，這樣就可以了，非常感謝你的幫忙，再見。

女：祝您有美好的一天，再見。

延伸聽寫 Answer Keys

Exercise A（請參考以下答案及解說。）

① How may I

② Is Mr. Lee in?（Lee 的尾音 [i] 跟後面 in 的母音字首 [ɪ]，連在一起念的時候只要稍微拉長一下 Lee 的尾音，接著發 in 的尾音 [n]，加上這句話是問句，所以 [n] 的尾音要往上揚。）

③ direct your call（t+y 連音會變成 [tʃ] 的音，your 弱讀為 [jər]，整個句子聽起來是 [daɪrek tʃər kɔl]，句尾的 [l] 要記得將舌頭抵住上齒齦才算發音完整。）

④ put you on hold

⑤ put you

⑥ leave a message

⑦ Extension（[t̬] 發彈舌音。）

Exercise B（請參考以下答案及解說。）

1. like to speak to
2. by that name
3. tell him（[h] 被省略，聽起來是 [telɪm]。）

Exercise C（請參考以下答案及解說，可弱讀的字詞以斜體表示。）

① Would you、② I'll wait、③ *I'm* afraid that、④ is on the phone

⑤ if it's alright、⑥ call her（[h] 被省略，[l] 跟 er 連音，聽起來是 [kɑlɚ]。）

Exercise D（請參考以下答案及解說。）

1. sales department
2. who's in charge of（連音。）
3. marketing department
4. PR office

Exercise E

① Ms Adams is on vocation.、② take a message

③ please speak up、④ so that they can

加值學更多！

關於「敲定會議時間」的對話情境、更多聽力技巧練習，線上下載，隨時想聽就聽！

Ch 3

Unit 20

- 商展——產品介紹
- 商務接待
  - ① 接待分公司同事
  - ② 公司導覽
  - ③ 介紹、引介

商展——產品介紹

情境概說

腳踏車銷售員正在向潛在客戶介紹公司產品的優勢，創造銷售機會。

Track 2001 S = Sales C = Potential customer ★ 請特別注意粗體字的部分 ★

S Hi, are you **tired of** carrying your bike upstairs?

C Haha, kind of, but **I thought it is what it is**.

S Have you ever **heard of** the Breeze 2000, the lightest bike in the world?

C Wow, it sounds cool, but no, I've never heard of it.

S Let me show you something that would blow your mind. Here's the Breeze 2000. It's an ideal bike for anyone looking for reliability and comfort in a city bicycle. The heart of the Breeze 2000 is a hand-made, light weight carbon fibre dual suspension frame which soaks up bumps on bumpy roads. It's just 200 US dollars and if you place an order today, you can get this limited-edition [1]**water bottle**. A startup founder just bought [2]**ten bikes** for all her employees. They want to encourage cycling. Anyway, did you get your free neck gaiter?

C Um, I don't think so.

S Here you go. Our tube-shaped accessory is so comfortable and chic. Although it's most commonly worn around the neck, it can also be worn many other ways, as a scarf, a hood, or even a hat.

C This is really nice. Thank you so much.

聽力提點

1. **water bottle**
   複合名詞的重音會落在修飾用的名詞上，以 water bottle 為例即會落在說明這個「瓶子」的功能為裝水之用的 water 這個字，聽起來會是 [ˋwɑtɚ bɑtəl]，而不會是 [wɑtɚ ˋbɑtəl]。
2. **ten bikes**
   當字尾是 [n]，後面若接雙唇音開頭的字會產生語音同化現象，[n] 會變成

[m]，所以這裡的 ten bikes 會變成是 tem bikes。這樣的變化主要也是為了讓口語發音時有滑順的聲音效果。

延伸聽寫 | Exercise A

解答參見第 294 頁

Track 2002

1. We're a leading manufacturer of thermal insulation fabric. With __________-__________-__________-__________ technology, we're changing the way we view clothes.
   我們是保暖布料製造商，憑藉最先進的技術，我們正在改變我們看待衣服的方式。
2. Our company was founded in 2000 and we are very proud of our ve-gan snacks made from all-natural, organic ingredients. __________ __________ like some?
   我們的公司成立於 2000 年，我們為全天然有機成分製成的純素食小吃感到自豪，你想要嚐嚐看嗎？
3. Are you having trouble getting your __________ __________ shinny and clean? This video presentation must make you excited about our new prod-uct, easy-clean kitchen sink. We export our products primarily to Europe and United States.
   您是否感覺到讓廚房水槽保持光澤和清潔感是很困難的？這個影片展示一定會讓您對我們的新產品——易潔淨廚房水槽——感到興奮和期待！我們的產品都出口到歐洲和美國這些地區。
4. Are you looking for camp cookware that's light but durable? We use titanium when other companies are still using aluminum or iron. __________ __________ __________ revolutionary.
   您在尋找輕便耐用的露營炊具嗎？當其他公司還在使用鋁或鐵的時候，我們已經使用鈦這種材質了，這讓我們具有劃時代意義。

Ch 3

實用字詞補充

1. **blow someone's mind**（口語）讓某人感到相當驚艷或是驚訝
   例 The ending of the movie really blew my mind.
   電影的結局讓我感到太震撼了。
2. **bumpy** 顛簸的

例 They drove along a bumpy and narrow road.

他們開在一條又窄又顛簸的路上。

3. **chic 時髦的、雅緻的**

例 I like your new bag. It's very chic.

我喜歡你的新包包，很時髦耶。

4. **limited edition 限量款**
5. **wholesaler 批發商**
6. **retailer 零售商**
7. **supplier 供應商**
8. **middleman 中間商**
9. **state-of-the-art 最先進的**

情境會話 A／翻譯

銷售業務：嗨，要把腳踏車搬上樓是不是讓你感到很厭煩啊？

潛在客戶：哈哈，大概吧，但是我以為這件事情不就只能如此嗎！

銷售業務：您有沒有聽說過世界上最輕的自行車 Breeze 2000 ？

潛在客戶：哇，聽起來很酷耶，沒有，我沒有聽說過 Breeze 2000。

銷售業務：讓我來向您展示一些會讓您大吃一驚的東西。這就是 Breeze2000。它是想要在城市自行車中尋求可靠性和舒適性的任何人心目中的理想自行車。Breeze 2000 有純手工製作的輕質碳纖維雙懸架，可吸收最崎嶇不平道路上的顛簸。一輛才 200 元美金，而且如果你今天就下訂單，你還可以得到這款限量版的水壺。有一家新創公司的老闆剛剛才買了十輛給所有員工，他們大概要鼓勵騎自行車吧，無論如何，您剛剛有沒有拿到免費贈送的多用途圍巾？

潛在客戶：嗯，沒有喔。

銷售業務：來，這個給你。我們的這個配件非常舒適而且很別緻。雖然通常大家是戴在脖子上啦，但其實還有很多其他種配戴方式耶，例如變成圍巾啦，頭巾甚至帽子。

潛在客戶：這很棒耶。非常謝謝你。

商務接待 ①

接待分公司同事

情境概說

邀請來公司訪查的分公司同事共進晚餐。

🎧 **Track 2003** A = Adam S = Stacy ★ 請特別注意粗體字的部分 ★

A Hi, Stacy, how's your day?

S Oh, thanks for asking, it's very good.

A *__Since you are around this weekend, some colleagues and I are going to try the new sushi place, and we were hoping you would join us for dinner.__*

S How nice! I love sushi so much. Of course, I'll be there.

A Great! See you later.

S Later.

聽力提點 🎧 Track 2004

*Since **you** are **around** this **weekend**, **some colleagues** and **I** are going to **try** the **new sushi place**, and **we** were **hoping you** would **join us** for **dinner**.

句子中重音 (sentence intonation) 的細節會因為每個人說話語調甚至是腔調而有抑揚頓挫的差異，但是大方向會是一致的，例如「虛字」（介系詞、助動詞、be 動詞、代名詞、連接詞等）通常不會是重音的位置。請跟著音檔念念看，念到虛字的時候音量是較低弱、小聲而輕快帶過的，而相對於虛字的「實字」是句子裡的重要資訊，在這裡用粗體表示，這些字的重音節聲音會相對高昂一點（以色字表示），速度也會慢一點點，另外記得要連音，除非是斷句的位置才能換氣。如何在長句子當中斷句換氣，請看以下分析說明：

① Since you are around this weekend, 標點符號可以停頓一下。

② some colleagues and I / and ... 主詞比較長的時候，在動詞之前會有一個很迅速的稍微停頓。

③ and we were hoping you would join us for dinner 連接詞之前也會稍微停頓一下。

Ch 3

延伸聽寫 | Exercise B

➜ 解答參見第 294 頁

Track 2005 請圈出句子當中「實詞」，並且搭配音檔進行跟讀練習。

1. Do you have any plans on Tuesday evening? Would you like to have dinner with Jimmy and I? My treat.
   你星期二晚上有約嗎？您想跟吉米和我共進晚餐嗎？我請客。
2. We are going to grab a bite! Do you want to join us?
   我們要去吃點東西！你想要一起來嗎？
3. How about we get some dinner after our meeting on Thursday? I know a great Korean BBQ. What do you say?
   星期四開會後我們去吃晚飯怎麼樣？我知道有一家很棒的韓國燒烤，你覺得呢？

實用字詞補充

1. **See you later 再見**
   * 不是「真的等一下會再碰面」的意思，不要因為中文直翻「待會見」而誤會，口語上就是再見的意思。
2. **Later 再見** *see you later 的更隨興、更簡短用法。
3. **What do you say? 你覺得呢？**
   例 A: What do you say we go grab a bite and catch a break?
   我們何不去吃點東西然後休息一下呢？
   B: Okay, it will be a long day. Let's get some coffee and dessert too.
   好啊，今天將會是很漫長的一天啊，我們也來點咖啡跟甜點吧！
   A: Good idea. 好主意。
4. **My treat. 我請客**

情境會話 B／翻譯

亞　當：嗨，史黛西，你今天過得怎麼樣？

史黛西：噢，謝謝你關心我，今天都很好。

亞　當：既然你這個週末還會在，我和一些同事要去試試看一家新的壽司店，我們希望你能和我們一起吃晚餐。

史黛西：太好了！我非常喜歡壽司。我當然要去的。

亞　當：太好了！回頭見。

史黛西：好喔。

商務接待 ②

公司導覽

情境概說

帶客人參觀公司及介紹產品特色。

Track 2006 S = Sales C = Potential clients ★ 請特別注意粗體字的部分 ★

S Please follow me this way. Let me show you our new UV & Sun-Resistant fabric. Have you seen our lab? In this video, you can see how we test our fabrics to make sure what kind of fabrics can effectively shield us from harmful UV radiation.

C Oh, I heard of it. You expose fabrics to UV rays… um… it's something called… hours to… fade…

S "Sun fade testing".

C Yeah, that's it! "Sun fade testing"

S [2 3 4]**Our fabrics are tested in a lab using special UV lights, and we then can know** [1]**how long it takes to show a noticeable color change**.

Ch 3

聽力提點 Track 2007

1. **and we then can know / how long it takes / to show a noticeable color change...**

   接續前一個對話提到的「斷句換氣」位置除了有「比較長的主詞之後」、「連接詞之前」、以及「標點符號」之外，還有像是這個例句中「子句」的位置及「介系詞」的位置前，通常也會輕短的停頓一下。

2. **斷句換氣的位置**

   我們用「/」來表示輕短的停頓：Our fabrics are tested in a lab using special UV lights/, and we then can know/ how long it takes/ to show a noticeable color change.

3. **句中出現實詞的位置**

   句子當中實詞的位置用粗體字來表示，而套色字標示該字的重音音節（念這些字的時候把音調拉高，自然會產生語音語調的抑揚頓挫）：Our **fabrics** are **tested** in a **lab** using **special UV lights,** and **we** then **can know how long** it takes to show a noticeable color change.

4. **語調重音**

除了前述的語音語調規則之外，**語調重音也是一個必須突破的重點**。語調重音的位置通常在每一次換氣之前的最後一個重音節，這個重音節要在起始點的位置提高音量，而且這個高音要比前面的語調重音節都要來得高，然後開始下降，關鍵是在最後要微微上揚。要在結尾微微上揚的原因是表示句子還沒有真正結束。

我們把「語調重音」用底線標示出來，最後直到「句尾」語調才會完全下降：

Our **fabrics** are **tested** in a **lab** using **special UV lights,/ and** we then **can know/ how long it takes/** to **show** a **noticeable** color **change./**

延伸聽寫 | Exercise C

解答參見第 294 頁

Track 2008 請用「/」來標記斷句換氣的位置，並且搭配音檔練習跟讀。

1. Would you like to see our winter collection displays, or would you like to have a cup of tea first?

   您要看看我們的冬季特選展示呢，或是您想要先來杯茶？

2. Please go along the hallway, and then you will see the smoking lounge on the left side.

   請沿著這條走廊走下去，然後你會看到吸菸室在您的左手邊。

Track 2009 請圈出句子中實詞的位置，並且搭配音檔練習跟讀。

3. Please turn left at the smoking lounge and take the elevator to the sixth floor.

   請在吸菸室那邊左轉，然後搭電梯到六樓。

4. Turn left after the restroom and take the stairs to the third floor.

   看到洗手間之後，往左邊走，然後接著走樓梯到三樓。

Track 2010 請用「/」來標記換氣位置並把句子中實詞重音的音節圈出來，語調重音的位置以底線標示，並且搭配音檔練習跟讀。

5. The thermal fabric lab is on the other side of the building.

   保暖纖維實驗室在大樓的另外一側。

6. The guest lounge is just around the corner.

貴賓休息區就在轉角那邊。

實用字詞補充

1. **go along the corridor 沿著走廊走下去**

   例 Don't worry. You just go along the corridor and the guest lounge is on the left side. You can't miss it. 別擔心，你只要沿著這個走廊走下去，貴賓休息室就在你的左手邊，很好找的。

2. **You can't miss it! 很容易找到的**

   例 Go to the next traffic light and make a right. You can't miss it.
   到下一個紅綠燈右轉，很醒目的，你一定找得到的。

3. **smoking lounge 吸菸室**

   * 或是 smoking area、smoking room、smoking cabin

情境會話 C／翻譯

業　　務：請往這邊走。讓我向您展示我們最新的抗紫外線和防曬布料。你看過我們的實驗室嗎？在這個影片當中，您可以看到我們如何測試布料以找出哪些布料能夠最有效的隔絕紫外線，不會傷害到我們人體。

潛在客戶：喔，我有聽過，你們會把布料拿去曝曬在紫外線下，那個叫做什麼啊？

業　　務：「耐曬試驗」。

潛在客戶：沒錯，我想說的就是這個。

業　　務：我們的布料在實驗室中進行特殊的紫外線測試觀察，然後我們才可以知道說一塊布料要產生顏色變化需要多長時間。

商務接待 ③

介紹、引介

情境概說

在商務場合要介紹人們彼此認識的時候，可以簡單記得一個原則，就是將「職位較低」那一方先介紹給「地位較高者」，而且在開始介紹之前，要先稱呼職位較高者的職位或是姓名。

Track 2011 J = Jonathan C = Ms. Chen ★ 請特別注意粗體字的部分 ★

J Good morning. Ms Chen.

C Nice to see you again, Jonathan. You look great today.

J Thank you, Ms Chen. Please follow me this way.

J **Ms Chen, I would like you to meet Sally May, our visitor from Family Supermarket. Ms May, this is our Vice President, Ms Chen.**

聽力提點

句中出現語調重音（高音）的位置以底線標示。【語調重音通常在換氣之前的最後一個重音音節，這個音會比其他字的重音高。需要留意的是語調重音也可能不在最後一個字上，而是要看說話者想強調的資訊在哪裡。】

Ms Chen,/ I would like you to meet <u>Sally May,</u>/ our visitor from <u>Family</u> Supermarket./ <u>Ms May,</u> /this is our <u>Vice President,</u>/ Ms Chen.|

延伸聽寫 | Exercise D

解答參見第 294 頁

Track 2012 請以「/」標示換氣位置，並且仔細聽有底線位置的語調重音。

1. Allow me to introduce myself. I am Harper Chen, the General Manger of Family Supermarket in Taiwan.

   請容我自我介紹，我是 Harper Chen，Family 超市的總經理。

2. I don't think we have met before. I am Vicky Song, a photographer for Impact magazine. It's an honor to meet you. What you have done for those underprivileged children is remarkable.

我想我們之前沒有見過，我是 Impact 雜誌的攝影師 Vicky Song，非常榮幸見到您，您替那些弱勢孩童所做的貢獻很令人崇敬。

實用字詞補充

This is... 這位是……

例 Mr. Stevens, this is Sammy Huang, one of our clients from Singapore. Sammy, this is my boss, Mr. Stevens.

史帝文斯先生，這位是黃小姐，我們在新加坡的客戶之一。珊米，這位是我老闆，史帝文斯先生。

情境會話 D／翻譯

強納森：早安，陳女士。

陳女士：強納森，很開心見到你，你今天看起來精神奕奕呢！

強納森：謝謝您，陳女士，請跟我來。

強納森：陳女士，我來介紹一下，這位是 Family 超市來參訪我們公司的莎莉梅。梅女士，這是我們的副總，陳女士。

延伸聽寫 Answer Keys

Exercise A（請參考以下答案及解說。）

1. state-of-the-art
2. Would you（連音 [wʊdʒə]。）
3. kitchen sink（這個複合名詞的重音跟前面提到的 water bottle 不一樣，因為 kitchen 是地點，而地點當中的某樣物品，兩個字都會是重音，聽起來是 [ˋkɪtʃənˋsɪŋk]。）
4. This makes us

Exercise B（實詞會用粗體字標示。）

1. Do you have any **plans** on **Tuesday evening**? Would **you like** to **have dinner** with **Jimmy** and **I**? My **treat**.
2. **We** are going to **grab** a **bite**! Do **you want** to **join us**?
3. **How about we get** some **dinner** after our **meeting** on **Thursday**? **I know** a **great Korean BBQ**. **What** do **you say**?

Exercise C（請參考以下答案及解說。）

▶ 斷句換氣位置以「/」來標示

1. Would you like to see our winter collection displays/, or/ would you like to have a cup of tea first?
2. Please go along the hallway/, and then you will see the smoking lounge/ on the left side.（標點符號、介系詞之前通常會稍微停一下。）

▶ 句子中實詞的位置以粗體字標示

3. **Please turn left** at the **smoking lounge** and **take** the **elevator** to the **sixth floor**.
4. **Turn left** after the **restroom** and **take** the **stairs** to the **third floor**.

▶ 實詞重音音節以套色字標示，語調重音以底線標示，換氣位置以「/」標示

5. The thermal fabric lab/ is on the other side of the building./
6. The guest lounge/ is just around the corner./

Exercise D

1. Allow me to introduce myself.| I am Harper Chen,/ the General Manger of Family Supermarket in Taiwan.|
2. I don't think/ we have met before.| I am Vicky Song,/ a photographer for Impact magazine.| It's an honor/ to meet you.| What you have done for those underprivileged children/ is remarkable.|

⊕ 加值學更多！

線上下載更多聽力技巧練習。

接待外國客户不可少的邀約客户餐敘、以及在餐廳用餐時的 small talk 通通給你，隨時想聽就聽！

Ch 3

Unit 21

在這個人人都可以是 youtuber 的時代，觀看 youtube 影片已成爲許多人的日常。所以追蹤自己喜歡的主題，邊看邊練習英文聽力也是很不錯的方式！現在就一起進入幾個頻道，熟悉一下 youtuber 們常用的語言吧！

・星座命理・美妝教主・瑜珈

・時間管理妙方・美味廚房

Youtuber A 星座命理

Track 2101 ★ 請特別注意粗體字的部分 ★

Debby: Hey there, everyone, what's up! What's going on! It is Debby, the Healing Tarot Reader, welcome back to my channel. Before we get started, I do want to give a **huge** shout out to my sponsor Daily Vibe…, you guys know how much I love Daily Vibe, I have my own personal subscription for like three years, if you have never heard of Daily Vibe before… Daily Vibe is a one of the best audio entertainments you can have. I always listen to audiobooks while I am cooking or taking a shower. What I like the most about Daily Vibe is that they also have classes that everyone can join. And last month Daily Vibe just launched its new membership, the Daily Vibe Premium. You can enjoy ad-free TV shows, comedies, and a whole new level of entertainment **choices**. If you sign up for a monthly subscription now, you will save 20%. Okay, without further ado, today's astrological prediction is all about good things, guys. Good things are coming to you. Here's the horoscope **message** you need to hear for the end of January, 2022, based on your **zodiac** sign.

聽力提點

choice / message / huge 比較 zodiac

字尾不發音的 e 會讓 c [k] 跟 g [g] 變成發音比較輕的 [s] 跟 [dʒ]。例如這裡的 choice 會念成 [tʃɔɪs] 而不是 [tʃɔɪk]；message 會念成 [mesɪdʒ] 而不是 [mesɪg]。

延伸聽寫 | Exercise A

解答參見第 312 頁

Track 2102

請用「/」標記斷句換氣的位置、底線標示語調重音、「|」表示句尾尾音下降，並且搭配音檔練習跟讀。

Hello! My loves! Welcome back to my channel. Today's video is a new pick-a-card reading. This one is your monthly, January of 2022, future prediction. I'm so excited about it right now. You can see we have five piles of cards here and you can take a moment or even pause the video if you like. If you are new here, don't worry. Just pick the pile that you feel strongly drawn toward! After you pick the pile, you can just scroll down to the description box to find the time stamps to watch your personal reading for the month of January.

翻譯

哈囉，親愛的，歡迎回到我的頻道，今天的影片呢是新的抽牌讀牌，是針對你 2022 年 1 月的每月運勢預測喔。我現在對此感覺非常興奮，你可以看到這邊有五疊牌卡，你可以稍待一下或是先暫停影片也可以，如果你是第一次看我的影片呢，不要擔心，就是看看哪一疊牌卡你覺得感覺有一股吸引力，就選那疊！選好之後，你就可以往下滑看資訊欄那邊，你可以找到時間軸，觀賞屬於你的 1 月份個人運勢預測喔。

實用字詞補充

1. **horoscope 星座運勢**

   例 I read my horoscope most days.
   我大多數日子都會看一下自己的星座運勢。

2. **Pick-a-card reading 大衆塔羅占卜**

   例 This is a free pick-a-card reading. You just need to follow your intuition, not your eyes, and pick a pile of cards that you feel most powerfully drawn to.
   這是免費的大衆塔羅占卜，你只需要跟著自己的直覺，而不是用眼睛看，你可以挑選其中一疊感覺對你最有吸引力的卡片。

3. **zodiac sign 星座**

   例 12 astrological signs, also called zodiac signs, include Aries, Taurus, Gemini, Cancer, Leo, Virgo, Libra, Scorpio, Sagittarius, Capricorn, Aquarius and Pisces.
   黃道十二宮，也稱為十二星座，包括白羊座，金牛座，雙子座，巨蟹座，獅子座，處女座，天秤座，天蠍座，射手座，摩羯座，水瓶座和雙魚座。

4. **Without further ado 廢話不多說，馬上、立刻**

   例 Without further ado, let me introduce tonight's guest, Justine Cole.
   我們廢話不多說，馬上來介紹今天晚上的貴賓賈斯丁．科爾。

5. **shout-out （口語）在媒體上向某人、某公司表達敬意**

   例 I would like to give a big shout-out to *Funtime Magazine*.
   我想向《歡樂時光雜誌》表達感謝。

6. **subscribe 訂閱**

Youtuber A／翻譯

黛比：嘿，大家好！都還好嗎？我是塔羅牌療癒師黛比，歡迎你們今天回到我的頻道，在我們開始之前，我想要謝謝我的贊助商「活力每天」，你們都知道我超喜歡「活力每天」，如果你沒有聽過「活力每天」，我本身訂閱「活力每天」也有三年啦……「活力每天」真的是你可找到的最好的音樂娛樂平台之一。我都是在做飯或洗澡時聽有聲書，我最喜歡「活力每天」的地方是，他們也有各種課程可以參加，上個月呢，「活力每天」推出了新會員方案「活力每天」白金版，你可以享受無廣告打擾的節目、喜劇以及全新的多樣娛樂選擇，如果你現在就訂閱，可以有八折折扣。好啦，廢話不多說，今天的運勢預測都是關於好事要發生的，大家，好事要來了，以下就是大家在 2022 年 1 月底需要聽到的 12 星座運勢預測。

美妝教主

Track 2103 ★ 請特別注意粗體字的部分 ★

Kathy: Hello, everyone, welcome to my channel, if you are new here, my name is Kathy Lin, for todays' video, I'll go over my best makeup tips for you guys to not just make sure your eyebrows are wonderfully structured for your face, get perfect skin and make everything look good, but also to look amazingly good in person. I feel like every time I run into some subscribers, they often comment about my make up, saying "wow, I am so surprised that your makeup actually looks so good in person". Okay, a good rule of thumb is a healthy and fresh complexion! A lot of people are so obsessed with perfect light porcelain skin but they end up with a "makeup cake face", a thick cakey layer of makeup. You don't want that, alright! Yes, we all have blemishes on our faces, no big deal, so the point is how we layer our makeup in a smart and proper way. **Okay**, [1]**I'm gonna go** with the Estee Lauder Double Wear foundation today. Why I love it so much is because it's vey watery. About foundation, a useful rule of thumb is less is more. Oh, wait, [2]**I haven't shared with you** how to choose your foundation. Alright, everyone of us has a skin tone and an undertone. For example, my skin tone is medium. That is obvious and easy for everyone to figure out, but the tricky part is figuring out your skin's undertone. First, there are three traditional undertones, warm, cool, and neutral. Some people may wonder why we have to make things so complicated. Well, basically, our undertone isn't the same thing as the color of our naked skin before we put on foundation, which means that even the fairest skin can have a warm undertone.

Ch 3

聽力提點

1. **I'm gonna**

縮讀 (reduction) 是口語當中很常見的現象，I'm gonna 是 I'm going to 簡化而來，不過在輕鬆而快速的對話當中，I'm gonna 有時也會再縮減為 I'muna，甚至連開頭的 I 都幾乎不見，聽起來剩下很輕快的一個 muna 的聲音。

2. **I haven't**

否定字尾縮寫的讀法 (n't contraction)。這裡聽起來不會是 [aɪ ˋhævənt] 這麼清晰的聲音。首先，haven't 這個否定字尾 n't 的 [n] 只會是一個很短的舌尖鼻音，要發好這個聲音，舌尖會輕輕往前，有點像要發出中文狀聲詞「嗯」或注音符號「ㄣ」，差別是中文的「嗯」比較像 [ʌn]，「ㄣ」比較像 [ɛn]，但字尾 [nt] 的 [n] 只有短短的鼻音，上下顎的嘴型並沒有改變。可以試著把嘴巴閉起來發一個微弱的鼻音，然後再微微把嘴巴張開發音。這裡的尾音 [t] 是 stop T，所以 haven't 聽起來是 [ˋhævənt]。此外，[h] 會被省略掉，字首的 [aɪ] 也變得輕而短促。

延伸聽寫 | Exercise B

解答參見第 312 頁

Track 2104

Youtuber: Hello, today, ①__________ __________ __________ doing an everyday super glowing skin makeup tutorial. I mean, radiant skin, radiant, guys! Also, today's video is in partnership with Zoca Classic. One of the reasons I love Zoca so so so much, I mean, they have a variety of makeup brands. ②__________ __________ a huge fan for a long long time. So, super excited to be partnering with them using the Benefit hyper glow palette that I've been using almost everyday, just love it, love it! Okay, I also use Giorgio Armani Luminous Silk foundation. You can totally feel the difference. You will be able to keep your skin super hydrated.

翻譯

網紅：大家好啊，今天呢，我要分享一個讓你每天像在發光一樣而且看起來健康好氣色的化妝教學，我是說，容光煥發的皮膚，容光煥發喔，大家！還有啊，今天這支影片是跟 Zoca Classic 合作的，我非常喜歡 Zoca，其中一個原因就是他們什麼化妝品牌的產品通通都有，我一直是 Zoca 的忠實粉絲，因此，今天非常開心可以合作，也會使用這款我幾乎每天都在用的 Benefit 超炫光彩妝盤，我超愛，超愛它的！好喔，我等一下也會用 Giorgio Armani Luminous Silk 粉底，你會感覺到它效果完全不一樣，你可以讓皮膚超水潤。

實用字詞補充

1. **in person 面對面、親自、本人**

例 They all expected that he would be there in person. 他們都希望他會親自到場。

2. **subscriber** 訂閱（雜誌、社群媒體頻道等）者

3. **rule of thumb** 經驗談

   例 Here's the general rule of thumb to follow: wash your whites and colors separately. 試著按照普遍經驗談這麼做：白色和有顏色的衣服要分開清洗。

4. **complexion** 膚色（整張臉的臉色）

   例 She has been staying up late for days so she has a dull complexion.
   她已經熬夜好幾天了，所以她膚色很暗沉。

5. **skin tone** 膚色

6. **undertone** 底色

7. **blemish** 瑕疵

   例 Skin blemishes are like freckles and scars. 肌膚的瑕疵像是雀斑，或是疤痕之類。

8. **fair skin** 白膚色

   例 The youtuber talked about makeup hacks for fair skin.
   這個網紅在影片裡面談淺白膚色的彩妝祕訣。

9. **makeup hacks** 彩妝技巧

   例 YouTube is a great place to learn new makeup hacks.
   YouTube 是個學習最新彩妝技巧的好地方。

Youtuber B／翻譯

凱西：哈囉，大家好，歡迎來到我的頻道，如果你是新朋友，我叫林凱西，在今天的影片裡面，我會為大家介紹我的化妝祕訣，絕對可以讓你的眉毛左右完美對稱，肌膚狀況超好，讓你看上去好極了，而且重點是，近距離看起來一樣漂亮。我每次啊遇到一些有在觀賞我影片的觀衆時，他們都常常會這麼說：「哇，我很驚訝你的妝面對面近距離一樣看起來那麼漂亮耶！」。好吧，重點妙方就是，健康和有精神的膚色！很多人都會瘋狂追求那種超完美的陶瓷娃娃一樣的膚色，然後最終卻畫出一個「蛋糕妝臉」，像是濃密的奶油蛋糕在臉上一樣，我們當然不要這樣啊，說真的，我們大家臉上都有瑕疵，這沒什麼大不了的，重點是我們到底如何用一種聰明而適當的方式一層一層的把妝上好。好喔，我今天要用雅詩蘭黛這一款「粉持久完美持妝粉底」來上底妝，我之所以超喜歡這一款的原因是它非常水潤，上底妝這件事情，最有用的經驗法則就是，少即是多。哦，等一下，我還沒有跟你們說要怎麼選擇粉底吧，來，我們每個人都有自己的膚色和底色，比如說，我的膚色是中等膚色，這個不難，很容易就知道你自己的膚色是什麼，但是比較煩的部分是要弄清楚每個人皮膚的底色。首先，有三種傳統分類的底色，暖色系、冷色系和中性，有些人可能會想說為什麼我們要把這件事情弄得這麼復雜，基本上呢，我們的底色跟我們沒有上粉底之前的裸膚色是兩回事喔，意思就是說，即使是最白皙的皮膚也可能是屬於要用暖色系底色的人。

Ch 3

瑜珈

Track 2105 ★ 請特別注意粗體字的部分 ★

Amelia: Hi, everyone, welcome to Yoga with Amelia, I am super excited today because we have a sequence for beginners. No matter whether you are interested in do**ing** Yoga, or you are a bit curious about yoga, this video is for you. This will help you build up strength. You can see I'm sitt**ing** on a yoga mat, but if you don't have a mat right now, it's absolutely fine. Don't worry. Also, I'm not us**ing** any props, which means you don't need any equipment. The most important thing is your open mind. It will be really simple and easy for you to follow. Okay, we're go**ing** to begin in a cross-legged position or the easy pose, or in any way that is comfortable for your hips and lower back. See if you can lift your shoulders up and then roll all the way back down. This is a basic posture and you want to feel your lower back. Are you ready?

聽力提點

doing / sitting / using / going

動詞字尾加上 ing 會多一個音節，這個音節都是非重音 (unstressed)，所以在句子當中通常都會是語調降低的位置。

延伸聽寫 | Exercise C

解答參見第 312 頁

Track 2106

1. **Youtuber**: Hello, everyone, thank you so much for ①__________ me today. Today I am ②__________ to bring you a quick stretch session, not too intense, don't worry. It is absolutely perfect for stress relief. We are going to be ③__________ on our breath and the whole session will calm you down. Without further ado, let's get started.

翻譯

網紅：大家好，非常感謝大家今天跟我一起，今天，我們會做一個很簡單快速的伸展教學，動作都不是太激烈的，別擔心喔，這個非常適合來緩解壓力。我們要開始專注在呼吸這件事情上，然後整個課程會讓你舒緩平靜下來。廢話不多說，我們開始吧。

2. **Youtuber**: We're going to start off by doing 10 deep breaths. Okay, then ④__________ __________ take our feet a little bit wider than shoulder width apart, so we can do some very nice deep bends like this, and some shoulder rolls like this. It's very important to warm up your body, to loosen it up.

   翻譯

   網紅：我們會從深呼吸 10 次開始，好，我們的腳要張開比肩膀稍寬一點，這樣我們就可以做一些很棒的深蹲，像這樣，還有肩膀伸展，像這樣。我們可以做到暖身，讓身體舒緩放鬆下來這是很重要的。

實用字詞補充

1. **sequence** 一系列
2. **props** 道具

   例 The common yoga props are mat, pillow and blocks.

   常見的瑜珈道具有瑜珈墊，枕頭和瑜珈練習磚。
3. **lower back** 下背

   例 Low back pain can be one of the world's biggest health problems.

   下背痛可能是世界上最大的健康問題之一。
4. **loosen (something) up**（運動之前）進行準備、熱身

   例 Every student has to do a few stretches to loosen up before they run.

   每個學生開始跑步之前都要伸展四肢來熱身。

Ch 3

Youtuber C／翻譯

Amelia：嗨，大家好，歡迎與 Amelia 一起來做瑜珈，我今天超開心的，因為我們要做這個適合所有瑜珈初學者的程序，無論你是對瑜珈感興趣，或是對瑜珈有點好奇，這個影片都很適合你，這會幫助你更有力氣。你可以看到我現在坐在瑜珈墊上，但是如果您現在手邊沒有瑜珈墊，那也沒關係喔。另外呢，我也沒有使用任何道具，意思就是說你完全不需要什麼設備就可以開始囉，最重要的是你放寬心，不要擔心，等一下的動作都是很容易理解的。好的，我們用這個盤腿姿勢或者應該說一個放鬆的姿勢開始，當然，你也可以用一個讓你的臀部和下背部舒服的姿勢開始。你試試看，是不是可以這樣抬起肩膀，然後一路往下捲下來，這是一個很基本的姿勢，您想感覺自己的下背部，您準備好要開始了嗎？

時間管理妙方

Track 2107 ★ 請特別注意粗體字的部分 ★

Youtuber: Probably one of the reasons you are watching this video right now is you are not making the most of the time you have. We've all been there, right, we had our plans and we thought all we need to do is to stick with the plans, but the truth is it just doesn't work. Why? Today I'm gonna share with you the time management tips that can help you **manage** your time better. Having a good understanding of your precious **resource**, time, will allow you to master it. Even better, you can accomplish more. First, you have to identify your ambition. Knowing your ambitions can maximize your productivity. Without seeing the big picture, it is really difficult for anyone to do as many things as you can. Second, don't underestimate the value of setting your goal. When we set goals and we try our best to achieve it but we fail. That can be frustrating. The feeling of failure can not only just bring us down, but also stop us from trying again. Setting a practical goal is golden. Third, rewards. Be generous to yourself! You work hard, of course you can play hard. Finally, we are living in a world where we are constantly being distracted by almost everything around us. To stay focused is what we all want to do but we fail to do it all the time, right? Say, your friend is texting you while you're trying to finish the last page of your paper, or your mom calls to ask you whether you can give her a ride, or your daughter, I mean, there are so many people, so many things that need your attention, and they might be taking too much of your time, I'm not saying that you should just ignore them or be a loner or something… but what I am trying to say is that life is a limited amount of time and energy. That's why I believe setting a clear goal would help you a lot to take care of everything, including your own goal, wisely.

聽力提點

manage / resource

字母 g 因為後面字尾 e 的關係，會發 [dʒ] 而不是 [g]，同樣的，字母 c 在這裡會發 [s] 而不是 [k]。

延伸聽寫 | Exercise D

解答參見第 312 頁

Track 2108

請用「/」標記斷句換氣的位置、底線標示語調重音、「|」表示句尾尾音下降，並且搭配音檔練習跟讀。

IG Live: Hey, hey, it's James, we are live, because it's Wednesday and it is the first day of Spring Break! Yeah! Well, for my family, today it's our "Taco Wednesday". I have no idea why we picked, um, Wednesday, haha, seriously, well, for those guys who don't know what I'm talking about, since we have friends from Japan, Malaysia, or Taiwan, I feel like I should introduce you to this… okay, so some of you probably have heard of Taco Tuesday, it's some sort of tradition in America, many Mexican restaurants offer special prices every Tuesday night to satisfy our taco addictions. It's pretty much like Happy Hour, if you know what I mean… anyway, oh, right, Lebron James, the Los Angeles Lakers basketball player, shared social media posts on instagram about his family's weekly taco dinners as well, and he said that it's their "Taco Tuesday". Anyway, my family, we have our "Taco Wednesday" every week, and sometimes "Taco Thursday" too… we just love it so much. It's super delicious! Ya, if you are interested in my family's secret taco recipe, please check the caption. Enjoy your weekend. Be safe! Bye bye!

翻譯

IG Live：嘿，嘿，我是詹姆士，我們在直播，因為今天是星期三，而且是春假的第一天！耶！好啦，對我的家人來說，今天是我們的「週三墨西哥玉米餅日」，我不知道為什麼我們選擇星期三，哈哈，天哪，好吧，對於那些不知道我在說什麼的朋友們，因為我們有來自日本，馬來西亞或台灣的朋友啊，我覺得我應該跟你們介紹一下……好喔，你們有些人可能有聽過所謂的週二墨西哥玉米餅之日，在美國這算是一種傳統，很多墨西哥餐館在每個星期二晚上都會以特價來滿足我們這些愛吃墨西哥玉米餅的人，就類似酒吧那種減價優惠時段一樣，我這樣說你應該就懂了吧……好啦，哦，對了，洛杉磯湖人隊的勒布朗．詹姆斯之前也有在 IG 上說他家人吃墨西哥玉米餅當晚餐，他說這是他們的「週二墨西哥玉米餅之日」，總之，我家呢，我們每週都會來個「週三墨西哥玉米餅之日」，有時也有「週四墨西哥玉米餅之日」……我們超超超愛吃墨西哥玉米餅的，真的太好吃了，如果你對我們家的獨門墨西哥玉米餅食譜感興趣的話，請看內文啦。週末愉快。注意安全喔！掰掰！

實用字詞補充

1. **loner** 孤僻的人，不合群的人
2. **happy hour**（酒吧等）優惠時段

Youtuber D／翻譯

Youtuber：你現在正在看這部影片的原因之一可能就是你其實沒有充分利用自己的時間，我們都有過這種經驗對吧，我們定好了計劃，我們認為我們絕對可以完成所有事情，我們要做的就是堅持計劃而已，但事實是，這根本行不通，為什麼會這樣呢？今天，我要跟大家分享時間管理技巧，這些技巧可以幫助大家更有效地管理時間。充分了解你寶貴的資源和時間，將使你能夠掌握它。更棒的是，你能夠在更短的時間內完成更多工作。首先，你一定要明白自己想達到的願景，了解你內心的雄心壯志可以有效地提高你的生產力，如果不去看大局，對於我們每個人來說，要每天盡可能做很多的事情確實是很困難的。其次，不要低估設定目標的價值。當我們設定目標的時候，我們總會盡力實現目標，但最後卻失敗了，這是相當令人喪氣的，這種失敗的感覺不僅會讓我們感到失望，而且還會讓我們不想再去嘗試，所以設定一個切實可行的目標是非常有利的。第三，獎勵。達成每個目標後，別忘了獎勵自己。請對自己慷慨大方一點！你努力工作了，當然可以努力地玩。最後，我們生活在一個不斷被周圍幾乎所有事物分心的世界中。保持專注是我們所有人都想做的，但是我們一直都做不到，對吧？假設你最近有空的朋友在你試圖完成論文的最後一頁時發短信給你，或者你的媽媽打電話問你是否可以搭便車，或者你的女兒，我的意思是，有那麼多的人，那麼多的事情需要你注意，他們可能會花費你很多時間，我並不是說你應該不要理他們，或者成為一個孤獨的人……但是我想說的是你的時間和精力有限。這就是為什麼我相信設定一個明確的目標將幫助你明智地照顧好所有事情，包括你自己的目標。

美味廚房

🎧 **Track 2109** ★ 請特別注意粗體字的部分 ★

Chef: Welcome, everyone, this is my daughter Lily, by **the** way. Recently, she is helping me to make breakfast for **the** whole family. We had a lot **of** fun, right, sweetheart! So I thought it would be a great idea **to** share with all **of** you how you can create wonderful family home cooking memories. Plus, I think it's just amazing, really, **to** cook with your kids. If you can cook meals together, it is a lot easier to let children know what exactly a healthy lifestyle is. We are all busy with work, school, all kinds of activities. Preparing food together gives us a chance **to** just catch up **and** connect with each other. Lovely. Great! Today, we together are going **to** make one pan breakfast. We do it every Sunday morning. It's a legit recipe. Okay, here we've got beautiful, beautiful smoked bacon and sausages. I always cut sausages **in** half. Often it means less than five minutes on the grill, and they will all get a lot crispier. Now, you can see **the** bacon **and** sausages **in the** frying pan start rendering, and it's time to put tomatoes **and** mushrooms in. Lily, can you put those beautiful tomatoes **and** mushrooms in. Nice. Lily, do you smell the bacon and sausages now? We all love this kind of smoky flavor. Yum. Guys, don't forget, you want your bacon **and** sausages to get beautiful brown color. Caramelization is the magic. So please be patient! It takes about 8 minutes. **And** later, Lily and I are gonna **to** crack four free range eggs **in** the frying pan. Wow, it smells so good now. I'm going to season it with some freshly ground black pepper and a pinch of sea salt. Look at **that**, one pan breakfast. I often serve it with slices of fresh sourdough bread. Hope you enjoy today's video! See you next time!

聽力提點

在這段 Youtube 內容當中有許多字音被弱讀，以下列出英文口語中經常被弱讀的 5 個字，請聆聽音檔多練習跟讀，便可以在聽力的過程當中更輕鬆快速地掌握對方的語意。

1. **the** 強讀 [ði]，弱讀 [ðə]。
2. **that** 強讀 [ðæt]，弱讀 [ðə]。（若 that 後面是母音，例如 that I，這時的尾音 [t] 就會發彈舌音跟雙母音 aɪ 連音）
3. **to** 強讀 [tu]，弱讀 [tə]。
4. **of** 強讀 [ɑv]，弱讀 [əv]。
5. **and** 強讀 [ænd]，弱讀 [ənd] 或是更短的 [ən]。

延伸聽寫 | Exercise E

解答參見第 312 頁

Track 2110

Chef: Guys, today's video is one ①__________ __________ been requested to do for months, and today is the day. It's Britain's most treasured national dish, the full English breakfast. Okay, here's our frying pan. Heat up! I always throw the sausages in first because they take the longest time to cook. And then cut one tomato in half. Before you put the tomato in, add some black pepper and a dash of salt. Okay, now it's the secret, brown sugar. I love to sprinkle a bit of brown sugar on it. Now, put the bacon, ②__________ __________ __________ __________. Oh, it looks really nice. Later, we will crack some eggs in. Can't wait! Okay, we also can throw some unsalted ③__________ __________ to give the mushrooms a bit of nutty flavor. Here comes my favorite, baked beans. Some people don't like it. I really don't know why. Just heat half a tin of beans. You can use a saucepan or microwave. It doesn't matter. Okay, get yourself a nice big plate ④__________ put everything on and finally spread a thick layer of butter on your toast. Ta-da!

翻譯

廚師：各位，今天這個影片呢，很多人要求我拍這個主題，問了好幾個月了，終於就是今天啦！介紹英國最珍貴的國菜，英式大早餐。好的，這是我們的煎鍋，加熱！我呢一定會先把香腸放進去，因為它們煮的時間最久，然後，把番茄切成兩半，在把番茄放進鍋子之前，加入一點黑胡椒粉和少許鹽，好喔，現在是祕訣，紅糖，我喜歡在上面撒一點紅糖，風味更好。現在，放入培根，菇類跟番茄，哇，現在看起來非常不錯喔。等一下，我們要打幾顆蛋進去，等不及了！好的，你可以加入一些無鹽奶油，讓蘑菇可以增添一點堅果香味，我最喜歡的烤豆來啦！有些人不喜歡它，我真的不知道為什麼？只需加熱半罐即可，你可以使用平底鍋或微波爐，都沒關係。好啦，給自己拿一個好的大盤子，把每一樣東西放上去，然後最後在烤麵包上塗一層厚厚的黃油。

實用字詞補充

1. **legit**（口語）很酷

   例 That video is legit! 那支影片好酷。

2. **pass (something) down** 傳承

   例 It's a family recipe passed down from my great-grandfather.
   這是我從曾祖父那輩傳下來的家族食譜。

3. **a pinch of** 一小撮

4. **a dash of** 少量的、一點點

   例 Add some yogurt, lemon juice and a dash of salt.
   加一點優格、檸檬汁，和一點點鹽。

5. **Ta-da**（狀聲詞）用來引起注意，表達興奮之情，或是揭曉什麼特別之物等等

Youtuber E／翻譯

主廚：歡迎大家，順便介紹一下，這是我的女兒莉莉，最近，她都會跟我一起幫全家人做早餐，我們玩得很開心，對吧，親愛的！所以我就想說應該要來跟大家分享一下，如何跟家人一起創造美好的烹飪回憶，特別是，我認為跟孩子一起做飯真是非常棒，如果你們可以一起做飯，那麼也比較容易讓孩子們知道什麼是健康的生活方式，我們大多忙於工作、學校、各種活動和責任義務，如果一起準備食物，我們有機會了解彼此發生什麼事情，好好相處，這是很溫馨美好的呀！今天，我們會一起做這道「一鍋早餐」，我們每個星期日早上都會做這道，這是一個超酷的做法喔。好，我們這邊準備了很棒很棒的煙燻培根和香腸，我都會把香腸切成兩半，如果是在烤架上差不多只需要不到五分鐘，而且它們會變得更加酥脆。現在，你可以看到煎鍋中的培根和香腸開始冒出油香了，現在是時候放入番茄和蘑菇，莉莉，你可以幫我把那些漂亮的西紅柿和蘑菇放到鍋子裡面嗎？很好，莉莉，你現在有聞到培根跟香腸的味道嗎？我們都很喜歡這種煙燻味，超美味的，對了，大家，千萬不要忘記，你想要你的培根和香腸變成漂亮的棕色，焦糖化的過程是關鍵，所以請耐心等待喔！大約需要 8 分鐘左右。等一下呢，我和莉莉會把四個放養雞的雞蛋直接打到鍋子裡。哇，好香喔，我要用一些現磨的黑胡椒和少許海鹽來調味，你們看看這樣的一鍋早餐，我通常會跟新鮮的酸種麵包切片一起吃。希望你喜歡今天的影片！下次見！

延伸聽寫 Answer Keys

Exercise A（請參考以下答案及解說。）

斷句換氣位置以「/」來標示，語調重音的位置用底線標示，句尾尾音下降用「|」表示：

Hello! My loves!/ Welcome back to my channel.| Today's video is a new pick-a-card reading.| This one is your monthly,/ January of 2022,/ future/ prediction.| I'm so excited about it right now.| You can see/ we have five piles of cards here,/ and you can take a moment/ or even pause the video if you like.| If you are new here,/ don't worry.| Just pick the pile/ that you feel strongly drawn toward!| After you pick the pile,/ you can just scroll down to the description box/ and find the time stamps/ to watch your personal reading/ for the month of January.|

Exercise B

① I'm going to、② I've been

Exercise C（請參考以下答案及解說。）

① joining、② going、③ focusing

④ we're gonna（前面提到的 I'm gonna 在輕鬆隨意的談話當中，可能會把 [g] 省略，變成聽起來像 Imuna 或甚至把 I 都省掉，聽起來只剩下 muna，但是在 He's gonna、She's gonna 等都不會發生這種省略，只有 I'm gonna 因為是說話者自己的意見表達，文意的重點在 gonna 的後面，所以常常會被自動縮減到一個短短的聲音而已。）

Exercise D（請參考以下答案及解說。）

斷句換氣位置以「/」來標示，語調重音的位置用底線標示，句尾尾音下降用「|」表示：

IG Live: Hey, hey,/ it's James,/ we are live,/ because it's Wednesday/ and it is the first day of Spring Break!| Yeah!| Well, for my family,/ today it's our "Taco Wednesday".| I have no idea why we picked Wednesday,/ haha, seriously,/ well, for those guys/ who don't know/ what I'm talking about,/ since we have friends from Japan, Malaysia, or Taiwan,/ I feel like I should introduce you to this.| Okay,/ so some of you probably have heard of Taco Tuesday,/ it's some sort of tradition in America,/ many Mexican restaurants offer special prices every Tuesday night/ to satisfy our taco addictions.| It's pretty much like Happy Hour,/ if you know what I mean…/ anyway, oh, right,/ Lebron James,/ the Los Angeles Lakers basketball player,/ shared social media posts on instagram/ about his family's weekly taco dinners as well,/ and he said/ that it's their "Taco Tuesdays".| Anyway,/ my family,/ we have our "Taco Wednesday"/ every week,/ and sometimes "Taco Thursday" too... / we just love it so much.| It's super delicious!| Ya, if you are interested/ in my family's secret taco recipe,/ please check the caption.| Enjoy your weekend.| Be safe!| Bye bye!|

Exercise E

① that I've、② mushrooms and tomatoes in、③ butter in、④ and

Unit 22

新冠肺炎的全球大爆發，讓人們無論在社交或生活型態方面都受到極大衝擊並帶來許多的改變。本單元一起來聽聽疫情時代的生活相關話題。

・股票投資・Clubhouse

・封城隔離・Covid-19 疫苗

情境會話 A 股票投資

Track 2201 A = Anita C = Carl ★ 請特別注意粗體字的部分 ★

A Did you get the chance to talk to Lee last night at the party?

C [1]**I did**, he was bragging about his huge profits. Sharing good news is one thing, but bragging about it is another. I don't want to say this, but it's just…

A **I know**, and I've never felt so… well, [2]**just to be clear**, a lot of people talk about their investments, and I'm totally fine with that… anyway… I was so embarrassed last night. What's wrong with him… I mean… is he… the way he talked last night makes me feel like he's another person…

C That's what I want to say… you know what… I am pretty sure he told me so many times that he's not interested in the stock market at all.

A I don't know what changed his mind, but many people are chasing the stock market with day trading because of the pandemic. I guess some of them are looking for entertainment and profits because they are bored.

C Actually, I sold all of my stocks last week.

A Short selling?

C No, I just see a better opportunity to invest elsewhere. How about you? Any interesting news?

A I was thinking it's time that I should adjust my portfolio since it has become inappropriate for my investing goals.

C Stock investing somehow has been filled with all kinds of strategies about when to buy a stock and how to get a deal.

A I would say, any strategy is a good one but if we are attracted by the promise of big gains, we probably are more likely to suffer big losses.

聽力提點

1. **I did.** 跟 **I did.**

套色字為語調重音位置，當改變語調的重音位置時，也可以改變說話者的情緒表達跟語意表示。**當重音換到 did 的時候**，則多表達了一層含義，強調 did

的語義。用中文口語來比喻，當有人問：「你昨天晚上在派對上有沒有跟 Lee 講到話？」，若我們一聽關鍵字 Lee 立刻心領神會對方為什麼要提到 Lee，馬上開啓小圈圈八卦閒聊模式，情緒感受進來，或許就會說「有啊～～～」這個「啊」會比前面的有還要高音甚至大聲，或許還會拉長音，換到英文這個語言，語音語調的改變一樣會有各種五花八門的變化，就看當下說話者的心情與意思表示。Anita 的回答 I know 的語音語調上揚並且拉長，表達認同 Carl 剛剛提出的關鍵點，並且表達自己不可置信的情緒感受。

2. **Just to be clear**

突然插入打斷的語句，這在口語當中很常見。當說話者話說到一半突然自己打斷自己，跳出原本說話的鋪陳，改換不同角度補充說明一些感受或情緒，補充完了之後，才又會再回到原本的語意表示文句裡。

延伸聽寫 | Exercise A

解答參見第 325 頁

Track 2202

請用「/」標記斷句換氣的位置、底線標示語調重音、「|」表示句尾尾音下降，並且搭配音檔練習跟讀。

Ch 3

Man: Alright, to make a profit, you have to know when the right time is to buy and to sell your stocks. Well, say you buy shares of stock at $30 with the intention of selling it, of course, say when it reaches $35. After a couple of days, that stock hits $33 and you think why not just hold it. All of sudden, the stock price drops back to $28. You tell yourself to at least wait until it hits $30 again. Well, unfortunately, it never happens. It's kind of an all-too-common scenario, isn't it?

翻譯

男士：好喔，想要獲利，你就得知道何時才是買賣你的股票的正確時機囉。好啊，假設你以 30 美元的價格買了一檔股票，買的時候打算等到價格漲到 35 美元的時候你就要賣，幾天後呢，股價來到 33 美元，你就想說再放放看好了，突然，股價跌到 28 美元，那你就跟自己說至少等到再回到 30 美元的時候吧，好吧，遺憾的是，股價就再也都沒有回到 30 美元了，這算是一個非常常見的故事情景，我說的沒錯吧？

實用字詞補充

1. **Just to be clear（口語）先聲明一下**（想要避免對方因為自己接續要講的話有所誤會而提示、提醒）
2. **all too 過於⋯⋯**（後面接形容詞或是副詞，通常用於強調較不樂見的情況）

   例 The problem has been occurring all too often.

   這個問題出現的頻率也太高了。

情境會話 A／翻譯

安妮塔：昨晚在聚會上有機會跟李聊到天嗎？

卡　爾：有啊，他一直在吹噓自己股票賺超多。跟別人分享好消息是一回事，但吹牛就是另一回事囉，我並不想這麼說，但這真的⋯⋯

安妮塔：我知道⋯⋯我從來沒有那麼⋯⋯哎呦⋯⋯我先講清楚喔，很多人都會講他們的投資想法那我對這個也是完全沒關係喔，但是，我昨天晚上真的超級尷尬耶，他到底怎麼一回事啊，我是⋯⋯他到底⋯⋯他昨天晚上那樣說話的樣子讓我覺得他根本是另外一個人。

卡　爾：我也是要說這個，我很確定他跟我說過好多次他對股市完全不感興趣喔。

安妮塔：不知道是什麼改變了他的想法，不過由於疫情的緣故，很多人都在股票市場裡瘋單日交易。我想其中有些人是因為太無聊而想要尋找娛樂和利潤吧。

卡　爾：其實，我上週賣掉了所有股票。

安妮塔：賣空？

卡　爾：不，我只是看到了在其他地方投資的更好機會，你呢？有什麼有趣的消息嗎？

安妮塔：我是一直在想說，也是時候該調整自己的投資組合了，畢竟它已經不太適合我現在的投資目標。

卡　爾：在某種程度上，股票投資已經充斥了有關何時購買股票以及如何達成交易的各種策略。

安妮塔：我想說，任何一種策略都是好方法，但是如果我們被大獲利的前景所吸引，那麼我們也許更有可能遭受重大損失。

Clubhouse

🎧 **Track 2203** L = Lina M = Michael ★ 請特別注意粗體字的部分 ★

L Have you been invited to Clubhouse? Do you know how to get a Clubhouse invite?

M The Clubhouse invite code can only be given by users who have been invited to the app by existing users.

L Is it a secret society or something?

M Hahaha, **a bit… anyway**, my supervisor invited me, and I haven't used my invites. So if you want, I can invite you.

L Yes, yes, yes, please invite me. I am really curious about [1]**how… how it can… well**… it's simply an audio-based social network. How can it [2]**become a… the most trending subject**?

M Thanks to one tweet from Elon Musk, I guess. **You can say it's the fast-rising startup**. Almost everybody is talking about this new social media app!

L The idea that anyone can chat with people from around the world is quite fascinating, but isn't it like listening in on someone else's phone call?

M Not really, but it's an interesting analogy! Look, inside the app, there are so many "chat rooms" you can enter. You can either silently listen to it or even actively participate in that conversation.

L Who creates those "rooms"?

M Oh, you can also create a room on any topic you like.

L I still don't get it. Why do suddenly so many people want to talk or listen to strangers?

M **Who knows?** The app is still in its beta phase. **It's hard to say** whether it will be the next big Social Media platform or not.

L Why is it invite only? **I mean**, if people have to be invited by an existing member, how is that possible for influencers or businesses to gain exposure?

M **We'll see how it goes!**

聽力提點

1. **比較多瑣碎的更正重說跟插入語句同時出現。**

   在真實的對話情境中，很常出現說話者說到一半突然跳開，然後又回到原點。有時候是因為想說的事情有各種角度，或是因為一時之間還在腦海裡面搜尋自己到底想要表達什麼，想要加強聽力絕對不能對於這種凌亂的句子感到有壓力，只要放輕鬆跟緊說話者一開始想要表達的意涵，跟著語音語調的起伏掌握最關鍵的資訊即可。

2. **become a... the most trending subject**

   說話者本來想要說 become a... 但是話才脫口就馬上想到要說 the most trending subject。

延伸聽寫 | Exercise B

解答參見第 325 頁

Track 2204 請試著把句子中實詞的位置標記出來，並搭配音檔進行跟讀練習。

The most interesting thing is all conversations on Clubhouse are audio-only, and when they finish, they disappear forever.

最有趣的是，Clubhouse 上的所有對話都是純音頻的，當它們結束時，會永遠消失。

實用字詞補充

1. **listening in on something 偷聽**

   例 When I was in high school, my parents listened in on my phone conversations.
   我高中的時候，父母會偷聽我講電話。

2. **analogy 比喻**

   例 The teacher drew an analogy between time and money.
   老師做了一個金錢與時間的比喻。

3. **influencer（對他人）有影響力的人（意見領袖、有影響力的網紅）**

   例 Do you think social media influencers are changing the world?
   你覺得社群媒體上的意見領袖、網紅等等正在改變這個世界嗎？

4. **see how it goes 靜觀後續發展**

   例 It's the only thing we can do now, but we need to try our best and see how it goes. 這是目前我們唯一能做的事情，但是我們就盡力而為，然後靜觀後續發展。

情境會話 B／翻譯

莉娜：您有被邀請加入 Clubhouse 了嗎？你知道怎樣才可以被邀請嗎？

麥可：Clubhouse 的邀請代碼只有已經使用這個應用程式的用戶才可以提供。

莉娜：這是一個祕密社團還是什麼啦？

麥可：哈哈哈，有點類似吧……無論如何，我的主管有邀請我，那我還沒有用掉我的邀請名額，如果你想的話，我可以邀請你。

莉娜：好啊，請邀請我，謝謝！我實在很好奇這個基本上以聲音交流的社交網絡為什麼會成為當下最流行的事情耶！

麥可：我猜大概是因為伊隆 · 馬斯克 (Elon Musk) 的推文吧！你也可以說這是一家快速崛起的新創事業，幾乎所有人都在討論這個新的社群軟體！

莉娜：誰都可以跟世界各地的人聊天，這個想法的確很吸引人，但這不就像是偷聽別人講電話的感覺嗎？

麥可：並非如此，不過這是一個有趣的比喻！你看，在 Clubhouse，你可以進去各種「聊天室」，可以安靜的聽，或是可以主動參與該對話。

莉娜：那是誰創造這些「房間」啊？

麥可：哦，你也可以就自己喜歡的主題創建一個房間。

莉娜：我還是不懂，為什麼突然有這麼多人想要跟陌生人說話或是聽陌生人說話？

麥可：誰知道？這支 app 還處於測試階段，很難說它到底會不會成為下一個大型社群平台。

莉娜：為什麼只有收到邀請才能使用？我的意思是，如果必須由現有成員邀請人們加入，那麼那些意見領袖、網紅或是各大企業媒體要怎樣才能利用這來增加曝光機會呢？

麥可：我們就靜觀其變囉！

情境會話 C 封城隔離

Track 2205 　J = Joseph　A = Annie　　★ 請特別注意粗體字的部分 ★

J Hey Annie, this is Joseph, is everything okay?

A **What can I say? Here we go again.** It's another snap lockdown.

J I'm so sorry. It's really frustrating, and you must be exhausted. I wish I could be there.

A I know.

J Hey, I'll send many many **care packages** to you. Make it like your birthday everyday.

A You don't need to do that. Online shopping is very convenient. Don't worry. I'll be fine.

J I hate that the only thing I can do is to send packages to you. It's… uh… it's really bad.

A Don't say that. [1]**It's not all bad**. At least you live in Taiwan. You're so lucky.

J Book a flight ticket now?

A You're crazy. I wish I could.

J It's been a year and the whole world is still struggling. There have been so many people stuck at home in self-isolation, unable to see their loved ones, but there… **there's nothing we can do to change the situation**… I just… uh… It sucks.

A Well, [2]**we can do some things**, washing our hands, using hand sanitizer, and wearing a mask.

J Yeah, that's right!

A During the lockdown, staying safe is so much easier than staying positive, but I think to beat the boredom and frustration, what we need the most is to stay positive to get through hard times.

J You are not alone. Don't forget that!

聽力提點

1. **It's not all bad.**
   句子重音放在 all，bad 是已經出現過的資訊，通常不會是重音的位置，女生的說話重點在 not all 上面。
2. **We can do some things.**
   句子重音位置也會出現在「對比的資訊上」，前面男生說 there's nothing we can do…，而對比 nothing，下一句女生回答的 some things，強調「還是有些事情是我們可以做的啊。」

延伸聽寫 | Exercise C

➔ 解答參見第 325 頁

Track 2206　請試著把句子中實詞的位置標記出來，並搭配音檔進行跟讀練習。

During the Covid-19 pandemic, sending a care package to your beloved family and friends is more significant than ever. You can book low-cost worldwide parcel delivery with Fastsender.

翻譯

在 Covid-19 大流行期間，向您摯愛的家人和朋友遞送關愛包裹比以往任何時候都還要重要。您可以以低廉價格使用 Fastsender 預訂全球投遞的包裹寄件。

實用字詞補充

1. **lockdown 封城**
2. **self-isolation 自我隔離** *quarantine（防疫情擴散採取的）隔離

情境會話 C／翻譯

約瑟夫：嗨，安妮，我是約瑟夫，一切都還好嗎？
安　妮：我能說什麼？哎，又來了，又要再一次封城。
約瑟夫：我很抱歉，這一切真的很令人沮喪，你也一定累壞了吧。真希望我可以在你身邊。
安　妮：我知道。
約瑟夫：嘿，我會寄很多很多包裹給您，讓你好像每天都在過生日一樣喔！
安　妮：你不用這樣啦，網上購物很方便啊，不用擔心我，我沒事的。
約瑟夫：哎，我唯一能做的就是寄包裹給你，這真的很討厭，這一切都糟透了。
安　妮：別那麼說。也不全都那麼糟啊，至少你人在台灣，你很幸運。
約瑟夫：要不要現在訂機票啊？

安　妮：你瘋了，我也希望我可以啊。

約瑟夫：已經一年了耶，整個世界卻還在掙扎，有那麼多人在家中自我隔離，見不到親愛的家人朋友，但我們卻對此無能為力，實在糟透了。

安　妮：話說，我們還是可以做一些事情喔，勤洗手，用洗手液，還有戴口罩。

約瑟夫：沒錯沒錯！

安　妮：在封城期間，保持安全比保持積極樂觀要容易多了，但是我認為要克服無聊和沮喪，我們最需要的是保持積極樂觀才能度過艱難時期啊。

約瑟夫：你並不孤單。別忘了喔！

Covid-19 疫苗

Track 2207 J = Jacob L = Larry ★ 請特別注意粗體字的部分 ★

J Hey, Larry, do you know how to find vaccine locations?

L I just checked the CDC website, and it's said that there are many ways for us to look for a vaccination provider, like visits vaccines.gov or even local pharmacy's website.

J Okay, and can we choose which COVID-19 vaccine we get?

L I'm not sure, **let me see**… umm…, here, it says… umm,… okay, yes, we can. Oh, wait, we also should be aware of the risk if we choose Johnson & Johnson's Janssen COVID-19 Vaccine. There are possible health problems, 15 reports of women who developed thrombosis after they got the vaccine.

J No… **what do you think?** Should we choose other vaccines?

L Yeah, maybe. It's said that thrombosis hasn't been linked to other vaccines liken Pfizer-BioNTech or Moderna.

J Oh, and we don't need to pay, **do we**?

L **Nope, we don't**. The federal government is providing it. It's free to all people living in the United States.

J I bet it concerns lots of people that COVID-19 vaccines may not be safe for them because of potential side effects after getting vaccinated.

L But the truth is widespread vaccination is the way to help stop the pandemic.

J Let's find a vaccination location now, **what do you say**?

*CDC: Centers for Disease Control and Prevention

Ch 3

延伸聽寫 | Exercise D

解答參見第 325 頁

Track 2208 請試著把句子中實詞的位置標記出來，並搭配音檔進行跟讀練習。

1. The vaccines produce protection and develop an immune response to the virus.

   疫苗可產生保護作用，並對病毒產生免疫反應。

2. It's noted that children under twelve years old cannot have the Pfizer COVID-19 vaccine.

請注意，未滿 12 歲的兒童不能接種輝瑞 COVID-19 疫苗。

實用字詞補充

What do you say?（口語）你覺得呢？

例 What do you say we sell our shares of the stock?

我們把股票賣掉吧，你覺得呢？

情境會話 D／翻譯

雅各：嘿，賴瑞，你知道我們要怎麼找到哪裡可以打疫苗嗎？

賴瑞：我剛剛查閱了 CDC 網站，據說我們可以通過多種方式來尋找疫苗接種提供者，例如訪問 vaccines.gov 甚至本地藥房的網站。

雅各：好的，我們可以選擇要接種的 COVID-19 疫苗嗎？

賴瑞：我不確定，讓我看……嗯，在這裡，這是說……嗯，是的，是的，我們可以。哦，等等，如果我們選擇強生的 Janssen COVID-19 疫苗，我們也應該意識到這個風險，可能存在健康問題。15 例婦女接種疫苗後出現血栓的報告。

雅各：不……你怎麼看？我們應該選擇其他疫苗嗎？

賴瑞：是的，也許。據說血栓形成與其他疫苗沒有關聯，例如輝瑞 BioNTech 或 Moderna。

雅各：哦，我們不用負擔疫苗費用對吧？

賴瑞：不用啊，聯邦政府買單，所有居住在美國的人都是免費的。

雅各：我敢打賭，很多人擔心接種疫苗後可能產生的副作用，所以認為 COVID-19 疫苗接種可能並不安全。

賴瑞：但事實就是，大家得接種疫苗才是阻止這個流行病的方法呀。

雅各：我們現在來找疫苗接種地點吧，你覺得如何呢？

*CDC：疾病控制與預防中心

延伸聽寫 Answer Keys

Exercise A

斷句換氣位置以「/」來標示，語調重音的位置用底線標示，句尾尾音下降用「|」表示：

Man: Alright/, to make a profit/, you have to know/ when the right time is/ to buy/ and to sell your stocks|. Well,/ say you buy shares of stock at $30/ with the intention of selling it/, of course,/ say when it reaches $35|. After a couple of days/, that stock hits $33/ and you think/ why not just hold it.| All of sudden/, the stock price drops back to $28|. You tell yourself to/ at least wait until/ it hits $30 again|. Well,/ unfortunately,/ it never happens.| It's kind of an/ all-too-common scenario/, isn't it?（尾音上揚）

Exercise B

句子當中實詞的位置也就是重音的位置，我們用套色字來表示：

The most interesting thing is all conversations on Clubhouse are audio-only, and when they finish, they disappear forever.

（forever 在這裡是被強調語意的副詞，所以也是重音位置。）

Exercise C

句子當中實詞的位置也就是重音的位置，我們用套色字來表示：

During the Covid-19 pandemic, sending a care package to your beloved family and friends is more significant than ever. You can book low-cost worldwide parcel delivery with Fastsender.

Exercise D

句子當中實詞的位置也就是重音的位置，我們用套色字來表示：

1. The vaccines produce protection and develop an immune response to the virus.
2. It's noted that children under 12-year old cannot have the Pfizer COVID-19 vaccine.

Ch 3

Unit 23

不會被廣播的時間限制住、眼睛也不需要被畫面綁架，可以隨時隨地用聽的來獲取娛樂或知識……本單元要帶你感受一下 Podcast 的魅力！

- 新聞頻道・音樂頻道
- 學習頻道・旅遊生活頻道

新聞頻道

Track 2301 ★ 請特別注意粗體字的部分 ★

Host: Why would a long-term couple like Bill and Melinda Gates get divorced? Unlike those glamorous celebrity couples, couples like Bill and Melinda Gates appear to be a reliable marriage model. **So it's kind of a shocker… you know… uh**, whenever someone announces they are splitting after so many years. It's hard to believe that their marriage would break down. A lot of people talk about what went wrong for the philanthropic power couple. And what about their philanthropic efforts? In the joint statement, they wrote "we have raised three incredible children and built a foundation that works all over the world to enable all people to lead healthy, productive lives. We continue to share a belief in that mission and will continue to work together at the foundation, but we no longer believe we can grow together as a couple in this next phase of our lives."

延伸聽寫 | Exercise A

解答參見第 338 頁

Track 2302 請試著把句子中實詞的位置標記出來，並搭配音檔進行跟讀練習。

How come two people in a long-standing marriage and the successful establishment of one of the world's largest foundations couldn't make it? The couple is known for their remarkably generous contributions to charity through their foundation. When they announced the divorce, many people were stunned.

翻譯

兩個人已經經營了長期的婚姻關係還共同建立世界上最大的基金會之一，怎麼會走不下去了？這對夫婦長久以來透過基金會對慈善事業慷慨奉獻，當他們宣布離婚時，很多人都為之震驚。

實用字詞補充

1. **shocker**（口語）令人震驚（或不快）之物（尤指新事物或新宣佈之事）
2. **philantropic** 樂善好施的

   例 The couple's contributions to philanthropic causes earned them awards.

   這對夫妻對慈善事業的貢獻為他們贏得了獎項。

Podcast A／翻譯

主持人：為什麼像比爾和梅琳達．蓋茨這樣踏入婚姻很長時間的夫妻，到最後還是離婚了呢？不同於那些光鮮亮麗的明星夫妻檔，比爾和梅琳達 · 蓋茨這樣的夫妻就像是一種令人感覺可靠的婚姻典範，所以，這個消息是有點令人震驚的……你知道的……嗯，不管是誰在結婚好多年之後竟然宣佈分手時，大家其實都會感到震驚啦，就感覺很難相信他們的婚姻會破裂。許多人談論這對慈善事業權力夫妻到底出了什麼問題，他們的慈善事業會怎麼樣呢？他們在聯合聲明中寫道：「我們一起養育三個完美出色的孩子，並且建立了一個跨足世界各個角落的慈善基金會，致力於讓所有人都能過上健康、富足的生活。我們將繼續對這一使命抱持信念前進，並將繼續在基金會裡攜手努力，但我們不會在人生的下一個階段以夫妻的身份一起成長。」

Ch 3

音樂頻道

Track 2303 E = Eddie M = Matt ★ 請特別注意粗體字的部分 ★

E Hello, music lovers, **this is** Eddie. **How are you doing!** The Jungle has officially debuted their first single in 2022. I think it really is a good time to release something inspiring, especially during the pandemic. We have the singer and songwriter, Matt with us, **hey man**, it's been a long time.

M Yeah, a long long time. Thank you for having me.

E Thank you Matt, thank you for sending the song over early. My wife and I were just lying on the sofa, listening to your music, and all of the sudden, we totally sink back into the ocean. It's like the coolest spiritual adventure.

M Wow, thanks man, you are the coolest! I should put your words on our cover.

E It's good, isn't it. Okay, The Jungle's first single, "*Sink Back Into the Ocean*", is just out today. Congratulations, Matt!

M Thank you… um… it's really something that we put our thought into… ya… like… you know… last year… a lot of people, you know, [1]**i-i-it's tough**, [2]**and I… and I think** it's really really challenging for almost everyone. Lots of people, you know, they can't go to live shows, or concerts, so we all feel like it's really good to release something like this to make people, you know, … um… I don't know, wow… um… man, … oh, no, it's embarrassing, I don't even know what I'm talking about right now. Man, where's my script?

E Oh… in no way do you need a script on my show, Matt.

M hahaha, **I know, I know… um… thanks though…** I am just a bit emotional and really excited about it. I tried to say something nice to, to encourage people, … but also … umm… immediately sensed that what I was trying to say it's a bit cliché. And… all of sudden I was speechless.

E You are totally forgiven, Matt. You are a musician, an artist. Your language is music.

M That one is pretty good. I love that.

E Alright, music lovers, *Sink Back Into the Ocean* **is just out**! **I don't want**

to give too much away, but no kidding, the music is unbelievable! You can stream it on Apple Music and Spotify. And Matt, congratulations again, man, I am really happy for you.

M Thank you, Eddie.

聽力提點

1. **i-i-its' tough**
   口語實境上有些時候會有這種像是口吃一樣的反應，為說話者在思索到底該怎麼表達的過程。
2. **and I... and I think**
   口語實境中會有這種說話者重複反覆同樣字句的例子，通常也是因為說話者正在思考下一句話要說什麼。

延伸聽寫 | Exercise B 解答參見第 338 頁

Track 2304 請試著把句子中實詞的位置標記出來，並搭配音檔進行跟讀練習。

1. We are back again with your annul countdown music, everybody. I know, 2021, what a year! Join me as we say goodbye to 2021 and welcome 2022. Since most of us are all staying in, we still can do it right! Let's party at home with this mix and have some fun. We will start it at 11:40 sharp. Stay tuned.

   翻譯
   大家好，我們回來啦，帶著我們要給大家的跨年音樂，我知道，2021 年，天哪，是怎麼樣無法用言語形容的一年啊！和我一起告別 2021 年並歡迎 2022 年吧，由於我們大多數人都還待在家裡，我們還是可以好好的跨年！讓我們在家裡跟著這集混音一起同樂吧，玩得開心喔，我們將會從 11:40 準時開始，別走開喔！

2. Listen up! If you think of starting a podcast just like this one, there's no other choice but to use Anchor app, that's it, since it's free and its tools are very easy. Also, Anchor will distribute your podcast for you.

   翻譯
   聽好喔！如果你想要像這樣開始製作你的 podcast 的話，你其實別無選擇，就是用 Anchor 應用程式就對了啦，因為它是免費的，而且應用工具都非常簡單，此外，Anchor 應用程式還會幫你發布你的 podcast。

實用字詞補充

1. **Hey man!**（用於稱呼，尤指對男子）老兄（弟）、朋友

   例 Hey, man, how are you doing? 嘿，老兄，你好嗎？

2. **Stay tuned** 敬請期待（別走開、別轉台）

   例 The fast-food chain said fans should stay tuned for the nationwide launch.
   這家速食連鎖店表示，粉絲們敬請期待全國發布會。

3. **put something into/in** 花費大量時間和精神投注於某事

   例 They have put a lot of time and effort into making it work.
   他們花費相當多的時間跟精神讓這件事情可以成功。

Podcast B／翻譯

艾迪：各位音樂同好，大家好，我是艾迪，大家都還好嗎！「叢林」樂團已經正式發行他們 2022 年的第一張單曲，我認為現在確實是發布一些鼓舞人心的東西的好時機，尤其是疫情期間。好，我們今天邀請到歌手也是詞曲作者，麥特，跟我們一起，嘿，好久不見啦。

麥特：很久很久不見了，謝謝你邀請我。

艾迪：謝謝麥特，感謝你之前就寄給我這首歌，我跟我老婆就躺在沙發上，聽你的音樂，突然之間，我們完完全全地沉入大海，簡直是一場最酷的精神冒險。

麥特：哇，謝謝你，你是最棒的！我應該把你說的這句話放到我們專輯封面。

艾迪：說的很棒，對吧！好喔，「叢林」樂團在 2022 年發行的第一張單曲《沉入大海》今天就發行了。恭喜你，麥特！

麥特：謝謝，嗯，這張專輯，我們想了非常多層面……你看……像去年整年，好多人，很艱難的，對幾乎我們每個人來說，這就是一個大挑戰，好多人，他們不能去看現場表演或演唱會，所以我們都覺得在這個時候發行這張單曲來讓人們……嗯……你知道，我是說……哎呦，天哪，太尷尬了，我根本不知道我現在在說什麼，歐，我的腳本在哪裡？

艾迪：你在我節目絕對不需要腳本啊，麥特。

麥特：哈哈哈，我知道，我心情有點激動，也很興奮。我本來是想要試著說一些好聽的話來鼓勵大家……但又馬上感覺到我想說的話根本就是陳腔濫調，然後我就一下子語塞了。

艾迪：誰會怪你啊，麥特，你是一個音樂家，一個藝術家耶，你的語言是音樂。

麥特：很好，我喜歡這個說法。

艾迪：好啦，愛好音樂的大家，單曲《沉入大海》剛發行！我不想破梗太多啦，但是沒在跟你開玩笑，這張單曲真的會讓你驚艷！你可以在 Apple 音樂或是 Spotify 等各大平台收聽到他們的最新單曲喔！麥特，再次恭喜你，我真的為你感到高興。

麥特：謝謝你，艾迪。

學習頻道

Track 2305 ★ 請特別注意粗體字的部分 ★

Welcome to a new episode from *English Daily* Podcast. I am Nat. Covid-19 has a bad affect on people's lives. Or effect? Effect and affect are good examples of today's topic. The two words look similar, have a similar spelling, or sound similar so many people get mixed up. But they actually have different meanings. In this episode, we are going to talk about easily confused words in English. A free download pdf with practice is highly recommended for those people who want to practice listening, you can find the link in the description box. Okay, about easily confused words, like effect and affect. Affect is a verb and it means to cause someone or something to change, like in "The humid weather has severely affected his health." However, Effect is a noun, not a verb and it means "the result of an influence", like in "Covid-19 has a bad effect on people's lives." Also, dessert and desert. Dessert means sweet food, like apple pies or cakes, but desert means an area covered with sand or rocks and very little rain. Okay, you might ask, are there tips for learning these easily confused words? The answer is yes, of course. Every time you learn a new word, don't forget to say it out loud. Saying it out loud again and again will help you remember it correctly. **Join us again for more learning tips. Goodbye.**

延伸聽寫 | Exercise C

解答參見第 338 頁

Track 2306 請試著把句子中實詞的位置標記出來，並搭配音檔進行跟讀練習。

This is the BBC. This podcast is supported by advertising outside the UK. To find out more, visit our website. Hello and welcome to the News Review from BBC learning English. Joining me today is Phoebe.

翻譯

這是英國廣播公司。本播客由英國境外的廣告贊助支持，想要了解更多消息，請到我們的網站。大家好，歡迎收聽 BBC 學習英語的新聞評論節目，今天跟我一起的是菲比。

Ch 3

Podcast C／翻譯

歡迎收聽《英語每日播客》最新一集，我是納特，Covid-19 對人們的生活造成不良影響 (affect)，還是應該說影響 (effect) ？ Affect 跟 effect 是今日主題的很好的例子，這兩個詞看起來很相似，拼寫相似，或者你要說聽起來也很相似，所以很多人會搞混，但是它們實際上具有不同的含義，在本集中，我們將討論英語中很容易混淆的單詞，強烈建議想要練習聽力的人免費下載 pdf 檔案練習，你可以在說明欄中找到雲端連結。好囉，關於容易混淆的單詞，例如 affect 和 effect，affect 是一個動詞，它意味著使某人或某物發生變化，例如這句，「潮濕的天氣嚴重影響了他的健康」，而 effect 則是名詞，不是動詞，它的意思是「影響的結果」，例如這句話「Covid-19 對人們的生活有不利的影響」。還有另外像是 dessert 和 desert 這兩個字，dessert 是指甜食，例如蘋果派或蛋糕，而 desert 是指被沙子或岩石覆蓋且幾乎沒有雨水的區域。好的，你可能會想問，有沒有技巧可以學好這些容易混淆的單詞？答案是肯定的。每次你學習一個新單詞時，請不要忘記大聲說出來。一遍又一遍地大聲說出來會幫助你正確記住每個單字，記得下次再收聽我們節目，獲得更多學習技巧，再見囉！

旅遊生活頻道

Track 2307　★ 請特別注意粗體字的部分 ★

This is the Traveller Chit Chat Podcast. **I'm your host**, Ginny Liao, **welcome to episode 188** of the Traveller Chit Chat Podcast. **Today I want to talk about** how to be a tourist at home. Wonderful ways of getting some sort of travel feelings may not necessarily be associated with immersing yourself in a foreign culture. We actually can gain benefits of travel in our hometown. Think of art galleries, theaters, gardens or even zoos in our hometown. Yes, I know, we have been there like thousands of times. How come revisiting those spots would become something adventurous? Okay, since last year, we have been staying at home, working from home. We basically do everything at home. I bet so many people are kind of fed up but there's not so much we can do about it. It's a battle against the virus, even though we all hate social distancing. I'm not sure when it might be okay to travel around the world again, but for many places like Taiwan, at least we can travel at home. I think it's an invaluable chance for us to explore those places near us. You know, to get to know more about the culture that defines who we are can be something inspiring and powerful. It can be an amazing journey if you just let yourself be a tourist in your own hometown. Grab the opportunity to look the city inside and out like you would never visit it again. Be curious about everything! There's always something new to learn, trust me. For example, I have lived in Taipei for more than twenty years, but I have never visited Taipei 101 observatory. Why? Isn't it a bit bizarre that for the foreigners, Taipei 101 is a must-see attraction, but for local people, it's like… oh yeah, it's famous, and it's just over there? I mean when we go to Tokyo, TokyoTower is a must-go, right! We want to get a sense of Tokyo's cityscape in all three dimensions. Getting a bird's eye perspective of a metropolitan is undeniably a fantastic travel experience. But I have never even thought about visiting the lookout point in Taipei. Well, maybe, once or twice, couple of my friends said hey lets' make a visit to the Taipei 101 observatory deck, but then we just put the idea on the back burner. So, I booked the ticket last night and I can't wait to appreciate the beautiful view of Taipei city. **How about you? What comes into your mind when you hear** "being a tourist in your hometown"? **Okay, if you like today's podcast, make sure to subscribe. Bye!**

延伸聽寫 | Exercise D

解答參見第 338 頁

Track 2308 請試著把句子中實詞的位置標記出來，並搭配音檔進行跟讀練習。

Today I have a special episode. It's about a recipe, well, my grandmother's recipe… anyway, I will explain more in a minute.

翻譯

今天我們是特輯，我們要說說食譜，好吧，應該是說我奶奶的食譜，總之呢，我等一下馬上就會跟大家解釋是什麼意思。

實用字詞補充

1. **on the back burner**（尤指因不緊急或不重要而）暫時擱置一旁

   例 We have no choice but to put the plan on the back burner.

   我們別無選擇只好先暫時把計畫擱置一旁。

2. **in a minute** 馬上，一會兒

   例 Don't worry! We will be there in a minute.

   不要擔心，我們馬上就到。

3. **chit chat** 聊天閒聊

   例 Even though it's just chit-chat, I really enjoy it.

   雖然不過是閒聊而已，我還是覺得很盡興。

4. **tourist attraction** 旅遊景點 *spot 旅遊景點

   例 The Skyscraper Center is the city's biggest tourist attraction.

   摩天大樓中心是該城市最大的旅遊勝地。

Podcast D／翻譯

這是旅行者聊聊播客，我是主持人廖潔妮，歡迎來到我們的第 188 集，今天，我想談一談如何成為一名在家鄉旅遊的人。獲得某種旅行感受的奇妙方式不一定要跟深陷外國文化有關連，實際上呢，我們可以從在家鄉遊歷來體驗旅行的好處，想一想那些家鄉的美術館、劇院、花園甚至動物園好了。對，我知道，我們去過那些地方幾百萬次了，參觀那些景點怎麼會有冒險的感覺呢？從去年開始，我們都一直待在家裡，在家工作。我們基本上做所有事情都在家裡，我敢

打賭，很多人有點受夠了，但我們能怎麼辦呢，這是一場與病毒的戰爭耶，即使我們都討厭保持社交距離這件事情，但是我們仍然必須這樣做，我不確定我們到底何時可以再次環遊世界，但對於台灣這樣的地方，至少我們可以在家附近旅行啊。我認為這是我們探索附近那些地方的寶貴機會，可以對於定義我們之所以是我們的文化有更多了解，這可能會帶給我們許多啓發，如果你讓自己成為遊歷家鄉的遊客，那將會是一段令人驚奇的旅程，抓緊這個機會把這座城市從裡到外看仔細，就好像你永遠不會再回到這個地方一樣，對一切都感到無比好奇！相信我，我們總會找到一些新的東西要學習，就好比說，我在台北生活了二十多年，但卻從來沒有去過台北 101 觀景台，為什麼？對外國人來說，台北 101 是必去的景點吧，但是對當地人來說，這就像……哦，是啊，它很有名，它不就在那邊嗎，這種對比其實有點奇怪吧？我的意思是說，當我們去到東京，東京鐵塔是必須要去的，對啊！我們想從各個面向清楚的看一看整個東京市景，鳥瞰大都市無疑是一種奇妙的旅行體驗，但是我真的還從未想過要去看整個台北市景，好吧，也許有一次或兩次，我的幾個朋友問說，嘿，不如我們去參觀台北 101 觀景台，但是後來這個想法就一直擱置也沒成行啊。所以，我昨晚訂了票，我現在是等不及要欣賞台北市的美景了，那你呢？當你聽到「在你的家鄉成為一名遊客」的時候，你會想到什麼？好吧，如果你喜歡今天的播客，請一定要訂閱喔。再見！

Ch 3

延伸聽寫 Answer Keys

Exercise A

句子當中實詞的位置也就是重音的位置，我們用套色字來表示：

How come two people in a long-standing marriage and the successful establishment of one of the world's largest foundations couldn't make it? The couple is known for their remarkably generous contributions to charity through their foundation. When they announced the divorce, many people were stunned.

Exercise B

句子當中實詞的位置也就是重音的位置，我們用套色字來表示：

1. We are back again with our annul countdown music, everybody. I know, 2021, what a year! Join me as we say goodbye to 2021 and welcome 2022. Since most of us are all staying in, we still can do it right! Let's party at home with this mix and have some fun. We will start it at 11:40 sharp. Stay tuned.
2. Listen up! If you think of starting a podcast just like this one, there's no other choice but to use Anchor app, that's it, since it's free and its tools are very easy. Also, Anchor will distribute your podcast for you.

Exercise C

句子當中實詞的位置也就是重音的位置，我們用套色字來表示：

This is the BBC. This podcast is supported by advertising outside the UK. To find out more, visit our website. Hello and welcome to the News Review from BBC learning English. Joining me today is Phoebe.

Exercise D

句子當中實詞的位置也就是重音的位置，我們用套色字來表示：

Today I have a special episode. It's about a recipe, well, my grandmother's recipe... anyway, I will explain more in a minute.

Unit 24

本單元的話題圍繞在未來經濟的「宅趨勢」：

・斜槓人生・Netflix・食物外送・宅經濟

情境會話 A 斜槓人生

同步練習

請仔細聆聽情境會話音檔，把每一句中斷句換氣的語調段落標記出來。

Track 2401　P = Peter　J = Jane　★ 請特別注意粗體字的部分 ★

P Have you talked to Sandy recently? I texted her, called her, but she just sent me some emojis and said that she was really busy. I mean, **busy doing what**?

J **Haven't you heard**?

P Heard what?

J Well, Sandy is a slashie now.

P Really, **didn't know that** she's a workaholic.

J **Why did you say that**? I think choosing to be a slashie is **a lot different from** being a workaholic.

P **That's something I don't understand**. I mean… the term "slashie" itself for sure sounds cool, except that you will be extremely busy being able to manage every job well, right! Seriously, some of my friends envy slashies. **They are so crazy about the idea that** you can work from home and kinda enjoy the feeling of liberation and freedom. I… I don't… I just don't think being a slashie is that good. Just think of the pressure. The erratic schedule is also really bad for one's health. The upsides of having several jobs can't possibly outweigh the downsides. **I'm telling you!**

J **I know what you mean**. You know what, *<u>**I did think about**</u> being a freelancer a couple of months ago, but in the end, I just couldn't make up my mind. **The flip side** of enjoying those jobs I like possibly can be that I end up working 20 hours a day, or seven days a week. It's too risky. I certainly don't want to live an extremely stressful life.

P **That's what I'm talking about**, but the gig economy is thriving **though**. It's estimated more than 1 million people are now working two jobs or more. **Can you believe that**?

J Well, **I do… I really do**. I guess there are a lot of reasons. Some people probably have no choice but to choose this kind of super busy work schedule because they can't secure a full-time job with a sufficient income to support their dreams.

P Indeed, or it allows people to fulfill different interests.

J Yes, like Sandy, you can't deny that she is really talented. She is a chef/blogger/photographer/gardener. It may be a glamorous new way for those people who are jacks-of-all-trades.

聽力提點

***I did think about...**

did 的音調上揚。通常助動詞不會是句子重音位置，很常見的例外是作為強調語意的時候，助動詞會念重音，例如這裡用 I did think about... 就像是中文的「我還真的有想過……」。

同步練習 | 解說 Track 2401

英語的斷句換氣通常會在以下幾個位置：1. 標點符號 2. 連接詞之前 3. 子句之前 4. 介系詞之前（除了 of 之外） 5. 主詞（很長的情況下）之後。以下對話的斷句換氣位置以「/」標示：

P Have you talked to Sandy recently?/ I texted her,/ called her,/ but she just sent me some emojis/ and said that she was really busy./ I mean,/ busy doing what?

J Haven't you heard?

P Heard what?

J Well,/ Sandy is a slashie now.

P Really,/ didn't know/ that she's a workaholic.

J Why did you say that?/ I think choosing to be a slashie/ is a lot different from being a workaholic.

P That's something I don't understand./ I mean/... the term "slashie" itself/ for sure sounds cool,/ except that you'll be extremely busy/ being able to manage every job well,/ right!/ Seriously,/ some of my friends envy slashies./ They are so crazy about the idea/ that you can work from home/ and kinda enjoy the feeling of liberation and freedom./ I/... I don't/... I just don't think being a slashie is that good./ Just think of the pressure./ The erratic schedule is also really bad for one's health./ The upsides of having several jobs/ can't possibly outweigh the downsides./ I'm telling you!

J I know what you mean./ You know what,/ I *did think about being a freelancer a couple of months ago,/ but in the end,/ I just couldn't make up my mind./ The flip side of enjoying those jobs I like/ possibly can be/ that I end up working 20 hours a day,/ or seven days a week./ It's too risky./ I certainly don't want to live an extremely stressful life.

P That's what I'm talking about,/ but the gig economy is thriving though./ It's estimated more than 1 million people/ are now working two jobs or more./ Can you believe that?

J Well,/I do/… I really do./ I guess there are a lot of reasons./ Some people probably have no choice/ but to choose this kind of super busy work schedule/ because they can't secure a full-time job/ with a sufficient income to support their dreams.

P Indeed,/ or it allows people to fulfill different interests.

J Yes,/ like Sandy,/ you can't deny/ that she is really talented./ She is a chef/blogger/ photographer/gardener./ It may be a glamorous new way/ for those people who are jacks-of-all-trades.

實用字詞補充

1. **slashie** 斜槓（有數種兼職的人）

   例 The term slashie means, instead of simply having one job, might have two or three part time or freelance roles.

   Slashie 一詞的意思是，不是僅僅有一份工作，而是可能有兩到三個兼職或自由職業者的角色。

2. **except that** 用於說明某件事情無法或是不可能為真

   例 I want to visit her, except that I'm so exhausted.

   我想去看她，只是我真的太累了。

3. **make up your mind** 下定決心

   例 I haven't made up my mind when to quit.

   我還沒下定決心什麼時候要辭職。

4. **flip side** 反面、負面

5. **gig economy** 零工經濟

   * 指勞工並非享有公司福利的正職員工，屬於獨立案件式的約聘人員 (contractor)。

   例 The gig economy is suddenly booming.

   零工經濟短時間內蓬勃發展。

情境會話 A／翻譯

彼得：你最近有跟姍蒂聊天嗎？我傳簡訊給她，打電話給她，她都只是回我一些表情符號，然後說她真的很忙，她到底是在忙什麼啊？

珍　：你沒聽說嗎？

彼得：聽說什麼？

珍　：姍蒂現在是斜槓人。

彼得：真的，我都不知道她原來是個工作狂啊。

珍　：你為什麼這麼說？我覺得選擇當斜槓人跟所謂的工作狂其實很不一樣。

彼得：這就是我一直不懂的地方，我的意思是說，「斜槓」這個詞本身聽起來是很酷沒錯，只是為了要可以把每一項工作都兼顧好，會超級忙耶，沒錯吧！說真的，我有一些朋友很羨慕這種斜槓人生，基本上就可以在家工作啊，享受沒有束縛且自由的感覺，但我……我是……我覺得斜槓人生根本也沒那麼好，你只要光想那個壓力就好，不穩定的工作時間表其實對人體健康也有害耶，我認為有好幾個兼職工作在手的好處不管怎樣都無法大過於壞處的，我講真的。

珍　：我懂你說的，你知道嗎，幾個月前我是有考慮過要成為一名自由業者，但最終我還是下不了決心。享受我喜歡的工作的另一面可能是我每天工作 20 個小時，或每週工作 7 天，太冒險了，我是一點也不想要過那種極度壓力的生活。

彼得：我就是這個意思！但是，這種零工經濟正在蓬勃發展耶，據估計，現在有超過 100 萬人正身兼兩份以上的工作，你相信嗎？

珍　：嗯，我相信啊，真的很有可能啊。我猜這有很多原因，有些人可能別無選擇，只能選擇這種超級忙碌的工作時間表，因為他們無法單靠全職工作來獲得足夠收入去支持他們的夢想。

彼得：確實啦，斜槓可以讓人們去實踐不同的興趣方向。

珍　：是啊，就像姍蒂一樣，你不能否認她真的很有才華，她是廚師／部落格主／攝影師／園藝師，對於那些十項全能的人來說，這的確是一種迷人的新工作方式。

Netflix

同步練習

請仔細聆聽情境會話音檔，把每一句中斷句換氣的語調段落標記出來。

Track 2402 T = Tina G = Georgina ★ 請特別注意粗體字的部分 ★

T Have you watched *The Crown* yet?

G No, I haven't. I don't know why you guys spend so much time on Netflix.

T Why not? Okay, first of all, Netflix is awesome. It has everything, from sitcoms to dramas to travel and talk shows. If you want to just lie on the sofa and chill out, Netflix is all you need. **Second of all… second of all… gee…** I forgot what I wanted to say… anyway, you got to watch *The Crown*, **you won't regret it, I promise**.

G I don't know… but *The Crown*, isn't it about Britain's royal family? **For me, it's like** watching discovery channel.

T Alright, **listen**, I don't like discovery channel either. The show is different, I can tell you. It's really iconic. I'm starting *The Crown* over again. This will be my third time watching.

G **You're kidding**.

T **Of course not**, it is not only highly entertaining, but it paints a nuanced and complicated portrait of a royal family. I even started looking for information about the World War I and World War II history because of *The Crown*.

G Wow, you, studying history! **That's a new one on me**!

T Haha, very funny. But you're right! It's like the first time I am really curious about what actually happened in history.

G TV shows can be really powerful.

T **They can.**

G **It just came to me that I've never binge watched TV series**. Maybe I should do it this long weekend.

T Let's do it together!

G Ya, sure, let's do it! You can stay at my place. It should be fun.

同步練習｜解說

Track 2402

以下對話的斷句換氣位置以「/」標示：

T Have you watched *The Crown* yet?

G No, I haven't./ I don't know why you guys spend so much time on Netflix.

T Why not?/ Okay,/ first of all,/ Netflix is awesome./ It has everything,/ from sitcoms to dramas to travel and talk shows./ If you want to just lie on the sofa/ and chill out/ Netflix is all you need./ Second of all…/ second of all…/ gee…/ I forgot what I wanted to say…/ anyway,/ you got to watch *The Crown*,/ you won't regret it,/ I promise.

G I don't know…/ but *The Crown*,/ isn't it about Britain's royal family?/ For me,/ it's like watching discovery channel.

T Alright,/ listen,/ I don't like discovery channel either./ The show is different,/ I'm telling you./ It's really iconic./ I'm starting *The Crown* over again./ This will be my third time watching./

G You're kidding.

T Of course not,/ it is not only highly entertaining,/ but it paints a nuanced and complicated portrait of a royal family./ I even started looking for information about the World War I and World War II history/ because of *The Crown*.

G Wow,/ you,/ studying history!/ That's a new one on me!

T Haha,/ very funny./ But you're right!/ It's like the first time I am really curious about/ what actually happened in history.

G TV shows can be really powerful.

T They can.

G It just came to me/ that I've never binge watched TV series./ Maybe I should do it this long weekend.

T Let's do it together!

G Ya,/ sure,/ let's do it! You can stay at my place./ It should be fun.

實用字詞補充

1. **Sitcoms** 情境喜劇 **(= situation comedy)**
2. **chill out** 冷靜、放鬆一下
3. **I can tell you**（用來強調表示你所說的）千真萬確

   *I'm telling you *I tell you
4. **That's a new one on me** 我從來沒聽說過

Ch 3

情境會話 B／翻譯

蒂　娜：你看過《王冠》了嗎？

喬治娜：還沒有，我實在不知道你們為什麼會在 Netflix 上花那麼多時間。

蒂　娜：為什麼不呢？好，首先呢，Netflix 超讚，它什麼都有，從情景喜劇到戲劇類到旅遊見聞，還有脫口秀都有耶，如果妳只想躺在沙發上休息一整天，有 Netflix 就夠了，還有，那個……哎呦，我忘了我剛剛想說什麼啦……不管怎樣，你真的一定要看《王冠》這部影集，你不會後悔的。

喬治娜：我不知道耶……但是這部影集不是關於英國王室嗎？對我來說，這就像在觀看探索頻道。

蒂　娜：好吧，聽著，我也不喜歡探索頻道。可是這節目真的不一樣，沒騙你。我還要重新開追這部劇耶，這是我第三次看了！

喬治娜：你在開玩笑吧。

蒂　娜：當然不是，這部不僅非常有趣，而且描繪了王室內部的那些很細膩又複雜的樣貌，也是因為這部戲，我甚至開始尋找有關第一次世界大戰和第二次世界大戰歷史的資料。

喬治娜：哇，你，學習歷史，這是破天荒的事情吧！

蒂　娜：好啦好啦，給你笑沒關係。但是沒錯，這是我第一次真正對歷史上實際發生的事情感到好奇喔。

喬治娜：電視節目真的是有辦法發揮很大的作用。

蒂　娜：真的。

喬治娜：我突然想到，我還從來沒有狂追過電視劇耶，也許我應該在這個連續假期來試試看。

蒂　娜：一起啊！

喬治娜：好啊，我們一起看劇！你可以待在我家，應該會很好玩。

食物外送

Track 2403　S = Sam　H = Holly　★ 請特別注意粗體字的部分 ★

S What's for dinner? I am starving.

H Should we order Chinese food or pizza?

S **I thought** we were going out for dinner, … um… but if you prefer to stay at home… ya, we can…

H No, no, no, of course we can go out. Look, I think food delivery service ruined me.

S **What do you mean?**

H Well, these couple of months, whenever I didn't feel like cooking, or I was too busy, I ordered food delivery.

S I **don't see why it's so bad**, especially during the coronavirus pandemic. Food delivery services comfort a lot of people.

H But the point is that it is too convenient to resist it. It makes me spend much much more. I just got my credit card bill yesterday and I was like what, is it mine? Anyway, I tracked how much I spent on foodpanda and Ubereats, and then I realized I have been literally eating up all my money with food delivery apps.

S **You're exaggerating!**

H Sadly no, I do need to quit my food delivery addiction. But it's really scary when it has become part of my daily routine. It's really challenging to break a habit like this. *<u>**Do not** let me use those apps again!</u>

S Well, I'd love to help. Go get your sweater. Let's go to the new Lebanese restaurant. I've got coupons.

H Good idea.

聽力提點

Do not let me use those apps again!

這裡不說 Don't 不只是沒有縮讀的差別而已，當口語表達時選擇不縮讀，有可能

Ch 3

是說話者想要表達不同的語意，不縮讀 not 表示了「千萬不要」的文意，就好比桌上有一鍋雞湯很燙，我們想要特別提醒小孩千萬不要伸手去摸，口語用 Do Not touch it 會比用 Don't touch it 更強烈。

延伸聽寫 | Exercise C

解答參見第 352 頁

Track 2404 請聆聽音檔，試著把句子中斷句換氣的位置標記出來。

Like me, **chances are** you've probably ordered food online at least once this month, okay, **who am I kidding**? You ordered food yesterday, and you are gonna do it again today. Am I right? Yes, guys, we are so obsessed with the food delivery thing. Have everything delivered to your door. Yeah, it's not just about convenience, you know what I'm talking about, it's not… it's more than that. We… well, I am a big fan of cooking at home. I think it's really great for your health, for the whole family. You get the idea. So, yeah! Okay, now everyone in my family is working remotely, and it's great that we can sit down and enjoy our meal together. But the question is, who should cook? My mom, she is doing like ten Zoom meetings a day and my dad,… well, let me put it this way, the only thing he can do in the kitchen is to make coffee. And I love cooking, but I don't want to cook every single day. Food delivery changes a lot of things, **if you see what I'm saying**.

翻譯

像我一樣，你很可能已經在網路上訂過至少一次食物吧，哎呀，我是在騙誰？你昨天有叫外送，今天還點外送，沒說錯對吧！是的，大家，我們非常痴迷於外送這件事，把任何東西直接送到家門口，對的，但是這不只是為了方便而已耶，你知道我的意思嗎？不是……它不僅僅是……我們……嗯，至少我是在家做飯的忠實擁護者，我認為這對你的健康和整個家庭都有好處，你懂我的意思的！所以說呢……，好，那問題是現在我家裡每個人都在遠距工作，那當然，大家可以坐下來一起享用美食是很好的事情，但問題是，誰要煮飯呢？我媽，她一天大概要開十個線上會議吧，那我爸呢，……好吧，讓我這樣說好了，他在廚房裡唯一能做的就是煮咖啡，我呢，我是喜歡煮飯，但問題是我不想每天都做飯啊，你懂我的意思了齁？其實外送服務真的改變了很多事情。

實用字詞補充

1. **(the) chances are** 可能是

   例 Chances are (**that**) she's been there before.

   很有可能的是，她早已經去過那個地方了。

2. **If you see what I'm saying** （用來詢問對方是否理解，尤其在沒有很清楚的情況下）你明白我的意思嗎？

   *see what I'm saying

情境會話 C／翻譯

山姆：晚餐吃什麼？我好餓喔！

荷莉：我們要叫中國菜還是披薩呢？

山姆：我以為我們要出去吃晚餐，嗯，但是如果你比較想在家裡的話……可以啊，我們就……

荷莉：不，不，不，我們當然可以出去吃，你看，我覺得這些外送服務真的毀了我啦。

山姆：什麼意思啊？

荷莉：哎，這幾個月來，每次當我不想做飯或是我太忙的時候，我就叫外賣啊。

山姆：我不知道為什麼這有你說的那麼糟糕耶，尤其是在冠狀病毒大流行期間，食物外送其實讓很多人感到蠻安慰的。

荷莉：但是重點是它太方便太難以抗拒了，這讓我花更多錢耶，昨天我收到信用卡帳單，我當下想說，等等，這是我的帳單嗎？總之，我回去看我在 foodpanda 和 Ubereats 上消費的記錄啊，然後我才意識到說我叫外送的消費習慣幾乎要花光我的錢了。

山姆：你在開玩笑吧？

荷莉：不幸的是我是說真的，我覺得我需要戒掉叫外送的習慣，但是當這種東西變成一種生活例行公事的時候真的很嚇人，想要打破這種習慣真的很困難。不要再讓我用那些 app 了！

山姆：嗯，我很樂意幫助你打破這個習慣，去拿你的毛衣，我們去那家新開的黎巴嫩餐廳。我有折價券。

荷莉：好主意。

情境會話 D 宅經濟

同步練習

請仔細聆聽情境會話音檔，把每一句中斷句換氣的語調段落標記出來。

Track 2405 A = Student A B = Student B ★ 請特別注意粗體字的部分 ★

A Hey, what are you reading?

B Oh hi, it's *The Wall Street Journal* about stay-at-home economy.

A Over the past year, the corona virus is boosting the growth of stay-at-home economy!

B Yeah, the pandemic is definitely fueling it. **Speaking of that**, do you think whenever it becomes normal again, you know, **whenever it is for us to** leave the house for work or shopping, will we go back to our life style before the pandemic?

A **That's a good question**. I believe that delivery platforms do make our lives a bit tolerable during the pandemic. If the convenience has become a routine or even a necessity, it is unlikely that we just **give it up overnight**.

B Also, for those companies that have made huge investments in the infrastructure needed for delivery services. **There's no going back**.

A **No matter what**, once a habit is established, **it's so difficult to break it**.

B **That's true**. I don't think we're going back to the same economy.

A **That's exactly what I think.**

同步練習｜解說 Track 2405

以下對話的斷句換氣位置以「/」標示：

A Hey, what are you reading?

B Oh hi, it's *The Wall Street Journal*/ about stay-at-home economy.

A Over the past year,/ the corona virus is boosting the growth of stay-at-home economy!

B Yeah, the pandemic is definitely fueling it./ Speaking of that,/ do you think/ whenever it becomes normal again,/ you know,/ whenever it is for us/ to leave the house for work or shopping,/ will we go back to our life style/ before the pandemic?

[A] That's a good question./ I believe/ that delivery platforms do make our lives a bit tolerable/ during the pandemic./ If the convenience has become a routine/ or even a necessity,/ it is unlikely/ that we just give it up overnight.

[B] Also,/ for those companies/ that have made huge investments/ in the infrastructure needed/ for delivery services./ There's no going back.

[A] No matter what,/ once a habit is established,/ it's so difficult to break it.

[B] That's true./ I don't think we're going back to the same economy.

[A] That's exactly what I think.

實用字詞補充

1. **the Stay-at-Home Economy 宅經濟**
2. **Speaking of something 說到這件事情**

   [例] Lisa is at a birthday party. Speaking of birthdays, Simon's is Sunday.

   麗莎在參加生日派對，說到生日這件事情，西蒙的生日是星期天耶！
3. **There's no going back 沒有回頭／反悔的可能了（因為已經決定）**

   * 很像中文口語會說，頭已經洗下去了，就是要做到底。

   [例] We've already signed the contract, so there's no going back.

   我們已經簽約了，就是要做下去。
4. **Kick the habit 戒除惡習、改掉舊習慣**

Ch 3

情境會話 D／翻譯

學生 A：嘿，你在看什麼？

學生 B：哦，嗨，我在看《華爾街日報》，有關於宅經濟。

學生 A：過去一年來，冠狀病毒算是促進宅經濟大成長齁！

學生 B：對啊，疫情真的大幅刺激宅經濟的成長，說到這一點，你覺得當這一切再次恢復正常，你知道，反正不管什麼時候，當我們可以離開家裡，去工作或去購物的時候，我們是不是會回到之前的生活狀態呢？

學生 A：這是一個很好的問題耶，我相信，在疫情期間，外送平台的確讓我們的生活變得比較能夠忍受一點，如果這種便利感已經變成一種常態甚至是必需品，我們就不太可能一夜之間放棄這種狀態吧！

學生 B：還有，像是對於那些在外送服務所需的各方面設施已經投注大幅資金的公司們，他們肯定是沒有回頭路了啊！

學生 A：無論如何，一旦習慣被養成了，就不容易被改變囉。

學生 B：是啊，我認為我們不太會再回到過去的經濟模式了。

學生 A：我也是這麼想的。

Exercise C

以下內容斷句換氣的位置以「/」標示：

Like me,/ chances are you've probably ordered food online/ at least once this month,/ okay,/ who am I kidding?/ You ordered food yesterday,/ and you are gonna do it again today./ Am I right?/ Yes,/ guys,/ we are so obsessed with the food delivery thing./ Have everything delivered to your door./ Yeah, /it's not just about convenience,/ you know what I'm talking about,/ it's not/… it's more than that./ We/… well,/ I am a big fan of cooking at home./ I think it's really great for your health,/ for the whole family./ You get the idea./ So, yeah!/ Okay,/ now everyone in my family is working remotely,/ and it's great that we can sit down/ and enjoy our meal together./ But the question is,/ who should cook?/ My mom,/ she is doing like ten Zoom meetings a day/ and my dad,/… well,/ let me put it this way,/ the only thing he can do/ in the kitchen/ is to make coffee./ And I love cooking,/ but I don't want to cook every single day./ Food delivery changes a lot of things,/ if you see what I'm saying.

Unit 25

科技讓我們的生活更加的便捷、輕鬆，但同時也帶來許多負面的影響，你有想過未來生活的樣貌嗎？一起來聽聽幾個與未來生活息息相關的熱門話題：

・電動車──特斯拉・移民火星計劃

・氣候變遷・電商 AI 廣告投放

電動車——特斯拉

同步練習

請仔細聆聽情境會話音檔，把每一句中斷句換氣的語調段落標記出來，並觀察每一個語調段的最後一個重音節之重音強度（高音）是否有所不同。

Track 2501　F = Flora　A = Alan　★ 請特別注意粗體字的部分 ★

F I've lost faith in Elon Musk. ***That's it.**

A Hahaha, you look like you are heartbroken, drama queen!

F It's too crazy. I want to give up dealing with bleeding stocks.

A **I know what you're saying**, bad news keep pouring in, right! And China is banning Tesla cars. Did you hear the news?

F **Whatever!** It feels like Musk is not doing Tesla's shareholders any favors. I think it's time for me to sell the stock.

A **Calm down! Well, if you ask me,** even though a large portion of Tesla's cash has been invested in Bitcoin, I don't think it means Musk chose Dogecoin over Tesla.

F Do you think Tesla's domination in manufacturing will increase over the next decade?

A **Who knows?** But some of my friends are about to go all in. To be honest, I don't think they are crazy. "Self-driving" cars are still a long way off, so it also means Tesla's stock price has room to grow!

聽力提點　Track 2502

***That's it.**

這篇對話中 That's it 的語調最高音位置在 That 而不是在句末的 it。如果最高音的位置變成 it，意思反而不同。聽聽看以下兩句的不同之處。

That's it.

重音位置在 that，意思會是「好了、夠了、到此為止了」。

That's it.

重音位置在 it，意思會是「正是如此」、「沒錯就是這件事情」、「沒錯就是……」。

同步練習 | 解說

Track 2501

句子裡可能會有一個以上的斷句換氣小段落，就像唱歌有抑揚頓挫的音調高低小段落一樣，每一個小段落的最後一個重音音節，就是句中的語調重音位置，要唸得比其他的音節重音還要高，然後迅速下降之後，再稍稍揚起，這個尾巴上揚的目的是要接續還沒有說完的下一個語調小段，因為必須等到句點的位置才能完全把語音語調降下來，通常句點前最後一個換氣小段落的語調重音位置會是所有重音當中最強烈（高）的。以下句中斷句換氣段落以「/」表示，而句中語調重音的音節則以色字表示：

F I lost faith/ in Elon Musk./ That's it.

A Hahaha,/ you look like you are heartbroken,/ drama queen!

F It's too crazy./ I want to give up/ dealing with bleeding stocks.

A I know what you're saying…/ bad news keep pouring in,/ right!/ And China is banning Tesla cars./ Did you heard the news?

F Whatever! It feels like Musk is not doing Tesla's shareholders any favors./ I think it's time for me/ to sell the stock.

A Calm down/… well/…If you ask me…/ even though a large portion of Tesla's cash/ has been invested in Bitcoin,/ I don't think it means Musk chose/ Dogecoin over Tesla.

F Do you think Tesla's domination/ in manufacturing will increase/ over the next decade?

A Who knows?/ But some of my friends are about to go all in./ To be honest,/ I don't think they are crazy./ 'Self-driving' cars are still a long way off,/ so it also means/ Tesla's stock price has room to grow!

實用字詞補充

1. **drama queen** 小題大做的人，反應激烈誇張的人 ＊較為揶揄的口語

   例 Don't be such a drama queen. It's really no big deal.

   不要小題大做好不好！這是沒什麼大不了的事情啊。

2. **cryptocurrency**

   （諸如比特幣一類的）加密電子貨幣

3. **all in**（撲克遊戲等中）下注所有籌碼

   例 After I raised back, she **went** all in.

   在我又加碼下注之後，她就把所有籌碼都下了。

Ch 3

情境會話 A／翻譯

芙羅拉：我對伊隆．馬斯克失去了信心。簡單來說就是這樣啦。

愛　倫：哈哈哈，你看起來傷心欲絕，很愛演耶！

芙羅拉：這太瘋狂了，我想放棄不管這些狂跌的股票了。

愛　倫：我知道，壞消息一直來，對吧！而且中國禁止特斯拉汽車，你聽說了嗎？

芙羅拉：隨便啦！感覺就像是馬斯克沒有給特斯拉的股東帶來任何好處啊，我認為現在該賣股票了。

愛　倫：你冷靜一點，我是覺得，就算特斯拉的資金有很大一部分投資到比特幣，這也不意味著馬斯克選擇了狗幣而不是特斯拉啊。

芙羅拉：你覺得未來十年內，特斯拉在製造業中的龍頭地位會變得如何？

愛　倫：誰知道？但是我有一些朋友要整個「梭哈」下注耶，老實說，我不認為他們瘋了。自動駕駛汽車還有很長的路要走，所以這也意味著特斯拉的股價未來還有增長空間啊！

情境會話 B

移民火星計劃

聆聽重點

請仔細聆聽情境會話音檔，看看是否每一個語調段最後一個重音節的重音強度（高音）都是該句最高音的位置，有沒有「例外」呢？

Track 2503　H = Hank　M = Miranda　★ 請特別注意粗體字的部分 ★

H [1]**Look at this photo, Starship SN8.** It's remarkable, isn't it?

M Didn't know you are interested in that. I feel sending humans to Mars is a pretty scary idea, not to mention permanent settlement on Mars… wow…

H **I beg to differ.** Human settlement on Mars is a brilliant inspiring project. Actually, I thought about signing up for the trip.

M [2]**You did?** How… Why…

H What? … okay… you think I'm crazy, right? Is that what you think?

M I'm saying… wait… I… I didn't mean that the whole thing is completely ridiculous, stupid or something…. I… well, can you really imagine a trip to Mars? I mean… really… You have to know that once the first humans safely arrive at Mars, there is no means for them to return to Earth. [3]**Mars will be their home forever**. That's really sad.

H Sad but adventurous, audacious, remarkable! It will just be one of the greatest adventures of all time. By the way, don't you think the whole idea can actually inspire us to make Earth a better place? To treasure everything we have?

M **I don' t see how**.

H Remember the awful feelings that you have every time you watch a disaster movie on Netflix? **It's like a wake up call**, telling us the importance of respecting the power of nature.

M For me, the idea of living on Mars is something against nature. Human beings obviously have destroyed so many things on Earth. If the reality were a Hollywood film, the ending should be something like we all die unfortunately. We are the perpetrators, the bad guys… **you know what I'm**

Ch 3

saying… It can't be like this, after we use up everything here, **so what, big deal,** haha… we are powerful enough to exploit resources on another planet?

H **Don't take it the wrong way**, but what you're saying is a little… cynical. **It's not that black-and-white**, you know that.

M Yeah, I agree.

聽力提點

Track 2504

如同前一段對話中的例子，同樣一句話 that's it，當改變其重音位置就可以表達不太一樣的語意，因此，雖然基本通則是把句子最末一段的最後一個重音節當作整個句子重音位置最強烈的表示，但卻也非僵化不變的。比方說，當說話者想要特別強調句子當中某些字，也可以把該字當作整句話裡面最高音的位置。請看以下本段對話的例子：

1. **Look at this photo,/ Starship SN8.**

   這一句話裡面有兩個語調段落，有兩個語調重音的位置 photo 跟 SN8，整句最高音的位置在句末最後一個語調重音 SN8，是一般的語音語調規則。

   Look at this photo, Starship SN8.

   這一句話的最高音變成 this，代表說話者想要特別強調「這一張相片」，而不是別張相片。

   Look at this photo.

   這一句話的最高音變成 Look，代表說話者的表達情緒都聚焦在「大家快來看看」這樣的語意上面。

2. **You did? / Did you? / Did you!**

   did 尾音上揚是用來表示驚訝，如果變成問句 Did you? 比較會是單純的在問對方「你有……嗎？」，有趣的是，如果重音再變成 Did you!，那意思就稍微轉了一下變成「你真的……了啊！」，也是有表達到驚訝之類的情緒表現。

3. **Mars will be their home forever.**

   強調 forever。

   Mars will be their home forever.

   強調 home。

實用字詞補充

1. **I beg to differ.** 禮貌表示不同意對方所說的意見

   例 You say it's impossible to solve the problem, but I beg to differ.

   你說要解決這個問題是不可能的，但是我並不這麼認為。

2. **not to mention** 除了……之外（還），更不用說還有……

   例 She is one of the smartest and most considerate, not to mention beautiful, woman I know.

   她是我認識的女性裡非常聰明又貼心的一位，更不要說她還有多漂亮迷人了。

3. **I don't see how / why / what...**（用於回應）我不明白……

   例 I don't see why you can't give them more time.

   我不能理解為什麼你就不能給他們多一點時間。

4. **a wake-up call** 警訊

   例 For the community, the tragic accident was a wake-up call.

   對整個社區來說，這個悲傷的事故警醒了大家。

5. **so what**（口語）就算那樣又如何

   例 So what if I give up at this moment—I have tried my best and that's enough.

   如果我在這個時間點放棄那又怎樣呢？我已經盡力了，這樣也就足夠了。

Ch 3

情境會話 B／翻譯

漢　克：看看這張照片，星艦 SN8。很了不起，不是嗎？

米蘭達：不知道你對這種事情有興趣耶，我覺得把人類送去火星是一個可怕的想法，更不用說要在火星上永久定居了。

漢　克：我不這麼認為，人類在火星上的定居這個計畫又傑出又有啓發性，實際上，我還曾經考慮過要報名火星之旅耶。

米蘭達：真的？怎麼會……為什麼……

漢　克：怎樣？……好吧……你覺得我瘋了對吧？你是這麼認為的嗎？

米蘭達：我是說……等等，我並不是說這整件事情是超荒謬或愚蠢之類的，好，你真的能夠想像出發去火星嗎？你要知道耶，一旦第一批人類安全抵達火星，他們就再也沒有辦法返回地球了，火星將成為他們永遠的家，很哀傷耶。

漢　克：哀傷沒錯，但是也充滿冒險精神，相當大膽，而且超群，這將不僅僅是我們這個時代最偉大的冒險之一而已，順便再說一句，您不認為整個想法實際上可以激發我們，讓我們想要讓地球變得更美好嗎？讓我們想要珍惜我們現在擁有的一切。

米蘭達：我不覺得耶，會嗎？

漢　克：還記得每次在 Netflix 上看災難電影時的糟糕感受嗎？那就像是警醒我們的聲音，告訴我們要尊重大地之母的力量。

米蘭達：對我來說剛好相反，我們人類很顯然地已經摧毀了地球上的許多東西，如果現實是一部好萊塢電影，那麼結局應該就像我們最後都不幸地死掉一樣，我們是肇事者，是壞人呀，怎麼可以是這樣，當我們耗盡這裡的一切之後，這又有什麼大不了的事，我們強大到可以再去剝削另一個星球上的資源？

漢　克：我這麼說你別往心裡去，但我覺得你這樣說有點憤世嫉俗。你知道的，不是那樣非黑即白的。

米蘭達：好吧，我同意。

氣候變遷

Track 2505 E = Ellison M = May ★ 請特別注意粗體字的部分 ★

E How'd the seminar go yesterday?

M Oh, it was really good. **And you know what**, I met some of my friends from college. **Time flies. Time flies.** The funny thing is during the coffee break *we ended up talking **about facial soft-tissue changes instead of climate change**. It was hilarious.

E Sounds like you had a really good time.

M Yeah, um…I don't know, climate change is pretty overwhelming for all of us.

E I guess the point would be how to curb negative feelings. Friendship, for example, changes a lot of things.

M Well, some of my friends are doing national projects and are having a great impact, but sometimes they still feel hopeless.

E **It is tough.** No matter what we do, we all need supports. Even hanging out with colleagues can suddenly boost my energy. That's why I love my office pantry so much. It's very clean and comfortable. You know, last Friday, Charlie, one of my fellow researchers, bounced a couple of ideas off me while I was making coffee. **It sounds annoying but not at all.** We even came up with some possible solutions to our project. So, for me, there's nothing like a relaxing but productive chat.

M I wish my colleagues would do that too.

E **What do you mean?**

M I'm pretty much surrounded by scientists who study climate change, global warming and climate-related health problems. Of course we care about it deeply, but interestingly, I don't know why, for some reason, climate change just doesn't come up in conversation. So weird…

E Maybe **it's like what you said**. It's just too overwhelming.

M But climate change is the biggest problem facing mankind.

E **That's it!** Because it's a disastrous, serious and challenging topic, it could feel like an abstract problem, or like something far far away.

M I guess you're right! But climate change is affecting every aspect of our lives now. Every once in a while, when I want to have a nice conversation about climate change I usually get the freeze response.

E Hey, sometimes superheroes just want a normal life.

M That's really nice. Maybe I am too harsh. With friends like you, who needs superheroes?

E Haha, I'll take that as a compliment.

聽力提點

Track 2506

***We ended up talking about facial soft tissue changes instead of climate change.**

句中最高音的位置在第一個 change，因為在**做對比資訊**，前面的面容老去的改變與氣候改變，兩個都是改變，但是卻是完全不同的兩件事情，說話者也會把自己在想要對比的資訊上面做最強烈的重音表達，而不會把最高音放在句點前的最後一個重音節。

實用字詞補充

1. **end up** 最後處於、以……告終

   例 The general ended up living in a nursing home.
   那位將軍最終住進了療養院。

2. **catch up with someone** 了解某人近況

   例 How often do you catch up with your friends?
   你多久會跟朋友聯繫近況一次呢？

3. **bounce sth off sb**（口語）探詢……對……的看法

   例 Do you have a minute? Can I bounce some ideas off you before the meeting?
   你有空嗎？我可以在會議之前就幾個想法看看你的意見如何嗎？

4. **every once in a while** 偶爾、有時候

   例 Dana and I meet for lunch (every) once in a while.
   我跟黛娜偶爾會碰面吃中飯。

5. **take it/that as a compliment** 把對方說的話當成誇讚收下了

   例 I take it as a compliment when my friends say I am naive.
   當我朋友說我太天真的時候，我就當他們在誇獎我了。

6. **What can I say?**（口語）我也不知道還能怎麼表達／解釋了。

情境會話 C／翻譯

艾力森：昨天的研討會怎麼樣？

梅　　：哦，很好啊。而且你知道嗎，我遇到了一些大學時代的朋友，真的是時光飛逝，時光飛逝啊。有趣的是，在喝咖啡的休息期間，我們到最後都在討論有關於臉上皮膚漸漸鬆弛的變化，而不是氣候變遷了。這很滑稽。

艾力森：聽起來很開心啊。

梅　　：是啦，嗯，我也不知道，氣候變遷這個議題真的是會讓人有種太巨大到令人無法承受的感覺。

艾力森：我想重點是，面對這種情況的時候要怎麼讓自己不要去感到消極，就像是，友情可以帶來很大的改變。

梅　　：對，他們有一些人做的是國家級的計畫，也正在發揮他們的影響力，但是他們有時候還是會感到無助啊。

艾力森：這真的不容易，無論我們做什麼事情，我們都需要支持。跟同事一起消磨時間都可以振奮我的精神呢！這就是為什麼我如此愛我的辦公室茶水間，非常乾淨舒適。你知道，上週五，我的研究員之一查理在我煮咖啡的時候提出一些想法問我的意見，聽起來好像很煩人對不對，但一點也不，我們聊的很開心，還為我們的計畫提出了一些可能的解決方案。所以啊，對我而言，沒有什麼比得過又放鬆又有生產力的聊天了。

梅　　：我希望我的同事也能做到這一點。

艾力森：什麼意思？

梅　　：我周圍幾乎都是科學家，他們研究氣候變遷、全球暖化以及跟氣候變遷有關的健康問題，我們當然都很在乎氣候變遷啊，但是有趣的是，我不知道為什麼，大概就是出於某些原因使然，我們閒聊都幾乎不會去談到氣候變遷耶，很怪耶。

艾力森：也許就像你說的那樣，一想到就很累人了。

梅　　：但是氣候變遷真的是人類面臨的最大的問題。

艾力森：就是因為這樣，因為這是一個災難性的、嚴肅的、又極具挑戰性的話題，這就是為什麼它會感覺起來很像是一個抽象的問題，或者感覺距離我們非常遙遠的事物。

梅　　：我想你說的是對的！可是氣候變化正在影響著我們生活的每一個方面，我偶爾都會想在閒聊的時候談到氣候變遷，不過通常空氣就瞬間凝結。

艾力森：嘿，有時候超級英雄只是想過一下正常的生活。

梅　　：哇，你真是太暖了，我大概有點太嚴厲了。有你這樣的朋友，誰還需要超級英雄呢？

艾力森：哈哈，我就當你在誇我囉！

電商 AI 廣告投放

Track 2507 D = Debra L = Louis ★ 請特別注意粗體字的部分 ★

D It's creepy that Instagram ads can be so accurate, don't you think? I just talked about vintage bags last night and now look what's on my Instagram feed.

L Don't you know that your phone listens to your conversations?

D How exactly do they do that? Are they like Siri?

L Well, there are plenty of ways for algorithms and artificial intelligence to "listen" to you, but I don't know how to explain it either. Loosely, they can use that data to target ads to you. That's… that's basically…

D Okay, but [1]**I wanna know** how to banish ads from my Instagram feed. [2]**We can do that, right?**

L [3]Yeah, there are many ways. For example, every time you come across sponsored posts, as long as you don't like, you can select "Hide This." Oh, and your phone can be silently listening to everything you say all the time, you know, so you have to disable those features, like "Hey Google".

D **Then I can completely get rid of them?**

L **Umm, I'm afraid not, sorry. What a bummer, huh!**

D Gee… I hate that… well… but I have to admit that it makes sense, though. It's all about business.

L With e-commerce ads, brands can efficiently drive awareness and increase their customer base.

D If I were an e-commerce store owner, I would love it so much.

L For me, advertising is not that annoying but thinking of the idea behind that makes me really uncomfortable. You know, what we like on social media, or what we google have all been collected. The Internet collects a frightening amount of data about every one of us. In that way, what we see on Instagram, or Facebook is actually what they assume we like. It means that to some extent, you aren't making a decision of buying a certain item on your own.

D **Stop it! I've got goosebumps!**

L Come on! I thought you're a big fan of sci-fi movies.

聽力提點

1. **I wanna know how to banish ads from my Instagram feed.**
   句子強調重點在 I 跟 banish。
2. **We can do that, right?**
   兩個語調重音位置，do 以及 right，整個句子的最高音位置在句子尾的語調重音上。
3. **Yeah, there are many ways.**
   Yeah 是全句最高音的位置，通常在對話情境中，如果有一問一答的狀況，提供答案的一方所提出的資訊則為重要的「新資訊」，新資訊就會是語調重音最強烈突出的位置。

實用字詞補充

1. **algorithms** 演算法
2. **What a bummer!**（口語）實在令人大失所望、掃興。

Ch 3

情境會話 D／翻譯

黛布拉：你不覺得 Instagram 廣告投放的這種準確度很讓人毛骨悚然嗎？昨天晚上我才剛剛談到了復古包包，你現在看看我的 instagram 上面的廣告內容。

路易斯：你不知道你的電話隨時都在聽你講話的內容嗎？

黛布拉：他們到底是怎麼做到的？像是 Siri 那樣嗎？

路易斯：嗯，演算法和人工智慧有很多方法可以 "監聽" 你，但是其實我也不知道怎麼解釋啦，簡而言之，他們可以使用這些數據來決定要投放什麼廣告給你。

黛布拉：好吧，我想知道我要怎麼從 instagram 裡面把廣告刪掉，有辦法做到的吧？

路易斯：是啊，有很多方法。例如，每次遇到贊助商的廣告的時候，只要你不喜歡，就可以選擇 "隱藏它"。喔，還有，你的手機也可以輕悄悄的偷聽你說的所有內容喔，所以你要禁用這些功能，像是 "Hey Google"。

黛布拉：這樣我就可以徹底擺脫它們了，是嗎？

路易斯：嗯，恐怕不是，對不起。真是太掃興了對不對，呵呵！

黛布拉：超級掃興啊。我真討厭廣告，但是我不得不承認這是有道理的。一切都與商機有關。

路易斯：藉由電子商務廣告，各個品牌可以有效地提高知名度並擴大自己的客戶群。

黛布拉：如果我是電商老闆，我當然會非常喜歡它。

路易斯：對我來說，廣告並不是那麼煩人，但如果考慮到背後的意義，我就真的很不舒服了。你想喔，我們在社交媒體上按了什麼東西讚，或者是我們在 Google 上搜索什麼東西，都被記錄下來了。網際網路收集了有關我們每個人的驚人數據，這樣長久下來，我們在 Instagram 或 Facebook 上看到的實際上是他們認為我們會喜歡的東西，這意味著在某種程度上來說，你決定購買某件商品的這件事情並不是完全出於自己的選擇。

黛布拉：別說了！我都起雞皮疙瘩了！

路易斯：我還想說你不是科幻電影的忠實擁護者嗎！

國家圖書館出版品預行編目資料

實境英文練聽力 / 劉怡均作. —— 初版. —— 臺北市：
波斯納出版有限公司, 2022.05
面； 公分

ISBN: 978-986-06892-8-0（平裝）

1. CST: 英語 2. CST: 讀本

805.18 111002379

實境英文練聽力

作　　者 / 劉怡均
執行編輯 / 朱曉瑩

出　　版 / 波斯納出版有限公司
地　　址 / 台北市 100 館前路 26 號 6 樓
電　　話 / (02) 2314-2525
傳　　真 / (02) 2312-3535
客服專線 / (02) 2314-3535
客服信箱 / btservice@betamedia.com.tw
郵撥帳號 / 19493777
帳戶名稱 / 波斯納出版有限公司

總 經 銷 / 時報文化出版企業股份有限公司
地　　址 / 桃園市龜山區萬壽路二段 351 號
電　　話 / (02) 2306-6842

出版日期 / 2022 年 5 月初版一刷
定　　價 / 480 元
I S B N / 978-986-06892-8-0

貝塔網址：www.betamedia.com.tw

喚醒你的英文語感！

Get a Feel for English !

喚醒你的英文語感！

Get a Feel for English !